Praise for Carsten Stroud's

NICEVILLE

"[A] thrill-ride. . . . As enthralling as a tale by the Brothers Grimm."
　　　　　　　　　　　　　　　　　　　—*The Wall Street Journal*

"Mesmerizing. . . . *Niceville* has claws as sharp as the soaring crows' talons."
　　　　　　　　　　　　　　　　　　　—*South Florida Sun-Sentinel*

"Terrific. . . . A mystery but also a ghost story, with a touch of horror. . . . This is a very sharp . . . view of traditional Southern Gothic."
　　　　　　　　　　　　　　　—*The Globe and Mail* (Toronto)

"A unique genre-bending novel that will haunt readers long after the last page. . . . *Niceville* is a town readers have to visit for themselves in order to believe."
　　　　　　　　　　　　　　　　　　　—*The Free Lance-Star*

"A simmering read; one part thriller, one part suspense, and taken with a hefty sprinkling of supernatural hot spice, it's one of the most compulsive page-turners of the year."
　　　　　　　　　　　　　　　—*The New York Journal of Books*

"[Stroud] literally gives plenty of bang for the buck."
　　　　　　　　　　　　　　　　　　　—*Booklist*

CARSTEN STROUD

Niceville

Carsten Stroud is the author of the *New York Times* bestselling true crime account *Close Pursuit*. His novels include *Sniper's Moon, Lizard Skin, Black Water Transit, Cuba Strait,* and *Cobraville.* He lives in Toronto.

NICEVILLE

NICEVILLE

CARSTEN STROUD

VINTAGE CRIME/BLACK LIZARD
A DIVISION OF RANDOM HOUSE, INC. | NEW YORK

FIRST VINTAGE CRIME/BLACK LIZARD EDITION, AUGUST 2013

The Library of Congress has cataloged the Knopf edition as follows:
Stroud, Carsten.
Niceville / by Carsten Stroud.—1st ed.
p. cm.
I. Married people—Fiction. 2. Missing children—Fiction. I. Title.
PR9199.3.S833N53 2012
813'.54—dc23 2011047306

Vintage ISBN: 978-0-307-74535-4

www.weeklylizard.com

Map by Robert Bull
Book design by Virginia Tan

Printed in the United States of America
10 9 8 7 6 5 4 3 2 1

For Linda Mair

Come from the Four Winds, O Breath,
And breathe upon these slain,
that they may live.

—Monument to the Confederate Dead,
Forsyth Park
Savannah, Georgia

Malicious men may die, but malice . . . never.

—Molière, *Tartuffe*

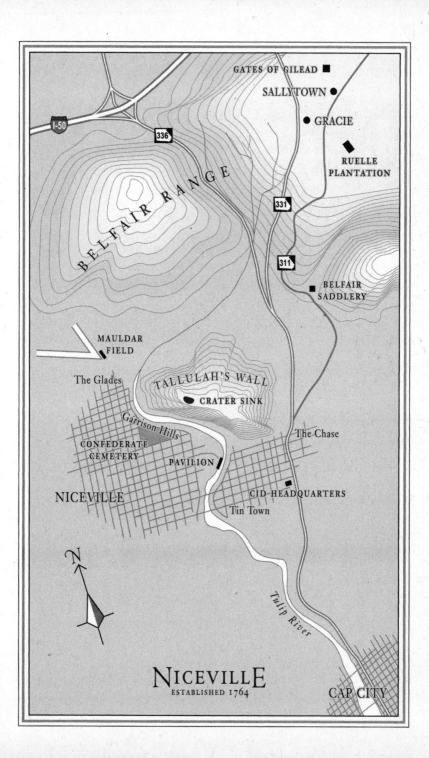

GATES OF GILEAD ■

SALLYTOWN ●

● GRACIE

◆ RUELLE PLANTATION

I-50

336

331

311

BELFAIR RANGE

■ BELFAIR SADDLERY

MAULDAR FIELD

The Glades

TALLULAH'S WALL

● CRATER SINK

Garrison Hills

The Chase

CONFEDERATE CEMETERY

PAVILION ▮

CID HEADQUARTERS ■

NICEVILLE

Tin Town

N

Tulip River

NICEVILLE
ESTABLISHED 1764

CAP CITY

NICEVILLE

Rainey Teague Doesn't Make It Home

In less than an hour the Niceville Police Department managed to ID the last person to see the missing kid. He was a shopkeeper named Alf Pennington, who ran a used-book store on North Gwinnett, near the intersection with Kingsbane Walk. This was right along the usual route the boy, whose name was Rainey Teague, took to get from Regiopolis Prep to his house in Garrison Hills.

It was a distance of about a mile, and the ten-year-old, a rambler who liked to take his time and look in all the shop windows, usually covered it in about thirty-five minutes.

Rainey's mother, Sylvia, a high-strung but levelheaded mom who was struggling with ovarian cancer, had the kid's after-school snack, ham-and-cheese and pickles, all laid out in the kitchen at the family home in Garrison Hills. She was sitting at her computer, poking around on Ancestry.com with half her attention on the front door, waiting as always for Rainey to come bouncing in, glancing now and then at the time marker on the task bar.

It was 3:24, and she was picturing her boy, the child of her later years, adopted from a foster home in Sallytown after she had endured years of fruitless in vitro treatments.

A pale blond kid with large brown eyes and a gangly way of going, given to sudden silences and strange moods—she's seeing him in her mind as if from a helicopter hovering just above the town, Niceville spread out beneath her, from the hazy brown hills of the Belfair Range in the north to the green thread of the Tulip River as it skirts the base of Tallulah's Wall and, widening into a ribbon, bends and turns through the heart of town. Far away to the southeast she can just make out the low coastal plains of marsh grass, and beyond that, the shimmering sea.

In this vision she sees him trudge along, his blue blazer over his shoulder, his stiff white collar unbuttoned, his gold and blue school tie tugged loose, his Harry Potter backpack dragging on his shoulders, his shoelaces undone. Now he's coming to the rail crossing at Peachtree and Cemetery Hill— of course he looks both ways—and now he's coming down the steep tree-lined avenue beside the rocky cliff that defines the Confederate graveyard.

Rainey.

Minutes from home.

She tapped away at the keyboard with delicate fingers, like someone playing a piano, her long black hair in her eyes, her ankles primly crossed, erect and concentrated, fighting the effects of the OxyContin she took for the pain.

She was on Ancestry because she was trying to solve a family question that had been troubling her for quite a while. At this stage of her research she felt that the answer lay in a family reunion that had taken place in 1910, at Johnny Mullryne's plantation near Savannah. Sylvia was distantly related to the Mullrynes, who had founded the plantation long before the War of Secession.

Later she told the uniform cop who caught the call that she got lost in that Ancestry search for a bit, time-drifting, she said, one of the effects of OxyContin, and when she looked at the clock again, this time with a tiny ripple of concern, it was 3:55. Rainey was ten minutes late.

She pushed her chair back from her computer desk and went down the long main hall towards the stained-glass door with the hand-carved mahogany arches and stepped out on the wide stone porch, a tall, slender woman in a crisp black dress, silver at her throat, wearing red patent leather ballet flats. She folded her arms across her chest and craned to the left to see if he was coming along the oak-shaded avenue.

Garrison Hills was one of the prettiest neighborhoods in Niceville and the sepia light of old money lay upon it, filtering through the live oaks and the gray wisps of Spanish moss, shining down on the lawns and shimmering on the roofs of the old mansions up and down the street.

There was no little boy shuffling along the walk. There was no one around at all. No matter how hard she stared, the street stayed empty.

She stood there for a while longer, her mild concern changing into exasperation and, after another three minutes, into a more active concern, though not yet shifting into panic.

She went back inside the house and picked up the phone that was on the antique sideboard by the entrance, hit button 3 and speed-dialed Rainey's cell phone number, listened to it ring, each ring ticking up her concern another degree. She counted fifteen and didn't wait for the sixteenth.

She pressed the disconnect button, then used the number 4 speed-dial key to ring up the registrar's office at Regiopolis Prep and got Father Casey on the third ring, who confirmed that Rainey had left the school at two minutes after three, part of the usual lemming stampede of chattering boys in their gray slacks and white shirts and blue blazers with the gold-thread crest of Regiopolis on the pockets.

Father Casey picked up on her tone right away and said he'd head out on foot to retrace Rainey's path along North Gwinnett all the way down to Long Reach Boulevard.

They confirmed each other's cell numbers and she picked up her car keys and went down the steps and into the double-car garage—her husband, Miles, an investment banker, was still at his office down in Cap City—where she started up her red Porsche Cayenne—red was her favorite color—and backed it down the cobbled drive, her head full of white noise and her chest wrapped in barbed wire.

Halfway along North Gwinnett she spotted Father Casey on foot in the dense crowd of strolling shoppers, a black-suited figure in a clerical collar, over six feet, built like a linebacker, his red face flushed with concern.

She pulled over and rolled down her window and they conferred for about a minute, people slowing to watch them talk, a good-looking young Jesuit in a bit of a lather talking in low and intense tones to a very pretty middle-aged woman in a bright red Cayenne.

At the end of that taut and urgent exchange Father Casey pushed away from the Cayenne and went to check out every alley and park between the school and Garrison Hills, and Sylvia Teague picked up her cell phone, took a deep breath, said a quick prayer to Saint Christopher, and called in the cops, who said they'd send a sergeant immediately and would she please stay right where she was.

So she did, and there she sat, in the leather-scented interior of the Cayenne, and she stared out at the traffic on North Gwinnett, waiting, trying not to think about anything at all, while the town of Niceville swirled around her, a sleepy Southern town where she had lived all of her life.

Regiopolis Prep and this part of North Gwinnett were deep in the dappled shadows of downtown Niceville, an old-fashioned place almost completely shaded by massive live oaks, their heavy branches knit together by dense traceries of power lines. The shops and most of the houses in the town were redbrick and brass in the Craftsman style, set back on shady avenues and wide cobbled streets lined with cast-iron streetlamps. Navy-blue-and-gold-colored streetcars as heavy as tanks rumbled past the Cayenne, their vibration shivering up through the steering wheel in her hands.

She looked out at the soft golden light, hazy with pollen and river mist that seemed always to lie over the town, softening every angle and giving Niceville the look and feel of an older and more graceful time. She told herself that nothing bad could happen in such a pretty place, could it?

In fact, Sylvia had always thought that Niceville would have been one of the loveliest places in the Deep South if it had not been built, God only knew why, in the looming shadow of Tallulah's Wall, a huge limestone cliff that dominated the northeastern part of the town—she could see it from where she was parked—a barrier wall draped with clinging vines and blue-green moss, a sheer cliff so wide and tall that parts of eastern Niceville stayed under its shadow until well past noon. There was a dense thicket of old-growth trees on top of the cliff, and inside this ancient forest was a large circular sinkhole, full of cold black water, no one knew how deep.

It was called Crater Sink.

Sylvia had once taken Rainey there, a picnic outing, but the spreading oaks and towering pines had seemed to lean in around them, full of whispering and creaking sounds, and the water of Crater Sink was cold and black and still and, through some trick of the light, its surface reflected nothing of the blue sky above it.

In the end they hadn't stayed long.

And now she was back to thinking about Rainey, and she realized that she had never really stopped thinking about him at all.

The first Niceville cruiser pulled up beside her Cayenne four minutes later, driven by a large redheaded female patrol sergeant named Mavis Crossfire, a seasoned pro in the prime of her career, who, like all good sergeants, radiated humor and cool competence, with an underlying stratum of latent menace.

Mavis Crossfire, who knew and liked the Teague family—
Garrison Hills was part of her patrol area—leaned on the
Cayenne's window and got the urgency of Sylvia's story as fast
as Father Casey had, a story she was inclined to take much
more seriously than a police sergeant in any other mid-sized
American town might have taken it at this early stage, because,
when it came to Missing Persons, Niceville had a stranger
abduction rate five times higher than the national average.

So Sergeant Mavis Crossfire was paying very close atten-
tion to Rainey Teague's disappearance, and, after listening to
Sylvia for about four minutes, she got on the radio and called
her duty captain, who got on his horn to Lieutenant Tyree
Sutter, the officer commanding the Belfair and Cullen County
Criminal Investigation Division.

About ten minutes after that, every cop in Niceville and
every county sheriff and all the local staties had gotten a digital
download of Rainey's photograph and description—Regiopolis
Prep kept digital photo files on every student—and every officer who could be spared was rolling on the Rainey Teague disappearance. This was a very creditable performance, as good as
the best city police force in the nation and a lot better than
most. Motivation counts.

Less than an hour later, a beat cop named Boots Jackson
called in from his riverside foot patrol along Patton's Hard,
walked into Alf Pennington's bookshop on North Gwinnett,
and developed the last confirmed sighting of Rainey Teague,
which he then promptly punched in to the HQ mainframe on
his handheld-computer link.

By this time the search perimeter had been expanded to
include all the Cullen County and Belfair County deputies as
well as the State Patrol guys as far north as Gracie and Sallytown, on the other side of the Belfair Range, and as far south
as Cap City, about fifty miles downrange.

Sitting at his desk at the CID headquarters on Powder
Ridge Road, Tyree Sutter, known as Tig, a blunt-featured

broken-nosed black man large enough to have his own gravity field, saw the Alf Pennington notation appear on his Coordinated Search Screen. He immediately handed the contact off to Detective Nick Kavanaugh, a thirty-two-year-old ex–Special Forces officer, a white guy, around six one, lean, hard as cordwood, with pale gray eyes and a shock of shiny black hair going white at the temples, who was standing in Tig's office door and staring at Tig like a wolf on a choke chain.

Kavanaugh was in his navy blue Crown Vic a minute later and flying up Long Reach Boulevard, following the bend of the Tulip, his strobes lit up but no siren, on his way to see Alf Pennington, pulling up to the curb outside Pennington's Book Nook at 1148 North Gwinnett less than twenty minutes later. The time was 6:17 p.m. and Rainey Teague had now been officially listed as missing for one hour and fourteen minutes.

Alf Pennington, late sixties, rail-thin, with a dowager's hump, bald as an eagle, with sharp black eyes and a down-turned mouth, looked up from behind his banker's desk as Nick came through the door, Alf's sour expression deepening as Nick weaved his way through the bookcases.

Not by nature a sunny person, Alf worked up a disapproving frown as Nick approached his desk, registering the slim well-tailored summer-weight dark blue suit—*too expensive for a cop*—*probably a bribe*—the unbuttoned jacket—*so he could get to his billy club, no doubt*—showing a pure white shirt, open at the neck, his tanned angular face shadowed in the dim light, the wary gray eyes, the shining gold badge clipped to his belt, the obvious bulge of a gun on his right hip.

"Hello. You must be the police. Would you like a coffee?"

"Thanks, no," said Nick in a pleasant baritone, looking around the shop, taking in the titles, breathing in the scent of must and wood polish and cigarette smoke, putting his hand out. "I'm Nick Kavanaugh. With the CID?"

"Yes," said Alf, giving him a quick shake and taking his hand back to see if his pinky ring was still there. Alf, a closet

Marxist from Vermont, didn't like cops very much. "Officer Jackson said you'd be by."

"And here I am. Officer Jackson says you saw Rainey Teague shortly after three? Can you describe him for me?"

"Done that already," said Alf, his Yankee accent jagged with short, sharp fricatives.

"I know," said Nick, deploying an apologetic smile to soften the request, "but it would be a big help."

Alf looked skyward, his black eyes rolling as he collected himself.

"See him every weekday. He's a lollygagger. Skinny kid, head too big, shaggy blond hair hanging down in his eyes, pale skin, snubby nose, big brown eyes like a cartoon squirrel, white shirt, tails hanging out, collar open, tie all loose, baggy gray pants, blue blazer with that Christer doodad on the pocket, dragging a Harry Potter knapsack behind him like it was full of bricks. That him?"

"That's him. What time was this?"

"Already said."

"Just once more?"

Alf sighed.

"Three oh five, 3:10, maybe. Usually see him then, coming home from that Christer school."

Nick was judging the street view from where Alf was sitting beside his desk. He had a pretty good sweep of North Gwinnett in front of him, the people going back and forth, the traffic streaming along, flashing steel in the afternoon light.

"You sitting here?" asked Nick.

"Ayup."

"Good look at him?"

"Ayup."

"Was he alone?"

"Ayup."

"Did he seem in a hurry, or agitated?"

Alf's frown deepened as he worked that through.

"You mean, like someone was following him?"

"Ayup," said Nick.

Alf, a sharp old file, picked up on Nick's mimicry and gave him a censorious frown, which Nick somehow managed to withstand.

"Nope. Just lollygagging. He stood there for a while, looking at the books."

"He ever come in?"

"Nope. Kids don't have any use for books nowadays. Always on those tweeters and such. He looks in, moves off next door. Uncle Moochie's."

"The pawnshop."

"Ayup. Every day the same thing, looks in here, waves at me, and then moves down to stare at all that crap in Uncle Moochie's window."

"They spoke with Uncle Moochie. He says he saw the kid yesterday, saw him the day before, and the day before that, but not today."

"Moochie," said Alf, as if that was explanation enough.

"Moochie's window is full of stuff a kid would like to look at," said Nick.

Alf considered this, blinked, said nothing.

"Have you ever seen anyone who looked like he might be following the Teague boy? Anyone in the street who was paying too much attention?"

"You mean like one of those peedo-philes?"

"Yeah. One of those."

"Nope. I did come to the door to look at the boy, him standing there, staring in at Moochie's window. Kid always spent a good five minutes in front of Moochie's, looking at all the pawn stuff. I figure, what you should do, you should go stand there for a while, yourself, see what you get."

"You think?"

"Ayup."

So Nick did.

The store where Uncle Moochie ran what he liked to call his brokerage service had been a fairly ornate barbershop back in the thirties, and it still had faint traces of gilt lettering in an arch across the front of the glass—SULLIVAN'S TONSORIAL ACADEMY—but the window was so jammed to the ceiling with antique clocks and gilt mirrors and pocket watches and china busts of pocket dogs and rusted Art Deco lamps and cameos and brooches and gaudy costume jewelry and tiny bronze nudes that it looked like a treasure chest. Nick could see how a kid would find the window fascinating.

According to Boot Jackson's field report, Nick was right on top of the last place on North Gwinnett where anyone had seen the kid.

No one in the shops farther down North Gwinnett had seen him go by, although he was a regular at Scoops in the next block, and people often saw him climbing the base of the bronze statue of the Confederate trooper in the parkette at the intersection of North Gwinnett and Bluebottle Way.

But not today.

Today, as far as the Niceville PD had been able to determine, this spot of sidewalk in front of Uncle Moochie's was the farthest Rainey Teague had gotten before . . . before *something* happened.

Pawnshops have security cameras, Nick was thinking. There it was, in the top left corner, one red eye blinking down at him.

Moochie, a morose Lebanese with a sagging face full of guile and sorrow, had once been enormous, but a severe case of ulcerative colitis had left him looking like a melting candle. He was a notorious fence but also a good street source for Nick, and he was happy to let Nick see the security video, leading him through the clutter and litter and overloaded display cases to the back of the narrow store, where, in an office that reeked of sweat and hashish, he opened up a cupboard concealing an LED monitor and pressed a few buttons on a panel.

"It's all digital. Auto-erases every twenty-four hours, if I don't cancel it," said Moochie, as the video began to roll backwards, the time marker flickering in the lower right-hand corner of the screen.

They stood there in Moochie's crowded office and watched the people in the video walk jerkily backwards through time as the seconds coiled up again. A minute and thirty-eight seconds ran off and Nick saw himself standing on the walk outside Moochie's, staring up at the video camera, and then Nick walked backwards away to the left of the picture. The marker spooled and flickered, the people in the video moving as in an old silent film, stiff and strange, as if they were all ghosts of the long-gone past.

Nick was very aware of Moochie beside him and for a time he wondered if Moochie himself was the last thing Rainey Teague saw.

Had Rainey come into the shop?

And if he had, what had happened then?

Was he upstairs right now, or in the basement?

The next shop along was Toonerville, a hobby shop with a big Lionel train going around and around in a miniature version of Niceville. Rainey never failed to go inside and talk to Mrs. Lianne Hardesty, who ran the shop. Rainey was a favorite there, but today, no Rainey.

Moochie?

Nick had never heard anything hinky about Moochie, no hint of a pedophile streak or any other kind of chicken-hawk leaning. His record, although far from edifying, contained nothing that indicated any sort of sexual impulses at all.

But you never knew.

Moochie grunted, hit a button, and the image froze with the time marker stopped at 1509:22. There was Rainey Teague, just stepping into the picture, seen from an angle above and to his right, so that the kid seemed foreshortened.

Moochie looked at Nick, who nodded, and Moochie hit a

button that advanced the frames one at a time. Rainey's clockwork figure ticked fully into the picture frame, exactly as Alf Pennington had described him, Harry Potter knapsack slung over his left shoulder, so full it was tilting him in that direction.

Nick's heart rate climbed as he watched the kid standing there, feeling a shadow of what Rainey's parents must be feeling right now, but even the shadow of that dread was cold and cutting.

Moochie kept the image moving, frame by frame, as Rainey came to a stop about a foot from the plate glass, shading his eyes to stare in at the pirate treasure, even, at one time, pressing his snub nose up against the glass, flattening it out in a comical way, his breath misting up the glass. People were moving past him in the image. No one was paying him any unusual attention.

"Freeze it there," Nick said.

He leaned down to look at the kid's face. The expression on it was utterly absorbed. He was staring at something in the display, and whatever he was looking at had completely fascinated him.

He was held there, as if by a spell, frozen and transfixed.

By what?

"Did he ever come into the shop?"

Moochie shook his head.

"I don't let the Regiopolis kids come in. They're all thieves. Little Ali Babas. Just like the street kids in Beirut."

"Do you know what he was looking at, in the window? Whatever it is, it's sure got his attention."

"He's looking at the mirror. I finally figured out it was that mirror," said Moochie, staring at the boy in the frozen frame. "From the way he's standing, it's right in front of him. He's looking right at it. It's the one in the gilt frame. It's very old, prewar at least. I mean the Civil War. It came out of Temple

Hill, the old Cotton mansion up in The Chase. Delia Cotton gave it to her housemaid, a lady named Alice Bayer, she lives in The Glades, and Alice came in one day and asked me for fifty dollars on it. I gave her two hundred. It's worth a thousand. I still have the ticket. Rainey liked to see himself in it, I think. He always stood there, looking into the mirror, anyway, just like that. Then he'd sort of shake himself out of it and off he'd go. The glass is rippled from age, so I guess it's sort of a fun-house thing for the kid."

Nick made a gesture and Moochie started inching the frames forward again, Nick looking for something, anything he could use. At time marker 1513:54 Rainey started to move his head backwards, his mouth opening. At 1513:55 he was starting to step back onto his left heel, and his mouth was opening wider.

At 1513:56 he wasn't in the picture at all.

The camera was aimed at an empty patch of sidewalk.

Rainey was gone.

"Is it the camera?" Nick asked.

Moochie was just gaping at the screen.

Nick asked him again.

"No. It never does that. It's brand-new. I got it put in by Securicom last year. Cost me three thousand dollars."

"Back it up."

Moochie did, one frame at a time.

Same thing.

First frame, Rainey's not there.

One frame back, there he is.

He's stepping onto his heel, with his mouth wide open.

Another frame back, he's still there, and now he's close to the window, but beginning to . . .

To what?

Recoil?

From what?

Something he saw in a mirror?

Or someone behind him, reflected in the mirror. What the hell was going on here?

"What's the recording stored on?"

"The hard drive," said Moochie, still staring at the screen.

"Is it removable?"

Moochie looked at him.

"Yes. But—"

"I'm going to need it. No. Wait. I'm going to need the whole system. Do you have a spare?"

Moochie was far from thrilled by this development.

"I still have the old camera, hooked up to a VCR."

"Run it again, one more time. This time go right through the sequence."

Moochie pressed ADVANCE.

They stood and watched as Rainey Teague stick-walked jerkily into the frame, leaned close to the glass, stayed there, his expression growing more fixed as the seconds passed, Rainey drawing closer and closer to the glass until his nose was pressed up against it and his breath was fogging the window.

Then the recoil.

He steps back.

And . . . vanishes.

The camera kept rolling. They both stood there and watched it, riveted, locked on, with the utter *wrongness* of the thing rippling up and down their spines. In the frames they saw the feet of passing strollers, always that patch of bare sidewalk, now and then a piece of paper flickering through or the shadow of a bird rippling across the screen, and in the background people passing by, perfectly oblivious.

They ran the frames on until a uniform cop appeared in the image, crossing from the direction of Pennington's Book Nook, reaching for the door of Uncle Moochie's.

Nick recognized the big bulky shape and the pale freckled

features of Boots Jackson, the Niceville cop assigned to canvass this block. They rolled it back and forth a few more times,
but it was always the same.

At 1513:55, Rainey Teague is right there.

At 1513:56, the kid is *gone*.

He doesn't leap out of the picture, or duck to one side, or
jump way up high, or fade away, or turn into a puff of smoke,
or get jerked away by the arms of a stranger.

He just flicks off, as if he were only a digital image and
somebody had hit ERASE.

Rainey Teague is just *gone*.

And he never comes back.

Of course in the harrowing days and nights that followed, as
the CID and the Niceville cops and everybody else who could
be spared tore up the state looking for the kid, no serious cop
believed even for a second that what the camera was showing
was literally the truth, that the kid had just snapped out of
existence.

It had to be some sort of computer glitch.

Or a trick, like something David Copperfield would do.

So they started with the security system that Moochie had
installed, examining it and testing it and retesting it, looking
for the glitch, looking for any sign that Moochie had rigged
the entire thing to cover up a simple kidnapping. The security
machine, a Motorola surveillance system, was sent off to the
FBI for a complete forensic examination. It came back without a flaw, showing zero signs of having been tampered with in
any way.

Next came Moochie himself, who was put through an
interrogation that would have done credit to the Syrian Secret
Police. He also came through without a hint of guilty knowledge.

They took his shop apart.

Nothing.

They took Delia Cotton's antique mirror to a lab and checked it for—well, they had no damned idea what, but whatever they were hoping for, it wasn't there. It was just a medium-sized antique mirror with a tarnished silver face inside a baroque gilt frame, with a handwritten linen card on the back:

With Long Regard — Glynis R.

So Uncle Moochie got his expensive security system back, with their apologies, although he refused to have anything more to do with the mirror, which finally ended up in Nick Kavanaugh's closet, and in the meantime they took Alf Pennington's Book Nook apart, which he endured stoically, seeing it as a final confirmation of the innate brutality of the Imperium. They found nothing.

They took Toonerville Hobby Shoppe apart.

Nothing.

They looked at every available frame of every available surveillance camera video up and down North Gwinnett between Bluebottle Way and Long Reach Boulevard.

Nothing.

Not a trace.

Naturally, Nick Kavanaugh went effectively nuts around the ninth sleepless day, and his wife, Kate, a family practice lawyer, at Tig Sutter's urging, slipped a couple of Valiums into his orange juice and packed him off to their bed, where he slept like the living dead for twelve hours straight.

While Nick was sleeping, Kate, after struggling with the idea for a time, called her father, Dillon Walker, who was a professor of military history up at the Virginia Military Institute in the Shenandoah Valley. It was late, but Walker, a widower who lived alone in faculty rooms on the edge of the parade square, answered the phone on the second ring. Kate heard his whispery bass voice in those familiar warm tones and she wished, as she often did, that her father lived closer to Niceville and that her mother, Lenore, the heart of Dillon Walker's life, had not been killed in a rollover on the interstate five years ago. Her father was never the same after that. Something important had gone out of him, some of his amiable fire. But he was sharp enough to hear the tightness in her voice when she said hello.

"Kate . . . how are you? Is everything okay?"

"I'm sorry to call so late, Dad. Did I wake you?"

Walker sat up in his leather club chair—while not actually asleep on his military-style cot, he *had* been dozing over a copy of *Pax Britannica*, James Morris' history of the British Empire under Victoria. Kate's voice had that faint quiver in it that was always there when she was stressed.

"No, sweet. I was up late reading. You sound a little worried. It's not Beth, is it? Or Reed?"

Beth, Kate's older sister, was in a toxic marriage to an ex–FBI agent named Byron Deitz, who was cordially loathed by everyone in the family. Reed was her brother, a state trooper who drove a pursuit car, a hard-edged young man who was never happier than when he was running down a speeder.

"No, Dad. Not Beth. Not Reed. It's about Nick."

"Dear God. He's not hurt?"

"No, no. He's fine. To tell you the truth I sort of slipped him a mickey so he could sleep. He's upstairs now, dead to the world. He's been on a case for days, and he's a total wreck."

There was a pause, as if she were trying to find a way to begin. Walker leaned over and stirred the fireplace embers into a soft yellow flickering, sat back in the worn leather chair, and picked up his scotch. Tepid and flat, but still Laphroaig.

He could hear Kate's breath over the phone, and pictured her there in their old family home, a slender auburn-haired

Irish rose with sapphire blue eyes and a fine-cut, elegant face, very much the picture of her mother, Lenore. He sipped at the scotch, set it down.

"You sound like you have a question, Kate. Is it about Nick's case?"

A silence.

Then, "I guess it is, Dad. The fact is, we've had another disappearance."

She heard her father's breathing stop, and knew she had touched a sore point between them. Several years ago her father had begun an informal personal inquiry into the high rate of stranger abductions in Niceville, only to quit the project abruptly after Lenore's death. He never picked it up again, and he had delicately but effectively evaded the topic ever since. When he spoke again his voice was as warm as always, but perhaps a little more wary.

"I see. And I guess this case is what's keeping Nick from sleeping? Was it really an abduction? A stranger abduction? Like all the others?"

"So far they seem to think so. Can I tell you about it? Would that be okay?"

"Please, Kate. Anything I can do."

Kate told him what they knew so far, Rainey Teague, on his way home from school, Uncle Moochie's pawnshop, the security camera, and the way the boy just disappeared into thin air. Walker listened and felt his throat tightening.

"The boy's name was Teague? Not Sylvia's boy?"

"Yes, Dad."

"God. That's awful. How is she?"

"Terrible. Falling apart."

"And Miles?"

"You know Miles. He's a typical Teague, and they all have that cold spot. But he gets quieter every day. They've both given up hope."

"Where does the case stand now?"

"Everyone's in it. Belfair and Cullen County, the state police, the Cap City office of the FBI."

"Do they have any leads?"

"Nothing. Nothing at all."

A pause.

Then he spoke again, with a kind of forced calm in his voice.

"Did anything—anomalous—happen?"

"*Anomalous*, Dad? Like what?"

"I don't know, really. I know you're asking me because of the research I was doing, but I don't know any more about this kind of thing now than I did then. That's why I quit. It was pointless."

"You quit when Mom died, Dad."

He was quiet again.

She waited.

She had crossed his line—she knew that—but she also knew she was his favorite child, the one he had always been closest to.

"I guess, by anomalous, I mean anything hard to explain."

"Other than the fact that Rainey just vanished into thin air while being filmed by a security camera?"

"In front of Uncle Moochie's pawnshop, right?"

"Yes."

"You said he was standing on the sidewalk, looking at something in Uncle Moochie's window?"

"Yes."

"What was it?"

"It was a mirror."

Silence from her father, but she could feel his tension, like a vibration humming down the wire.

"What sort of mirror?"

"An antique. Moochie said it was pre–Civil War. It came from Temple Hill. Delia Cotton gave it to the lady who does the cleaning and shopping."

"Teagues and Cottons," he said in a flat tone.

"Yes. Two of the old families."

More silence.

Finally . . .

"Can you describe the mirror?"

"Gold frame, baroque, ancient glass, with the silvering coming off the back. Maybe seventeenth-century Irish. Or French. About thirty inches by thirty inches. Heavy. Has an antique linen calling card glued to the back."

"What was on the card?"

"Very fine handwriting, in turquoise ink. 'With long regard . . . Glynis R.' "

A taut silence again. Kate could hear him breathing, slow and steady, as if he were trying to calm himself. When he spoke again, all the genial warmth had left his voice.

"Where is it now? The mirror? Still at Moochie's?"

"No. It's here. It's upstairs, actually. In our bedroom closet. Why?"

Walker was quiet for so long that Kate began to think he had fallen asleep.

"Dad? You there?"

"Yes. Sorry. I was thinking."

This sounded like . . . not a lie, because he never lied to her, but at least an evasion.

"Can you make any sense out of all this, Dad? The connections between the old families? Nick tried to establish who Glynis R. was, but Delia said she had no idea. Does the name mean anything to you?"

"No. No, it doesn't."

Again that sense of . . . wary distance.

Evasion.

"What should we do, Dad? I'd like to help Nick. And Sylvia's family. Rainey was—is—such a sweet kid. I know it's late, Dad. I know you need to sleep. So do I. Can you think of anything at all?"

She waited.

"Do you *use* the mirror?"

"No. Of course not. It's evidence, sort of."

"You should give it back to Delia. Or to her cleaning lady. As soon as possible. I'm sure it's quite valuable."

"As I said, right now it's part of the case. At least Nick thinks so. Anything else, Dad?"

"Yes. Don't *ever* use it. The mirror."

"I'm not sure I understand."

"Neither do I."

She tried to be light.

"Is it cursed?" she asked with a smile. "Like if we break it, we'll get seven years of bad luck?"

"Maybe you should do just that."

"Do what?"

"Break it. Smash it. Throw the pieces into Crater Sink."

"You're teasing me now."

A silence.

"Yes. I'm just teasing you. I'm sorry not to have been more helpful. Honey, I need to sleep. You do too. How about you call me in the morning? Around eleven? We can talk some more?"

"I will, Dad. Love you."

"Love you too, Kate. Love you very much."

Kate never quite got around to calling Dillon Walker at eleven the next morning, mainly because of the flurry of activity following a call that came at daybreak, Tig on the line to say that Sylvia Teague's red Porsche Cayenne had just been found by a patrol cruiser doing a routine check of the parking area near Crater Sink. Sylvia's ballet flats were found at the rim of the sink itself. Of Sylvia Teague, no trace was found, in spite of the deployment of a robot dive camera which was brought in by Marty Coors, head of the State Police HQ in Cap City.

The camera went down and down into the sink, lights spearing out into the cold black water a way, only to die out, overwhelmed by the darkness. The control cable ran out at a thousand feet.

The attached sonar mapping system showed nothing but rock face and more rock face with a side channel running out of the sinkhole at nine hundred and eighty feet, leading, everyone assumed, eventually to the Tulip River in the valley below the cliff face.

If Sylvia Teague *had* gone into Crater Sink—and so far no suicide note had been found, and suicide was only one of several possibilities—they'd have to wait for natural processes to bring her back up again.

Or maybe she had been dragged into the side channel by a random current, which meant that perhaps someday what was left of her would come bobbing up in the Tulip River itself.

The Crater Sink search took most of the tenth day, with Nick, haggard and running on amphetamines, there for every minute of it. He stayed there until around six that same evening, the evening of the tenth day, when he got a call from Mavis Crossfire, who told him Rainey Teague had been found.

Nick got to the Confederate cemetery across the road from Garrison Hills just as the sun was setting. He saw the police vans clustered around a low hill on one of the meandering stone pathways that led through the rocky, uneven slopes of the graveyard, weaving past hundreds and hundreds of white stone crosses—here and there a few Stars of David—towards what was called New Hill, a part of the Civil War graveyard that had been set aside for the more prominent civilians of Niceville history.

New Hill had perhaps fifty miniature stone temples, most of them in the Palladian style, mostly family crypts with names like HAGGARD and TEAGUE, COTTON and WALKER, GWINNETT and MULLRYNE and MERCER and RUELLE carved into their lintels.

Each temple was made of marble blocks and each one had a solid oak door, locked and sealed, and then further protected by an iron grate. The ground in the cemetery was stony, so some of the lesser graves were simply a low mounded barrow of red clay brick with a long marble or stone cap, the barrow set deep into the ground and mounded all around with earth and grass. The crypt was accessible only by a low iron grating at one end, always padlocked.

The cops were gathered around one of these low mounds, watching two firemen with sledges who were attacking the roof of the crypt. Nick could hear their sledges clang with each blow, and he saw brick dust rising up in the glimmer of the headlights and the halogen work lamps that had been set up all around the mound.

Everyone turned to watch as Nick parked his Crown Vic down the slope and walked slowly up the hill to where they were working. Mavis Crossfire stepped out of the crowd— Nick could see the rangy form and Marine Corps crew cut of Marty Coors, the CO of the local state troopers, above the heads of the other cops, turning to stare at Nick, his face solemn and hard, his eyes full of uncertainty.

"Nick," said Mavis, coming up to shake his hand. "He's here."

Nick looked past her, at the mound, at the men slowly hammering it into brick chips and marble splinters.

"He's in there? How do you know? That crypt hasn't been open for more than a hundred years. They're all like that. The padlocks are all rusted and seized. The bars are half in the ground and they're all grown over."

"Yes. That's true. That's all true. Nick, are you okay?"

Nick looked at her.

"Hell, no, I'm not okay. Are you?"

Mavis gave him a smile that changed into an odd look.

"No. I'm not. None of us are. How we know he's in there, Nick? We can *hear* him."

Nick looked at her for a long time.

Mavis nodded, her expression blank, except for a wary look in her eyes and a pallor in her skin.

"Yeah. That's right. I didn't want to tell you before you got here. Didn't want you to die in a crash racing over here. The groundskeeper heard something in the afternoon. Sounded like maybe a bird, but then he thought maybe not. He traced it to this mound here."

"Who's in it?"

"Guy named Ethan Ruelle. Died in 1921. In a duel on Christmas Eve, so the groundskeeper is saying. One of the fire guys has a sound sensor, the kind they use to search for people in a collapse? He stuck it up against the roof of that thing. We all heard it plain."

"Heard what?"

"A kid. Crying."

Nick looked at her, and then past her at the workers, at the cops standing around, the ambulance waiting a ways back, lights churning red and blue, casting a crazy hectic flicker across the graveyard.

"It's a trick," he said finally, his temper flaring. "This whole thing has been some kind of sick stunt. Someone is jerking us around, Mavis. It's all just some kind of twisted game."

"If it is, it's a damn good one," said Mavis, taking no offense, speaking in a soothing tone. "The guy tapped on the stone and the crying got worse. *Something's* in there. We all think—maybe I should say we all *hope*—it's Rainey."

They heard a muffled *crump*, a gravelly tumble, and then everyone was talking loud and fast.

Nick and Mavis got to the mound just as Marty Coors stepped up and put his Maglite into the hole the fire guys had opened. There was a terrified face looking up at them, big round brown eyes, dirty blond hair, his dusty cheeks streaked with tear tracks, his mouth round and stretched as he went way back and down for the scream he finally came up with a few seconds later. It rang out across the graves and a flock of crows went exploding up out of a stand of linden.

The boy was Rainey Teague, and he was alive.

When they got him out a few minutes later, still in his school uniform, they realized he had been placed inside a long wooden box, a coffin, and the coffin wasn't empty.

Rainey Teague had been cradled in the withered embrace of a corpse, presumably the remains of Ethan Ruelle. They had no idea how this had been done, how the tomb had been opened without any sign of tampering, or by whom, or why, but Rainey Teague was alive. They took him to Lady Grace, where, over the next five hours, he slipped slowly but inexorably into a catatonic state.

He was still lying there three days later when his father, Miles Teague, came to see his boy once again in the ICU unit. Rainey was lying in the middle of all the usual medical machinery, IV drips and beeping monitors and catheter racks and catheter drains.

The ICU docs told Miles—a blunt-bodied Black Irish man in his early fifties, with a well-cut, handsome face going rapidly to hell—before withdrawing to leave the man alone with his son, that Rainey's catatonia was not an uncommon response to unimaginable trauma.

Miles Teague stared down at his son for two hours, watching him breathe in and out, then he leaned down and kissed him on the forehead, straightened up and went out to the parking lot and climbed into his big black Benz. He drove himself back to the family home in Garrison Hills, where he was found the next morning, in the same clothes, in a marble folly at the bottom of the garden, a handmade Purdey shotgun lying by his body and his head blown off at the shoulders.

Friday Afternoon

Coker's Afternoon Required
Some Concentration

The two-way radio in Coker's pocket started to buzz, like a palmetto bug in a bottle. Coker was down deep inside himself, trying to see it all unfold. This Zen trick used to come naturally, but that was a long time back. He was looking through the yellow pampas grass at the snaky stretch of blacktop curving towards him through the long green valley, the heavy rifle in his hands as solid and warm as the neck of a horse.

The two-way buzzed again.

Coker pulled the handset out, thumbed the key.

"Yes."

"We're at mile marker 47."

Danziger's voice was flat and calm, but tight. Coker could hear the sirens in the background, hear the hissing rush of wind, and the rumble of tires on the pebbled surface of the highway.

"What have you got?"

Coker listened to a short hard-edged exchange between Danziger and Merle Zane, the driver, both voices a little adrenalized, which was only natural.

"So far only four," said Danziger, coming back, "They're right on us but staying back. We've got one news chopper with us, but far as we can see no cops in the air yet. Anything up ahead?"

Coker looked down at the little portable TV on the ground beside him. On the tiny plasma screen he could see a dull black bullet-shaped car with a front like a clenched fist, Merle Zane's Chrysler Magnum, flying down a curving ribbon of county road, patchwork farmlands all around, with four cars in close pursuit, two charcoal-gray and black Crown Vics, what looked like a black and tan deputy sheriff car, also a Crown Vic, and one dark blue unmarked car, a flying brick with big fat tires and a rack of black steel bumper bars right up front.

The image was coming from a local news chopper follow-ing the chase. Coker could see the roof-rack lights on the patrol cars flickering red and blue.

Coker twisted the VOLUME button and heard the hyperven-tilating commentary of a young female newscaster describing the chase. The image pulled back as the chopper lifted to clear a line of transmission towers, briefly showing a rolling blue country with low brown hills far off to the south.

Coker was waiting in those low brown hills.

He picked up the radio, keyed it.

"So far no roadblocks, road is clear. Confirm you have four units. Two state and a deputy. The blue Dodge Charger is one of their chase units. A hemi, three sixty-eight mill, a roll-cage, those heavy-duty ram bars. They've got him laying back in the pack but at the first chance he'll pull around and climb right up your tailpipe. He'll use those bumper bars on your off-side taillight, put you into a spin. Don't let him get close."

"We won't," said Danziger. "So nobody up ahead?"

Danziger's tone was still flat, but Coker could hear the ten-sion in his throat. Coker was monitoring the police frequen-cies, listening to the cross talk between dispatch and the pursuit cars.

"They've called for units from Sectors Four and Nine, but

so far only two units can respond, and they're twenty miles off, on the other side of the Belfair Range. They're spread all over the county and most of their guys are up on the interstate, helping with traffic around the crash site. That's where their chopper is too."

"Okay," said Danziger. "Good—"

Coker heard a solid thump, and the sound of glass cracking, and then Merle Zane's voice, swearing softly.

"Christ. They're shooting at us."

Coker glanced down at the television, heard the announcer's excited voice, her words tumbling out in a rush. The banner along the bottom of the screen read HAPPENING NOW! POLICE CHASE ROUTE 311 SOUTH SKYCAM NEWS POLICE CHASE! HAPPENING NOW! but the crawl did not name her. Coker figured whoever she was, she was having a hell of a good time.

Good for you.

Get it while you can, kid.

"Like I said. You're letting them get too close."

Coker heard the sound of a pistol firing, a series of sharp percussive cracks, and then Merle Zane's voice.

"Danziger's shooting back."

"Well, tell him don't, Merle. Shooting back just motivates them. He oughta know that. Tell him to keep his head down or they'll take it off."

He heard Merle Zane barking at Danziger, heard Danziger's heated reply, but the shooting stopped, and then Merle was talking again.

"Mile marker 40. We're two miles out."

"I'm here," he said, and clicked off.

He turned the sound on the plasma screen down and shut off the police radio. Didn't really matter what the State guys were doing right now.

Whatever it was, it was too late.

The news chopper—now *that* was a problem.

He looked at the TV screen, trying to get an idea of how

high up the chopper was, the angles, the kind of machine. Most of the news and some of the police choppers in the state were Eurocopter 350s. What he could hear of the rotor noise and the engine sounded like that's what this one was. Nice fast machine.

But light and thin-skinned.

A flying egg.

He leaned back against a tree trunk, eased the rifle in his lap, took a slow breath, and opened himself up to what was going on around him.

In a stand of cottonwoods on the far side of the road a bunch of crows were bickering with another bunch of crows. The wind off the flatlands was stirring the pampas grass, making its shaggy heads bob and its brittle stalks hiss and chatter as they rubbed together. The afternoon sun was blood-warm on his left cheek. He looked up. The sky was a cloudless blue. Down the slope of the hill a possum was digging in the red earth, its tail showing like a curved black stick above the pale yellow grass. Three hawks were circling overhead, wings spread and fixed, gliding in lazy circles, riding the thermals as the day's heat cooked off the lowlands. The air smelled of sweetgrass, clover, hot earth, and baking tarmac. It reminded him of Billings and the sweetgrass coulees down in the Bighorn valley. In the distance, faint but growing, Coker could hear the wail of sirens.

He looked down at the TV screen, saw the line of cars following Merle's black Magnum, that dark blue interceptor weaving up through the pack, closing in on Merle as the two-lane started to rise up into the grassy foothills of the Belfair Range.

Across the street the crows fell silent, as if listening, and then they exploded upwards in one swirling black cloud, amber light shimmering on their wings.

He felt the drumbeat of a chopper, coming in low, hidden by the tree line, and then, under the siren wail, the squealing

of tires as Merle pushed the Magnum through a curve a quarter mile away.

The sirens grew more shrill, crazy echoes bouncing off the
hills all around, mixed up with the snarling sound of engines
racing.

Coker hefted the rifle, put on a pair of ear protectors, let
out a long slow breath, got into a seated brace, resting the
rifle's bipod on a stump in front of him, and depressed the
stock until the squared-off muzzle brake was covering the top
of the tree line.

The rifle was a semi-auto five-shot. He had five rounds in
the box mag, and three more full mags in the canvas bag on
the ground beside him. Coker figured that if he needed those
extra mags, he'd be dead by sunset.

He did not put his eye close to the Leupold scope until he
saw the shiny red ball of the news chopper appear above the
trees. Then he leaned into the scope, set the stock in tight,
braced for the machine's mule-kick recoil, eased his finger
onto the serrated ridges of the trigger blade, pressing down on
it until he could just feel the sear begin to engage. Stopped.
Held it.

The chopper was slipping left, skimming the tree line, following the curve of the hills, intent on the chase, a steady
glide, hardly moving at all, so the newsgirl could get a good
smooth camera pan. Coker could see two pale figures through
the canopy bubble. The newsgirl would be in the copilot seat,
on the left side of the canopy, working the radio and the camera and talking her talk.

The pilot would be in the right-hand seat, busy with the
cyclic and the collective and the pedals, his mind totally taken
up with situational awareness, with thinking about power lines
and tree branches and big dumb suicidal geese and all the
other air traffic that might be zipping around in the pursuit
zone.

Even if the pilot had been looking right at Coker's position, all he would have seen was a little scrap of tan cloth in a field of pampas grass, maybe a long black rod sticking up.

Coker locked down on the sight image, inhaled, breathed out slow, held it at half, stilled himself.

Squeezed the trigger.

The Barrett bucked in his grip, slamming back into his right shoulder, the muzzle-brake gasses flaring out sideways. The chopper image in his scope was momentarily obscured by the heat ripple but Coker saw the pilot take the .50-caliber round right in the middle of his chest.

Basically, the guy exploded, the hydrostatic shock wave blowing through the water-filled tissues of his body at the speed of sound, like an asteroid slamming into the sea.

Coker had seen it before, many times, a center mass hit like that. Usually, when you got down to the vehicle, you found the driver's head hanging by strings, both eye sockets blown right out, ears and mouth running black blood, and nothing left of his upper body but pink vertebrae and gaping ribs.

Firepower, thought Coker. *You gotta love it.*

With no living hands on the cyclic and the collective, the chopper staggered, dipped, and then, vibrating crazily, went into a sideways roll.

In the TV screen Coker watched the camera image as the sky and the ground traded places. The TV picture turned into a whirling blur as the cottonwood trees came rushing up.

Faintly, through the sound-canceling earphones, he heard a high shriek of raw terror, thin as a silver wire, coming from the TV speakers. The newsgirl, filing her last best story, an up-close and personal eyewitness report right from the scene of a fatal chopper crash.

Happening Now!

The thought made him smile, putting a cold yellow glitter in his pale brown eyes, his hard mouth tightening.

He felt the concussion through the earth as the chopper hit hard on the far side of the tree line. Out of the corner of his right eye he saw orange fire come billowing up, but by then he had shifted his position, reset himself, the rifle scope now zeroed in on the highway as Merle's Magnum came flying up the curve towards Coker's position.

Coker had taken a stand that allowed him to see down the entire length of the S-curve as the cars came directly at him. It would give him the most time-on-target and a field of fire that would stretch right down the line of cars.

Technically, if this were a Recon Marine ambush, there would be a five-man fire team on the long side of an L-shaped barrier, a chain of command-linked claymore mines at the forward edge—seven hundred steel balls embedded in a curved packet of C-4 plastic explosive, with those lovely words embossed on the front: FACE TOWARDS ENEMY. Click the clacker and off they all go in a blinding roar and a hailstorm of steel to shred the poor bastards in the kill zone, followed up by a mad minute from every rifle and automatic weapon in the squad and, God willing, a mortar to seal the deal.

But this afternoon there was only Coker and his Barrett .50, at the top of the S-curve, watching them come. He could see Merle's thin white face behind the wheel, and Danziger's flash of dirty blond hair. Everything slowed down.

To the left side of Merle's black car he had a pretty good slice of the dark blue interceptor coming up.

Not all of it.

But enough.

He put the second shot of his five-round mag into the hood of the chase car. The super-heated engine block exploded in every direction, including chunks of hot iron that flew backwards right through the firewall and into the driver's face, chest, and belly. The car swerved as the driver's hands dragged the wheel to the right.

It slammed into a line of trees, blood spattered across the inside of the windscreen and sheeted over the air bag. The cruiser settled, and began to steam.

Now Coker had a clear line on the second car, the black-and-white sheriff's car. One man behind the wheel. Coker could see his face turning as he flew by the wreck of the interceptor, see his mouth open in shock. He recognized the guy, an earnest young Cullen County cop named Billy Goodhew.

At that moment Merle Zane and Charlie Danziger flew by Coker's position, horn blaring, Danziger staring out through the passenger window.

Coker never turned his head, was only dimly aware of them passing. You could have fired a 9 mm next to his ear right then and he would not have flinched.

Coker's third round took Billy Goodhew's head and upper body off and spattered it all over the prisoner partition behind him. It also took out the rear window and, in one of those weird accidents that happen in firefights, sent a glittering sun-drenched sheet of the deputy's arterial blood and brain tissue across the windshield of the patrol unit on his tail.

Both state cars broke hard, tires smoking, grilles dipping down, cutting left and right, coming to a tail-to-tail blocking position, overlapped, trying to establish a defensive stand.

Coker put his fourth round into the driver's side of the windshield on the left-hand car, saw the roof stipple with fragments and the shattered window cover itself with a sheet of black blood. Nobody popped out of the passenger door, so Coker figured the driver was alone.

Poor bastard.

Thanks to the recession, most of the state and county guys had been cut back to singles, even at night. It was a goddam disgrace. Fucking bean counters down in Cap City. They'd never have to make a DUI stop at two in the morning, all alone out on a deserted highway, pulling over some overloaded black Escalade with tinted windows and God-only-knows-what waiting inside it.

Coker turned his attention to the other car, which was stopped now, a lone trooper climbing out from behind the wheel, a shotgun in his left hand, a radio in his right, his Stetson jammed on all wrong and a wide-eyed holy shit expression on his round white face.

The kid turned and scooted around to the defilade side of the unit, out of Coker's direct line of fire, trying to put as much heavy metal between himself and whatever was shooting at him as he could.

Coker let him get set, even let him get off a round, just to make sure he knew where the center of his mass would be, and then he put his fifth round straight through the entire width of the car and blew the kid into bloody chunks.

The trooper's shotgun clattered backwards.

And the quiet came down.

A moment of pressurized silence, Coker's heart thudding in his ribs. And then he got up, shook his head to clear the ringing, and looked around him as if seeing the place for the first time.

The stillness was unsettling and in spite of the ear protection his hearing was vague and muffled, as if the world were wrapped in a bubble. His shoulder throbbed from the kick of the Barrett.

On the far side of the road a small forest fire had broken out and a pillar of white smoke was rising up into the sky.

The cottonwood smoke smelled nice, tangy and biting. Reminded him of Christmas back in Billings. Happy times. Coker breathed it in for a while, feeling the world come slowly back to normal.

He turned on the scanner and listened to the cross talk for a moment. All he heard was panic. Nobody knew what the hell had just happened and everybody was telling everybody else what to do about it at the top of their lungs.

He figured he had time for a quick cleanup.

Just to be on the safe side, he removed the empty box mag, slammed a new one home, released the bolt to chamber a round, flicked the safety to horizontal, and shouldered the rifle, all twenty pounds of it, on a patrol sling, where he could swing it around and bring it to bear if he had to.

He pulled out a Colt Python and walked down the road to the squad cars and put a big soft-nosed .357 round into every intact skull he could find, reloaded, and did what he could with whatever was left of whoever was left.

Then he extracted, with some difficulty because of the latex gloves he was wearing and the bits of tissue and blood and bone all over the interior, all the hard disks from the various dashboard cameras. That done, he stepped backwards out of the area, looking to see if he was leaving bloody boot tracks at the crime scene.

Coker went back and policed his shooting position, gathered up his five spent casings, kicked away his boot marks and scuff traces, double-checked the area once more, and then walked over the low brush-covered hill to his cruiser, a big black and tan Crown Vic with county markings.

He popped the trunk, broke the Barrett down, easing the hot barrel out of the lock, wiped the machine with a silicone-saturated cloth, and tucked it away in sections inside its carrying case.

Then he peeled off his bloodstained overalls, stuffed them into a brown paper bag, slammed the trunk, checked his uniform in the side mirror—he looked pretty good, all things considered—got in behind the wheel, and slowly drove away from the scene. In his rearview mirror a thin spiral of smoke was rising into the sky. The crows had come back, now that all the excitement was over, and a few of the hungrier ones were settling onto the roofs of the squad cars, drawn by the scent of fresh blood.

The sun was sliding down and long blue shadows stretched

across the highway. A honey-colored light strobed along the side of his face as he drove through a stand of cottonwoods. On his police radio the air was crackling with cross talk, but it sounded like somebody at HQ—probably Mickey Hancock— was finally getting a grip on things. Soon they'd be calling him in, along with every other cop in the western hemisphere.

Coker sighed, looking out at the world rolling by with a satisfied mind. He smiled, put on his Ray-Bans, lit himself a cigarette, pulled the smoke in deep. His shift was just starting, with what looked to be a long, hectic night ahead. He was, however, consoled by the warmth and the lovely light. It promised to be a pretty evening.

Bock's Afternoon Was Disappointing

"All rise," and so they all rose, as Judge Theodore W. Monroe came back into the courtroom, his robes swirling behind him like portents of doom. The courthouse had originally been a Catholic church, and it still had ten wood-frame leaded-glass windows along either side, old whitewashed wooden plank walls, and a row of ceiling fans down the cedar-vaulted middle to stir, without much effect, the humid air, which, after all these years, still carried the scent of sandalwood incense.

Judge Monroe, a hatchet-faced old warrior with small black eyes and a thin smile, sat where there once would have been an altar but now there was a high carved wooden bench with an oil painting of a Civil War cavalry battle—Brandy Station on the second day—and a giant but faded American flag hanging behind. The flag had only forty-eight stars, but since neither Alaska nor Hawaii had written him to complain it was still hanging up there behind Judge Monroe's gray and bristly head.

He nodded curtly at the other people in the room, all eight of them, the unhappy ex-couple at two separate tables, standing by their lawyers, the clerk of the court, the court deputy, and a familiar elderly couple at the rear, the Fogartys, Dwayne and Dora, both retired deputy sheriffs, childless, amiable and well liked by the court staff, as alike in appearance as hermaphroditic toads. The Fogartys attended almost every trial, large and small, like retired horses that can't stay away from the track.

Judge Monroe's steel eyeglass frames glittered in the late-afternoon sunlight streaming in through the western windows. He straightened his papers into a pile, lifted them up, and tapped the fat sheaf into squared-off order on the desk, and laid it down again, resting his blue-veined hands on top.

"Kate—Ms. Kavanaugh—is there anything you would like to add before I render my decision?"

While he was presiding over a case, as a matter of ethics, Ted Monroe worked to suppress his soft spot for Kate Kavanaugh, who had effectively taken over his family law practice when he was elected to the bench. He and Kate's father, Dillon Walker, had both gone up to the University of Virginia, many long years ago now, and Ted Monroe had watched Kate grow from a long-legged coltish child with wild auburn hair and wary blue eyes into this self-contained and forceful young lawyer now appearing before him. Her marriage two years ago to an ex–Special Forces officer she had met while attending Georgetown Law in D.C. had broken the hearts of at least three young Niceville men.

Monroe had worried about the match—Nick's heart, according to Tig Sutter, was still in the covert wars, but after Tig had managed to talk Nick into taking a job with the CID instead of going on to the judge advocates, Nick had seemed to settle into the insular Niceville world without too much difficulty, quickly building a reputation as a hard cop, ruthless but fair. Ted Monroe, who had met him several times, inside the court and out, felt there was something troubling the man, something buried deep, but it had been his experience that this was true of most men who had lived complicated lives.

In short, as Ted Monroe sat there on the leather chair looking out at the scene that lay before him, he felt that Kate Kavanaugh was a happy young woman who was exactly where she was supposed to be and doing precisely what she was born to do.

Kate glanced briefly at her client, a meager and bruised-looking young woman with home-streaked hair and a pinched look in her thin face. The woman stared wide-eyed back at Kate, her tiny red hands raw as they twisted a scrap of blue polka-dot scarf. Kate gave her a reassuring smile and turned back to the bench.

"Thank you, Your Honor. Only that, should the court grant sole custody to my client, Miss Dellums wishes to inform the court that she intends, if the court allows, to accept an employment offer in Sallytown, which would involve a move of eighty-eight miles away from her ex-husband, Mr. Bock, whose employment with the Niceville Utility Commission would very likely prevent him from following, and that this move may affect the nature and construction of the court's directions concerning subsequent rules of access to the daughter."

"Thank you, Ms. Kavanaugh, for being scrupulous, but the court was aware of that development, and has already taken it into account. Miss Barrow?" He turned to the other table, addressing a tall, broad-shouldered woman in a well-cut gray pantsuit, with a pink complexion, no makeup at all, a wild aura of steel gray hair, and an air of disorder and distraction that clung to her like cigarette smoke.

"Thank you, Your Honor. Only to stress once again that my client—" Here she turned to indicate a Mr. Christian Antony Bock, a short, rather bulging young man with wide-set gray eyes, bright pink cheeks, full, feminine lips, and a blunt, petulant face, his features not quite forming into a unified whole, as if he had been composed of spare parts left over from a more successful incarnation. His nose was flat and dotted with blackheads, his skin patchy and pockmarked, his thin black hair receding, even at his young age, into an inverted vee, which had the effect of seeming to crowd all of his features into the lower third of his face.

Most people react to the random defects of their physical appearance with equanimity and humor and thereby manage, with grace, to transcend these defects and make themselves appealing, very often lovable. Tony Bock was not one of those people.

Bock straightened his sloping shoulders, adopting a parody of the military's at-ease position, and assumed what he thought was an ingratiating look as Miss Barrow turned back to the judge.

"Only to stress again that Mr. Bock has voluntarily and successfully undergone an anger-management class, that he has fully paid his entire arrears of child support, that he has paid for the damage that was accidentally done to his ex-wife's front porch and car, that he has voluntarily enrolled in a parenting-skills seminar that begins next week, and that he restates his desire to be a kind and loving presence in his daughter's life, if the court will only grant him the opportunity."

Judge Monroe's eyeglasses glittered again as he raised and lowered his head in a perfunctory acknowledgment of the statement.

Everyone in the courtroom was reasonably certain that barring a stroke of lightning, Judge Theodore W. Monroe was about to come down very hard on somebody. He had his vulture face on.

He did not disappoint.

"Duly noted, Miss Barrow, and the court thanks both counselors for their professionalism and clarity during what has been, at times, a very contentious and emotional hearing."

He paused here, set his fountain pen down on the papers in front of him, leaned back in his wingback chair, which creaked under his weight, oddly loud in the silent courtroom, clasped his arthritic hands over his belt buckle, and let his detached gaze move slowly over the upturned faces staring back at him.

"Well, so . . . having heard the arguments of both sides, and taking into full account all the various depositions filed and the petitions made, and the reports filed by Children and Family Services and the Belfair and Cullen County Domestic Violence Advisory Panel, this court has decided to grant full and sole custody of Anna Marie Bock—now Anna Marie Dellums—to her mother, Colleen Claire Dellums—and that Mr. Christian Antony Bock, formerly Miss Dellum's husband and the biological father of Anna Marie, will have no contact of any kind, either written—Miss Barrow, restrain your client—"

Bock, his face darkening, had begun to object, but his lawyer shut him down with a hoarse whisper.

Judge Monroe let a long moment pass while he glared down at Mr. Bock's inflamed face.

"I will repeat. Mr. Bock will have no contact of any kind, either supervised or unsupervised, until such time as an independent family review committee shall make a determination of the likelihood of Mr. Bock repeating the pattern of manipulation, deceit, bad faith, cruelty, aggression, and abusive and assaultive behavior that has been so well documented in this court. I do not rule out," said Monroe, gesturing with a claw-like hand knotted by age, "some sort of supervised contact in the future, but only after an assessment such as I have described has been made and the results delivered to me for my consideration. I have also directed and required the various law enforcement agencies involved to ensure that there is no contact of any kind—written, electronic, visual, televisual, sema-phoric, hieroglyphic, telepathic, in a séance—no contact of any kind will occur between Mr. Bock and any member of the Dellums family. Hear me now, Mr. Bock . . ."

He fixed Bock with a cold gray eye.

"I will regard even a casual encounter on the street as a matter to be carefully reviewed. I will consider the unexpected arrival on Miss Dellums' front porch of a white dove with a sprig of laurel in its beak to be a flagrant breach of this order and I am ready, Mr. Bock, quite ready, to enforce your full compliance with this restriction upon you in any way within my power, up to and including your incarceration upon a bench warrant for such time as the statutes and my judicial discretion may allow."

A stir from his lawyer, framing an objection.

The judge lifted a hand, bony fingers spread out, his head turning from side to side.

"No, Miss Barrow, with all respect, please do not offer a comment, if you will, at this time. I have just one final statement for the record, and then we may all go about our daily lives in peace. Let the record show that I am now directly addressing Mr. Bock. Do you hear me, Mr. Bock? Are you paying close attention?"

"Yes, Your Honor," said Bock, in an artificially small voice, but with a grating undertone, like stone sliding on stone. For a short, almost dwarfish man he could radiate a lot of mulish resentment, which he generally did only when he was alone in a room with someone or something smaller and weaker. But today, for the first time, he showed it to the whole court, and Kate Kavanaugh took careful note.

"Good. I do not approve of you, Mr. Bock. Not at all. Were it in my power to see you out of Niceville, out of the state entirely, I would do it. You have depths, Mr. Bock, and are not at all what you present to the world. I have encountered your like before, in my long life, and I imagine I will again before I go to my Maker. But I wish you to know, Mr. Bock, that I have *seen* you, and I have *noted* you, and that for as long as I am on the bench and you are within my jurisdiction, I shall have my eye upon you. Do you understand what I am saying to you, Mr. Bock?"

A long, strained silence during which Mr. Bock struggled to find an acceptable face to put before the world. To Kate Kavanaugh, who deeply loathed the nasty little man for what he had done and had tried to do to Anna Marie and her mother over the last eight months, it was like watching one of the minor demons trying on various freshly skinned human faces.

The one Bock finally picked was only half human and when she saw it a deep chill raced through her body. Bock was careful to show it to her only, in a flash of a sidelong scowl, and had a more human one in place as he faced Judge Monroe.

"I do, Your Honor," he said, in a penitent voice, inserting a tactical throat catch and blinking his eyes rapidly. "And may I say that I will try very hard to spend whatever time I have left in my life doing everything in my power to make you feel very different about me. You. My wife. My child. All of you."

Judge Monroe considered him for a time, his blue lips tight and his fingers steepled on the desk in front of him.

"Will you now, Mr. Bock?"

Bock nodded, his hands hanging down at his sides, his eyes averted from the shining disks of the judge's glasses, now trained upon him.

"I will, sir. I promise you all that I will."

Judge Monroe said nothing for a long moment.

"I believe you, Mr. Bock. I believe that for the first time in my courtroom you are speaking the literal truth. Duly noted. Court is now adjourned."

Delia Cotton's Afternoon Was Hard to Explain

Delia Cotton lived alone, quite happily alone, right up until the evening of her disappearance. She was an erect, full-figured, and elegant lady with soft brown eyes, once a heart-breaker and even now a rare beauty with a pale autumnal glow and a full head of rich silvery hair swept high and held in place with a Cartier diamond pin, bought for her in Venice by a long-dead lover.

She had enjoyed a long and complicated life filled with personal and professional success, and she had known many charming and brilliant and utterly engaging people who, by the time she had reached eighty-four, bored her to distraction.

Except for the ones who were dead and therefore could be depended upon not to grate on a woman's nerves. She was now down to two regular visitors, aside from the ladies in her book club: Alice Bayer, who drove over from The Glades five times a week to clean, bring groceries, restock her bar, and tend to Mildred Pierce, her Maine Coon cat, and Gray Haggard—his real given name, God bless him—who came around occasionally to do some gardening and routine maintenance and, from a safe distance, in a tastefully unobtrusive way, quietly adore her.

Delia cherished her privacy, and her memories, many sweet, some bitter, and all far enough in the past to have lost either their savor or their sting, and she dearly loved Temple Hill, her rambling old Victorian pile buried deep inside the tree-shaded privileges of The Chase.

Tonight, around sunset, with a lance of sunlight shining through the oaks and laying a golden glow on the rolling lawn, she was sitting in the ornate octagonal window-walled room that her husband had liked to call the bandbox when the front doorbell bonged softly in the outer darkness of the great hall.

She did not hear it right away, because up until a few minutes ago, she had been watching, with deepening depression, the urgent reporting of some hideous atrocity that had been inflicted earlier in the day upon several young highway patrol officers, up in the northern part of the state. Four dead, slaughtered in their cars. Not to mention two newspeople in a helicopter who had been killed when their machine crashed.

The cop killings had driven another story, a fatal truck rollover on the interstate, right off the television.

Watching all this, she recalled . . . who was it?

Hannah Arendt?

Dorothy Parker?

Someone such as that, who said, "One should not be required to know of events over which one could have no hope of influence."

Finally, heartsick, she had turned the television off and was now listening to Ofra Harnoy play a series of Vivaldi sonatas—glacial, precise, and perfectly depressing—music to slice your wrists to, but oddly soothing.

The doorbell had a low vibrating bronze note, rather like a cello, so it took a moment for the sound to register.

She sighed, looked at the clock above the fireplace, set her scotch down carefully, picked up the television remote, turned the set on, and switched the input to CAMERA ONE.

A pretty young girl of an indeterminate age, late teens or

perhaps older, perhaps not, auburn curls, nicely curved, unlike the current crop of praying-mantis girls. She was wearing an old-fashioned light cotton sundress, pale green, and shiny red slippers like Dorothy's. She was waiting on the verandah, lit by the glow of Delia's porch light, staring intently at the front door, apparently unaware of the camera.

Her pale and heart-shaped face was solemn, her pale hazel eyes unsmiling. She was holding Delia's Maine Coon cat, Mildred Pierce, in her arms, the huge animal almost too much for her to lift, struggling in her grip, the cat's dense striped fur matted and wet-looking.

Blood?

Delia touched a button by her chair.

Her voice, coming from a speaker by the door, seemed to startle the girl.

"Child, what are you doing with my cat?"

The girl jumped, and Mildred Pierce writhed in her arms, but she did not release her. Delia, knowing Mildred Pierce, thought the girl was stronger than she looked.

"Miss Cotton? I'm Clara, from across the way? I think your cat got in a fight?"

Delia knew the people across the way only as recent arrivals, renters, from out of state, a young married couple who had taken over the old Freitag place on Woodcrest after the last of that uppity bunch of stiff-necked Prussians had finally died two months ago. Delia did not know the renters at all, did not know they had a child, but since each house in The Chase sat on almost two acres of lawn and forest, well back from the road, the houses often gated and walled, it was quite usual for even longtime neighbors to know little if anything about the people living near them.

Delia looked at the image in the television, saw what looked like blood on the girl's arms and on her pretty green dress. Delia had no affection for Mildred Pierce, a cranky and disputatious cat with imperious ways, but her heart went out to the girl, who was getting the cat's blood on her pretty green dress.

"Wait there . . ."

"Clara," said the girl, lifting her chin and shifting the weight of the cat in her arms.

"Clara," said Delia, softly repeating the name as if trying to remember other Claras she had known, feeling a slight flutter of something strange, something *wrong*, in the back of her mind, a fleeting wisp of an ancient sin, a shameful family event buried somewhere in the distant past, connected to the girl's name. But the memory, or the thought, or the fancy, slipped away from her like a koi in a pond. She sighed, turning off the TV and getting slowly to her feet.

"I'll be right there."

"Good," said Clara, smiling sweetly up into the camera now, although Delia could no longer see her. Which was too bad, because if Delia had seen Clara smile and seen the light that was in her hazel eyes she might not have opened the door.

Charlie Danziger
and Merle Zane Disagree

Two and a half miles into the brown foothills of the Belfair Range, as you run south on the winding pitted asphalt of Route 311, there's a rutted track on the right, hidden in the brush, that leads off the highway and into the cool green darkness of the old forest, a dense mix of alders and oaks and pines. The track curves away around a bend and seems to dissolve into the trees.

After a few hundred yards, the track breaks out into a clearing, in the middle of which stands—or stood—an old pale blue barn, sagging under the weight of all the years since the Great Depression, during which it finally ceased to operate as the Belfair Pike General Store and Saddlery.

The sheet-metal roof of the barn had collapsed in several places, exposing square-cut beams a hundred and fifty years old, slick with mold and rot. The interior was dim and hot and reeked of spilled oil and manure and decades of accumulated bat scat.

Merle Zane and Charlie Danziger had been sitting inside this barn for three hours, breathing through their mouths, patiently waiting for the manhunt to pass over.

Although a critical part of the plan, this was also a tense

period, a necessary risk to run with a chance that a state chopper flying over would notice this obscure patch of blue deep in the old forest and send a squad car in for a closer look.

The only warning they would get, if this were to happen, would be a short cell phone call from Coker, who, as a sergeant with the Belfair County patrol, was out there in the hunt with the rest of the posse. So far this call had not come.

Merle Zane was a craggy-faced Franco-Irish guy in his middle forties with a shaved head and a flame scar on the left side of his neck. Merle was extremely fit, a martial artist, calm and self-contained. The turnings of fate and the fact that his father was a mechanic and auto body man who had specialized in stolen car parts had led him into stock car racing until, one day in a Louisiana town called Cocodrie, a couple of pit mechanics started yapping at him about how he was hogging the wall on the off-side turn. Zane's forceful counter argument included the deployment of a tire iron.

A Cocodrie judge whose view of the exchange differed from Merle's invited Merle to attend the notorious Angola prison, which was essentially a gladiator school granting any survivor an advanced degree in sheer brutality. Merle had survived it somehow, getting an early release seven years ago.

Since then Zane had been in the employ of a pair of car dealers who ran auctions up and down the eastern seaboard, mainly dealing in muscle cars from the sixties and seventies. Since the muscle car auction business often blurred the line between simple fraud and grand theft auto, the owners of the business, two Armenian American kids whose family motto was "Your money and my experience will become my money and your experience," needed someone like Merle Zane around the office, where his duties covered the spectrum from Corvettes to personal security.

Although working with the Bardashi Boys was like sharing a hot tub with anaerobic algae, the job paid reasonably well. But Zane hoped one day to have his own charter boat service on Florida's Gulf coast and had been quietly on the lookout for a business opportunity that would make that happen.

This opportunity came along one day in the form of Charlie Danziger, a tall cowboy-looking older man with a big white handlebar mustache, an easy smile, and a hoarse, whispery voice. Danziger, born in Bozeman, Montana, at the other end of the state from his old friend Coker, was an ex-highway patrol officer, cashiered early due to a job-related disability— addicted to OxyContin after being injured on the job—who was now working as a regional manager for a Wells Fargo unit doing business along the eastern seaboard.

Charlie Danziger and Coker had met in the Marine Corps, so long ago that neither man could quite remember where, although they sort of recalled that they were being strafed at the time. They were both stationed at Quantico, Virginia, by the end of their time in the Corps, and since they had both come to like the Deep South a lot better than the Far West, they eventually ended up in different law enforcement agencies down around Niceville.

Charlie Danziger and Merle Zane had met at a used-car auction in Atlanta. Danziger was looking to buy a Shelby Cobra Mustang, and they soon discovered some mutual acquaintances among the Angola Gladiator School Alumni. After some background checking, Danziger invited Merle to take part in a confiscatory enterprise involving the First Third Bank in a rural supply town called Gracie. Four men were needed, including a good wheelman.

The fourth man, not directly involved in the robbery, had been paid—anonymously—to create a diversion in another part of the state, which, it was felt, he either would or would not do.

As it turned out, he had succeeded in creating the diversion in a way that approached catastrophic.

At any rate, back in the planning stage, Danziger's scheme, including the part involving his friend Coker and Coker's Bar-

rett .50, had struck Merle Zane as totally ruthless but tactically sound, and since the cops who had arrested him at Cocodrie and his keepers at Angola had not endeared the law
enforcement community to him, he had come on board for a
33 percent share in the operation, the most dangerous part of
which—the actual sharing—had yet to take place.

So now the two men were waiting, with declining patience,
in the humid and ammonia-stinking confines of the Belfair
Pike General Store, a good quarter mile into the tangled old
forest south-southeast of Route 311.

Since both men were chain-smokers and neither of them
was ready to step outside the barn to have one and since the
hay-dust-and-bat-guano-fueled explosion that would have
immediately followed lighting one up inside the barn would
likely attract the wrong sort of attention, the two were reduced
to sitting a few yards apart, Merle on an overturned oil drum
and Charlie Danziger on a rickety three-legged stool, both
staring into the middle distance as the light outside slowly
changed from greenish yellow to pink to gold.

Now and then they heard the mutter of a helicopter in the
distance, and the Doppler wail of a passing patrol car as the
state and county guys raced back and forth and up and down
and, when the opportunity presented itself, sideways.

There was a definite sense inside the barn, unspoken but
growing, that the hunt had peaked and passed over and was
now moving outwards, expanding the perimeter to include
larger sections of the county and then the state.

The take, the haul, the *proceeds*, not yet inventoried, were
contained in four large black canvas duffel bags and temporarily concealed in a concrete subbasement in a far corner, the
hatch hidden under a pile of barn boards and car tires.

The black Magnum, wiped down and stripped clean of
every possible identifier, had been rolled into an empty horse
stall, covered with a tarp, and left to gather dust.

Two nearly identical beige sedans, one a recent Ford and

the other an older Chevy, sat just inside the barn doors, equipped with plausible plates and papers, ready to take Merle and Danziger away in opposite directions.

Now that the adrenaline was ebbing and a leaden fatigue was setting in, both men were ready to take their cut and go, Merle to return to his job with the Bardashi boys and Charlie Danziger to finish up the details here and go back, for a while at least, to his life with Wells Fargo. In the vernacular, it was long past Miller Time, and the waiting was hard.

On the other hand, a payday of 33 percent of an estimated two and a half million dollars was a consoling thought, and both men were professionally resigned to the situation.

And if all went well, Merle Zane was thinking, this could be the beginning of a beautiful—or at least profitable— friendship.

At this taut point, Danziger's cell phone rang, a muted chirp in the pocket of his brown leather jacket. Merle straightened up on his oil drum, reaching instinctively for the mid-sized Taurus nine-mill in his belt. Danziger held up a hand, his callused leathery palm out, shaking his head.

"Yeah?"

Merle could not hear what was being said on the other end, only that whatever it was made Danziger's face tighten up.

Danziger put the cell phone to his chest.

"Go check the perimeter. Coker says there may be civilians inside the fence line."

"Not cops?"

"Says no. Maybe hunters. Go look. Be careful."

Merle pulled out his Taurus and stepped softly over to the barn doors, leaning down to look out through the gaps in the boarding. All he could see was weeds and the top of the lane where it opened up into the clearing. He was reaching for the door handle when Charlie Danziger shot him in the back, a rushed shot, hitting Merle in the lower back instead of the spine, a complication which proved to be quite troublesome later on.

The impact slammed Merle up against the barn doors and he crashed through the rotten wood, turning as he fell, landing on his back in the dust outside. He rolled to his left as a second shot scored the dirt a foot away from his thigh.

The barn wall was now between Zane and Danziger. He heard Danziger's boots scraping on the concrete floor of the barn. Merle fired four quick shots in a horizontal line at roughly chest height along the wooden slats.

He heard Danziger cry out, a startled grunt, followed by the satisfying tumble of a body hitting the floor hard. A second later the barn boards began to shred as Charlie Danziger, apparently still very much in the game, began firing blind, straight through the wall. One stray round caught Zane in the right shoulder, a glancing impact, but the blunt shock threw him back to the ground again.

He rolled, got back up, stumbling backwards as he emptied the Taurus into the barn, concentrating his shots in and around the area where he thought he could see the dim outline of Danziger's body through the bullet holes in the barn boards.

He stitched up the boards in a Charlie Danziger–shaped pattern—eleven more rounds—and then the slide locked back and he was out of ammunition. Merle turned and stumbled into the woods, lungs on fire and head spinning, crashing through the brush like a gut-shot buck, thinking, *So much for the beautiful friendship.*

Gray Haggard Comes at a Bad Time

Gray Haggard had once been briefly and happily married, but the young Margaret Mercer whom he had adored beyond words was so long in the past now that he had trouble bringing her image to mind, other than her soft brown eyes and her auburn hair and her round full body and that she had been a daring and sometimes astonishing lover.

But Margaret Mercer was long gone from the world and it had always seemed to him unfair that he should manage to survive the Kasserine Pass and that god-awful landing at Gela in Sicily and finally go through the abattoir of Omaha Beach and come out of it with nothing more than a chest full of shrapnel, while back in Niceville his heart's desire had fallen prey to a female mosquito loaded up with the encephalitis virus.

His relationship with the Almighty had been a distant one ever since and now that he was closing in on eighty-five he often gave thought to what he was going to say to God should they ever end up on speaking terms again.

These were the sorts of thoughts he was thinking as he drove his 1952 lime green and hot pink Packard around the curve of the tree-shaded lane that led up to Temple Hill. It was late in the day to tend to Delia's garden—the light of the evening was almost gone—but his alternative had been to drive all the way up to Sallytown to the Gates of Gilead Palliative Care Center and watch an old friend named Plug Zabriskie descend deeper into his terminal dementia.

So a bit of shuffling around in Delia's forsythia bushes and perhaps some time spent fiddling with her malfunctioning sprinkler system—that is, the *house's* malfunctioning sprinkler system—he had an idea that Delia's sprinkler system was in tip-top shape . . . now there was another thing he needed to take up with God, if they'd ever let him get close enough. One of the benefits of age was supposed to be a certain easing of the more frantic carnal imaginings and yet here he was having sinful thoughts about Delia Cotton's sprinkler system. Haggard slowed to a halt, the sinful ideas dying slowly away as he stared at the entrance to Delia's estate. The wrought-iron gates were wide open. Delia always kept them closed.

Always.

He braked the Packard in the entrance and extracted his long, lean frame from behind the wheel, straightening up with an effort and peering over his glasses at the big house up on the rise, a tall, bent old man wearing tan slacks and a plaid shirt, gardening boots, with a tanned, hawkish face, a crest of snow white hair, and clear blue eyes with a fan of deep wrinkles at each corner.

He was looking at *another* puzzle.

Delia's house, called Temple Hill, was a classic High Victorian mansion, with a wide curving porch running all the way around the building, gingerbread carvings and gables and turrets here and there, and very fine stained-glass windows in all the rooms.

Tonight these rooms were shining like red and violet and green jewels in the fading light. It looked like Delia had turned on every light in the entire house. It stood out in the blue evening like a cruise ship on the far horizon.

As he was wondering about the open gate and the house all lit up like this, he heard the sound of music floating down the grassy hillside—a deep resonant droning melody, a cello or a viola or perhaps an organ.

The sound, although very graceful and moving, was also very loud, and loud was one of the many modern innovations that Delia did not approve of.

Gray stood there for a moment, taking it all in and wondering what the hell Delia was up to, and then he got back into the Packard and rolled up the cobblestone drive, parking the car in the wide turning circle a few yards from her front steps.

The front door was wide open and the hallway was filled with shimmering light from the massive crystal chandelier that dominated the foyer. The cello music flowed out of the house in a river of honey-colored sound.

He stood there beside the car for a moment, wondering if he had been taken back in time to those buttermilk days before the goddam Nips hit Pearl and he'd gone to serve with the First Infantry, a distant age that was, in his long memory, a glowing bygone era full of balls and cotillions and picnics along the Tulip with leggy girls in gauzy dresses and wide straw hats and baskets full of fresh strawberries, a time of light and music that had filled all the old homes in The Chase, until the war opened up under everybody's feet and they all fell into the fire.

But tonight Delia's rambling old Victorian stood open, full of lovely music, an invitation to a dance.

Gray called out Delia's name a couple of times but doubted that she could have heard his voice over the cello sonata that was pouring out of every window and streaming through the doorways.

He sighed and straightened up his shirt and smoothed out his slacks and walked unsteadily up the steps to the open door, hesitating at the threshold. He was aware that his breathing had become difficult and the skin and muscles across his shoulders were tightening as if he were expecting an assault. He shook that off with an effort, gathering himself, and knocked heavily on the frame of the door.

"Delia? You home? Delia, it's Gray."

No call.

No movement.

Just the music ebbing and flowing all around him, like an undertow now, pulling him in. He came slowly down the hall, walking, out of habit, to one side of the long Persian runner that Delia hated to see abused by a gardener's shoes.

He reached the door to the music room, which seemed to be the source of the cello sonata, looked in, saw the elegant octagonal space filled with light and sound. The cello music was coming from Delia's old but powerful hi-fi set.

This close to the source, and at this volume, the cello sounded less honeyed and more like the deep bass growling of a monstrous creature buried under the parquet floor, the heavy vibration thrumming through the soles of his feet and crawling up his shins.

Every lamp in the room was on, including the big Tiffany dome in the center of the ceiling. He walked in a few more feet, looking around, saw nothing out of place and no sign of any disorder.

There was a crystal glass with an amber liquid in it, half full. He picked it up.

Scotch, now warm and flat.

The chair where Delia liked to sit and watch TV was dented and ruffled, her white fox comforter in a heap on the parquet floor, as if she had been in the middle of something when either the phone rang or the doorbell sounded.

No. Not the phone.

There it was, the cordless handset that Mrs. Bayer had insisted she buy, just in case.

He stared down at the chair for a time, trying to put his impressions together into something useful, and failing. He was reaching out to shut off the music when he noticed movement beyond the closed French doors that led into Delia's wood-paneled dining room.

The glass panes in the doors were old and rippled, but it looked to Gray, as he peered through them, as if something—no, someone—was on top of the rosewood table in the center of the room. He could make out a blurred shell pink figure, spinning and spinning, arms spread wide, head back, and pale white face lifted up to the crystal chandelier that hung over the table.

Even through the antique glass he could see that whoever was standing—whoever was *dancing*—on top of the table, it was not Delia.

Delia had a full head of silver-white hair. This figure—unmistakably a woman—had shoulder-length auburn hair that flared out in an arc as she spun in circles on the table.

Gray stood there looking at the woman for a long, timeless period, transfixed by the fury and the grace of her dance. After a moment, he realized that the woman was quite naked.

This feverish vision, the dancing nude woman flickering like fire through the rippled glass of Delia Cotton's French doors, combined with the deep, resonant rumble of the cello vibrating through the entire house, even through his own fragile bones, held him fixed and frozen, as if he had been hypnotized. Something about that dancing figure was disturbingly familiar, and precisely as the name came to him—*Margaret*—the nude woman stopped spinning and turned to face him through the glass.

She opened her arms and opened her body to him and stood there, clearly waiting for him to come in to her, her face and body rippling and shifting as he watched.

Thinking that he might be having a stroke, or that he was at the threshold of some great illuminating event, possibly even his death, but not so very fond of his life that either of these possibilities carried much weight, Gray Haggard began to move towards the figure on the far side of the glass, like a man in a dream.

He reached the doors—*Margaret*—took the gilt handles in his rough, dry hands, his clear blue eyes fixed on the naked woman—*Margaret*—who was waiting on the other side of the glass, her arms open, her lush white body and her full breasts glowing like alabaster in the diamond-hard light—*Margaret*— Gray turned the handles and threw the doors open.

The dining room was utterly black.

Totally dark.

He could see nothing at all, as if a black cloth had been thrown over him.

He shook his head, blinking, thinking—*a stroke I'm having a stroke*—but then he saw pale light on either side of him, flickering and silvery. He looked down at the rippled glass in one of the doors and saw the naked woman *inside* the glass panes, still waiting with her arms open, smiling out at him. His chest tightened and one knee began to quiver. He looked back into the featureless dark of the dining room.

He heard a voice.

It might have been Delia Cotton's voice.

Run, Gray, run.

For the love of God run.

Gray Haggard was about to slam the doors shut and run when something exploded out of the black like a huge flock of crows, flying directly at him.

He caught a brief flash of jagged black beaks and coal black eyes with a green light in them. The air was full of the fluttering of wings. The black cloud struck him full in the upper body and face with crushing force, a blinding violet light full of sizzling red wires flared up inside his skull, and he went down, falling backwards into the music room, the floor slamming into his back, his head striking the parquet tiles hard. Dazed, stunned, he was aware that the black cloud had settled down onto him like dust, that it was coating him like oil, that it covered him like a shroud, that it was burning its way into him like lava, penetrating him in every place. He felt himself being fed upon.

This went on for much longer than his mind could deal with it. Towards the end he was not himself. The thing kept feeding and a long while later Gray Haggard was gone from the living world.

Kate and Nick Connect

Kate was driving home when her cell phone rang. It was Nick, calling from his cruiser, by the background noise.

"How'd it go with Bock?"

Kate's mood, darkened by the look she had seen on Bock's face, lifted at the sound of Nick's voice.

"We beat the bastard," she said.

"Good. But we talked about him. I still think you need to watch him. You still have your Glock in the glove box?"

Kate rolled her eyes. Nick tended to be a bit extreme when it came to the defense of his family. Since Kate was the only wife he had, as far as she knew, she got all his attention.

"Nick, stand down, okay? You don't have to be on point about me all the time. Look what happened in Savannah last week."

"Hey. Guys begged for it. So I just tuned them up a little."

"Nick. They were just a couple of steroidal jerks in Forsyth Park. And if that was just a tune-up, I'd hate to see the whole program. And right across the street from the hotel we were staying in. Everybody in the lobby saw it happen."

"Nice hotel, though. Great pool."

"You're changing the subject."

"I'm sure as heck trying."

"Nick . . ."

"Look, I went too far in Savannah. Won't happen again. But you're out there driving around with everything I give a damn about in the world."

"Yeah?" she said, point made and backing off. "What about the Oakland Raiders? Don't you love them too?"

"They're not in Oakland anymore. And anyway they all have guns."

"So do I. Where are you?"

Nick's voice changed again.

"You heard about the Gracie thing?"

"Yes. It was terrible. Have they put you on it?"

"Not yet. The First Third is a national bank, so it will go to the Feds and to Marty Coors at State."

"So where are you?"

"I'm out at the scene. I'm walking it with Jimmy Candles and Marty."

"How come, if it's not going to be given to CID?"

Nick's answer was careful.

Guarded.

"Well, mainly because I'm ex-military, and Marty asked me to."

Kate was silent for a moment.

When she had first met him, he had shown up at one of her criminal justice courses, in his full Class A's, a chest full of ribbons, as dark-skinned as a Bedouin, all his edges on, cold gray eyes, a sharp-cut face so lean he looked half starved, a wiry frame so hard it looked as if you could cut yourself on him.

Kate, although she had grown up in a military family and had a younger brother in the Federal Law Enforcement Training Center at Glynco, was as quietly left-wing and vaguely antiwar as a girl from the South could get.

Didn't matter a damn bit.

For reasons she could never explain, to herself or any of her shocked classmates, most of whom were earnest young liberal women just like her, Kate was instantly transfixed by Nick, utterly fascinated by his compact body, his strangely liquid walk, his aura of latent menace, as if he were a leopard who had climbed out of his pit at the zoo and was now pacing around McDonough Hall sizing up the gazelles. She had dug around a bit and found out that he was there to try on the law, having been offered a slot in the Army's Judge Advocate General's branch.

When she had finally gotten up the nerve to talk to him, in the atrium at the Williams Law Library, his wry and totally unexpected smile and the way it changed the lines around his eyes had lit a slow fire in her belly.

By the end of their first month together she would have opened a vein to take him home to Niceville. By the end of the fall semester, she had managed it. Her father, in honor of Nick's first visit to Niceville, had come down from VMI to throw a semiformal bun fight for him at the Anora Mercer Golf and Country Club, where Nick first ran into Tig Sutter. By the end of the party Tig Sutter would have done anything to get this guy into the Belfair and Cullen County Criminal Investigation Division. By the end of the school term, Tig Sutter had, somehow, managed to do it.

To Kate's amazement and delight, Nick had taken an early out from the Army, giving up on JAG as a career and accepting a spot on Tig's newly minted CID unit. He'd explained it to her in a way that seemed persuasive—loved her, loved the town, a chance to make a life for both of them—but she had the idea that, although he meant every word—lying wasn't in him—there was something he was keeping from her, something to do with his service, something, she suspected, that had happened to him overseas. Figuring that Tig Sutter would know, since he was the guy who had hired Nick and he was ex-Army himself, she tried to oil it out of him over several near-lethal mojiitos at the Moot Court bar.

Tig, who hated deception, had danced around it, confirming by his obvious unease that there really was something hidden there, so Kate kept at it, pushing the boundaries of their friendship a bit, but in the end he would only tell her, with affection, but firmly and finally, that although Nick's service record was immaculate, covert combat always takes place in a cloud of ambiguity, and that whatever happens, or doesn't happen, on a particular mission should stay there. That was the Army way, and it was Tig's way, and if one day Nick wanted to tell her about it, whatever it was, or it wasn't, if there actually *was* anything to tell, he would, but in his own good time.

In the meantime, Tig told her he was happy for her, and Nick was a very lucky guy but he really needed to put her in a cab right now because there were two of her and the middle one was all blurry.

Nick, true to his word, had done a full year's course at Glynco in six weeks and four days, a record for the Federal Law Enforcement Training Center, making a solid friend out of Kate's brother, Reed, while they were there together, and coming out third in his class. They had finally gotten married two years ago, and he was *still* here, still in Niceville, still with her, her husband, the capstone of her life, right now a soothing baritone rumble at the other end of the line, still talking about the shooting, patient, as he always was with her, laying the thing out for her.

"The shooter was probably ex-military, but other than that, not much. Pretty cold killing. I figure the weapon was a Barrett, a .50-caliber rifle anyway, but instead of it just disabling the engine, the block blew up and a hunk of shrapnel killed the driver. Then he picked them off one by one as they drove into his sights. It's possible that he killed the other three because once the first man was dead, it was just the orderly thing to do. Like housekeeping."

"Because once anyone dies in a robbery, the penalty in this state is always death?"

"That's it. But it's just as likely that the shooter meant to kill them right from the start. He had already killed the two people in the chopper."

"But why kill the cops too? If he could just disable the cars?"

"From a military point of view, it's just more efficient. No survivors, no witnesses, no risk."

"Oh, Nick—such an ugly thing."

"Not really. Just military."

"You coming home?"

"Be there in a while."

"How long's a while?"

"Before dark. You really still have that Glock?"

"I do. It's right here in the glove box."

"Is it loaded?"

"If it isn't it's a paperweight."

"Honey, please take it with you."

"Do I *look* like Dirty Harriet?"

"I don't know. Squint, and say, 'Do you feel lucky?' "

"I'll take the gun."

"Good. Love you."

"Love you back. Stay safe. Bye."

Charlie Danziger Considers His Options

After a long interlude during which he gave some thought to the caprices of fate, Danziger came carefully out of the barn, his legs unsteady, his fingers bloody on his shirt, his face white and slick.

He dropped to his knees, pulled out his cell. His mouth was dry and a weary weight was dragging him down.

The cell was buzzing as he put it to his ear.

"Shut up," he explained, in a hoarse, growling whisper. "I'm shot. Yeah. Shot. Like with bullets?"

A pause while he listened to Coker.

"Lung, I think. It's sucking."

More listening.

"Yeah, I have some plastic in the car. But I'm going to have to get to a medic."

Coker talking again.

"A through-and-through? I can't tell. I gotta find a mirror."

More talk from Coker.

"No. Merle's gone. But I hit him. I saw him take the round."

A crackle from the cell.

"Small of the back. Lower right. He went through the barn boards and it all went to shit."

He listened for a time, his craggy face white and his lips blue.

"Yeah, well, I'm not used to shooting a guy in the back. I guess you have to practice."

More buzzing from the cell phone speaker.

"No," said Danziger, shaking his head. "Not by myself. We'll deal with him later."

More heated talk, this time with swearing. Danziger listened for a while, said no again a couple of times, added a *fuck you* for emphasis, and clicked off.

He got to his feet and staggered back into the barn. With his free hand, he riffled around in the Chevy until he found the plastic bag the manual had come in. There was duct tape on a nail next to the door. He used the edge of an old wood-saw to rip off three long strips.

Then he tried to take his shirt off with one hand while using the other to press down on the bullet hole in his chest. After a time he gave that up and just ripped the fabric away, tearing the shirt to pieces and exposing an ugly purple-black hole in the fleshy part of his chest about three inches below his right nipple. Every time he breathed out, pink bubbles of blood would foam up out of the hole.

It wasn't bleeding that much, which meant most of the blood was staying inside his chest. Given enough time, his chest cavity would fill up and he'd drown in his own blood. Unless it had nicked an artery, in which case the same thing would happen, only at warp speed, and he'd have about three minutes to live. He'd have to wait and see.

Coker had asked him if the wound was a through-and-through. This would be a good thing to know, he decided, so he opened up the shreds of his shirt, trying to figure out which shred had been part of the back of the shirt. Far as he could see, there was no exit hole in any of these pieces.

Gotta make sure, he thought.

He walked back over to the Chevy and tried to get a look at his back in the passenger-side mirror. He used that side because the mirror was convex and gave him a wider view.

Aside from learning that objects in this mirror were closer than they appeared, he saw nothing but unbroken skin on his back.

No through-and-through. The slug was still inside him. This was not good news. If the slug took some of his shirt inside with it, which they usually did, then that dirty bit of cloth was going to make the wound septic.

So, what with a sucking chest wound, a dirty nine-mill slug stuck somewhere inside him, and the related internal bleeding, Charlie Danziger was in a bad place.

Danziger used what was left of his shirt to press down on the wound again. This hurt a lot, so he stopped doing it and settled for just getting the area around the wound dry enough so the duct tape would stick to it. He managed, after several tries, to tape the plastic film down on three sides, remembering to leave the fourth side open.

As soon as he got the plastic in place, the sheet flattened out against his ribs as the lung contracted. The plastic being open on one side meant that it worked like a valve, closing to allow the lung to get some negative pressure going and pull in some air, but opening back up to allow air out so the lung could expand again. People who do not have sucking chest wounds call this process breathing. Being able to breathe made a few other things more feasible, like getting the hell out of Dodge. It took him ten painful minutes to get the duffel bags into the trunk of the beige Chevy. Money might be the root of all evil, but two million in stolen cash was mainly a hernia risk.

He started the car, rolled it out into the clearing, got out, scanned the forest all around looking for any sign of Merle Zane. The light was fading quickly. Or maybe he was dying.

Didn't guys say in those old movies, *Wyatt, everything's getting dark* when they were dying of a gunshot wound? He looked down at his cowboy boots—his best navy blue Lucchese cowboy boots—and noticed that they were spotted with blood.

It was a comfort to him that if he was about to die, at least he'd be doing it with his boots on, in the tradition of all the great gunfighters.

But, since he wasn't quite dead as of yet, there was nothing left to do but light up a road flare and toss it into the barn. He was two hundred yards down the track when the twilight sky behind him turned into red fire.

Tony Bock Has an Epiphany

Lanai Lane was one avenue in a long, spreading fan of inter-
lacing streets, each of them lined with identical small yellow
brick Art Deco bungalows alternating with identical ranch-
style homes, all built back in the early fifties as part of a housing development called The Glades.

The Glades once stood apart from Niceville, cherishing an
air of suburban exclusivity, but over the years Niceville had
slowly grown out to envelop it and now even the name—The
Glades—was remembered only by what remained of those
bright young families, fresh from the Second World War, who
had moved in to do their part in the construction of the Great
American Dream.

Most of these postwar families had flourished along with
their hope-filled nation, planted trees and gardens, built
fences and watered lawns and walked across those green lawns
on soft summer evenings to meet the neighbors and share
some iced drinks and watch their kids grow up through the
Eisenhower years, the Nixon years, the Vietnam War, the
counterculture, the nineties, Reagan, Clinton, September 11,
and the wars that followed on.

During the inexorable progression of these times, the

original Glades families had grown old and lost their mates and were seeing less and less of their kids while their friends and neighbors died off steadily, names being ticked off a list.

Now, in a brand-new century, the live oaks planted as skinny saplings before the Civil War were large enough to reach across the narrow roads and touch branches, a broad green canopy draped in Spanish moss and sheltering a sun-dappled timeworn community composed mainly of solitary old women living on pensions, a few renters escaping from Tin Town, and here and there a black or Hispanic or Muslim family passing through on their way up the reasonably steady achievement ladder of Niceville society.

In a few of the old Glades houses, where the elderly solitaries who owned them were willing to take a chance on a stranger, for the money or the company or the safety, some lone male would take up residence in a basement suite or an apartment over a garage, usually someone new to Niceville and trying to find a job, or a businessman just transferred in and scouting out a place to set up his family.

At 3156 Lanai Lane, the solitary man in the flat over the garage, resident there for eight months, ever since he had been forcibly removed from the family home on Saddle Creek Drive, was a newly divorced man by the name of Tony Bock.

This warm Friday evening a joyless Tony Bock parked his lime green Toyota Camry in the tiny space allotted to him by his landlady, a Mrs. Millie Kinnear.

Bock gave her a sardonic wave as she twitched the curtain open to scowl at him—they were not on good terms—as he passed down the lane to the rear of the house, where he pushed the rusty chain-link gate open, stepping carefully through the random clumps of dog crap that stuccoed Mrs. Kinnear's scruffy patch of backyard.

Then, and slowly, with a bitter burn in his belly, he climbed the creaking wooden stairs to his three-room flat above Mrs. Kinnear's garage.

Home again home again hippity-hop, he said to himself, opening the door. He'd always said this to the Effin Cee when he got home from work. She used to smile when he said this, but after his coming home started to mean she was going to get smacked around some more she stopped smiling when he said it. But he kept right on saying it anyway.

Bock was that sort of guy.

The apartment smelled of stale coffee and the Chinese takeout he'd had for breakfast but was otherwise very neat and orderly, if rather severely overstuffed, being packed full of everything the Effin Cee had let him take, mainly what had been in his private gentleman's retreat in the basement back at Saddle Creek Drive.

What he had been *allowed* to take, under the watchful eyes of a couple of plus-size Niceville cops, consisted of a large brown leather sectional sofa with a matching ottoman, a brand-new forty-two-inch flat-screen Sony Bravia on a black lacquer sideboard, a bar fridge right beside the sectional, well stocked with Stella Artois beers, a narrow desk along the window wall with a Dell PC and a twenty-six-inch HD monitor, a ham radio set, a CB radio, a Direct TV satellite dish, a second computer, a silver Sony laptop actually owned by the NUC— the Niceville Utility Commission—his employer, but his to use as he pleased on his off hours, and a high-speed broadband Internet connection that, after losing a long and vexatious argument with Mrs. Kinnear, who was tighter than a gerbil's colon, Bock had personally paid to have installed.

There was a small galley kitchen, a cramped and window-less bedroom barely big enough to hold his singleton cot, a bathroom that was not much of an improvement on a Porta-Potty, and a porch overlooking Mrs. Kinnear's grue-some backyard, where, if he was so inclined, he could sit on a soft summer evening with a cold Stella in his hand and watch Mrs. Kinnear's demented shi-tzu—a perfect name for the lit-tle rodent, since his capacity for fecal production seemed inexhaustible—do his business all over the lawn, in between random episodes of high-pitched yapping.

However, tonight Bock did not choose to do so, because, on the way home from the courthouse, still writhing under the lash of Judge Monroe's scathing words, he had experienced a kind of dark-side epiphany.

Bock was a proud man, and not utterly uneducated. He was, after all, a graduate of East-Central-Mid-State-Poly and held an Advanced Degree in Eco-Sustainable Energy Systems with a minor in Information Technology. Therefore Judge Monroe's complete dismissal of his entire person had bitten deep into his soul and the marks remained there still, a festering sore that would have to be cauterized in the fires of retributive justice.

The question was how, and his recent epiphany revealed the first stirrings of an answer. A lone man seeking justice against an oppressive system had to move with subtlety and guile. Since they were all so damned sure of their better angels, maybe that was where they were most vulnerable. The central idea of his epiphany was to attack them obliquely. How? He had the resources right in front of him, the computers and the Internet.

Therefore, tonight, instead of his usual hectic interlude with Internet porn, he popped himself a frosty Stella, sat down at his desk, opened up a Word document, and began to type.

A few letters.

A beginning.

THE INNOCENCE PROJECT

He sat back, stared at the words floating in the middle of a glowing white field, pulsing with possibilities, gathering himself, feeling a hot rush in his lower belly.

Innocence was exactly the word.

Bock's short but memorable experience of the world had

led him to conclude that no one was *innocent*. Certainly not the Effin Cee, and that little bitch of a daughter—who probably wasn't even his—was not much better.

How about Miss Barrow, his dozer-dyke lawyer?

Hell no.

She'd probably taken a bribe to lose his case. And there were lurid rumors about her private life circling the town.

How about Judge Monroe?

Everybody thought he was a pillar of the judicial community. But nobody was a pillar, not if you looked close enough. Every pillar had cracks around the base.

The Kavanaugh woman?

There walked the woman he *really* wanted to nail, another Effin Cee he was going to totally fuck with, the bitch who was going to pay for messing with Tony Bock. Bock didn't know much about her—her husband, Nick, was some kind of plain-clothes cop with a reputation for being a hard-ass.

Thinking about her, he got onto Google and typed in her name, Kate Kavanaugh, born a Walker, found a bunch of links to sites like Court News and Niceville Who's Who, along with a whack of citations in law journals and law clerk for appeals court cases. A busy little beaver, this chick.

A link to her father, Dillon Walker, a big-shot professor up at VMI, and then a whole lot of irritating crap about how the Walkers went way back in the history of the state, all the way back to what these redneck crackers around here still called the War Between the States—slave-trading cotton-dealing slime-balls—more crap about the Founding Four, the Cottons, the Teagues, the Haggards, and the Walkers—nothing he could really mine for deep shit to shovel on her head. But nobody was innocent, not in this tight-ass town.

Hell, even the name was a lie.

Niceville.

How about the guy who was laying pipe to her?

Her husband, the cop, Nick Kavanaugh.

Bock googled him, got links to some newspaper articles about his service in Special Forces—Silver Star, Bronzes with a Vee, whatever that was, couple of Purples. Interesting that he was out of the Army so soon, after all that glory . . . guy was only thirty-two . . . lots of war left for a glory-sucker like this asshole . . . wonder why he's out . . .

Bock tried a link into Army Records, found it firewalled, tried a few tricks, and managed to get into a level seven info-link maintained by an antiwar website called WikiLeaks.

It was called www.fukthawarpigs.org, and now it got more interesting.

In the middle of all the sixties rhetoric and anti-American raving, there was a mention of an incident in Yemen, filed by somebody from Doctors Without Borders, involving a Fifth Special Forces unit, headed up by a guy named Cavanah—*Cavanah?* First name initial only, an *N.* These guys were deployed around a place called Wadi Doan—several women had been killed because . . . because why?

Hard to figure it out.

Something to do with suicide bombers dressing up in full-body burkas and getting too close to coalition soldiers . . . there was some kind of video file attached to the site. Bock hit it and watched forty-seven seconds of a grainy digital mpeg of three women in black walking single file down a narrow alley in between low mud-brown walls, a Humvee at the far end of the alley, five U.S. Army soldiers standing around it, watching them come on, the troopers as taut as Dobermans in a junk-yard.

There was no sound, just the fixed images of these Arab broads in head-to-toe black, walking like zombies—some sort of action at the far end, by the Humvee, the military figures spreading out, one man coming forward, hand raised, the women keep coming, the soldier is clearly shouting at them—he lifts a weapon of some sort—the film jumps a bit, as if the guy taking the video is startled by something—when he gets back on the alley the three women are down and the soldiers are coming up on them . . .

No.

Fuck it.

The site was too crazy.

Whole thing looked like a setup, otherwise who would be taking the video in the first place?

Bad provenance, bad spelling, bunch of wing nuts. Lousy video. No source cited.

Better set the Nick and Kate thing aside for now, at least until his skills improved. Make a mistake with that guy, from what Bock had heard about him, it was going to end in tears.

Start out small.

Stay away from the obvious targets, the fucking lawyers, that sanctimonious prick of a judge, the Effin Cee and her bastard bitch, while he figured out how to manage this.

His theory was that everybody had a crime or a sin or something shameful and disgusting buried in his past, something that could shame or even ruin him.

Or her.

It was an interesting proposition, and proving it could be a lot of fun.

But he had to be . . . subtle.

Start with someone totally unconnected.

He had to pick a name out of a hat, totally at random, then do the homework, find out all there was to know, circle around like a tiger, stay in the long grass and work it all out. Find out how to ruin a life by remote control.

He already had some possibles, people whose dirty secrets he had "happened upon" in the course of his day job. Risky to use too many of them, because a smart cop, given enough incidents, would figure out what the linkages were.

No, stick to random, and be anonymous. Implacable. Do a few dry runs to warm up, take on people no one would ever be able to connect to him, while he studied and adapted and improved. That way, if he made some early mistakes—and everybody did—he wouldn't be on anybody's list.

But where to start?

He sat back in the chair, had some more of his Stella Artois.

Where to start?

He needed a *victim*, somebody he had no connection with, but somebody who was . . . vulnerable. Somebody with secrets hidden away. He sat there and stared at the screen for a while, his rat-mind nibbling away at the problem.

Where was there an obvious nexus between the information universe and people with secrets?

Criminals.

Criminal records required access to the National Crime Information Center, which he did not have and could not easily get.

How about employment records?

Human resources files?

Hard to get at those without leaving a trace.

Come on, Tony.

Think.

Secrets.

Okay.

Sex offenders had secrets.

Was there a National Sex Offender Registry?

A couple of taps showed him a site called the Dru Sjodin National Sex Offender Public Website. If he agreed to accept the terms, he could enter any name and the website would tell him if that name had ever been on any city, state, or federal sex offender list.

He sat back and looked at it, thinking hard. There was no point in just entering random names from the Niceville phone book and hoping to get lucky. He had to start at the other end.

Sex offenders liked to be around kids, didn't they? So how many guys in Niceville worked around kids? Social workers. Cops. Playground supervisors. Coaches. Teachers.

But they'd all have been checked out, right? As a city employee he knew that everyone who was bonded and every-one who applied for any kind of license to work with kids or in schools or in hospitals or church groups had to be checked out for anything criminal.

But how well?

How far back?

How . . . *carefully*?

Worth a shot, he decided.

Worth a shot.

How Things Were Going for Merle Zane

For a long time Merle just ran, through the brush and the branches, over deadfalls and under boughs, getting his face lashed and his hands bloody as he put as much distance between himself and Charlie Danziger as he could manage in as short a time as possible.

A few hundred yards into the forest the dense underbrush gave way to a padded carpet of dry pine needles. The trunks of the trees were spaced much farther apart in this section of the forest and even in the dim light he found he could cover the open ground much more easily.

He was vaguely aware that the forest had changed in some indefinable way, and now the golden twilight that poured down from the canopy and shimmered in between the upright pillars of the trees and spread itself on the red carpet of pine needles reminded Merle of being inside a huge silent temple.

His vision was blurry and his head was light, but all in all he felt better than he would have expected to after getting shot in the back. He didn't take too much comfort from this. Although he had never been shot before, he knew that in the long run, unless he could get some medical attention, he was in pretty big trouble.

He could see that the wound in his right shoulder was just a glancing one. It occurred to him that only someone who had actually been shot was qualified to use the word *just* when describing it.

But other than being ugly and bleeding like a stiff punch in the nose would bleed, he wasn't too worried about it. It was the bullet hole in his back that sort of preyed on his mind.

For the first few minutes after he got hit there wasn't a whole lot of pain. It was more like somebody had smacked him in the small of his back with a baseball bat. Everything around the impact area had gone numb, as if it had been frozen.

Then the cold and the numbness began to fade away and the pain had set in. And this was serious pain. Ten minutes after it first started in on him he was sitting on the ground gasping and sweating with his back up against a tree and his legs splayed out in front of him, and he was, as the saying goes, in a world of hurt.

He looked up at the sky, pale glowing gold and blue through the black tracery of the branches. It was early spring yet, so the trees hadn't fully leafed out. The first of the stars glittered up there and a crescent moon was gliding through wisps of cloud.

He put his head back on the rough bark of the pine and stared up at the evening sky for a while, trying to will the pain away, which he had heard from his karate instructor that you could do if you tried hard enough and had the mental strength to go all Zen on the very idea of pain, which was really nothing but an illusion manufactured by your corporeal body and could easily be controlled and overcome by the forceful application of a truly transcendental mind. This turned out not to be true.

A Problem Arises for Byron Deitz

Byron Deitz looked exactly like a guy with his name ought to look—a thick-necked heavy-bodied no-neck sort of guy with a shaved skull and a hard, unfriendly face and small, mean black eyes.

If he was in the movies he'd have to play one of the evil baldheaded guys with black goatees who always end up getting a balsa-wood chair broken over their heads by the curvy chick in a thong bikini who's only trying to stop him from pounding on the good-guy hero with the long blond hair.

Byron Deitz would have totally deserved this treatment since he was a guy who spent a lot of his time looking at people and things he didn't like and working out how to drive right over them.

As a matter of fact, Deitz was driving right now, in his supercharged bright yellow Hummer, and listening to Lady Gaga's "Poker Face" with the volume set to STUN, doing a scary one-forty down Side Road 336, taking a shortcut through the Belfair Range, heading for hearth and home—his very big damn hearth and home—in The Chase, as it happened, just a few blocks away from Delia Cotton's old Victorian, where, right at this exact same moment, something odd and deeply disturbing was happening.

Byron Deitz figured he could get away with doing a slick one-forty down SR 336 because every cop in the known universe was everywhere else looking for those outrageous pukes who had cherry-popped the First Third in Gracie and then eighty-sixed four cops and a news chopper over there on 311.

Deitz had to admit that whoever they were, these pukes, they had serious balls. That was shit-house-rat-crazy-fucking-brave. He'd have loved to have seen the look on the faces of the other cops in the chase when the first guy took a full-metal round straight up the beezer. *Holy Freaking Shit* wouldn't quite have done justice to that moment.

Deitz figured the sniper had to be military or an elite federal sharpshooter.

And stony cold.

A deeply ruthless prick.

A guy like that, Deitz would be proud to walk him all the way to the execution chamber and pour him three fingers of bourbon before they strapped him down. Part of him was hoping they'd get away with it. But they wouldn't.

Pukes, even crazy-brave pukes, never got away with shit. Byron Deitz, who was ex-FBI, knew something about pukes. The "ex" part of Deitz's career with the FBI wasn't entirely his idea, but he'd gone along with it because the alternative was five to nine in Leavenworth.

So now his career jacket was hermetically sealed by the order of a federal court judge, as part of a plea agreement, and therefore his professional reputation remained relatively unstained, other than in the long and darkly brooding memories of those four unfortunate men who had made the mistake of going into business with him. They were now pulling what should have been Byron Deitz's five to nine in Leavenworth.

Anyway, that unhappy time was all in the misty past, in his

rearview mirror, as he liked to say, and all those grumpy former henchmen were just speed bumps on the four-lane interstate of his career. So, all in all, on this honey-colored Friday evening Life Was Good for Byron Deitz.

Life Was Good partly because Deitz was making an outrageous amount of money running BD Securicom, an outfit providing perimeter security and on-site counterespionage services to several of the high-tech research firms that had established themselves in the northwestern suburbs of Niceville, in a gated high-security compound known as Quantum Park, home to a number of very anonymous feeder firms that subcontracted R and D for more well-known outfits with names like Lawrence Livermore, Motorola, General Dynamics, Raytheon, KBR, Northrop Grumman, and Lockheed Martin.

The sprawling park in which these firms resided featured perimeter sensors and infrared trip wires and motion detectors and transplanted sago palms and overflight interdiction systems and rolling lawns and a private golf course and countersurveillance jammers and an artificial lake where a large flock of trumpeter swans whose wing bones had been professionally snapped were required to glide gracefully about amidst the koi and the water lilies. How the hell a gaboon viper like Byron Deitz had managed to insinuate himself into this lucrative gig was a question that kept his competition awake at night.

But he had pulled it off somehow, and he was rocketing through the rolling brown slopes of the Belfair Range, with Lady Gaga's volume set on STUN and a nervous but lovely wife and two nervous kids waiting for him in his mansion in The Chase, and he was thinking that all was right with the universe when his truck phone rang.

The phone was linked through the Hummer's OnStar system, so the call shut Lady Gaga up in mid-screech with a gentle bell-like tolling.

Deitz glanced at the caller ID on the Hummer's LCD screen—PHIL HOLLIMAN—frowned, shook his head, and touched the ANSWER button on the steering wheel.

"You're not supposed to use this number."

"Had to. We got an issue."

"I'm waiting."

"You heard about the bank thing in Gracie?"

"How could I miss it? It's everywhere. They know about it on the moon."

"Yeah. Well. I heard from our guy."

Deitz felt his belly go cold and take a slow roll to the left. Because the First Third in Gracie handled all the payroll and banking for Quantum Park, Deitz had a man inside the bank.

Deitz swallowed twice.

"Yeah?"

"Our guy in Gracie," the voice said, with an edge.

"I got that part, Phil. What'd he say?"

"The guys—two of them—went through the vault, jamming shit in their bags. The Fargo truck had just dropped off all the cash for the ATMs in the sector, plus all the migrants working on the ADM farms, also the draw for Quantum Park."

"Coincidence?"

"I doubt it. Shit like that is never luck."

"So they got . . . what?"

A pause.

Giving Deitz bad news was best done over a phone. "Fuck of a lot of cash, mainly. They figure over two mill."

"Mainly cash? What the fuck is *mainly*?"

A silence, during which Byron Deitz heard a sound in his skull like walnuts cracking. He was grinding his teeth, an irritating habit that drove his wife and family bats. He had no idea he was doing it, and often wondered where the hell that weird walnut-cracking sound was coming from.

"They got into some of the lockboxes—"

"Oh shit."

"Yeah. After they're gone, there's an inventory. Our guy can't find the—"

"Don't say another fucking thing."

Silence while Phil Holliman, on the other end of the line, didn't say another fucking thing.

"Okay," said Deitz, focusing. "Is he sure?"

"Oh. I can talk now?"

Sarcasm.

Phil Holliman was like that, a sarcastic prick. With a nasty temper. But good at his job.

"Don't be a dick."

"The drawer is open but not totally cleaned out. Only thing they got was some bonds and . . . the . . . ahh, item."

Deitz was watching the road uncoiling at him, a long black snake with a white streak down its back.

A skunk snake, he was thinking. Just what he didn't need right now.

"Fuck. We gotta *find* those fucking pukes."

"Mind you, might be random," said Phil. "Might be nothing to worry about. I figure it was the stainless-steel jewel case that caught their—"

"Random? Know what, Phil? I don't believe in *random*. Why take the item at all? And when they open it and they see what's inside it, with that Raytheon logo all over it, you think that's going to make them say, hey, move on, nothing to see here. No. This is enemy action. We *move* on this. First thing you do, you get our guy in Gracie a box somewhere and take him apart. No way anybody knew the thing was there unless he shot his fucking mouth off. I wanna know to who. Got that?"

"Does he get *out* of the box?"

"Up to you."

"Be best if he did. Him not being around wouldn't look too good. It would be, like, lousy optics."

"Yeah. Okay. I got that. Maybe I'll go see him myself. But

you should drop by his place—tomorrow morning, early—throw one of your monkey-rangs and scare the living shit out of him. Tell him I'll be by the bank at noon, for a chat. Tell him he better be in a talky mood."

"Right there at the bank?"

"Why not? It was a Quantum Park payroll? I got every right to ask questions. Also, look into the Fargo guys, the drivers, see if they were talking too much, and if so, to who. Go up the ladder at Fargo and see who in management had the day off. Look for the one guy with a real good alibi, because that'll sure as shit be the perp. If it was an inside job, other than somebody in the bank, Fargo is the best bet. Another thing, I hear some asshole laid his rig down up on the interstate, just before the robbery. Is that right?"

"Yeah. It was a full load of rebar, came off a Steiger Freightways flatbed. A rollover. Some of the rebar got rammed straight through a minivan, laid some heavy pipe right through a coupla old church ladies. Hey, probably the stiffest rods they ever got to ride their whole lives."

Phil Holliman thought that was pretty funny, but it was totally wasted on Deitz.

"Thing like that," said Deitz, oblivious, "it woulda tied up all the state guys, including their choppers, medevac, traffic management, right?"

"Yeah. That's exactly what happened."

"And then somebody hits the First Third?"

"Yeah. Are you thinking—"

"I am. Did the driver live?"

"Yeah. At least I think so."

"Find out. Get his name. Find out where he is right now. Find a way to get to him. I'll bet my left nut that puke knows something."

"Yeah. Okay, I'll do that. But the Feds are all over this. This is about dead cops. We start poking into it, they'll wanna know why."

"Like I said, they took a lot of money belonging to Quantum Park, and that's sure as shit *our* business. Anyway, that's a risk we gotta take. The main thing, I don't want this . . . item . . . out there, hanging over our heads. You listening?"

"The Feds won't like it. Not smart to get them fired up. They'll come sniffing."

Deitz thought it over.

"Kavanaugh. Nick Kavanaugh. I'll start there. Maybe I can get close enough to the case to get one move ahead. Meantime, you work the angles, get some money on the street. Anybody asks, say we're showing solidarity with our fallen brothers. Trying to help, you follow? One way or another, we gotta find these pukes, burn them down to the bone, get the thing back."

"Nick's County. Dead cops. A national bank. That's Fed. County won't be near this case."

"No. But State CID will and he's in real tight with State CID. And the Feds, that Boonie Hackendorff guy, the Agent in Charge, they all love him in Cap City. Nick's a war hero. He'll hear stuff."

"Maybe. But will he tell *you*?"

A good question.

Deitz thought this over.

So did Phil Holliman, who had locked horns with Nick Kavanaugh a while back and gotten a piece of himself snapped clean off.

"Yeah," said Deitz, finally. "He's family, isn't he? My brother-in-law, remember? I married his wife's sister?"

Holliman knew Beth, Deitz's wife and Kate Kavanaugh's older sister. Also the older sister to Kate's brother, Reed, a pursuit cop for State who was colder than outer space and crazier than a wolverine on meth. Both men knew that Deitz was smacking Beth around on a pretty regular basis. Knowing Nick and Reed the way he did, in Nick's case from bitter personal experience, Holliman figured someday soon Byron

Deitz was going to open his front door and find two off-duty cops there and then Deitz's lights would get duly punched out. But he said nothing.

What was the point?

A difficult silence followed.

Deitz knew what Phil wasn't saying, but he didn't give a damn about that. He was still a cop, no matter what that U.S. attorney said about it.

And cops were like family.

On the far end of the line Phil Holliman was thinking there was some irony in Deitz using a word like *family* considering the state of his own, but Deitz wasn't a guy you could say was all loaded up with insight and awareness and all that shit.

So he just kept his mouth shut and listened to Deitz rant and rave.

"Anyway, whatever we're doing, we got to do it fast. We got some serious Chinks flying in Saturday, to look at the *item*. And the window at . . . the source . . . closes on Monday night. It's gotta be back in their inventory by then, or the black choppers will be flying up our ass. Go get this done."

He snapped the call off, tried some deep breathing to calm himself. He could see the lights of Niceville coming on down in the valley, see the microwave masts blinking red on the top of the limestone bluffs that overlooked the town. This was *his* town and he had built himself a good life here and these pukes who took his fucking *item* were going to sincerely wish they hadn't.

Friday Night

Merle Zane Meets
the Woman in the Forest

After giving up on all that transcendental horseshit, Merle came up with the much simpler alternative plan of passing out from the pain. This had its risks, such as shock and death, but Merle decided that being dead, while inconvenient in many ways, had the advantage of being painless.

He closed his eyes and rolled his head back and started to slip his cables, as the sailors like to say, when they mean to drift quietly out of the harbor without troubling to raise their anchors.

"You all right?" said a voice in his head, but not the nasty grating voice that was always criticizing and accusing him, a voice that, he had realized a long while back, belonged to his maternal grandmother, Murielle, who had always disapproved of him, and not entirely without reason.

Merle opened his eyes.

The dark was almost complete and the last of the golden temple light was leaving the forest. But he could see well enough to make out a shape standing in front of him, looking down at him.

Caught, he said to himself, almost with relief. *Now I'll get some medical attention. Anyway, technically, if you died during the getaway then you weren't really getting away, were you?*

Finding this argument persuasive, Merle forced himself to sit up, blinking at the silhouetted figure. As he moved, the pain sheeted through him with terrible intensity and he flinched a bit. The figure, slender, too slender for a cop, stepped quickly back and leveled what looked like a small-caliber rifle at him.

"What's *wrong* with you?" said the voice, a woman's voice, in a soft Virginian accent, wary but not actively hostile.

"I've been shot," said Merle, trying to get his legs to work, trying to get the world to stop tilting crazily to the left. "In the back."

"Who shot you?" asked the woman. "Federals?"

"No," said Merle, realizing from the suspicious way she said "*Federals*" that whoever this woman was, she probably wasn't with the cops.

"Not the Feds. A business partner."

"Shot you in the back?"

"Yes."

"Sounds like a bad partner."

Merle tried for a smile.

"I'm leaning that way."

She might have smiled back. It was too dark to tell, but there was a flash of white in her face.

"I heard you thrashing around in the valley. I thought you might be a hurt deer. Can you get up?" she asked in a flat, careful tone. She stepped back, holding the rifle steady, not aiming it right at him, but close enough.

"I think so."

"You do it, then."

Merle got a palm on the ground, which helped to stop the earth from turning over underneath him, turned to his right, got a knee braced, and managed to get to all fours.

He put a hand on the tree trunk, readied himself, and pushed himself upright, feeling the world spin and then slow.

His jeans were soaked with blood and his boots squelched as he turned to face the woman with the rifle.

In the dying light he could see that she was shapely, with shoulder-length hair, some dark color, possibly black, wearing jeans and heavy boots, a plaid shirt. Her skin seemed to glow in the last of the twilight.

"Let me see the wound."

Merle twisted, lifted his bloody shirt. She leaned down to peer at the black hole in his body, straightened up.

"Ugly. Don't see an exit wound. If the slug's in there, I guess it'll have to come out. You got any cash money?"

Merle considered the irony of having committed a wild-ass daylight bank robbery at gunpoint, escaping a statewide drag-net after being accessory to the assassination of four cops, in the process taking a bullet in the back from one of his own guys, only to end up being mugged like a patsy by a gypsy-looking girl-woman with what looked like a cap-and-ball squirrel gun about a hundred and fifty years old. *Life is an ever-unfolding panoply of marvels*, he was thinking.

"I have maybe two hundred dollars in my wallet. All I have. I doubt there's an ATM around here."

"Give it up," she said, a hard note, but not threatening. Merle extracted his blood-soaked wallet, handed it over to her. She kept the muzzle centered on his belly as she snatched the wallet away. Merle, swaying, watched her think things over.

"You got a gun on you there. I see it sticking out. Hand that over too."

He pulled his Taurus out of his belt, held it out to her. She took it, turned it in the dim light.

"What kind of a gun is this? Colt .45?"

"It's a Taurus. A nine-millimeter."

She frowned at it, and then shoved it into what looked like a canvas bag hanging from her shoulder.

"Can you walk?"

Merle gave it some thought, pushed himself free of the tree, did not immediately fall on his face.

"I think so."

"I have a place up the valley. It's about a quarter mile. Think you can walk that far?"

"I can. You really think you can deal with a bullet wound?"

She showed her teeth.

"I board horses, sir. Breed 'em too. I guess if I can pull a breech foal live out of a dead mare, I can see to your bullet holes."

The thing seemed to be decided.

Somehow Merle covered the ground, a long, unsteady walk up a generally rising slope covered in those soft pine needles, weaving his way without the girl's help through a towering stand of old pines and beeches and live oaks, putting one foot in front of another with the woman always a few feet behind him. He could feel the muzzle of her rifle zeroed on his back and was wondering if he was being helped or taken prisoner. Probably both. At this point, he didn't give a damn.

He just wanted something for the pain and to get that goddam slug taken out of his back. If she did that, she could call the cops and collect the reward, whatever it was, and the hell with it. He'd get the needle for his part in the shooting of those cops but that was a long way off and therefore, at this point anyway, purely hypothetical.

The woman seemed pretty calm, all things considered, but this was the South, and she was obviously country, not city, and he had observed that they grew a different kind of woman down here.

During the last few hundred yards, Friday evening came down to full dark and the only light around was what looked like a big wood-frame white-painted farmhouse at the top of the rise.

A string of large clear-glass electric bulbs, yellow and flickering, lit up the grounds like a used-car lot. There was a big rickety-looking barn beyond the house, with a rusted corrugated iron roof. He could smell horses, and hay, and fresh manure. No dogs around, which was odd, for a farmhouse. There was a *pockety-pockety* sound coming from the far side of the barn.

It took him a moment to figure out it was some kind of gas-driven generator. The interior of the house was glowing with a warm yellow light, and a thin ribbon of smoke was rising straight up into the starry night.

The woman stopped him at the gate, turning to look back down the long valley. There was a red glow in the east, and an acrid whiff of burning oil.

"A fire, down by the Belfair Pike," she said, turning around to look at him. "Looks like the Saddlery is going up. You and your partner have anything to do with that?"

"I think my partner may have."

She shook her head, watching the glow light up shreds of cloud in the night sky.

"Bad things happened there, a while ago. But it was too bad you had to burn it down. It was a useful place, in its time."

Merle felt a look of humble contrition was the safest response, so he gave her one. He could see her better now. In the harsh electric glare of the yard lights, her eyes were a pale shade of green and her skin was tanned that coffee-with-cream color Gaelic or Scottish people get if they're out in the sun a lot. Her black hair was thick and long and Merle saw that she was not pretty—too strong-featured for that—but certainly very attractive.

No makeup at all. Her hands on the rifle were rough and red and she had what looked like dried blood under her fingernails.

She felt him looking at her hands and smiled. When she did, Merle raised her age from mid-twenties to maybe early thirties. Her teeth were uneven, with a slight gap between the two front ones.

"I was killing chickens when I heard you crashing around down the valley. Strip down and come into the kitchen. I'll see what we can do."

Merle hesitated.

"Well, you're not tracking all that blood and gore into the parlor, my friend."

She set the rifle and her khaki-colored canvas bag down by the door. In the light from the overhead bulbs Merle saw that the bag had some markings on the side, faded but still legible.

1ST INF DIV AEF

She straightened up, looked at him for a time in the light of the porch, her expression puzzled.

"What are you, anyway? You look French."

"My dad's from Marseille," said Merle. "My mother's Irish, from Dublin, and I was born in Harrisburg, so I don't know where that leaves me."

"Guess you're an American," she said, a half smile flitting across her careworn features.

"Well, don't be shy," she said, indicating his shirt. "I've seen a naked man before."

With her help he was able to peel his bloody boots off. She used a skinning knife she had tucked into her belt to slice off whatever clothing wouldn't come off any other way. She stepped back, looked him over with a cool, critical eye.

"What the devil have you got on your neck there?" she said, indicating the dark purple flame scar that ran up from Zane's left pec and wound itself around the left side of his neck.

Zane reached up and touched the thing, something he had acquired after a long and drunken evening in Phuket, when he had stumbled on his way up a staircase while following a whore and dropped the lantern he was carrying, setting the bamboo house on fire.

Specifically, he got the burn itself when he went back into the flames to get the whore, who, once he had set her down safely outside, attacked him with her fingernails for setting her business on fire.

"I got burned. In a fire," he added redundantly. She shook her head, opened her mouth to say something, said nothing, and carried on with her cold-blooded assessment of his body.

"You keep yourself up okay," she said, giving him a slow up and down. "No fat on you. Good muscles. You got a rip in your shoulder there, looks like a grazing wound. He shot at you twice?"

"More than twice."

"Did he? You manage to get any shots off while he was doing that?"

"Fifteen rounds. I hit him at least once."

This seemed to please her.

"Good for you. Although one hit in fifteen is pretty poor shooting. You need some practice, I guess."

"He was shooting back at me at the time. That tends to spoil your concentration."

"I guess it does. That's a mean big hole in your back. Put your hands up on the wall there."

Merle did as he was told. Although he didn't like the position—it reminded him of getting busted by those cops in Cocodrie or getting a cavity search from the yard bulls at Angola—he found he needed the support.

She went inside and he heard the sound of a tap running. Over behind the barn the generator picked up speed, which meant that the water pump was electric and it was powered by that generator.

He hadn't seen any phone or power wires running into the house either. Or anything like a satellite dish on the roof.

She came back out through the screen door carrying a large wooden bucket and some rough towels, which she dipped in the water and then used to wipe him down, as if he were a horse that had been rode hard and put away wet.

The water was ice cold, as if it had been pumped up from glacier melt. She did the work without shyness, as brisk and thorough as an ER nurse, her expression turning grim as she studied the wound in his back, finally touching it with a fingertip, but gently.

"Not a big slug, I guess. You're lucky it didn't nick your spine. Okay, you'll do."

She straightened up, handing him a towel to dry off with. While he dabbed at himself she opened the door and stepped back to let him go through.

The house looked as if nothing had been done to it since the Depression. It was sparsely furnished, mostly bare wood pieces, oval hooked rugs here and there, in rust and green and gold, one large brown leather couch in front of a big stone fireplace, a wood fire blazing on the hearth, a few framed photos set out along the top of the mantel.

There was a four-slot gun rack above the fireplace, with two Winchesters, one carbine, and a long rifle with a tubular scope, both browned, with octagonal barrels, he noticed. Antiques, but in mint condition. Under that, one very old fowling piece, also cap-and-ball, resting on the bars.

And on the top bar, a long angular and mean-looking weapon that Merle thought might be a BAR, a Browning automatic rifle, a 30.06 full-auto monster that hadn't been used in the field since the end of World War II.

The darker side of Merle's nature figured he was looking at about fifty thousand dollars' worth of antique weapons on that rack alone. He put the thought aside. He figured he was already in enough trouble.

It looked like the eating got done in the kitchen, at the big trestle table. There was a woodstove and some kind of icebox from the thirties. There was no formal dining room. A flight of plain wooden stairs rose up into the darkness at the turning of the landing. Music was coming from somewhere, thin and scratchy, some kind of jazzy number with a lot of horns in it. The name of the song floated unbidden into his mind. "Moonlight Serenade," by Glenn Miller.

He had a couple of seconds to take it all in and was looking down at the worn-out floorboards just inside the kitchen door when the wooden slats just sort of rose up at him, at first quite slowly and then a hell of a lot faster. He felt her hands pluck at him, but she wasn't quick enough. He went down like a man diving off a cliff, hit hard, bounced once, passed out cold, and that was the official end of Merle Zane's Friday.

Coker's Shift Ends Dramatically

Coker's shift ran a lot later than he wanted it to, but all the off-duty guys had come in to help look for the shooters and provide moral support for the survivors, so bailing on all that gung-ho Semper Fi brotherhood-of-the-badge horseshit, and the holy righteous wrath that went with it, would have looked pretty cold-assed.

Around eleven he and a couple of his platoon mates, Jimmy Candles and Mickey Hancock, the shift boss, dropped over to Cedars of Lebanon to see the families of the guys who had gotten killed that day.

This was where the bodies had been taken for the final ME's report, which was being prepared right now, the forensic autopsies, and all that CSI poodle-fakery.

Coker wasn't too worried about them finding anything they could use. The only place CSI clues ever solved anything serious was on television.

Even if they figured out the weapon, the good old U.S. of A. was jam-packed with Barrett .50s in civilian hands, thanks to the NRA.

There was Billy Goodhew's sexy young wife over there, looking weepy, her nose running. Billy Goodhew had been in the county car following right behind the dark blue interceptor, a kind of goofy but brave and highly motivated guy with two tiny girls named Bea and Lillian. Billy had gotten Coker's second round smack in his kisser. Coker had seen him take it—he liked the kid but it had to be done, and what're you going to do?

Money for the taking?

Take it.

The world was a mean place and people had to look after their interests, and one of Coker's interests was in not ever being as dirt-poor and utterly miserable as his alcoholic parents had been.

Taking a long view, for cops, and for combat soldiers, it was Coker's firm belief that the major glory of the job, and most of the thrill of it, was that you could get killed doing it.

Every now and then somebody actually died on the job. Coker felt that line-of-duty death was like the jalapeños on a chimichanga; it added spice to patrol work that could be pretty damn boring most of the time.

Anyway, there it was: Billy Goodhew was going to his grave without a head and his casket welded shut and Coker and Mickey Hancock and Jimmy Candles, as the senior vets in the platoon, felt they ought to go around and see the families, who were sitting in the lobby of Cedars with about fifty other people, mostly relatives, a few friends.

No newspeople allowed inside.

The newspeople were flitting around out there in the parking lot like a circling cloud of vampire bats, maybe ten or eleven satellite trucks from all the local affiliates and the national cable outfits.

On the way from his patrol car Coker got blocked by a wispy but loudmouthed and universally loathed Cap City news guy named Junior Marvin Felker Junior—known to the cops for reasons lost in time as Mother Felker—who stepped up sprightly and stuck a fat furry mike in Coker's face and asked him how it felt to have all those dearly beloved cop bud-dies shot dead in one day.

Coker, always ready to help Mother Felker have a bad day, helped him chew on his fat furry mike for a good long while until Jimmy Candles and Mickey Hancock finally got him to let go. They left Felker lying on his back with blood running from his mouth, screaming something about lawsuits and damages and freedom of the press, in the middle of a glare of lights and mikes, surrounded by all the other hapless media mooks—including his own camera guys—who had done noth-ing at all to stop what Coker was doing but had somehow managed to get it all on tape.

Inside the hospital it was all white lights and the smell of Lysol and diapers and stale coffee and cigarette smoke and a crowd of red faces and a lot of uniforms—state, county, Nice-ville PD, even some guys in suits who looked federal, a little apart from the others—and of course everybody crying and weeping and wailing or sitting around with that dead-eyed stunned look that people always got when something deeply massive has slammed into their lives. Four cops dead, one of them county. It was like an asteroid had smacked into the place.

Coker and Jimmy Candles and Mickey Hancock stiffened themselves, took a deep breath, and waded into the crowd and manfully did all they could manfully do to comfort people who could not be comforted and to promise to smite a mighty smiting upon the killers.

Reed Walker was there too, still wearing his black SWAT-style rig and a Kevlar vest, a long, lean blade of a guy over six feet, with shiny black hair and movie-star good looks, except for the cool flatness of his eyes and the hard line of his mouth.

Walker drove a chase car for the State Patrol and had never wanted to do anything else. He was an adrenaline addict, crazy-brave, and, in Coker's opinion, probably doomed. Reed saw Coker in the press and came across, threading through the crowd like a matte black barracuda.

"Reed," said Coker, "I'm sorry about Darcy."

Coker knew Reed Walker wasn't going to mist up over Darcy. If anything, he had gone colder. Coker recalled that Darcy Beaumont and Reed Walker had gone through chase school together. Darcy was driving the blue Magnum that had caught Coker's second round. Too bad. What's writ stays writ.

Reed shook his hand, looked around the room.

"You're a shooter, sir," he said, in a low voice, his deferential tone as thin as window frost. "What do you make out of a guy who could take out four guys with four shots?"

Coker gave it some thought. Walker wasn't asking about training or background. That the shooter had to be a pro went without saying. A lot of amateurs can stitch up a shooting dummy neat as pins. Killing men requires something special. Killing four in cold blood, that requires a pro.

"I figure a rogue cop," said Coker, telling the kid the truth, "or maybe a Delta-level sniper home from the wars. Somebody used to killing humans."

Walker turned to look at him.

"Sir, if it ever comes around that you have these guys in your sights, you know, like in a standoff or a takedown? Just kill them, okay?"

"Son, if these guys ever get caught in something like that, you can bet they'll never get out of it alive. A guy chilly enough to do what he did, that guy will not be coming in standing up. They'll have to kill him. If they can. He won't give them a choice. He'll go down hard."

Generally, Coker hated to lie to anybody. Not because he had a moral objection. It was just that lying to somebody was a sort of cowardice, like you couldn't handle what they might do if you gave it to them straight. So, as much as he could, he was telling this kid the truth.

Walker seemed to get this.

"If it ever happens, sir, I hope I'm there."

"If I can manage it, I'll see that you are."

Walker smiled.

"Thank you, sir. I'll look forward to it."

So will I, thought Coker, smiling at the guy, thinking that if he had a clean shot at Reed Walker he'd sure as hell take him out first.

Be careful what you wish for, Reed.

Reed moved off into the crowd again, part of it but not in it, as if he had a space around him that no living person was ever going to fill.

Looking at his back, Coker thought Reed was a cop born to die young. Somebody recognized Reed, an ER nurse he used to date, and she wrapped him up in a hug. The crowds closed around them like a wave, and Coker got pulled into the undertow himself.

After a confusing flurry of hugs and tears and bleary red eyes and a lot of listening and nodding, Coker found himself by the water cooler with Billy Goodhew's wife crying into his badge and his two girls, Bea and Lillian, staring up at him with their big blue eyes and their pale white faces and their open, shocked mouths.

Looking down at them over the top of Billy Goodhew's wife's green-apple-shampoo-smelling blond hair—her husband's dead less than a full day and she takes the time to shampoo her hair?—Coker tried to feel something like guilt, or even pity, but he couldn't quite get there.

Feeling things had always been a problem for him, even back in the Corps, but he had learned to fake it pretty well, since faking empathy was a basic job requirement in uniform police work.

The closest he got to feeling anything tonight was feeling Georgia Goodhew's luscious tits pressing up against him—she had a real fine chassis—and feeling that maybe he should make it a point to drop by her house later in the week and see if he could comfort her some more. Coker hugged her in close and let her smear her black eyelash crap all over his number three service tunic, wondering if he could actually nail her, wondering what she'd be like when she really got her siren on, and also wondering whether that greasy black mascara crap would ever come out of his shirt.

Later, when he finally got home to his big old rancher in The Glades and rolled his duty car into his garage and climbed out, he was not at all surprised to find the muzzle of Charlie Danziger's pistol shoved hard into the back of his skull.

Saturday Morning

Nick and Kate Wake Up to Storms

By the morning, as if sensing that Niceville needed a good shower, the clouds had rolled in from the southwest and a blood-warm rain was hammering against Nick's bedroom window. He was already awake, had been lying in the growing gray light listening to the tidal ebb and flow of Kate's breathing, the warmth of her body along his left side, the scent of her on his skin and on his lips and in his hair. Considering how the night had passed, he should have been warmed by a sensual afterglow, calmly adrift in the blessed memory.

But Nick was not drifting.

Nick was lying there waiting for the alarm to go off and trying to find the nerve to talk to Kate about something so volatile that he was afraid to start, having to do with an old Army friend and the favor Nick had asked of him. He was wondering whether he would still be living at home by the time they finished talking about it.

Kate, a lovely woman and one of the sweetest-natured girls Nick had ever met, also had a volcanic temper, and when she started to heat up a wise man got the hell out of range. It had taken Nick a while to get this straight and he still had a small scar on the side of his temple where he'd zigged when he should have zagged and caught a high-velocity coffee mug on its way past his head. She had been terribly sorry she'd drawn blood, but not sorry that she'd hit him.

Kate stirred at his side and he felt that subtle but palpable change in her aura as she slowly woke up to this gloomy Saturday morning.

"Nick," she said, reaching for him, "how long have you been awake?"

He rolled onto an elbow and stroked a strand of auburn hair out of her eyes, looking down at her. She smiled up at him, her expression soft and full of trust and affection.

They had a good marriage, a very good marriage, and Nick knew he was a lucky man.

"Awake? Maybe an hour. You were having a dream."

"Was I?"

"Yes. You remember it?"

She closed her eyes, thought.

"Yes. Something stupid about a woman in a green dress and her big ugly cat. She wanted to come inside the house and for some reason I didn't want her to come inside."

She looked up at him.

"You don't look all that rested either. Were you thinking about the shootings?"

Nick's face hardened up for a moment, and then softened again.

"For a while, yeah."

"Will you have to do anything more about them? Other than walking the site with Marty and Jimmy?"

"Probably not. The Feds will take it over, because the First Third is a national bank. We won't get much of it, other than some stuff around the edges."

"I guess Reed will be going to the funerals. Will you?"

Nick shook his head, looked away.

Kate remembered that Nick had probably seen enough military funerals to last him a lifetime.

She changed the subject.

"You went for a run, after I fell asleep, didn't you?"

She gave him an up-from-under look.

"I'm amazed you had the strength."

Nick smiled down at her.

"I had to get out of the house. You were going to kill me. So I had a shower and then I went for a run along Patton's Hard."

Nick didn't feel like telling her that he had gone to Patton's Hard to take care of some pressing business—what he liked to call a "no-warrant takedown." Nick had some reason to believe there was a serial rapist operating in the area, a snake-mean sadistic pig who had, so far at least, been too smart to get caught.

So Nick went out every night on Patton's Hard, looking for him. And last night, there he was, large as life, in a track suit, squatting in the bushes a few feet off the running path, waiting for a victim.

He never saw Nick coming.

Afterwards, something very strange—while Nick was running homeward along the narrow track that ran through the woods by the Tulip, he had been overtaken and nearly knocked down by a huge runaway horse.

In the brief glance he got as it flashed through the pools of lamplight along the path, it looked like some kind of work-horse, a Clyde or a Belgian, anyway a gigantic animal, golden brown, with a long pale mane and four massive white hooves.

A horse big enough to shake the ground as it thundered past him in the dark, snorting and chuffing, its harness jingling and heavy hooves pounding the earth. It had disappeared into the night, hoofbeats fading into silence, and then, as he stood there in shock, staring after it, a sudden cold wind off the river had chilled him to the core.

Later he'd wondered if it had happened at all. Either way, he wasn't telling Kate about any of it. She hated Patton's Hard, seeing it as nothing but a dark and dangerous path through a dense forest of hanging willows, a place that she avoided even in the daylight.

Kate frowned.

"I wish you wouldn't run along the river late at night. It's not safe. You know what happened there last month, those two poor girls."

Nick gave her a look.

"Kate—"

"I know. Hoo-Rah and Gitter Dun and Semper Fi and all that manly horseshit."

"Gitter Dun is Larry the Cable Guy and Semper Fi is Corps, babe. I was Army, remember? Special Forces is Army?"

Kate knew that Nick craved the Special Forces the way a lifelong smoker craved his cigarette. It was a mystery to her how a man who already had eight years of front-line combat still hadn't gotten himself enough war. But now that he was here in Niceville—by his own choice—it was time for him to show up and be *present* in their life together. She was going to bring him all the way back, one way or another.

The moon clock on the bedside table began to flash, lighting up the dark attic room with a vivid yellow flare.

She sat up, naked, tapped the SLEEP button, and turned to kiss him, a deep, searching kiss. She felt him respond, felt his heat, and smiled to herself.

One way or another.

Breakfast, a while later, was toast and juice and black coffee, and over the litter of toast bits and jam and cutlery Kate, dressed in a tight blue skirt and crisp white blouse and ready for work—she had a meeting with a Belfair County social worker—caught Nick's hand as he raised his cup.

"I almost forgot. I ran into Lacy Steinert at the courthouse. She wants you to go see her."

Nick set the cup down, ran a hand through his short black hair in that way he had. Kate thought he looked like a man with something on his mind. She had no idea what it was, but it was eating away at him. Maybe he'd get around to telling her what it was sometime soon.

"What's she want?" he said, a wary tone.

Kate's expression shifted, the humor and the light leaving it. Outside, the rain was sheeting down and a thick gray fog was lifting in the street, rising up to the treetops like a flood. There was a short silence while she listened to the thunder of rain on their roof and looked at her husband across their breakfast table.

"Rainey Teague," she said softly.

Nick flinched, as she'd known he would, his gray eyes lowering for a second. The Rainey Teague case had put a large hole in Nick's heart. Kate knew this as well as anyone and that's why she had questioned Lacy pretty hard, and then thought long and deep about it before she brought it up with Nick this morning.

"Did Lacy say what she had?"

Kate shrugged, tried for a light touch.

"You know Lacy. Always working the system."

Lacy Steinert was a parole and probation officer with County Corrections, a stand-up and a fine woman, but she was also a hustler for her clients and was always looking for pleas and deals for one hard-done-by perp or another.

"I know her," said Nick, his face still tight.

Kate took a breath, then the plunge.

"It's about Lemon Featherlight—"

"I know him. Ex-Corps. Two tours, Bronze with a Vee, Purple Heart, a war hero. Honorable discharge and it all goes south. Now he's a confidential informant for Tony Branko at Niceville PD Drug Squad. He's a Seminole from Islamorada, down in the Keys. Hangs around the club district south of Tulip Bend. Ecstasy, OxyContin, Percodan, Demerol—

anything prescription, he can get it. Sells it to the carriage trade, when he can. Sells himself too, so we hear."

"Okay," said Kate. "The carriage trade. That's the connection. Lacy says he's telling her he was selling Demerol to Sylvia Teague."

Nick said nothing, but she could see the words sinking in.

"For the cancer?"

"This is what she's saying."

"Kate, Sylvia Teague was a very wealthy woman, and they get the best care there is. She could get whatever she needed from her doctor, up to and including heroin. Before Rainey went missing she had her own morphine drip. She could just press the button on the monitor whenever she wanted and get all the ease in the world. And how would she ever cross lines with a guy like Lemon?"

Kate hesitated, and then went on.

"He's telling Lacy they met two years ago at the Pavilion on Tulip Bend. She was there with some friends—lunch or something—and Lemon Featherlight was walking through— he's a good-looking man, dresses well—one of Lacy's friends waved to him and he came over."

"Lacy get this friend's name?"

Kate shrugged.

"You'll have to talk to Lacy about that."

"I'm still not getting the point."

Kate paused, looked at Nick.

"Lacy says Lemon got pretty close to Sylvia. Lemon says they became . . . friends."

Nick thought that over.

"I'm still in the dark. Where does this go?"

"Lemon Featherlight says Sylvia used to invite him home. Sometimes Miles would be there . . ."

Kate let it hang there.

Nick had some coffee, his gray eyes lowered. She could see his mind working.

"The *three* of them?"

Kate tilted her head to the left, gave him a wry look, older than her years.

"This is not entirely unknown in Niceville, Nick. Or in the rest of the world. Some pretty wild things went on in the twenties, and then again in the eighties. Even in the best families, so I hear."

"Not in mine."

"Sweetheart, your family's in Los Angeles. You grew up surfing off Santa Monica pier with your sister. Your father is an entertainment lawyer and your mother runs a hospital and they're both as frigidly unappealing as banana-flavored Popsicles. How they ever got you and Nora I'll never understand. They must have been trying out a new yoga move when they fell over and accidentally had sex."

Nick had to smile at that. She was dead right. His parents got intensely passionate about the die-off in the delta smelt population, but they really didn't give a damn about actual humans. They'd had two kids, Nick and his twin sister, Nora, reacted with quiet horror at the brute physicality of the birth process, cutesy-named the results Nick and Nora as if they were a pair of teacup Yorkies. Then they went out ASAP and got themselves vasectomies and tubal ligations, one each, and that was that for that. Kate smiled, touched his cheek.

"Nick, I keep telling you, Niceville is different, even more than the way the whole South is different. Maybe it's the heat, maybe there really is something weird in Crater Sink. Niceville has a strange pulse. Remember, I grew up here."

"That why your dad lives so far away from it?"

Kate smiled at him. Ever since she had asked her father about the Rainey Teague disappearance a year ago, he had gracefully but continually managed to avoid talking about it at all, other than to ask her, now and then, in a careful tone, whether she still had "that damned old mirror" upstairs.

Which they did.

Kate didn't answer Nick's question, which was clearly rhetorical. He had moved on to Lemon Featherlight anyway.

"Featherlight's gone to see Rainey maybe twelve times in the last year. I guess you already know that?"

Kate did, and said so.

"Yeah, well, Tony Branko looked into it, asked him what the connection was. Featherlight just said he felt sorry for the kid. Branko figured there was more, but Featherlight can close down pretty tight when he wants to, and Branko didn't see the harm in it anyway. What you're telling me, things get a little clearer, don't they? Branko's too damn soft on Featherlight, because he was Corps himself and he thinks Featherlight got royally screwed by the MPs. Wait till he hears this news. Is Lemon Featherlight saying he knows *anything* useful about what happened to Rainey?"

She shook her head, still watching him to see where he was going to come down on this. "No idea. Lacy just says, come by and see her."

Nick was silent for a while longer. This wasn't the time to bring up *the other thing*. Anyway, what Kate was saying had pretty much driven it out of his mind. He'd figure out what to say later.

"Damn. Lemon Featherlight and Sylvia—"

"And Miles. You can handle it, Nick. You're a tough guy. Whatever it is Lemon Featherlight has to say, you should probably go and listen."

"I liked the Teagues. I liked thinking well of them. Maybe I won't want to hear it."

"I know," said Kate, touching his hand. "Who does? But that's what you do, isn't it?"

Coker and Danziger
Have a Frank Exchange of Views

When Danziger came to that Saturday morning, his first impression was that he was lying at the bottom of a swimming pool staring up through ten feet of clear blue water at a match-head sun that was floating in a sky of pale green. It was lovely and warm and relaxing down here and he was giving some thought to staying put for the rest of the day when a dark shadow fell across the sun and he heard a deep booming voice that must have been coming from the pool drain because it seemed to be all around him. The voice was vaguely familiar and he closed his eyes trying to place it.

"Hey, Charlie, you dickhead. Wake the fuck up."

That helped. Coker.

He opened his eyes.

He was looking up at Coker, who was looking down at him, silhouetted against a bright halogen lamp of some sort. Coker's face, never a kindly one, looked like a death mask, staring down at him with a cold yellow glitter in his pale brown eyes.

"And don't you for fuck's sake say where am I," growled Coker, who had a cigarette in his mouth. His silhouette was wreathed in smoke, and ashes from the tip were drifting down onto Danziger's face.

"Where am I?" said Danziger.

Coker stepped back.

"You're at Donny Falcone's place."

"How'd I get here?"

"Last night at my house. I get home; you're in the garage. You stick a pistol in my ear and then pass out on the floor like a mall-rat on roofies. I carried you inside, patched you up a bit, figured you needed to get that slug outta your chest, so I called Donny."

Danziger thought that over.

"Donny's a *dentist*. I was shot. I needed a medic, Coker, not a dental flossing."

A voice from farther away, somebody else in the background. The low drawling voice of Donny Falcone himself, not at all friendly.

"I was medic enough to put you out and pull a nine-mil slug out of your fucking chest, Charlie. And sew you up nice and neat afterwards."

Danziger lifted himself up in the chair. It took awhile and hurt like hell. The room swirled a bit and went pale. He looked around, saw Donny Falcone looking back at him. Donny was a big black-eyed young Sicilian with George Clooney good looks and teeth so white that when he smiled you just wanted to smack him. Donny wasn't smiling right now.

In fact, he looked like a man who had just become an accessory after the fact to four—no, six—counts of felony murder, if you counted the two people in the news chopper.

This was a pretty accurate précis of his situation, and it was a situation he would never have allowed himself to be in if he hadn't indulged himself in a sexual fetish that involved using his anesthetized female patients as unwitting models in erotic photo-essays on the motif of partly naked and very attractive women posed shamelessly in dental chairs while gassed out of their gourds.

This form of artistic expression, which, had it involved crucifixes stuck in buckets of rhino poop or naked dead lesbian nuns floating in glass tanks full of formaldehyde, would have gotten him a nude lap dance with a happy ending from the head of acquisitions at the Tate Modern.

Instead, it brought him into Coker's gravitational field in a roundabout way, beginning with the fact that Donny Falcone had—briefly—employed a young and very pretty Cherokee dental hygienist named Twyla Littlebasket, who had stumbled onto one of Donny's "hobby shots" while borrowing his office computer.

After some heated negotiations, Twyla Littlebasket had been very well paid to go suddenly deaf and blind. This turned out to be a short-term fix. After cashing Donny's generous check and blowing half the money on a first-class tour of Europe and a scarlet Beemer, Twyla, upon reflection, decided that it was a matter of feminist duty to take this whole squalid story to her father, Morgan Littlebasket. Chief of their clan, a highly respected Niceville resident, and a man who was seen by all as a figure of adamantine integrity. Daddy would know what to do about Donny Falcone.

But Daddy, otherwise a kindly old man, was also puritanically austere in matters touching upon sexuality. His manner around Twyla and her older sister, Bluebell, had, during their teenage years, grown ever more frigidly distant and had verged on grimly disapproving as their bodies had blossomed into ripe young womanhood.

The fact that she had so befouled herself—and her clan— by accepting a bribe from a criminally deviant Italian dentist was a moral failure he might eventually forgive but he would never forget.

So Twyla, faltering in her resolve, ended up going with the only other independent and strong male connection she had, namely Coker, who was her part-time lover.

Coker elected to try the Donny Falcone case in Coker's Court of No Appeal, where Donny Falcone was duly pronounced Guilty as Sin and sentenced to pay a hefty monthly fine, in cash, to an account Coker had established in a galaxy far, far away, the proceeds of which Coker felt it only right to share with Twyla Littlebasket. Having some extortionate leverage on a perverted Sicilian dentist may not seem, at first glance, all that useful, but it had just saved Charlie Danziger's life.

Coker stubbed out his cigarette in the ceramic spit-up thingie next to the dentist chair and leaned down into Danziger's face, breathing cigarette fumes and something minty-zesty fresh all over Danziger's face.

"I see the *proceeds* aren't in your fucking car, Charlie. Can you enlighten me as regards to this unhappy eventuation?"

"There's no such word as 'eventuation,' you ignorant cracker. And yes, they are not in the car because you damn well know why. You'd have done the same, you were in my position."

Coker pulled back out of Danziger's face and lit up another Camel, offering one to Danziger and lighting it up for him with a gold Zippo bearing a worn-down crest of the United States Marine Corps.

Danziger sucked in the smoke, winced a bit at the pain in his side, glancing down at the sewn-up incision in his chest with quiet satisfaction and then back up at Coker, whose craggy hard-bitten face wreathed in cigarette smoke was making him look like Clint Eastwood's ugly older brother.

Coker breathed the smoke out through his nostrils, the two plumes drifting into the downlight from the halogen lamp.

"Yeah," he said, flashing a wolfish grin, "I guess I woulda. I gotta say I'm also a tad pissed at you for not dealing with Merle."

Danziger winced at the recollection and shook his head sadly.

"He's a nimble little fucker, I'll give him that. Flitted into the undergrowth like some kind of magical pixie and disappeared. Got any suggestions?"

Coker sighed, looked down at his cigarette, twirled it between his index finger and his thumb like a tiny baton—a signature trick he had—and flicked it back into his mouth.

"Way I see it, he's either dead in the woods or he got himself doctored up and now he's laying back in the tall grass getting ready to even things up. We can't afford to just hope for him being dead. The guys who showed up at the barn fire said they saw some blood at the edge of the forest, but the dogs got nothing after a few yards. So I'm thinking he's still out there."

"You're a gun-hand, Coker. Saddle up and go git him."

Coker shook his head.

"That's not going to fly now. I can't be loping about the woodlands yelling, '*Come out come out dear Merle come out come out wherever you are*' and firing randomly into the undergrowth. Only thing we can do is reopen negotiations."

"Yeah? How we planning to do that?"

Coker held up his cell phone.

"I—or maybe you—are going to call him up on his cell, ask for a meet. If he agrees, and we can manage it, we kill him. If we can't, then we piece him off fair and square. He's got as much skin in this cluster-fuck as we do."

Danziger pretended to think this over. What he was actually thinking was that being friends with Coker was kind of like having a python as a pet. You had to keep him well fed and amused all the time, and it would never do to let him think you were nervous around him. About Merle Zane, what Coker was suggesting was pretty much what Danziger had already decided was the only sensible solution.

"We kill him if we can, and if we can't, we piece him off?"

"That's the plan."

"Okay. I'm in."

Coker smiled, smacked the top of the dental tray, making the steel tools clatter.

"Great. And now you got the slug out and you're all doctored up, how about you go and get the *proceeds* and we divvy it up—Donny here's going to get a taste, aren't you, Donny?—and then we can all go about the Lord's work with a clear conscience."

Danziger inhaled the smoke, let it out slow.

"Nope."

"Nope? Why nope?"

"I can't go get it right now. I gotta be available to talk to the Feds today."

Coker looked a bit off balance.

"Why are the Feds wanting to talk to you today?"

Danziger gave him a sideways look.

"Because I'm the regional manager of Wells Fargo and we popped that bank about a half hour after one of my trucks dropped off the payroll for half of Quantum Park. That's why. The Feds don't like coincidences."

Coker blinked down at him, pulling on his cigarette, sucking his cheeks in as he did it, which made his eyes look even scarier.

"Did we think of this?"

Danziger, who was getting tired of looking up at Coker looking down at him, pushed himself out of the chair and looked around the office for his shirt. Donny was a step ahead.

"You didn't have a shirt," said Donny. "You can have one of mine. Also, I think you can fit into a pair of my jeans. Your boots are okay. Spotted up with blood some. You're going to have to take a blood thinner in case you throw a clot. I have some OxyContin too. When that freezing wears off, you're going to be in a lot of pain."

"I'm in a lot of pain right now."

Falcone nodded, got up, and walked back into his dispensary, fatigue in every line, a portrait of the dentist as a hanged man. While he was out of the room Danziger turned to Coker, who was leaning up against a rack of dental tools.

"Where's my cell phone? Not the one we used on the job. My own phone."

Coker reached into the pocket of his range jacket, tossed the cell to Danziger, who flipped it open and hit the ON button.

He looked at the screen for a couple of minutes, and then held the screen up to Coker.

"There you go. Seventeen calls, starting about ten minutes after the robbery. Nine from Cletus Boone at the depot—I left him in charge—four from Marty Coors at State, and the last three are from Boonie Hackendorff at the Feebs office down in Cap City. I called Boonie back last night around eleven—"

"With a bullet in you?"

"Had to. I knew they were going to wanna see me."

"Boonie ask you where you were calling from?"

"Yeah. I said I was calling from Canticle Key, outside of Metairie, fly-fishing off a pirogue. Said my cell was off because I was on my goddam vacation and how the fuck would I know that somebody was going to hit the First Third in Gracie."

"Can you prove where you were?"

"He can't prove I wasn't. Besides, if Boonie ever gets *that* suspicious, we're fucked anyway."

"You use your cell? Because if you did—"

Danziger was shaking his head.

"No. I made a Skype call from my laptop. You can't trace those to a cell tower."

Coker gave Danziger a look of approval.

"Sharp, Charlie. Very sharp. Now what?"

"I said I was driving up right away, going all night. I'm

going to call in, say here I am, go see him at his office, as soon as I get a shirt."

Coker looked at Danziger's bare chest, at the general color of the man, which, if Coker had been an interior decorator instead of a cop, he would have described as a cross between taupe and ecru.

"How the hell are you going to get through a grilling with the Feds with a hole in your chest? You can't afford to fall on your face right in the middle of a meet with the Feds, start barfing up blood and shit. And what about the *proceeds*?"

"We'll divvy up the proceeds after I'm done with Boonie, okay? You pulling duty tonight?"

"No. The Feds don't want us tracking mud all over this cluster-fuck. It belongs to the State CID and the Feebs. I'm off until Monday."

"Okay—you call Zane, set up a meet."

Coker thought it over.

"Do the split—or the hit, if he gives us a chance do it all at once?"

"Yeah. Why not?"

"Even me?" asked Donny, walking back in the room carrying a crisp white shirt and jeans and a big soft suede jacket. "I mean, the split, not the hit."

"Yeah," said Coker, shooting a glance at Danziger and then cutting away, which Danziger correctly interpreted as *maybe we'll hit Donny too, just to be safe*.

"Yeah, even you."

Then he had a final thought.

"Hey, what if it goes all wrong at Boonie's? Say you *do* pass out, or you start bleeding all over the carpet, some crazy shit. What about the money then? Maybe I should go get it now?"

Danziger went back a long way with Coker, knew him pretty well, which was why he was giving the answer a long thought. If Coker decided that Danziger was jerking him around, he was just as likely to shoot him right now.

"It's at your place."

Coker was not delighted by this news.

"*My* place? Where at my place? On my front porch, all wrapped up in a black bag with LOOT on the side, maybe a big red ribbon and a note with teddy bears on it?"

"It's lying on the rafters in the roof of your garage. Black canvas bags. No teddy bears."

Coker watched as Danziger got himself into Donny's shirt and the leather jacket.

"You're an unpredictable son of a bitch, Charlie. I'll give you that."

"Yeah?" said Charlie, pulling a cigarette out of Coker's pack and lighting it up, squinting at him through the smoke. "Well, there it is."

"Yeah," said Coker, grinning back at him. "There it is."

"*Ecco la cosa,*" said Donny.

They both looked at him through the smoke. Donny shrugged his shoulders.

"What did you just say?" asked Coker.

"I said, *ecco la cosa.* There it is."

A thoughtful pause.

"Well, don't," said Coker, after a moment.

"Yeah," put in Danziger. "Don't."

"Why not?" asked Donny in a hurt tone.

Danziger and Coker exchanged looks.

"Because it just sounds . . ."

"Weird," said Danziger.

"Yeah," said Coker. "Weird."

Nick Kavanaugh
Gets Some Disappointing News

Beau Norlett, back from a week's leave, caught Nick as he came in through the door, the office reeking of burned coffee, the weekend crew sitting around in their shirtsleeves, holsters and cuffs showing, everyone talking low, a cold gray rain streaming down the windows.

"Nick," said Beau, with a broad smile. "How was Savannah?"

Nick gave him a look.

Had he heard about what had happened in Forsyth Park? Probably not.

"Nice town. A little buggy. But pretty."

"Yeah? I never been there. May wants to go. Says it's really romantic, like Paris. You ever been to Paris, Nick?"

"Yes."

Beau, forgetting himself, sat looking up at Nick, expecting something more. Then he remembered that Nick hardly ever said something more.

"Okay. Hey, that was some bad shit, up in Gracie, wasn't it?"

"It was."

"Tig says you walked the scene with Marty Coors?"

"I did."

Beau waited.

Nick said nothing.

"Yeah. Well. Uh, Tig wants to see you. Asked me to say."

Beau Norlett was a nice kid, blue-black, solid as a bridge abutment, with a round bald head, sloping shoulders, great hands, as light on his feet as a tango dancer, but he could hit a crack-house door like a runaway freight.

He had been a famous linebacker when he was at Saint Mary's, might have made Notre Dame or Ole Miss with some luck. If you were looking for somebody to take a door down, he was your guy. If you were looking for cop smarts, you were still looking. But Nick thought the kid had potential.

Nick smiled, went down to the coffee room, poured himself a hot bitter cup and walked on through the crowded office to Tig's hideout, a corner glassed-in cubby with a view across the motor pool to the marble dome of the city hall. Rain was sleeting straight down and the dome looked like a round wet rock sitting on a pile of bricks.

In the northeast, looming high over the town like a storm front, blurred by the rain, he could just make out Tallulah's Wall, which made him think of Crater Sink, which brought the Teague case back in full HDTV.

Even before Sylvia Teague went into Crater Sink—if she really had—Nick had always thought that Tallulah's Wall had a kind of sickness cloud floating over it, and if anybody had told him that even the Indians who used to live here had stayed away from the place he'd have believed it.

Most small towns would have made a feature like Tallulah's Wall and Crater Sink a theme park and put ads in *USA Today* trying to drum up tourism, but not Niceville.

Early on, Nick had asked Reed Walker why Tallulah's Wall had everybody in Niceville so spooked. Reed had stared at his hands for a while and then started up a story about something that was said to have happened at Crater Sink back in the twenties, or maybe earlier, or later, he wasn't sure, then he seemed to think better of it, ordered two more beers, and managed to change the subject.

Nick stood in the hall outside Tig's office for a while, turning the memory over, his mind in neutral, watching the cloud banks get caught on Tallulah's Wall, spilling their cargo of gray rain down on the town.

On the far side of the Dome of the Rock, as they called City Hall, because the mayor's name was Little Rock Mauldar, Nick could see a section of the Tulip River, running mud brown and churning fast after two hours of hard rain. He shook himself loose from the dull gray landscape, the dull gray morning, and walked into Tig Sutter's office.

Tig looked up as Nick came in, an up-from-under over the rim of his steel gray reading glasses. He leaned back in his wooden swivel chair, making the thing creak like a cellar door in a horror movie.

"Nick. How's the Lovely?"

"Still with me."

"Probably just hanging around to see what the heck you'll do next. I hear she nailed that Bock asshole."

Nick smiled at that.

"She did."

"I always liked Ted Monroe. He's a damn good judge of character. Kate say how Bock took it?"

"Poorly."

"Screw him."

"Metaphorically?"

"Either way. Take a pew, Nick."

Nick plucked a wooden chair from under a picture of the president. The president, his chin cocked just so, his eyes all squinty, a thin-lipped smile like a gunfighter, was staring off into the middle distance, as if he could see some sunny green uplands that he was going to lead you to.

Nick sat, lightly, on the chair's forward edge, his forearms on his knees, the plastic cup turning in his long-fingered hands. Tig had some of his, Nick had some of his, and they sat there for a time in a companionable silence. Tig was shifting around in his chair a bit and Nick realized the man was nervous about something.

"Okay, well, first some hard news. Nick, I got a letter from a Colonel Dale Sievewright, down at Benning. It was about your request to re-up for combat deployment with the Fifth SF again . . . ?"

Nick looked at him but said nothing.

Tig shrugged.

"You were gonna pull out on me?"

"I was," said Nick. "No offense, Tig."

"None taken. I hired you, I didn't buy your ugly white ass down at the Wally Mart. I know you miss the action. I was worried a little that maybe you and Kate were having some trouble at home?"

Nick was quiet for a time. When he spoke there was something moving under the tight skin over his cheekbones, a pale glimmer in his eyes.

"No. Kate is . . . Kate. She couldn't be better. When she comes in the door, she makes my day. It's just . . ."

Tig set the cup down, creaked back in the chair again.

"Pale?"

Nick sipped at the cup, said nothing for a time.

"Yes. That's a good word. Like all the color went away. I mean, Kate wants me to put a deck on the back. So I go down to Billy Dials, I walk around, look at the cedar, I can't seem to figure out why in the hell Kate would want a cedar deck. I mean, what's a cedar deck for?"

"You know. Beer. Football. Barbecues."

"Barbecues," said Nick, looking into his cup. "Barbecues make me think of Fallujah, those contractors hanging from meat hooks on that bridge."

Tig looked out the window at the rain sheeting down.

There was thunder rolling around in the distance, getting closer, and lightning flaring up inside the cloud mass. A crappy morning if there ever was one.

"I have spent considerable time trying to forget that, Nick, so thanks for the reminder. You think Fallujah smelled like barbecue, try watching an Abrams burn up with a whole crew inside. You talk this over with Kate before you sent the letter?"

Nick shook his head.

"Okay. Well, no need to spook her with it now. I'm sorry to say this, I really am, although I'm happy not to be losing you, but Sievewright turned you down."

Nick nodded, took it in, his face closing up.

"The Wadi Doan?"

Tig nodded, his expression kindly.

"The Wadi Doan. Al Kuribayah. Yemen. That's not going to go away, Nick. Not your fault, nobody ever thought that. They were okay with JAG, but another combat deployment . . . I guess not."

"The optics."

"And that video."

Nick said nothing.

Tig let it slide.

Nick, ready to change the topic, said, "Anything for us on what happened yesterday?"

Tig rubbed his cheeks with both hands, looking suddenly old.

"You walked the site. What'd you think?"

Nick told him.

Tig nodded, having come to the same conclusion on his own. Cold-assed murder, plain and simple.

"We getting a piece of anything?" Nick asked.

"There'll be one hell of a funeral, for one thing," said Tig, looking out the window at the rain coming down. "There'll be uniforms coming in to Cap City from all over the country, far away as Canada, England. Christ, four guys. Plus the two people in the Live Eye chopper."

"The hell with the people in the chopper. Media vultures."

Nick didn't like the media. Tig, who felt the same way but had to work with them, liked to keep Nick far away from people with cameras and microphones. He changed the subject.

"I'd really like you to go, if you would. Next Friday? For our unit? Maybe you could take Beau?"

Nick looked down at his hands.

"I've had it with military funerals, Tig."

"So have I," said Tig, lowering his voice and leaning across his desk. "But I don't want us represented by some of these here younger guys, God love 'em, none of them know how to wear dress blues. Don't even know how to wear a business suit, for that. You do. And Beau will do whatever you tell him. He wants to be you when he grows up. Come on. I'm asking here."

Nick was quiet, remembering all the funerals he had been to, not all of them in crisp dress blues with taps playing, some of them just six guys in ragged BDUs standing around a smoking crater, shoveling gravel over what was left of a friend.

"Okay. I'll go. One of the guys was a friend of Reed's, so he's going. Kate'd like me to go too."

Nick's mind went back to the bank robbery.

"About Gracie, anybody looking at the rollover on the interstate?"

"The eighteen-wheeler?"

"Yeah. It bothers me. A full load of rebar, spreads it all over six lanes of traffic, spears a van full of church ladies. Two killed, but the driver walks."

Tig looked at Nick, thinking it over.

"You're thinking about the timing?"

"I am. When'd it roll over?"

Tig shuffled some papers, picked up a printout, riffled through it.

"Fourteen forty-one hours."

"There you go. These people hit the bank in Gracie, what, forty minutes later? Worked out pretty good for them, didn't it, since almost every available unit, ground and air, was tied up with the rollover? Anybody looking into the driver?"

Tig shook his head.

"Not that I know of."

"What's his name?"

Tig flipped up the edge of a printout, ran a finger down the paragraph.

"Lyle Preston Crowder. Six years with Steiger Freightways. No criminal sheet and no record of DUI or anything else. Other than a lousy credit history, which nowadays who doesn't have, he's shiny as a new dime."

"Where is he now?"

"He was banged up. Pretty hysterical. They've got him sedated and under guard at Sorrows down in Cap City."

"Guard? Guard from what?"

"The people in the minivan had husbands and fathers. People around here like to settle their own beefs. There's been some talk."

"Okay. I get that. Anyway, you might say something to Boonie."

Tig nodded, made a note on a yellow pad.

"I will. So. Work. How's your sheet?"

Nick sat back, drained his cup.

"I have a meet with Lacy Steinert, over in Tin Town. She says one of her clients wants to talk about the Rainey Teague case. Might know something."

"What client?"

"Lemon Featherlight."

"Yeah. I heard he got flaked for ecstasy by the goddam DEA. What's he want?"

"A deal on the DEA bust, be my guess."

"You think Lemon's worth looking at?"

Nick shrugged.

"Lacy's good people. If she thinks there's something in it, can't hurt to go have a coffee. I'd like to clear that one."

"Yeah. So would I."

There was no need to say anything else. They felt the same way about the Rainey Teague thing, and they both knew it.

"A year back, isn't it?" said Tig, as if he wasn't aware of that down to the hour.

"To the day," said Nick.

"How's the kid doing?"

"Still at Lady Grace. Still in a coma."

"Rainey was adopted, if I remember? Kate still acting as guardian?"

"She is. She's related to Sylvia, and she knows family law. The original adoption thing was handled by a lawyer name of Leah Searle—dead now—had a practice up in Sallytown. Rainey was in some sort of foster home up there. Birth parents apparently died in a barn fire. Kid was made a ward of the county and put into foster care. Kate got the papers from Sylvia's place after she . . ."

"Disappeared," said Tig, who knew that Nick, until he saw her body, was never going to acknowledge her suicide.

"Yeah, since then. Leah Searle died the next year, but Kate went over all the papers. Rainey's the only heir. Kate's got power of attorney for Rainey, sees to his finances and monitors the Teague portfolio, which is huge. Kept the house as it was, so if Rainey ever comes around, everything will be the way it was on the day he was taken. Gardeners. Cleaners. Has it checked every day by some people from Armed Response."

"Kate. Gotta love her. One of my favorite people. Can't believe you were thinking of going back into the shit, a lady like that at home."

On their terms this was an intrusion, but Tig felt it strongly, so he just let it stand.

Nick understood it.

Tig was right.

A moment passed in silence.

"Okay," said Tig, changing the tone. "You go see Lacy, let's hear what Lemon has to say."

"I will," said Nick. "We have anything else?"

"Yeah," said Tig, looking troubled. "Vice got an anonymous tip. I didn't like to hear it."

"They get a voice?"

"No. It was an e-mail. Sort of. But the IP was stripped out, or it was from a computer link we haven't got a line on yet. I don't get all that cyber-shit stuff, Nick. Anyway, like I said, untraceable. Anonymous."

Nick looked at his hands. Snitches were how it all worked, but nobody liked to work with them.

"What was the tip?"

Tig moved his shoulders, hesitated, and then handed a printout across to Nick.

The custodian at saint innocent orthodox has a history of child sex abuse going back to 1982. His name is kevin david his crimes were committed under the name kevin david dennison his dob is 1956/06/23. look first in maryland. He also is online on AIM as katydee999. You should look at him. a friend.

Nick read it, handed the sheet back. "Jesus. *A friend.* Man, I really hate this kind of anonymous shit."

Tig's face said the same thing.

"So do I. I ran this Kevin David guy and he looks pretty solid. Custodian. Wife died of cancer last year. Grown kids. Has a house up in Sallytown. Lives alone. Nothing against him. I asked around on the quiet. Everybody at the church thinks he's a saint."

"What about Maryland?"

"I'm waiting for a sheet and a photo. Age and general description is right, but there's a lot of Kevin Dennisons in the world. I gotta be sure before I let Vice go burn down a guy's life."

"Any whiff of anything?"

Tig looked down.

"Yeah. He has a cell phone cluster."

"You mean his GPS records. That was fast."

"My sister's family goes to Saint Innocent. They have a girl. I was motivated. I called a friend at Comcast."

"Where's the cluster?"

"Schoolyards. Playgrounds."

"Oh hell."

"Yeah," said Tig. "Oh hell."

"You want me to do this?"

Tig shook his head.

"Vice already has it. I didn't want to look like I was getting in the way."

Nick looked at the printout again.

"This e-mail, someone who would send this out, Tig, is a slug. Guy's capable of a whole lot worse. We should find out who this asshole actually is."

"You want to do that?"

Nick shook his head.

"I don't get this cyber shit any better than you do. Do we have anybody around who can look into it? Like one of those tattooed geeks in dispatch?"

"No. Not like this. Mainly they all sit around and twatter each other on their twats."

"I think that's *Twitter*, Tig."

"Whatever. What about your brother-in-law, that Deitz guy? Doesn't he have a whole boxcar full of computer wing nuts in that outfit of his?"

Nick wasn't very happy with Byron Deitz—something was going sour inside the guy—but he would definitely have guys who could track a cyber trail like this.

"Okay with me. I'd rather you asked him."

Tig was aware that there was some tension between Nick and his brother-in-law.

"Sure. I'll ask Deitz myself. Off the record, like. But I got something for you to do yourself. Take your mind off this Army thing. You know Delia Cotton, the Sulfur King's widow, up in The Chase?"

"I know the Cotton mansion. Called Temple Hill. Big yellow-brick place, wraparound porch, lots of that white gingerbread crap in every corner."

"Well, she's gone missing."

Nick sat up, life coming back into his frame.

"Missing?"

"Yes. Got a cleaning lady named Alice Bayer. Went there today to deliver some groceries, found the door open, music playing. Half a scotch on the table. House wide open and Delia Cotton gone. Cat gone too, some kind of Maine Coon cat. Name of Mildred Pierce. Maybe also the yard man, fellow named Gray Haggard. His Packard was in the drive, but no sign of him either."

"Relatives?"

"All dead. Maybe a few friends in her book club. Patrol guys did some leg work, got diddly. She's gone, Nick. With her yard man. Gone like the snows of yesteryear. That's Proust, you know."

Nick shook his head.

"Actually, I don't think so."

Tig lost his smug smile.

"Not Proust?"

"No. I mean, he said something *like* it—about the remembrance of things past, sort of. But he never said anything about the snows of yesteryear."

"Then who the fuck did?"

"I think it was some dead Frog. Gimme a minute. Villon. Yes. François Villon."

"What did he say?"

Nick took a moment.

"I think he said, *Où sont les neiges d'antan?*"

"Which means?"

"Where are the snows of yesteryear."

Tig remained unconvinced.

"You sure?"

"I'd have to google it. But I'm pretty sure."

Tig looked unhappy.

"Man. I've been throwing that quote around for years. Now I feel like a mook."

"Maybe. But you've still got your looks. Who's catching the Cotton thing?"

"You are. Delia was one of ours. I know the family; they were real good to my dad. Cottons were also one of the Founding Four. A fine lady too."

Nick stood up, put the chair back under the president's dreamy eyes, his faraway look.

"Can I have Beau?"

"Beau? He's pretty raw."

"He's not going to get any better unless we take him around some. Otherwise, he's just filling a chair and filing shit and losing his nerve."

"Okay. Take Beau. It'll give him a taste. We'll see what he's got too. One other thing," said Tig, as Nick turned to leave. His casual tone became a bit forced. "You run on Patton's Hard, don't you? Down there by the Tulip?"

"Yes."

"You run there last night?"

"Yes. Every night."

"Last night?"

"Every night."

"You see a big white guy down there, wearing a blue track suit, a muscle guy?"

"Nope. Why?"

"Well, Boots Jackson's got the motorcycle beat for Patton's Hard—"

"I know Boots. He found the last guy who had seen Rainey."

"Yeah. Alf Pennington. Anyway, Boots found this guy there around two in the morning, looked like he'd been mugged. Banged around pretty good. Like he had been worked over by a pro. He'll never look at the same face in his mirror again. Ribs cracked. Nose all over on one side. Cheekbone cracked like an eggshell. Both testicles ruptured and crushed. Effectively castrated, the medics are saying. Also may lose his right eye. Said he was just out jogging and somebody jumped him. Came out of the dark. A random attack."

Nick shrugged.

"Well, his story held up until Boots got him to the ER medics. They were cleaning him up and a big plastic Baggie fell out of his track suit pocket. Skate laces. Roll of duct tape. Baby oil. A box cutter."

"Tools for rape."

"Yes. Tools for a rape. So Boots ran him and he was wanted up in Charleston for forcible sexual assault. Looks like a chain of attacks on young women, mostly joggers, going way back."

"Not Ziggy Danich? Vice has been after him for months. Never able to pin anything on him."

"Yeah. I know. I remember you asking about him a while back."

"So they got him, finally?"

"Looks like it will stand up. Reasonable search, chain of evidence. Ziggy might be the guy who did those two young girls down by the Tulip two weeks ago. They're doing the DNA now."

Tig stopped, seemed to wait for Nick to say something, which didn't happen.

"So you didn't see anything?"

"No. Not a thing."

"Thing is, guy said he had no idea who attacked him, never saw it coming, no idea where the rape stuff came from. Said it must have been planted."

"They all say that."

Tig nodded. "They do."

He looked troubled, moved a couple of things around on his desk and then moved them back.

Nick waited, but Tig seemed to be done.

He wasn't.

"And you got nothing to add, Nick?"

"Not a thing. Good for Boots. Oughta get an attaboy for nailing that cockroach. Nobody else could. Sometimes you just get lucky."

Tig was quiet. Then he said, "Well, it doesn't pay to get too damned lucky. This kind of thing happened again, we'd have to figure we had some sort of vigilante thing going on. Remember that guy last year, in The Glades, we found him lying beside his car, in his garage, somebody took a bat to him? Every bone in both legs smacked into splinters? Never gonna walk again?"

"DeShawn Coles. Ran underage whores out of the Double Deuce in Tin Town. Mean as a razorback hog. We were looking at him for pouring bleach down the throat of a little runaway named Shaniqua Throne, but she died before she could ID anybody."

"Yeah. Him. Thing is, once, it's chance, twice, it's a coincidence. Three times—that's different. Gotta start looking at it. A vigilante, hell, even the Feds would start looking at that. And the press would suck it up like a dual-bag Dyson. They'd never lay off till the guy was caught."

"Yeah," said Nick. "I can see that."

"Yeah. So can I."

Now Tig was finished.

Point made.

Some air came back into the room.

"Okay," said Nick. "Well, I'll go jump on the Cotton thing, then?"

"Yes," said Tig, leaning back and folding his arms across his big bony chest, cracking a broad smile. "Right after the Teague thing. Check that out, and then go see what happened to Delia Cotton. You go do that. Maybe it'll take your edges off."

"I have edges?"

"Just go, will you?"

Tony Bock
Can't Leave Well Enough Alone

Like the boy in the fairy tale who stole these magic beans from the evil giant and planted them in his garden by the light of the silvery moon and then woke up the next day all crazy with excitement to see what radical magical delight had popped out of the . . . well, Tony Bock woke up in his over-the-garage flat in The Glades late on Saturday morning in that kind of state, anxious to see what his e-mail to the County CID about this Kevin David Dennison had wrought. It was a question about which Bock, in the cold light of dawn, was sorely conflicted.

He was partly on fire to see what had happened and partly sick with dread that in some totally unexpected way he had thoroughly buggered up his life with some obscure but legally cataclysmic blunder—abuse of the Internet? crossing phone lines in the commission of felony privacy invasion?—and was therefore about to reap the ugly reapings of his heedless night before.

No, he had to know NOW.

Bock couldn't even wait to brush his teeth or have some coffee or even get decently dressed. He sat down and fired up his computer, started a search string looking for any news of *Kevin David Dennison Saint Innocent Orthodox Niceville CID* and was, a few minutes later, oddly relieved when the string retrieved nothing at all.

So, as of this point, no action from the forces of justice. His heart rate began to return to normal. He leaned back and reached—out of habit—for one of the few cold Stellas that had survived his winnowing hand the night before.

He popped the cap with an opener shaped like a naked woman, leaned back in his chair, sipping from the bottle, and began considering the state of his world. Okay. Fine. Nothing yet.

He would have to be patient.

Remember the spider who waits?

The lion that lieth in the long grasses?

Fine.

A pause here for self-examination.

What exactly was he feeling?

Now that his fear was gone, or at least temporarily abated, Bock was feeling . . .

. . . *disappointed.*

He had, without reason, hoped that there might be something like an arrest notice—a suicide after a running gun battle with the cops was too much to hope for—or that at least there would be some kind of ripple on the surface of the Niceville community that suggested an investigation was under way. And, he suddenly realized, there might well be.

After all, the cops weren't going to *alert the media* on the basis of an anonymous e-mail tip, no matter how well composed and electrifying.

No, of course; they were quietly looking into the thing first, which was only right and proper.

Bock reminded himself, again, that in this new enterprise, he would have to be patient . . .

. . . and judicious . . .

. . . and . . .

. . . well . . . fuck that.

Let's face it—he was still pretty disappointed.

He called up the e-mail he had sent to Lieutenant Commander Tyree Sutter, CO of the Cullen and Belfair County Criminal Investigation Division, and stared at it for a time.

The custodian at saint innocent orthodox has a history of child sex abuse going back to 1982. His name is kevin david his crimes were committed under the name kevin david dennison his dob is 1956/06/23. look first in maryland. He also is online on AIM as katydee999. You should look at him. a friend.

He leaned into the keyboard, thought about it for a moment, and then forwarded this same e-mail—through a server somewhere east of Eden—to the city editor at the *Niceville Register*, the station manager at WEZE EZ JAZZn'ROCK, based in Gracie, to the manager at the Cap City Fox News affiliate, and to rector.parish@stinnocentorthodox.org.

This exercise provided a frisson that lasted not nearly long enough, since this sort of activity bears some parallels to crack addiction.

After a short time, he was edgy again, feeling that there was still useful work to be done here.

He tilted the bottle up, drained it to half, listening in a distracted way to the staccato yapping of Mrs. Kinnear's demented shi-tzu and staring at the screen. Something was surfacing. He could feel it working up, something inspired at first by the sight of his own nakedness and then becoming more specific as he recalled some of the insights he had gained into the people of Niceville in the course of his day job.

Not the *natural* course, since the job description didn't include snooping through boxes of tax records in the basement or poking around in old family albums up in the attic. Amazing the stuff that people hang on to, or forget they ever had, or think they'll get away with keeping.

For example, the cosmetic surgeon with a cardboard box full of counterfeit med school diplomas. The retired letter carrier who had seventeen bags of undelivered mail in her furnace room. The pharmacist with several cartons of stolen prescription drugs in her closet.

And there was a guy, a bank manager type, had this nice big rancher near Mauldar Field, a pillar of the community, who was taking peep shots of his teenage daughters in the bathroom.

Bock, in the course of his professional labors at the banker's house, had found the tiny camera in the ceiling of the shower stall, concealed in the fan housing. After some detective work, he had traced the fiber-optic cable to a still-frame recorder in the attic, hidden inside a trunk full of old clothes.

Bock had managed to copy the contents of the camera's hard drive, getting at least a thousand different shots of the girls over several years, doing all the things one normally does in a bathroom, the girls of course totally oblivious, which was the whole point.

Bock had savored the shots for a very long time—they gave him a godlike sense of *power* over these half-grown girls—seeing what no man had yet seen, watching them do all their secret female rituals.

But even that sick thrill wore off after a while, as they will, and Bock had posted the shots—anonymously—on this voyeur website, shredding his own copies as soon as the download was complete.

But what *was* the guy's *name*?

Can't mess with a guy's life without a name.

It'd be in his work records, on the Niceville Utility laptop, wouldn't it? One of his first out-calls, maybe five, six years back?

Very risky to tap that source, Bock thought, trying to calm himself down.

Remember the rules.

No linkages.

But if he only used *one*, then there'd be no linkage, right? You can't draw a line between one dot and no dot.

No.

Not a *banker.*

The guy wasn't a *banker.*

What do you call a guy who *comptrols* stuff?

A *comptroller,* right?

It was rising up in the back of his mind. The trunk in the attic was filled with old clothes, but they were *weird* old clothes, leathers and feathers and beady folky thingies . . .

. . . *flowers* . . .

. . . *boxes* . . .

. . . *tiny purses* . . .

It was all in there somewhere . . .

Think, Bock, think . . .

Visualize . . .

Wicker?

Straw?

Weavings?

And then it all came back in a rush.

Littlebasket.

Morgan Littlebasket.

He googled it, and there he was, a craggy-faced leathery old buzzard, smiling out like a Redskin Rushmore from the website banner of something called the Cherokee Nation Trust, based in Sallytown. Some more googling delivered up a news photo dated five months ago, the guy posing with two very foxy-looking young daughters at a graveside, with a caption underneath—

A tableau of mourning as Cherokee Clan Chief Morgan Little-basket stands with his daughters Twyla and Bluebell Littlebas-ket at the grave of his wife, Lucy Bluebell Littlebasket (*neé* Tallpony).

Bock could feel his blood rising as he looked at the two pretty young women in their mourning dresses, holding fresh-cut flowers, so solemn and sad and brave at the funeral of their sainted mother, and here was the All-Seeing Eye of Tony Bock looking down upon them and knowing pretty much all there was to know about what was under those tight black dresses.

But the *shots*.

The *proof*.

He had shredded his own.

They were gone forever.

And he had no reason to believe that the twisted old pervert would still have his spy camera hidden in that trunk, even if Bock could talk his way back into the house, which would be a damned stupid thing to do in the first place.

But Bock *needed* those shots.

Would they still be on that pervo voyeur website? Maybe in some sort of National Pervo Library of Sexual Congress?

Possibly.

He held his fingers over the keyboard, hesitating, like a boy selecting a chocolate from a gift box, his mouth open and his thick lips wet. The fact that he was, in effect, about to commit a kind of suicide was not clear to him at the time.

Beau Norlett Meets Brandy Gule

Nick took the unmarked navy blue Crown Vic. He let Beau Norlett drive because otherwise, with nothing to occupy him, Beau tended to chatter and Nick wanted to have some time to think about being turned down for a re-up by Dale himself, a personal no from a good friend and therefore deeply cutting.

Dale Sievewright and Nick Kavanaugh went back a long way, long before Yemen, all the way back to Benning and Fort Campbell. Dale's saying no to Nick's reenlistment when the whole Army was being bled white and even the motor pool pogues and the weekend wannabe warriors were pulling multiple redeployments—it just really shook him up.

He came out of his complicated thoughts vaguely aware that Beau was humming to himself, some sort of gospel number—he and May were Pentecostals—they were on Lower Powder Springs going crosstown towards the probation offices in Tin Town, and Niceville was ticking along in its own sweet way, the haphazard tangle of streets and avenues shaded with oaks and pines and beeches, Spanish moss hanging down, the streets and sidewalks packed with people and traffic, everybody coming and going in the steady gray rain, their figures blurred through the windshield glass, the Crown Vic's tires hissing on the road, fog drifting over it all.

"Beau, you have your blues, don't you?"

Beau looked over at him, back out to the road.

"Well, you know, sometimes I get a bit down, you know, I mean the job don't—"

"Dress blues, Beau. Dress blues."

Beau ducked his head, a smile lighting him up.

"Oh, man, Nick, I thought you was asking—"

"Tig wants us to go down to Cap City on Friday. Represent the unit. That's a full-dress thing."

Norlett looked worried.

"Ahh, look, the catch is, Nick, I kinda gained some weight since I bought them. Don't know if I could get—"

Here realization dawned upon him.

"You mean Tig wants us *both* to go. Me going with *you*? You and me? For the unit?"

"That's the plan. How much weight?"

"I . . . maybe fifteen, twenty pounds. Doubt I could button up the tunic."

"You've got four days. Get Gabriel to let it out for you. Wear a corset if you have to. Gabriel has them in the stockroom. Don't be ashamed. Dress blues are a bitch to wear well. A lot of guys use a corset to get trim. Do it if you have to. I want you looking strack. This means a lot to Tig."

Beau's face knotted up.

"Strack?"

"It's an Army term. Strictly According to Regulations. Strack."

Beau didn't get it. Nick sighed and left him with the problem. In a minute Beau had forgotten it, his expression opening up again, delighted, his happy face as shiny as a banister.

"I will, Nick—I mean, I'm honored to be asked—"

"Here it is," said Nick, cutting in.

They were rolling up to a low strip mall on the edge of Tin

Town, Niceville's version of a dangerous slum, a run-down neighborhood that had grown up along the muddy banks of the Tulip River a mile north of Tulip Bend, which was the beginning of the club and tourist districts.

Tin Town was everything Americans have come to expect in a dangerous slum, twenty-five maybe thirty square blocks of crumbling wooden bungalows, fenced-off lots, car wreckers, bars, mom-and-pop stores all barred up like forts, trailer parks walled in behind rusted chain-link fences, bricked-up speaks, and roach-infested crack houses.

The main industry ruling the place was a lethal combination of grinding hard times, blood-simple gunsels, pointless death, and blue ruin.

The strip mall had a busted-down 1950s-era sign at one end with letters spelling THE MIRACLE MILE peeling off like the mange.

The Miracle Mile, which was neither a miracle nor a mile, contained about fifteen ramshackle stores in a ragged rambling row, the eaves sagging and tiles missing from the roofs.

The local branch of Belfair and Cullen County Probation and Correctional Services—known in Tin Town as the Probe—had a white-painted steel grate covering the old glass window wall, a storefront operation sandwiched in between a dollar store and a porn shop.

The porn shop—the most prosperous business in the strip—had a blue neon sign in front that flashed out the name WIGGLES AND GIGGLES over and over again. Every time he saw that sign Nick wanted to put a bullet in it.

As Beau brought the car to a stop in the slot in front of the Probe, four dingo-dog-looking black kids in ragged hip-hop togs started to shuffle off to the far end of the strip, one kid looking back over his shoulder, feral eyes sharp under his sideways cap. Beau and Nick looked at them in silence.

"Which kid is holding?" Nick asked.

Beau gave it a minute.

"The one with the gym bag, because if we chase him he can throw it over a fence and then we have to prove possession."

"Very good. See the Goth chick in the Doc Martens? Down by the Helpy Selfy?"

Beau's eyes slid over to an anorexic white girl with black holes for eyes and spiky blue hair. She had on a pair of shredded purple stay-ups and a black leather jacket six sizes too large.

She was leaning against the wall outside the milk store, popping her gum and staring fixedly out into the street. She couldn't have looked any more guilty if she'd been whistling the theme from *Mayberry R.F.D.*

"You want me to do a field interview?"

"I do," said Nick.

He got out of the passenger side, leaned down and spoke to Beau through the open window.

"Just be careful. Watch her hands. Her street name's Iris but her real name is Brandy Gule. She may deal shit for Lemon Featherlight, we don't know yet, but her being here this morning when we're supposed to have a talk with Lemon tells us something. That's why I want you to have her in the car when I get back. I want a chance to talk to her. Hear me, Beau, look at me. She looks fifteen, but she's twenty-four, a runaway from a small town in the Carolinas.

"She looks like a kid."

His voice was soft, sympathetic. Nick leaned in to get a straight line on Beau's eyes.

"She's *not*, Beau. You gotta get that. She killed a jail guard with a nail file. Stuck it in his eye. And then she tore his jugular open. He bled to death on the floor of her cell. Camera shows her sitting there on the cot, chewing gum, watching while he thrashes around on the tiles."

Beau winced.

"What'd he do?"

"He tried to rape her. Had done it before."

Nick patted the top of the car, glanced back at the hip-hoppers sliding around the corner, did not look at Brandy Gule, and walked off, pushing through the smeared glass doors of the storefront office.

The interior was lit by a ceiling full of fluorescent bars. The thick air moved sluggishly around the room, stirred by a large fan with blades shaped like angel wings. The floor tiles, almost exactly the color of rubber dog vomit, were peeling up at the edges.

The waiting area had five cheap folding lawn chairs, mix and match, lined up against the wall, all of them empty this early on a Saturday, since most of the clients for the Probe were still lying on their backs in a tangle of crusty bedding, staring up at the ceiling and trying to figure out what the hell had made them do what they think they might have done the night before.

The girl behind the counter was new to Nick, a black-haired number with hard eyes and a sour twist to her lips. She glanced up briefly as Nick closed the door, frowned at him, put her head down, and went back to clacking away at her keyboard, staring fixedly at the screen. Nick let it slide, said good morning, got nothing back.

"Lacy in the back?"

"She's got a client," said the girl, with an edge, not looking up. Nick figured she didn't like cops. A lot of people didn't like cops. Some days even he didn't like cops. Nick held his temper, spoke in a reasonable tone.

"I'm with County CID. She asked to see me. Said it was urgent. Tell her Nick—"

The woman looked up.

"I'm aware that you're with the police, Detective Kavanaugh. Everyone who comes into this office knows what you are. You're very well known on the street. Ms. Steinert is very busy. When she's free, I'll tell her you're here."

Having, as she clearly felt, put the Pig back in his poke, she went back to her keyboard. Nick looked down at the top of her head, studying the part in her shining black hair. Her glossy black nails were too long for the keyboard and they had pink peace signs stuck onto them. *The footprint of the Great American Chicken*, thought Nick. Her tight black skirt was pulled halfway up her thighs. She had fine thighs.

"What's your name?" he asked, trying out his best smile on the top of her head. Something in his voice got through to her. She heard the edge in it.

She looked up, now a little wary.

"Gwen Schwinner."

Back to the typing, radiating dislike.

"Nice to meet you, Gwen," he said to the top of her head. "Call me Nick. How about you go get Lacy right now, Gwen? Pretty please."

Nick braced himself for a scathing look, but Gwen kept her head down, although she had stopped typing. Maybe she was working out what kind of scathing she was going to unleash on him. In the end, she sighed theatrically, got to her feet, and trudged wearily away from the counter—she had very nice hips as well as those truly fine thighs—and down the narrow plastered hallway to the closed door where Lacy Steinert was listening to a crack whore with lung cancer explain why it wasn't her fault that she was a crack whore with lung cancer. She glared back up the hall at Nick, who waggled his fingers and smiled at her, and then she rapped on the wall, got a "come in," and opened the door.

The crack whore, forty miles of bad road named LaReena Dawntay, was dabbing at her red-rimmed eyes and snotty nose with a crumpled wad of tissue. Her coffee-colored skin was coarse and pebbly and her legs looked like scabby twigs.

She glared up at Gwen and went back to sobbing. Gwen looked at Lacy, who looked back with an open friendly expression while handing a box of tissues across to LaReena.

"There's a Detective Kavanaugh here."

She said this in the same tone as you'd say "the toilets are backing up again."

Lacy Steinert was a compact middle-aged black woman with jade green Chinese eyes and sharp Cherokee cheekbones. She had started out as a state highway patrol officer, got shot in the hip by the eight-year-old daughter of a guy she was trying to Breathalyze. The round nicked her sciatic nerve and guaranteed her a future of severe and chronic pain.

She invalided out to a liaison desk at Cap City HQ, which bored her to tears, so she got herself transferred to Cullen and Belfair County Probation and Corrections and now here she was at the Probe in Tin Town coping with crack whores named LaReena and fourteen-year-old gang bangers with the life expectancy—if not the smarts—of a mayfly.

"Thanks, Gwen. Can you do me a favor?"

"Yes, Miss Steinert."

"Can you get a cab for Miss Dawntay here? She's got to go to Lady Grace for an infusion. Give her a voucher out of the box and tell the driver to be sure he walks her inside. You'll go inside, won't you, LaReena? You really can't miss these treatments. They can help you live a normal life."

As if.

But LaReena Dawntay nodded, staring down at her hands. Lacy considered her for a moment—*dead in six months*—and then looked back at Gwen.

"And then could you go next door to Wiggles and ask Mr. Featherlight to step across?"

Going to Wiggles for any reason other than to toss in a Molotov cocktail did not recommend itself to Gwen Schwinner, but she merely nodded and offered a hand to LaReena.

Lacy walked the two of them to the door and stood in the hall, watching as Gwen and LaReena went back up the hall, both women ignoring Nick Kavanaugh, who was leaning on the counter and grinning back at Lacy.

"Nick. Come on back."

He pushed himself off the counter and came down the hall—not a big man but somehow filling it from side to side, a hard-edged man with cool gray eyes and good lines around them. He was wearing a crisp black dress shirt, open at the collar to show a section of tanned neck, charcoal slacks, well cut, and a pair of slim black wing tips. He had his bright gold CID badge clipped to his belt and a large stainless-steel Colt Python in a holster on his right side. He looked . . . *fine* . . . she thought. She leaned up to get a cheek kiss from Nick and inhaled his scent, which reminded her of tropical beaches and drinks with umbrellas in them.

His hands on her shoulders were strong and warm and having him up close like this was probably going to be the best part of her day.

They broke and she led him into her office, a bare-bones affair with a poster of a sailboat gliding across a teal blue lagoon to a palm island with clouds floating above it.

"Thanks for coming, Nick."

"Always happy to see you, Lacy."

"Me too. I was surprised when Kate told me you had some time. I figured you'd be all over this Gracie shooting."

"No. Cap City Feds have it. We're not wanted at the dance."

"Boonie Hackendorff?"

"Boonie's a good cop, Lacy, under that dipshit beard."

"If you say so. Did you know any of the guys?"

He shook his head.

"Not if you mean like friends. Darcy Beaumont was tight with Kate's brother, Reed, and the Goodhew kid had helped us out once on a biker thing. But no, not like that. You?"

She shook her head.

"No, me neither."

There was nothing else to say and it was damned depressing to think about it, so they didn't.

"Anyway, where's our guy?"

"He's got a client next door at Wiggles. He'll be here in a minute."

"He's still *dealing*, even now?"

Lacy lifted her shoulders, said, in a fake Spanish accent, "I know nothing. I am from Barcelona."

"Manuel. *Fawlty Towers.*"

That got a big smile.

"I'm trying to find Lemon something better to do with his life."

"Such as?"

"If he can beat this ecstasy bust, I think he might be willing to go into one of our Better Chance programs. He taught himself how to fix helicopters when he was with Recon in Iraq. A good aircraft mechanic can pull down more than you and me together."

"You're putting a lot of faith and effort into a hustler, Lacy."

"Hope springs eternal."

"It sure does in you."

He liked her for that, among other things.

"So. You want to lay it out for me?"

She did. Lemon Featherlight's status as a street source for the Niceville Drug Squad guys had apparently meant dick to the Cap City DEA unit, who set him up on an ecstasy sting for reasons which, it seemed to Lacy Steinert, arose chiefly out of sheer boredom.

Nick, who secretly felt that the DEA was an agency with no reason to live, was thinking about a reply when there were steps in the hall and then a tall tanned figure, blade-slim but broad at the shoulders, filled the doorway.

Nick got up and turned to face him as Lemon Featherlight paused at the threshold.

Featherlight was wearing well-cut navy blue trousers, some kind of Italian slippers in dark green leather, a white shirt open a couple of buttons to show a well-muscled chest. He had a fine-boned face with eyes as sea green as Lacy's and the same Chinese eyes. It struck Nick that they could have been brother and sister.

Featherlight's black hair, parted in the middle and combed straight back, was long and as shiny as a raven's wing. He looked back at Nick with a direct but nonchallenging expression, and, after a moment, put out a tentative hand.

Nick took it, a firm dry hand, with a powerful grip, shook it once, looking back at Lemon Featherlight in that way he had, expressionless but searching, a cool light in his gray eyes.

"Detective Kavanaugh. Thanks for coming," said Featherlight in a baritone whisper, a trace of that flat twangy South Florida accent. Lacy, aware that Nick had other things to do, got right to it.

"I've filled Nick in on your situation. He's making no promises, but I think the best thing you can do is sit down and tell him what you know."

Featherlight took a wooden chair, pushed it back against the wall to give himself some distance from Lacy and Nick, paused a moment.

"Where should I start?"

Nick, leaning on the wall next to the door, his arms folded across his shirt, said, "You were involved with the Teagues. Tell me how."

Featherlight went quiet for a moment, seeming to gather himself, and then looked up at Nick.

"Thing is, she was a nice lady. People, they have their ways, Nick. This trio thing was theirs. The two of them. Mr. Teague, his thing was he liked to watch."

"This was at the house in Garrison Hills?"

"Yes. Always at the house. Only safe place."

"How'd they explain you to the neighbors?"

"They didn't," he said simply. "You know Garrison Hills, that big house of theirs. That wall of cedars and the drive goes way back from the street. Behind the house there's that ravine and then the forest and then the bluffs going up to Tallulah's Wall. It was a private place. They had no people, staff or gardeners. Miles always picked me up in the Benz—all that tinted glass—and he always drove me home. No cabs, ever. We'd talk, both ways, about life, or work, whatever came up, which sounds weird, but if he was okay with it, so was I. They paid cash, treated me well."

"How'd you meet Sylvia in the first place?"

"The Pavilion. Couple years back. She was with some friends. One of the ladies knew me, called me over. We all had something to drink. I liked her right away. I could see she was in pain."

"How?"

Featherlight flashed a tentative smile.

"In my line, you get to think like a doctor. Somebody comes to see you, they're hurting, you don't even have to ask for what. With Sylvia it was around her eyes. She left after a glass and her friend told me about the ovarian cancer, about her needing something for the pain."

"Something her doctor wouldn't give her?"

Featherlight shrugged.

"She wanted not to have to ask him all the time. She wanted her own. It was a control thing."

"So it was just sex and painkillers?" said Nick, with an edge.

"No. At first it was just the Demerol and the OxyContin. We met a few times, talked some. The other thing, she brought that up. I think her friend said I was available. Next week we had drinks with Miles—with her husband. We all got along. It moved on from there."

"Were you still involved with them when the boy was taken?"

"Yeah, but it stopped the day Rainey was taken. I never heard from them again. They were both dead within two weeks. That whole thing . . . the security tape at Uncle Moochie's . . . the barrow . . . you guys never worked it out, did you?"

"No. Maybe we should have looked at you. Tony Branko told me you were going to see Rainey in the hospital."

"Yes. I tried to go every couple of weeks. He was a good kid. Sometimes I got the idea he could even hear me talking to him."

"So what was it? Guilt? Maybe you had something to do with the disappearance and now you're feeling a little sleazy about it?"

Featherlight flared up at that, but kept it under control. He looked straight at Nick, a flat, challenging glare, and then shook his head once.

"No. That could *never* be me. I *liked* that kid. He was really into football. Before the Corps I was a walk-on for the Gators. We used to talk about how Saint Mary's was going to do this year. He wanted to play linebacker for Saint Mary's and then maybe go on to state. Nobody who knew him could hurt that kid. And if anybody had tried around me, I'd have killed them."

He spoke with heat and a tightness in his throat that was convincing.

"And I asked around, Nick, when it happened. I don't think anybody on the street had anything to do with it. I talked to a lot of people—about Uncle Moochie, if anybody on the street had ever heard anything—I got nothing but that he was a pretty good fence. I looked up that Alf Pennington guy from the Book Nook, figured maybe he had done something back in Vermont and that was why he was down here—"

"You didn't figure we had already done all that?"

"I wanted to find him myself, if I could . . . but nobody knew anything. Not even the short eyes and the bicycle seat sniffers. I sweated a few of them, but no, whatever it was, it came from . . . outside."

Nick thought *outside* was an interesting word to use in this connection. He had used it himself, when trying to work it all out.

Outside.

"Any thoughts on who did it?"

He looked up at Nick.

"Can I ask you something?"

"Sure."

"How long did it take you to get Rainey out of that grave?"

"About an hour. I was only in at the end."

"Why so long?"

"The grating was rusted shut and the barrow was mostly buried in the earth."

"And the bricks?"

"Hadn't been touched in over a hundred years. The mound was almost completely grassed over."

"I heard it took a couple of firemen to open it up, and they had to use sledges."

Nick could still hear the steely clank of iron on stone, and the faint shrieks from inside the tomb as each hammer blow slammed into the barrow.

"Yes. The tomb was sealed shut. No sign that it had been opened since they put the coffin inside it."

"But Rainey was trapped inside it, wasn't he?"

"Yeah. He was."

"You ever figure *that* out, Nick? How he got inside without the grave being touched? I mean, that's just . . . *wrong*, isn't it?"

Nick waited, saying nothing, thinking exactly the same thing. The whole thing had been *wrong* from the get-go.

But Nick didn't believe that there really was an *outside*. One day he'd get an explanation for all of it, someone would figure out the trick and then the trick would lead them to the trickster.

"Well, whatever . . . it scared the shit out of me," said

Featherlight. "There's something really strange about it. You think so too, don't you?"

"Why am I here, Lemon?"

Featherlight looked at his hands.

"I should have talked to you about this a year ago. But I didn't want you looking at me and thinking . . . maybe him. You understand?"

"Tell me why I'm here."

Featherlight went back inside for a time.

"You ever hear of a thing called Ancestry dot com? A website where you can research your family? You pay a fee; it has access to county records, census and military lists, Mormon files, parish hall stuff?"

"I've heard of it."

"Before Rainey disappeared, like maybe two days before, I was at the house, we were all just sitting around the pool and talking. Rainey was playing in the pool, Miles gets a call, he has to go back to the office. He asks me if I want to leave, I look at Sylvia, she says she'd like me to stay for supper. This is okay with Miles and he leaves. After Rainey goes to bed, she's a bit looped from the wine, she asks me how much I know about my people. My tribe."

"The Seminoles?" asked Lacy.

He glanced at her, a rueful smile.

"Everybody up here thinks I'm a Seminole. I'm not. My people were Mayaimi, not Seminole. They named Miami after us. Anyway, she started with that tribal stuff but went on into her own family. She had been using this Ancestry program to look up her family history."

"Why wasn't she just going to the archives?" asked Lacy, intrigued. "They'd have her family's whole story there."

"That was it," said Featherlight. "She didn't want anyone in town to know what she was doing."

"And what *was* she doing," asked Nick, "that she wouldn't want the town clerk to know about?"

"I never found out. But it was something that worried her, like she was afraid of what she might find. I got the idea that whatever it was, it went back. A hundred years. Maybe more. She was saying the records were okay until the end of the Civil War, when things fell apart in the South. And there was that fire in the town hall here, back in 1935, where the archives were destroyed. It was like she was on the trail of something, and it meant a lot to her, but she was also worried about it. Anyway, I put it down to the wine, but then it all happened and after that I never saw her again. And the thing is, where did they find Rainey? In a grave. Right after Sylvia jumps into Crater Sink. Like they were connected."

"*Connected*," said Lacy. "How?"

"Maybe it was a trade."

"A trade?"

"Maybe she went so that Rainey could come back."

"Jesus, Lemon," said Nick.

"Back from where?" asked Lacy.

"I don't know. Back from outside. Maybe Crater Sink leads to the outside, and Sylvia knew it."

"We don't know that she went into Crater Sink," said Nick.

"But wasn't her car there, at the end of the road? And her shoes?"

"Yes," said Nick in a flat tone. "Doesn't mean she jumped into it."

"Then where is she?"

"I don't know."

Featherlight, sensing Nick's mood, sat back, looked at Lacy and then back at Nick.

"So, well, that's what I wanted to say."

"That Sylvia was worried about something in her past, and she was using the Ancestry program to look into it without letting the town clerk know what she was doing? And that when Rainey was taken, she killed herself so whoever was holding Rainey could send him back from—"

"From outside."

"From outside. Like she had made a deal?"

Featherlight shrugged.

"A deal with who?" asked Nick.

"I don't know. But I think the answer is in there some-where."

"Where?"

"In the past. I think that's where you need to look, if you want to figure out what happened."

Nick was quiet, looking at Lemon.

"And that's it?"

"Yes," said Featherlight.

Nick was thinking about the Teague family, studying Lemon Featherlight's face. Lemon looked as if he had retreated into a smaller space, like it was where he always went to wait for bad news.

"Well, Nick?" said Lacy.

"Where'd she do this online checking?"

"From her office at the house."

"Her home computer?"

"Yes," said Lemon Featherlight. "She had a big Dell sys-tem."

Nick remembered it. He had driven Kate over to the Teague place last month, keeping her company on one of her usual walkabouts, Kate making sure the house was being kept up properly. The Dell was on Sylvia's desk in her office.

During the search for Rainey, they'd gone through it for clues, but he didn't remember anything about this Ancestry search engine. But there was . . . something . . . here.

He could feel it.

"I'm going to check this out, Lemon. If there's something in it, I'll call Cap City and see what I can do."

"He doesn't have a lot of time," said Lacy. "He has a bail hearing next—"

There was movement in the hallway, steps coming down it, rapid and sharp. Gwen Schwinner appeared in the doorway, glanced around, focused on Nick.

"Did you come here with a large black detective?"

"Yes."

"You'd better get out there. I think he's been stabbed."

Merle Zane
Gets an Offer He Can't Refuse

Somehow the woman must have gotten Merle into a bed because that's where he was when the heat of the sun shining in through the drapes woke him up. He was facedown on a lumpy feather pillow covered with coarse striped ticking, like they gave you at Angola. He had a brief surge of panic, thinking he was back there, but then he thought about the sunlight on his cheek and knew he sure as hell wasn't in Angola, because, like another famous location, Angola was where the sun did not shine.

He lifted his head off the pillow, which required him to flex the muscles in his lower back, which helped him to locate himself in space and time—on his face in a hard bed in a sun-filled room with a hole in his back from Charlie Danziger's Sig Sauer.

Merle tensed himself, and rolled over slowly, expecting a wave of pain but getting only a sharp tugging sensation in his lower back, as if he had barbed wire wrapped around him.

He looked down at his naked torso and saw a wide band of unbleached cloth, maybe linen or cotton, wrapped tightly around his midsection. He reached around and felt for the wound in his back. Under the cloth he could feel a row of

rough stitching. The move stretched his shoulder and the pain
drew his attention to a row of stitching there as well, in a crude
cross-hatched pattern that reminded him of the way a body
gets stitched up after an autopsy. The skin around the wound
was painted with some kind of deep reddish-orange stain—
iodine, he realized.

He swung his legs over and sat upright at the side of the
bed, taking in the room. He was in the woman's farmhouse,
and not a jail, he was pretty sure of that, and, from the shape of
the roof, in an attic room, small, and hot, but clean, with a
rough-planked wooden floor and hand-plastered walls and an
old beamed roof.

There was one tall window at the far end of the narrow
room, a wooden sash with thick rippled glass, framed by a pair
of gauzy curtains that fluttered in the breeze. The window was
open and a fat bumblebee was buzzing around in the space.
Through the window he could hear the singsong rise and fall
of cicadas in the trees, the plaintive *whoot-whoot* of a pair of
mourning doves, and, closer, above the muttering putter of
the ancient generator, the sound of a harness jingling, the
snuffle and stamp and whinny of a horse—from the depth and
force of the whinny, a very big damn horse.

He got up and crossed, unsteadily, to the window, looked
out across a sea of forest canopy painted in the pale deciduous
greens of early spring and pierced by the darker spear tips of
lodgepole pines, green forest rolling toward a horizon of
blue-brown hills far away to the south.

Nearer in he could see a large cleared section of tilled
earth, hemmed on three sides by the forest, a patchwork of
fields, some pale green with spring wheat, some darker green
with the first shoots of what he thought, from the white blos-
soms, might be potatoes, and at the far end the pale gold of
canola, all of this stretching out for almost a mile into the blue
distance.

At the far end he could see figures stooping over the dark

brown earth, hacking away at it with picks and shovels, A work party, from what he could make out without binoculars, digging drainage ditches or a foundation for a shed or something like that.

Beyond that distant plot there were more dark figures clustered around the heavier bulk of a tractor, dragging a skid loaded with what looked like a mound of small round river rocks.

Farm labor, he thought. *Better you than me.*

Looking up, he saw a sky that was clear and pure, without a cloud or even the scratch mark of a jet contrail, and the air smelled of hay, wheat, sweetgrass, budding flowers, turned earth.

He looked down at the yard below him and saw the woman standing by a powerfully built workhorse, a Belgian or a Clyde—cars were his main thing but he knew horses and crops from the huge work farms back at Angola. The horse had a shining hide the color of old rosewood, four very long and feathery white fetlocks, a white blaze, and a blond mane that flowed down the side of his muscled neck.

Merle figured this animal would have to weigh in at twenty-five hundred pounds. They had teams of them at Angola, none of them nearly as magnificent as this one, and yet each one was valued in excess of a hundred thousand dollars.

The impression of genteel poverty Merle had formed in the dark of the evening was being rapidly revised. The place was primitive, and he could see no modern farm machinery, other than the tractor and the generator, but he figured the overall worth of the farm at somewhere between two and three million.

The woman was soaping the horse down with a foamy sponge that she dipped in a wooden bucket on the ground beside her. She was wearing the same jeans as she had the night before, a man's jeans, too big for her narrow waist, and a faded plaid shirt, also much too big for her. She was barefoot and her tanned feet were coated in muddy water. Her hair, set free, fell in a shining black cascade down her shoulders and the muscles in her strong left arm flexed and relaxed as she scrubbed away at the horse's withers and barrel.

He watched her for a while, in a kind of trance, and was about to turn away and look for his clothes when she glanced up and saw him. She straightened, dropped the sponge into the soapy water, and used her hand to shade her eyes from the sun.

"You're up."

"I am," he said, with a smile. "That's a magnificent animal. He's a Clyde, isn't he?"

The woman turned to stroke the horse's neck, smiling with pleasure at the compliment.

"He is. His name is Jupiter. You know horses, Mr. Zane?"

"I've worked with Clydes," said Merle, leaving out the bit about doing it at a maximum-security prison called Angola.

"I approve of a man who understands horses. We thought we might have lost you. How do you feel?"

He thought, but didn't say, that he was glad not to be either dead or in jail. What he did say was, "You stitched me up. Thank you."

"You're welcome," she said, with a half smile, showing those fine but uneven teeth, her tanned face creasing and the lines around her eyes deepening. "I got that slug out of you too. Painted you up with iodine and sulfa powder. If you don't go septic I guess you'll live. I laid out some of my husband's clothes for you. Also his safety razor and some shave cream are in the bathroom. With the stitches so fresh I don't recommend you take a shower but you got a pretty good scrubbing last night. Your old clothes are soaking in a tub of lye out back. I doubt the blood will all come out, but we'll see. You hungry?"

Merle decided he was starving, and said so, and a few minutes later he was shaved and dressed in old-fashioned jeans and heavy farm boots, the soles worn down to the nails, a stiff white collarless shirt that smelled very strongly of mothballs, and he and the woman were sitting down in the austere kitchen, across the wooden table from each other, eating some sort of grainy porridge that she had spooned into bowls without a lot of ceremony.

She set a jug of molasses down and poured out two glasses of something cold and amber-colored. Apple cider, he realized. A pot of cowboy coffee was heating up on the stovetop. Clearly this woman liked things simple. There wasn't a Pop-Tart or a box of Cheerios anywhere in sight.

She sat straight and watched him eat the first couple of spoonfuls, her pale green eyes bright against the rough tan of her skin, her black hair hanging straight down on either side of her face. She wore no makeup at all and showed signs of a hard life lived mainly outdoors, but she was, in the warm light of the morning, very beautiful, in an unadorned and countrified sort of way. Her expression was thoughtful and remote, as if she hadn't quite decided what to do with him yet.

From somewhere deeper inside the main floor he heard the tinny sound of music playing, and then a man's voice, from the barking cadence some sort of radio ad.

If she has a radio, Merle thought, *she knows what happened in Gracie and she knows what I am.*

If she did, she wasn't talking about it. Maybe the cops were already on the way. Not much he could do about that. She seemed to feel no need to say anything at all right now, but Merle did.

"I want to thank you for what you did. My name is Merle Zane. I'm sorry, miss, I don't know your name yet?"

There was a pause while she seemed to come back to the here and now from some place quite far away.

"My name is Glynis. Glynis Ruelle," she said, in a low

voice with that Tidewater lilt in it, pronouncing the last name "Roo-elle," giving it a kind of New Orleans Creole twist. "I was born Glynis Mercer, but I've been a Ruelle now for twenty years. And where you are is Ruelle Plantation. We breed Clydes, got good cash crops of wheat and rapeseed and potatoes. Been in the Ruelle family since before the War Between the States."

"I saw people out in the fields."

Some indefinable emotion crossed her face. She lifted her head—she had a great profile—and looked off in the direction of the fields.

"Not many left. They die off or disappear. I'm always trying to find new help for the harvest. Albert Lee takes the Blue Bird down to town now and then, and men come back, migrants, mainly, but then maybe I'm too particular. All the help we have lives in the Annex, a barracks we built down by Little Cut Creek. The help seem to like it better that way."

"You said you run this place alone."

She gave him a sidelong look.

"These days I do. But I seem to be up to it."

Merle was conscious of sitting across from her in what she had described as her husband's clothes.

"Your husband . . . he's traveling?"

This brought a wry smile.

"John went into the wars and got himself killed."

"I'm sorry."

"So am I," she said, with a flash of heat. "But it was a damn foolish war in the first place. The president should never have taken it up. I didn't want John to go, but he was in the reserves so he went with the First Infantry. A married man with a farm, they shouldn't have called on him, but they did. I guess they had their reasons, and they did them no credit. But the thing was done. His younger brother, Ethan, went too. Ethan came back, at least some of him did, but now the running of this place is up to me. But I'm not angry with John. He felt he had to go with his unit. I blame that dimwitted grinning fool of a president for taking up a needless war."

Merle, not being a huge fan of that particular president either, didn't disagree with her. But since he was an accessory to the murder of four cops he didn't feel that a detailed discussion of service to country and how it had affected her family was a subject he should get into. Her next question drove it off his list entirely.

"Are you a man of violence, Mr. Zane?"

Merle was going to say no, since he had never thought of himself that way, but given the events of the past couple of days, and what it had been necessary to do to survive Angola, he felt he needed to think about that again. Mrs. Ruelle watched him do it, patient, contained, seeming to have no particular expectations.

"Yes," he said. "I didn't intend to go that way, but I guess that's where I am."

"You had a pistol with you. From what you told me, you stood your ground while another man was shooting at you. With one bullet in you already and a grazing wound on your shoulder."

"Things happened fast. I did what I had to. I can't say I shot well, since I emptied my gun and I think I only hit him once."

She frowned and made a dismissive gesture.

"Not the point. That happens to everyone, even in a disorderly mêlée such as yours. Even in a formal duel, attended by seconds, it happens. John Gwinnett Mercer, my grandfather, exchanged seven pistol balls with London Teague in an encounter having to do with the untimely passing of London's third wife, Anora Mercer. Anora was John's godchild, and held in high regard by all who knew her, so I am told. I do not like to re-tell private family matters, but it is true that the Teague family and our line, the Mercers and the Ruelles, have had a very long-standing enmity, going back many generations, all the way back to Ireland. The Teagues conspired with Major Sirr during the Irish rising in 1798. This has never been forgotten, although the Teagues have given many new offenses since then."

Here she broke off again, and studied Merle's face in silence for a time, as if trying to come to a decision about him.

"Well, about that fight, London and my grandfather came to their stand at Johnny Mullryne's plantation in Savannah, pistols being the weapons, since London, being challenged, had the selection. The New Irish Code requires that, once leveled, the pistols must be discharged within three seconds, aiming longer than that being considered unworthy of a gentleman. You must also remember that these old smoothbore pistols were not accurate weapons, which in a way explains the way the fight went."

She stopped here, took a sip of her cider, shaking her head, as if grimly amused. Merle, caught up in the story, sat motionless.

She went on.

"Seven rounds were exchanged this way, at twenty yards, a very drawn-out affair for a pistol duel, since after each exchange of fire the seconds are required to step in and urge the gentlemen to concede that honor has been served . . ."

She paused here, smiled at him, went on.

"But oh no. Not them. Not *those* two. So on and on it went."

She stopped again here, and went away somewhere, and Merle had the absurd feeling that she was remembering a fight she had seen herself. In a moment, she came back.

"Well, both men lived, although John was scored by a ball along his cheek that blinded his eye and he got another in his thigh and London received a ball in the left hip—his leg with-

ered all that winter and he never walked again. By the Irish
rules, honor had been fully satisfied with such serious wounds,
and the seconds should have ended the matter right there."

She sighed, ran a hand through her shiny black hair, and
sat back, giving him a long look over the rim of her cider glass,
a cool sea green appraisal.

"Well, I can go on, can't I? I do apologize. On the subject
of the Teague family, I am afraid I can be a bit of a bore. As I
said, there is a long and bitter history between our families, as
this old story shows. It came down through the decades, and it
lives on with us today, all these years later, while the modern
world spins all around us like a top, and we Ruelles stand
unmoving, a fixed point, stuck in the past. So. Enough of this.
My point is, Mr. Zane, you stood your ground."

Merle, stung by her compliment, feeling unworthy of it,
had a sudden urge to come clean with her.

"You have a radio on, Glynis. I can hear it. You *must* have
heard what happened in Gracie yesterday. You have a phone
too, I think."

"Yes. I have one. I don't like the telephone very much. The
bell is disconnected. If I want to call out, I do. I don't like the
idea that somebody can ring a bell in my home anytime they
like and expect me to come running and answer it. I do get the
news from the radio, but it's all about the wars and buildings
falling down and hurricanes in the Gulf and how the economy
is going bust again and what some celebrity whore is doing for
the holidays. You do have the air of a man on the run, Mr.
Zane. Did you kill someone for money?"

He was going to give her a complicated reply, but something about her made that seem a low and greasy thing to do,
so he just said, "Yes, I did."

"I see. Who'd you kill?"

"Police officers."

Her face hardened.

"Federal men?"

She smiled at him, and for a few seconds he felt a cold ripple come up from the floor, and then it was gone, and she was touching his hand with her warm, dry fingertips and looking at him in a direct unblinking way that felt like a silent interrogation and there was something sensual humming in the coffee-and-cider-scented air between them.

"Then I'll do what I can to help you. I won't call the federals and I don't want any of their blood money. But there is something, Merle, something that I would like you to do for me. I would try to do it myself, but there are some things I cannot do, and I find this is one of them. I would try again, perhaps to fail again. I hesitate to ask such a thing of you . . ."

"Just name it, Glynis. Whatever it is."

"Thank you. I need you to kill someone."

"No. State policemen."

"Over the money?"

"Yes."

"A bank?"

"Yes."

"The one in Sallytown?"

"No. The First Third in Gracie."

"I don't know that bank. Is it national?"

"Yes. I think so."

"So it's a federal matter. Where's the money now?"

"The man who shot me has it."

"Are the federals after you?"

"Yes. I think there's probably a reward, if you call them."

She seemed to be puzzled by the suggestion.

"Call who? The *federals*? The federals killed my husban with their stupid war. The federals can all go to hell. And have no sympathy for bankers. Are you going to try to get th money back from this man who shot you?"

Merle looked at his hands, and then leaned back into the chair, tensing as he put weight on his wound, and then easing himself into it.

"Yes," he said, deciding right then. "I am. But not right now. They have no way to spend it. The idea was to keep it hidden for a couple of years. I know who they are. I have time."

"Good. I like a man with patience. In the meantime, you need a safe place. There is a lot of work to do here. If I help you, will you help me?"

He studied her delicate but uncompromising features, the lines around her eyes, the forceful set of what was quite a lovely mouth. She stared back at him, her gaze level and unwavering, waiting with a stillness he admired,

She had what his mother used to call Chinese Silence.

"Yes," he said. "I will."

This seemed to seal some kind of pact.

Saturday Afternoon

Danziger Consults with the Feds

Boonie Hackendorff and Charlie Danziger belonged to the same National Guard unit and so the first few minutes in Hackendorff's FBI offices on the sixty-second floor of the Bucky Cullen Federal Complex in downtown Cap City were spent in going over the chances of either of them being called up to go fight the Ayatollahs of Iran anytime soon.

The final verdict came down somewhere between slim and damn slim. In celebration, Hackendorff poured Danziger a couple of fingers of Jim Beam and leaned back in his old leather chair, propping his size twelve boots on his desk.

The shining spires and glass towers and castellated condos of downtown Cap City spread out behind him beyond a wall of tinted windows, all the city lights turned on against the gloom and mist of a dark and rainy afternoon. The Feebs did themselves proud in Cap City, with a big suite of corner offices in the best complex in town.

Danziger stared out at the city lights for a second, thinking about what he was going to say, and then he considered Boonie, who was grinning back at him through one of those damned ugly sharp-trimmed full-face beards that big round guys like Boonie Hackendorff delude themselves into thinking give their faces an actual jawline.

They were wrong, but that didn't mean Boonie Hackendorff was any kind of a fool. He watched with a thinned-out smile and suddenly narrowed eyes as Danziger eased himself into a more amiable position on the stuffed couch across the room, lifted the glass in answer to Boonie's salute, and they each pulled a good bit of it down. Glancing at his boots, Danziger saw the spatters of his own blood on the blue leather and hoped that Boonie was far enough away to miss that detail.

"What's that on your boots, Charlie?"

Danziger shook his head sadly, looking down at the boots again.

"Blood," he said. "My blood. I stabbed myself cutting chum."

"Stabbed yourself? Where?"

Charlie tapped his chest, right on top of the bullet wound.

"I was using a filleting knife. Slipped and stuck myself right here in the tit. Bled like a bitch. Still hurts like stink."

Boonie started to snicker, and ended up laughing so hard he had tears in his eyes. He was enjoying himself so much that even Charlie started to smile, if only because when Boonie laughed it was oddly contagious.

"You dumb-ass old bastard. I never heard of such a thing."

"Fuck that noise," said Danziger. "You hooked your own self in the ass two years ago, when you and me and Marty were fly-fishing up on the Snake."

"My ass is a hell of a lot bigger than your tit, Charlie. It was hard to avoid. You always wear cowboy boots while you're fishing?"

"Boonie, I wear cowboy boots while I'm fucking. I plan to die in cowboy boots. While fucking."

Boonie nodded, looked at his own boots.

"I would too, if I could get anybody to fuck me. You're moving funny too. That because you stabbed your own tit?"

"Damn right," said Danziger. "Chest muscle hurt so much I could only use my left arm, so I was rowing around in fucking circles, fucking rowed that damn pirogue against the wind for two hours."

"Doesn't the thing have a motor?"

"Plugs fouled. I nearly jerked my left arm off trying to pull-start it, had to give it up, and then I one-arm-rowed that slug bucket five miles to the fucking dock. I'm thinking of giving up fishing entirely. Too fucking dangerous."

"Catch anything?"

"Crabs."

"You already got those."

"Old joke, Boonie."

"Yes, it is. I find they're the best."

"How you doing with this Gracie thing?"

Boonie patted his shirt for the cigarettes he didn't smoke anymore, winced the way he always winced when he remembered that he didn't smoke them anymore.

"I was hoping you could help us out there, Charlie."

Danziger smiled back at him through his big white handlebar mustache, showing tobacco-yellow teeth.

"I know what you're thinking. You're thinking it was an inside job."

"Hard not to," said Boonie.

"No, it ain't. I think so too."

He leaned back, groaned a bit from the pain, and pulled out a USB flash drive from an inside pocket of the suede jacket he had borrowed from Donny Falcone, handed it across to Boonie.

"I downloaded this from our Personnel office. It's a complete list of every employee we got who was in a position to have any knowledge of what was on that route truck, or who was going to be driving. Basically, everybody who could have ratted us out."

Boonie twirled the drive in his fat pink hands.

"Thanks, Charlie. We usually have to subpoena this kinda shit."

Danziger made a hard face, sighing heavily.

"Not from me, Boonie. Four cops dead. Fuck due process. If any of my guys had anything to do with this, I'll bring the shotgun and you bring the shovel and we can bury what's left."

"Your name on this list?"

"Hell yes. I'm a suspect too. I get that. You gotta look at everybody, Boonie, be a fool not to."

"You not nervous?"

Danziger tried to shrug, decided against it, lifted his big hands instead.

"You're a good cop, Boonie, in spite of being a lousy fly-caster. I figure I can trust you to catch the right guys. You always do, I 'collect. Is there anything else I can do to help this thing along?"

Boonie thought about it.

"You ever hear of a guy named Lyle Crowder?"

"Yeah. He was the driver of that rollover on the interstate. Dumb fuck. I hope he's hurting."

Boonie was quiet for a while.

Danziger let him be quiet. His chest was throbbing and he needed to take an OxyContin. And sleep for a week. Boonie looked up again, sighed.

"We got him under a suicide watch, actually."

Danziger blinked at that.

"Suicide watch?"

"Yeah. He feels pretty bad about it. Those dead ladies. He's, I mean, like . . . *despondent*? Is that the word?"

"Sounds about right."

"He's also heard, dumb guards told him, the dinks, that the families of the ladies in that van, they're all talking ugly stuff, what they're going to do to him, he ever gets out."

"Remorse is a terrible burden. Or so I'm told. Never tried it myself. Are you going to charge him?"

"Don't know yet. Witnesses all saw something different. We're looking at the truck to see if anything mechanical went wrong. Crowder says a blue Toyota cut him off on the down-grade, says he overcorrected, the flatbed started to come around, he turned into that, caught the shoulder—and it all went to shit. He's banged up pretty bad, ribs and hips, but he'll pull through."

"When'd the trailer go over?"

Boonie didn't have to look this up.

"Fourteen forty-one hours, roughly."

"And they hit the bank when?"

"Forty-two minutes later."

"While every law enforcement officer in three states was farting around the wreckage playing grab-ass and talking on their radios. Yes?"

Boonie had to smile at that.

"I'm not admitting to any personal grab-ass."

"I'm speaking metaphorically, Boonie."

"Well, if you think we haven't looked at Lyle Crowder, you'd be wrong. We're looking at him right now. And all we're seeing is an amiable young guy with no family who worked real hard for Steiger for six years and before that did a lot of freelance trucking with his own Kenworth until the recession came and the bank took his rig away."

"Yeah? What bank was that?"

"Not the First Third, Charlie."

"So credit-wise, he's a fuckup?"

"Hey, this economy, so's Jesus Christ. Why are you pick-ing on this poor damn driver, Charlie?"

Danziger's expression got more stony.

"Because no matter how this comes out, Fargo's going to look like shit. My division especially. Even if we all show up as clean as a rubber ducky's dingle. Fargo's still going to take the hit with the general trade. And so will I. Remember, I washed out of State—"

Boonie sat up, waved a finger in the air.

"No. You got injured in the line of duty, Charlie, and got all tangled up with hillbilly heroin on account of the pain. Nobody blamed you for that."

"I don't see a badge on my fucking chest," Danziger said, flushing red.

Boonie sympathized with him for a while, and Danziger's mood cooled down. Everybody knew that Charlie Danziger had been screwed by the Internal Affairs guys. Boonie lived in fear of it happening to him. So did everybody in law enforcement. Criminals occasionally showed mercy. IAD did not. If they set out to rat-fuck you, you could consider yourself rat-fucked.

"Sorry I blew up a bit," said Danziger, after Boonie had topped up their glasses. His anger had been very real but he never liked to let it show, especially since the Gracie bank robbery had been his way of getting back at IAD and all the rest of those Rear Echelon Motherfuckers at HQ.

"No harm done," said Boonie, looking carefully at Charlie over the lip of his glass. "When are you back at work?"

"Monday morning," said Danziger, looking past Boonie's shoulders at the glittering sweep of towers and pillars that made up Cap City, thinking maybe when all this blew over he'd come down here and buy himself a real nice condo with a high-up view of the Tulip and the Cap City skyline.

"While you're here, can you think of anybody can put you in Metairie yesterday?"

Danziger gave it some thought, or at least he looked like he was giving it some thought.

"Not right off. I moor the pirogue at Canticle Key. People were coming and going. You could ask Cyril—wait a minute. Wait a minute."

Boonie looked happy to wait until Judgment Day.

"I bought gas. Couple of times on my way back up. I likely

got the receipts in my car. That'll have the time date, the location on it. I mean, doesn't put *me* in the car, but it's something."

Danziger wouldn't have been offering gas receipts at all if he hadn't made a point of buying gas on his way home from Metairie the week before and then changing the dates with a scanner and Photoshop and printing them out again. He'd bought the gas from two little mom-and-pop stations three hundred miles apart, knowing that the receipts were printed on scrap paper and that neither mom nor pop kept any kind of accurate records. Risky, but offering them didn't mean that Boonie would remember to actually collect them. What Boonie would remember was the offer, which was all Danziger really wanted.

"Got any credit card receipts?"

"Don't use credit cards anymore, Boonie. I mean, I got 'em, but I don't like 'em."

Boonie leaned over, scribbled something on a sheet, hesitated, looked up with a frown.

"Can-tik—what? How you spell that?"

Danziger spelled out *Canticle Key* and then gave him the phone number of the gas tender, Cyril Fond Du Lac, an amiable old Cajun who would quite probably back up Danziger's story because his days and nights were all a blur of marijuana and whiskey anyway. Nothing Cyril could say would hurt Danziger, and might even help. In the meantime, what with drawing attention to Crowder and offering up the flash drive and the gas receipts and generally being up-front and cooperative, Danziger felt he was looking as innocent as a man could look.

"Well, thanks for coming in," said Boonie, lifting the flash drive. "Okay if I call you, I see anything on this that looks interesting?"

"Yeah. I'll be on my cell, anytime you need me, don't care

when, day or night. I want these assholes as much as you do. You sure you don't wanna go sweat that Crowder puke a bit, just to see what comes out?"

"You're not the only guy thinks we should look harder at him. I got a call from Tig Sutter—"

"That old warthog. How's he doin'?"

"Sounded busy. They got a whack of shit happening in Niceville. Some wealthy old broad gone missing, they caught that rapist who did those two girls on Patton's Hard, and Nick Kavanaugh thinks he might have a lead in the Rainey Teague case."

"Good for him. It don't surprise me. You were on that Teague thing too, weren't you?"

Boonie's shining face dimmed.

"I was."

"Ever make any sense of it?"

"You don't want to know what I think about that case, Charlie."

"Sure I do."

Boonie looked up at the president's picture as if he could see an answer there.

"It's complicated. You *sure* you want to know?"

"I got nothing better to do. You got any more bourbon?"

Boonie poured them each a hefty splash, brought Danziger his, and sat back down.

"Okay. Here goes. Brace yourself for some stats I been putting together—"

"*You* been putting together?"

"I'm not as dumb as I look, Charlie."

"I never thought you were, Boonie."

Boonie ignored that.

When he spoke, it was in the voice of a completely different Boonie, Boonie the solid FBI investigator under the good-old-boy facade.

"Okay. This is the backgrounder. Your average town the

size of Niceville, population between twenty and thirty thousand people, once you set aside the custody dispute kidnaps and the occasional incident like a teen having a fight with her dad over a curfew and taking Greyhound Therapy and being found six weeks later at her ex-boyfriend's house in Duluth—"

"Lyla Boone."

"Lyla Boone, exactly. So the average American town has maybe one or two suspected stranger abductions every five years, most of which turn out, after some digging, to have some connection between the victim and the perp. Like, say, a gang banger who gets kidnapped and murdered by a member of a rival gang, a guy he doesn't know, then his case would get tagged by us as a case of stranger abduction, but then, once the facts get worked out, the file would later get amended—"

"But it *never* does get amended, does it?"

"Nope. Least hardly ever. Human error. Not enough resources. So it goes into the stats as a stranger abduction. Along with thousands more just like that across the country. So all the civilians and all the media dinks are thinking, fuck, our children aren't safe, the streets are fulla pervos slavering after every little Binky and Boopsie. But the fact is, Charlie, real honest-to-God stranger abductions are extremely rare. A one in a million shot. So how many stranger abductions you figure Niceville has?"

"I don't know. I did wonder about it. When I was on the job, I figured we had a lot more than made any kind of sense."

"Damn right. Niceville has logged one hundred and seventy-nine confirmed and completely random SAs since records first started being kept back in 1928. This is a disappearance rate of, like, a little over two a year, Charlie, which is completely whacked. It's so far above the national average that Niceville gets cited every year at the FBI training courses at Quantico—"

"Not enough to get you guys to actually do something about it."

This seemed to sting.

"That's not true. We *are* doing something. Right now we're—"

"Anybody ever look into this, like a criminologist or somebody?"

"Yeah. Nick's wife, Kate—her dad is Dillon Walker, Reed Walker's dad too, he's a professor of military history at VMI. He got into this thing a few years back, but he gave it up when his wife got killed."

"I remember that. Six years ago. I was duty sergeant and took the call. Had to cut what was left of her out of the wreckage. She died in my arms, raving about something she saw in her rearview mirror . . . had her blood all over me . . . man, I'll *never* forget that night."

"Never caught the guy either, did you? Guy in the SUV, supposed to have run her off the road?"

"I never believed there was one, Boonie. I think the poor lady was off her meds. She was doing a hundred and forty when she rolled it, according to the OnStar GPS thing, how fast she was going, how fast she was covering the ground. A hundred and forty, easy. Over she goes. OnStar sends the rollover signal and I'm the second car on the scene. Last thing she ever said to me was *she uses the mirrors.*"

"*She uses the mirrors?* What the fuck does that mean?"

"No idea. She just kept saying it. *She uses the mirrors.* But try telling Reed Walker that. He was convinced it was some drunk driver, because one of the witnesses said he thought he saw somebody in a gray Lexus cut her off. He's out every day in his pursuit car, still looking, stopping every gray Lexus SUV he can find."

"Reed's a fucking fruitcake. If he reaches fifty I'll paint my toes with gentian violet and take up the zither. Anyway, that sort of took the heart out of the professor, and he gave it all up. Other than that, some pencil-neck statistician at MIT did a paper called . . . wait a minute, I got it memorized . . . 'Non-

Randomized Scatter Patterns and the Law of Statistical Regression as It Relates to Anomalous Abduction Phenomenology.' "

"Fuck me."

"Roger that. Anyway, in the paper he mentions what he calls the Niceville Disappearances—you know, like the Bermuda Triangle—all in caps, right? Get this—he calls them—wait a minute—you'll fucking love this, Charlie—an artifact of a Boolean scatter-back loop that created an apparent uptick in disappearance stats that was . . . shit, wait a minute, I got it here somewhere."

Boonie scrabbled around in his desk while Charlie, still a cop under it all, waited him out with genuine interest. He had spent a lot of his professional life wondering what the hell was wrong with Niceville for exactly this reason. Boonie found the paper, slipped on his reading glasses, leaned back in his chair.

"Okay. Brace yourself. He called it a Boolean scatter-back loop that created an apparent uptick in disappearance stats that was really just a semantic glitch in the reporting protocols."

"Fuck me sideways."

"Roger that too. Wait a minute. Yeah, here we go—he compared the Niceville Disappearances to reports of Alien Abduction—"

"Dumb shit."

"Not so dumb. Got him on *Good Morning America*, but the book deal fell through, so I hear, so that was that for the pencil-neck."

"So how many again, over the years?"

"One hundred and seventy-nine confirmed and completely random SAs. Only seventeen of these incidents have been solved: three sex-related abductions, where the bodies were found, the perp caught and executed—"

"Claude James Picton."

"Yep. Him. Five more were wives or girlfriends or daughters getting away from bad men, and the rest were random, bankrupts trying for a new life or insurance frauds or prostitutes giving up and going back home. Of the remaining one hundred and sixty-two people—men, women, sometimes kids—not a single trace has ever been found."

"Shit. That many?"

"That many."

"Anything ever link them all up?"

Boonie looked very pleased with himself.

"That's what I was trying to tell you. That's what we're doing right now. We're going over the entire list, we got all these computers, we got people downstairs entering all the stats of every one of these cases, all one hundred and sixty-two, and when they're done, we're going to cross-check them all and dig out anything that links them all together. Sound good?"

"Sounds more like a rat-fuck from the get-go, Boonie. These abductions go back how far?"

"Far back as 1928, anyway. Probably longer."

"So it's not going to be the same guy doing this, is it?"

"No. Maybe. Might be. Could be. Or maybe his sons."

"Boonie, all respect, you're totally whacked."

"Yeah? Nick Kavanaugh doesn't think so."

"What's Nick got to do with it? He's not in Missing Persons."

Boonie looked offended.

"It was his idea."

"Nick's? Was it? Got it from Kate's dad, maybe? Well, I wish him well, then. Nick's a good man."

Boonie brooded over the thing for a while, and then let it go.

"Yeah. Nick's a good cop too, for somebody from away. Nick's the one told Tig to call us about Crowder. We also heard from Phil Holliman—"

"Byron Deitz's muscle guy?"

"Yeah. He says Deitz really wants to help, any way he can. Phil says Deitz thinks the driver's dirty."

"So's Byron Deitz," said Danziger, who didn't like Deitz at all. "What the fuck business is it of his?"

"BD Securicom does all the intel and security work for Quantum Park. The bank at Gracie holds the payroll for most of Quantum Park. You know that."

"Yeah. Half their cash draw was on our truck. But Byron Deitz has no need to be sticking his ugly face in. You tell Holliman you're already looking at the driver?"

"Yeah."

"Holliman back off?"

Boonie had to think about that.

"Well, he said so."

"You believe him?"

"No, I don't, now you come to ask. I don't trust Phil Holliman. Or Byron Deitz. Deitz is taking this bank thing real personal. No doubt he'd like to get some knuckle-time with Lyle Crowder, just to make sure."

"Did you tell Holliman where Crowder was?"

Boonie actually went pink.

"Yeah, I let it slip, as a matter of fact."

"Where is Crowder now?"

"We got him in a sealed ward at Sorrows," said Boonie, letting it slip again. "Got two guys with him."

"Good guys?"

"Arnie Sparks and Tom Tibbet."

"They're both pretty new, Boonie."

"Yeah. But they're who I had to spare. Everybody else is out knocking on snitches and shaking out the whorehouses. Marty Coors has all his guys on it too. Hell, be a good time to rob another bank, all these guys out looking for cop killers."

"Don't say that out loud, Boonie, you don't know who might be listening. One thing, I were you, I'd move this Crowder guy."

Boonie was quiet for a full minute.

"You really think so, Charlie?"

"I do. I really think—"

Something in his jacket buzzed and then beeped. He looked at the call display, made a *sorry-gotta-take-it* gesture at Boonie, who grinned and waved him on. Danziger picked up the phone, flicked it open. "Danziger," he said into the cell.

"Charlie, it's Coker. I been going through the *proceeds*," he said. Danziger made it a point not to glance up at Boonie.

"Is that right?"

"You remember a flat box, two inches thick, stainless steel, maybe ten by eight?"

"Yeah, I believe I do."

"You figured jewels or some shit, right?"

"Yeah. Say. Hold on a minute, will you?"

He lifted the phone, smiled a big happy smile.

"It's Coker, Boonie. Hey, Coker, I'm down here at Boonie's place."

"Yo, Coker," Boonie called out. "You miserable old fuck. How they hanging?"

Danziger gave Boonie a nice good-old-boy smile so cheerful and friendly it hurt his cheeks and then got back on the phone.

"Boonie wants to know how they hanging?"

A pause.

"Shit. You're *still at Boonie's*?"

"You bet. We're having some JB and shooting the breeze."

"Fuck. Well, you can tell Boonie they're not hanging at all. You can tell him they've fully retracted and they took my dick up with them."

"Yeah. No shit. That's interesting."

"No shit. I opened the steel box, Charlie. Now I'm looking at this weird techno-gizmo thing lying here, round and flat, some sort of cyber-robot-Frisbee, and it has a Raytheon GNS logo on it. You figure Raytheon is making robot Frisbees, Charlie, or is this some sorta ultra-top-secret spy shit you stole that is going to jam us deep in the Dumpster of fucking doom with the CIA?"

"That's something to think about, for sure."

"That's not all. I'm staring at this robot-spy-Frisbee and then my cell phone rings."

"Well, there it is. Look, nice talking—"

"It's *Merle Zane* calling. His number anyway, on account of he got cut off. You coming back to help out or you going to play hide-the-floppy with Boonie Hackendorff all day?"

"Well, you give her a big wet kiss from me, okay? Talk at you later."

He snapped the phone shut, got to his feet.

"Gotta run?" said Boonie, draining his Jim Beam and setting the glass down with a satisfied smile. Danziger stood up, finished his off, came over and placed it gently down on Boonie's desk, shook Boonie's hand. Boonie shook back hard enough to jerk Danziger's chest wound and send a bolt of pain up his throat, but Danziger had other things to think about right now.

"Yeah. Gotta run," he said, but he managed to keep it down to a walk until he got to the curb.

Nick and Beau Find Time to Reflect

It was past midday—it was turning into a long Saturday shift—by the time they got Brandy Gule and Lemon Featherlight sorted out and Beau Norlett's butt attended to. He hadn't been stabbed, he explained in a stage whisper, for Nick's ears alone—he'd been bitten on the back of his, as he put it, "upper thigh region" while he was carrying Gule, upside down and squalling like a bearcat, to the car—"uncooperative ain't in it," said a chastened Beau a while later.

But when the good-looking typist chick from Lacy's office had come out to see what the screaming was all about, Beau hadn't found it in him to tell her he'd been bitten on the ass by the skinny Goth chick now kicking the living daylights out of the backseat of their cruiser.

So instead he'd mumbled something vague about being "sorta stabbed like," at which point she'd turned sharply on her spikes and stalked back inside to relay the happy news to Detective Kavanaugh.

After the initial flurry of talk and countertalk, Beau Norlett availed himself of the facilities in the back of The Probe offices to examine, privately, with the help of the bathroom mirror and a stepladder, the damage done to his "upper thigh region," which turned out to be a superficial but nasty semi-circular wound on his right cheek, now in the process of turning purple.

But no blood had been drawn, and Beau was in no way anxious to lay any sort of a charge on the girl, for reasons blindingly obvious to all, so Nick let that part slide, trying to keep the grin off his face.

This being decided, Lemon Featherlight managed to talk Nick into letting him take Brandy Gule back to her walk-up flat over the needle exchange on Bauxite Row, giving Nick his personal word that she'd be available to him anytime he wanted, and that she was really just sort of a harmless stalker chick with a major thing for him and that he was just trying to keep her safe in a kind of older-wiser-brother-feral-wing-nut-Goth-biker-chick arrangement.

Nick wished him the best of luck with that, and they parted, if not as friends, then as men with a slightly better understanding of each other, and as Nick and Beau rolled the cruiser away from the Miracle Mile, each man had a lot to think about.

Beau rode shotgun, listing severely to his left in order to keep his right butt cheek elevated, and listened with a glum expression to the lecture Nick felt compelled to give him about safe methods for arresting feral biker chicks with excellent teeth and the will to apply them where they could do the most harm, and what might have happened if he'd slung the girl over his shoulder the *other* way around, her feet hanging down his back, thereby presenting her fangs with a much more sensitive target area than his oversized butt cheeks.

When Nick was finished, as they were wheeling up Long Reach Boulevard on the eastern side of the Tulip, with the rain slacking off and the skies breaking up and the forested hills of The Chase rising on their right, Tallulah's Wall looming over all of it, Beau, looking as pale as he could manage, said, "Nick, sir, is there any way we could just sorta . . . kinda . . ."

Nick knew where this was going.

"I'm sure as shit not telling anyone back at the office that my partner got his entire assal region bitten off by a girl no bigger than a salt shaker, if that's what's worrying you."

Beau worked this through, emerging at last with the shiny new idea that Nick, in spite of recent shameful events, had just referred to him as "my partner." This put a glow on him that you could read by in the dark.

"Thank you, Nick. It won't happen again."

"If it does, I'm getting it on film and it's going on You-Tube. We're about five minutes from Delia Cotton's place. You spoke to Missing Persons while I was on the phone to Lacy. What'd you get from them?"

Beau lost his smile, changing into a concentrated professional frown as he pulled out a fat and brand-new black notepad with the logo of the CID embossed on the front, a bright golden disk.

He flipped it open, wincing as a sharp left turn through the stone gates of The Chase shifted his weight onto his right butt cheek, then began to read aloud from his notes.

"Cotton, Delia, DOB 1920—"

"Beau."

"Yes sir."

"Just summarize, okay?"

"Summarize?"

"Yeah."

Beau, disappointed—in a *CSI* frame of mind, he had written it all out in longhand complete with footnotes—reluctantly put his new notebook back into his suit pocket, took a deep breath.

"Well, mainly she's all that's left of the money side of the Cotton family, one of the Founding Four families, eighty-four years old, lives alone at Temple Hill, that's the name of her house at six eight two Upper Chase Run. Still has a driver's license, has a 1975 Cadillac Fleetwood, navy blue, in the shop for a busted axle. Missing Persons says her shopping lady, named Alice Bayer, sixty-three, she lives in The Glades, drove by the house early this morning with a load of groceries, there was a pink and lime green '52 Packard in the drive which she recognized as belonging to an old man who does fix-up and gardening for Miss Cotton, name of Gray Haggard—that's another one of those Founding Four, isn't it?"

"The Haggards, the Cottons, the Teagues—"

"And your missus, right, Nick? Missus Kate?"

"Kate's part Walker, yes."

"Anyway, Alice Bayer sees the house is all lit up, windows and doors all open, music playing so loud it was rattling the glass—"

"*Summarize*, Beau."

"Goes through the house, shuts off the music, sees nothing unusual other than there's nobody home, far as she can see nothing taken, but she says she all of a sudden got . . . the jim-jams."

"That means the place gave her a fright."

"Jimjams? Never heard of them. Anyway, she calls the security people for The Chase—"

"Armed Response. Owned by Byron Deitz."

"Yep. Armed Response arrives, they do a walk-through, Miss Delia's gone, no sign of this Gray Haggard guy, no sign of violence. By this time Alice Bayer is having a fit, so one of the security guys takes her back home—she lives on Virtue Place in The Glades and she'll be happy to talk to us if we want. Armed Response has a call-in-case list and they get on the horn to all those people—she has a book club and all these ladies are it—nobody knows nothing, so Armed Response calls NPD and NPD calls Missing and Missing tells Tig and Tig tags us—how's that for summarizing?—and here we are."

Which they were, as they rounded a long tree-shaded curve of cobblestone road lined in black wrought iron covered in vines and Temple Hill, Delia Cotton's mammoth Victorian pile, emerged massively from behind a wall of willows and live oaks draped in Spanish moss.

A red and black Armed Response Jeep and a slate gray NPD patrol car were parked on either side of the open gate, two uniforms leaning side by side on the hood of the patrol car, a solid bald-headed young black man in the complicated red and white regalia of Armed Response and an older white woman with red cheeks and rich red hair and shiny gold sergeant stripes on her dark blue NPD tunic.

They both watched as Nick and Beau rolled up in their navy blue Crown Vic. Across the street a small crowd of Chase residents had gathered, mostly elderly people, but a few young couples. They all had that avid, slightly glazed look civilians get when the cops show up.

The lady sergeant pushed herself off the hood and came around to Nick's side, smiling as she recognized him.

"Nick, old horse, you're catching this?"

"I am, Mavis. You're looking lovely today."

The sergeant rolled her eyes, smiling down at him. She had strong arms and big shoulders and a beefy body and looked like most sergeants look—cool, amiable, calm, risky to piss off.

Lovely? Possibly not.

Nick smiled back, introduced Beau Norlett to Staff Sergeant Mavis Crossfire of the Niceville Police Department.

Beau leaned across to shake her hand, got it well and truly shook, managed to get it back mostly unmangled.

"So, Nick, why you?" asked the sergeant, puzzled. "This is something for MP, I woulda thought?"

"So would I. Tig has a soft spot for Delia Cotton, so he wants to cover it personally."

"Lotta Missings going on around town, don't ya think, Nick?"

"I do. So does the mayor. Little Rock's finally got his hair on fire—missing people can't vote for him—and now he's got Boonie Hackendorff all worked up. Anybody Boonie can spare is going back over the last ninety years, looking for a pattern."

"Ninety years?"

"Yep. Every record. Something like one hundred and sixty-two people."

"Well, good luck to them," said Mavis. "I been wondering when Little Rock would get wise to all our *day-sah-para-cee-dos*. Damn strange, you come to think, for a small city like Niceville."

She straightened up, called out to the young black man in the Armed Response uniform.

"Dale, come on over and meet yourself a genuine war hero."

Nick winced but plastered on a smile as the Armed Response guy stepped up and offered his hand.

"Nice to meet you, Detective Kavanaugh. I'm Dale Jonquil."

He pronounced it "JON-kwill," and said it with a straight face, although a lot of people who knew that a jonquil was a kind of daffodil liked to make smart-ass comments about it.

Once, anyway.

Nick, who wouldn't have known a jonquil from a jackhammer, smiled, shook his hand, introduced Beau.

"Dale is Special Forces too, Nick," said Mavis.

Nick looked at the man more closely. Jonquil looked back, a cool, quiet consideration.

"Who you with?" asked Nick.

"Twentieth Special Forces Group. Third Battalion."

"National Guard? Based in Florida?"

"Yes sir. We liaised with Air Force SF at Hurlburt Field in Mary Esther but mainly we backed up the Seventh at Fort Bragg. Not much going on in our Area of Operations, which is mainly Mexico and Latin America."

"Except the *narcotraficante* wars along the border."

"Yeah, but we're not allowed to get into that, at least not yet. So, no service like yours, if I can say so, sir. Everybody in Special Ops Command knows about you, sir. It's a real privilege to meet you."

"Well, I'm glad you're home safe, Dale. Can you tell me what's your read up there?"

He nodded toward Temple Hill, and was surprised to find the young man's expression closing up.

"Sir, I honestly don't know what to make of it. That nice old lady is plain gone. And so's her gardener. Sergeant Crossfire and I walked through, it wasn't like there was anything out of . . . out of place, like? But neither of us felt . . ."

"Like staying," said Mavis, her tone flat.

Nick took that in.

"Well, maybe Beau and I should go see for ourselves."

"You do that," said Mavis.

Nick put the car in gear, stopped and looked across the street at the crowd of neighbors.

"Either of you talk to these people?"

"Yes sir," said Dale Jonquil. "I took down their names and phone numbers. Nobody saw anything out of the ordinary, other than they thought there might be a big party going on, because the lights were on all night and they could hear music coming from the house. But this is The Chase, sir, and people tend to value their privacy, so nobody made a call to us or went across to look."

"Thanks, Dale. Mavis. You going to wait?"

Mavis shook her head.

"We got a Barricaded EDP over at Saint Innocent. I gotta go supervise. Dale's going to stay. This house was in his sector."

Nick was about to roll past that, but then he didn't. An EDP was an Emotionally Disturbed Person, and a Barricaded EDP was the second most dangerous patrol call in the book.

"Saint Innocent *Orthodox*? On Peachtree?"

Mavis said it was, and was puzzled by the look on his face.

"Got a name for the EDP?"

"Hold on," she said, unhooking her radio.

"Delta Zero this is Echo Six Actual. Have we got a name for the EDP at Saint Innocent? Yeah? Okay, I'm five minutes away. Tell the guys to sit tight."

She snapped the rig back on her belt.

"Some guy named Kevin Dennison. Supposed to be the custodian. He has the pastor and a couple of kids locked up in the rectory."

"Christ," said Nick.

"You *know* this guy?"

Nick filled her in on the anonymous e-mail Tig had gotten that morning. Mavis took it in, her expression hardening up.

"Jeez. You guys go all ape-shit on the man?"

"No. Not on some anonymous tip. Tig wanted to go slow, didn't want to burn the guy's life down until we heard back from Maryland."

"Well *somebody* wanted to fuck with this guy. A reporter from the *Register* called the pastor, said they got a tip about a child molester supposed to be working there, and then the satellite trucks rolled up a couple minutes later. Dennison went totally bats. Locked himself in the office. You sure nobody at CID made a call?"

"I don't think so. But if somebody has, you can bet he'll be out on his ass by the end of the day. In the meantime, go easy with this guy, if you can. He might be innocent."

"If I can. Innocent or not, he's kicked over the trash can now. Something will have to be done."

"I understand. And you be careful, okay? We gotta do this thing here. Keep me in the loop about Dennison, if you can?"

Mavis said she would.

Nick turned to the Armed Response guy.

"Dale, give us an hour at the house. Just stay down here, hold the AO and keep the gawkers at a good distance, if you don't mind."

"Yes sir," said Jonquil, coming on point.

Nick was about to pull away when Mavis put her hand on his forearm.

"Nick, while you're up there, mind you mind the mirrors."

"Mind the mirrors?"

A troubled expression moved across her open, friendly features while she worked at an answer.

"Well, I—we—Dale and me both—we sort of . . . *saw* things, in the mirrors. Dale saw a pretty girl in a green sundress, holding a big old coon cat. I mean, he sees her reflection in a mirror, but when he looks around, there's nothing behind him."

"*You* see anything, Mavis?"

Mavis lost her easy manner.

"Yeah. Doesn't matter what I thought I saw. Some stupid thing out of my own damn brain. Nothing I care to get into here. Maybe over a beer. What I think, the house is full of cut glass, crystal, big shiny windows, mirrors and metal and polished things everywhere, like it's the inside of a rose vase, sort of, or like maybe one of those *collide-oh-scope* thingys, so when you move around the house you think you're seeing things out of the corner of your eye, but when you look, nothing is there. So, like I said, don't let the mirrors spook you."

"That's not quite what you said, Mavis."

She was silent for a moment, patted his forearm and straightened up.

"No, I guess it isn't. I'm at home tonight, after six. Call if you feel like talking."

"You think I will?"

Mavis shrugged, gave him another forearm pat. Nick

looked up at her for a moment, and then he eased the accel-
erator down and they rolled up the long curved drive towards
the big house, parking the car in a turnout paved in red brick
in front of a separate three-door garage. Nick put the cruiser
in next to a large antique Packard in official Florida colors.

Both men climbed out, feeling the light mist of rain that
was sifting down through the shredding clouds, here and there
a patch of clear blue showing. The front lawn smelled of grass
cuttings and the gardens were lush and wet, a riot of magno-
lias and bougainvillea and Japanese maples.

Beau tried the door on the Packard, popped the latch, and
leaned into the interior, basically poking around inside to see
what there was to see.

Nick left him to it and walked across the drive towards the
stairs that led up to the big curved front porch, floored in
strips of painted wood, set out here and there with graceful
bentwood chairs.

The door to the house was wide open, showing a lush
Persian-patterned carpet that led away into the interior hall, a
passage gleaming with polished wood and jeweled light from
Art Nouveau shades and sconces along the wall.

The main hall took a straight shot past what looked like a
door into a huge bandbox on his right and another door
opened onto a book-lined reading room on his left, running
all the way to a large white-painted kitchen at the back of the
house, a distance of maybe sixty feet.

He stopped at the front door, listening to the house creak
and groan and pop as the day's heat warmed its old wooden
bones.

He looked up at the corner above the entry and saw a small
camera fixed on a swivel, its red light a tiny ruby dot in the
blue shadows under the porch roof. A surveillance camera, he
realized, making a note to check for video.

When he looked back down into the hallway there was a
dark figure at the far end of the hall, silhouetted in the light

from the kitchen. His breath stopped dead, a flood of glacier ice poured down his spine, and his heart began to thrum in his chest like a feathering prop.

He blinked, but the image remained, a tall black figure, completely covered from head to foot in shapeless black robes, faceless and dead still.

A Muslim woman, in a black burka.

In a flash of white light his skin went numb and his revolver was in his hand before he had the thought—Beau, seeing the sudden flash of movement, came up the steps behind him, soft and quick, his own pistol out—Nick was aiming the Colt down the long dark hall at the still, black shape, his chest pounding and his throat aching and tight.

Beau was at his side, his weapon also aimed down the long hall.

"What is it?" he asked in a low whisper.

"The woman in black, at the end of the hall," said Nick, in a choked-off voice, more of a snarl, and as tight as a drumhead, "If she twitches, put two in her head. *Not* in the body. In her head."

Beau, trying to see what Nick had seen first, not sure what the hell was going on but seeing only a vague black shape shimmering there, followed as Nick moved quickly forward, his weapon up, his sights fixed on the head of the black figure sixty feet away. There is no way one can describe what was going on in his head right then as a normal police reaction.

Beau, at a loss but game, covered him, following carefully as Nick moved down the ornate wood-paneled hall towards the black figure, Beau close behind, his pistol down and to the right, Beau checking each side room as they passed it by.

About two-thirds of the way down the hall, the image of a tall thick-bodied Muslim woman in a full black burka abruptly resolved itself into a partially open glass door, and, reflected in the glass, a black pillar carved in hieroglyphics, in a niche by the kitchen entrance.

Nick halted in mid-stride, causing Beau to almost step on his heels, and there he stood, locked in place, his left leg vibrating wildly. He swallowed, with difficulty, lowered his gun, turned away and put his back up against the wall, breathing in short sharp gasps, both legs now trembling violently, his skin gray and wet.

"Nick, what's the matter. Nick. You okay?"

Nick held up his hand, palm out, working to get himself under control, making a vague gesture for Beau to go on ahead and check out the kitchen.

Beau stood there for a long moment, wondering if Nick was having a heart attack, and then he moved off down the hall and walked out into the bright open area of an all-white kitchen.

Nick stayed in the relative gloom of the hallway, staring into nothing as he tried to get his head out of Al Kuribayeh and the Wadi Doan, seeing again the spiky stone village at the bottom of a jagged valley surrounded by sandstone walls a thousand feet high.

He heard the wind in the creosote shrubs and the thudding chatter of automatic weapons echoing around the valley. He closed his eyes and put his head back against the wall.

The floorboards creaked near him and he opened his eyes to find Beau there, looking at him with a worried expression.

"Nick, what'd you see? What was there?"

Nick wasn't going to try to explain the Wadi Doan to Beau, or to anyone else.

"I'm sorry I freaked you. I thought I saw . . . a woman . . . at the end of the hall. I thought she might have a gun in her hand. What did *you* see?"

Beau shook his head, blinking at Nick.

"Man . . . I don't know. I saw this black pillar thing here, looked sorta ripply in the glass. But nothing like a woman."

With an effort, Nick got himself back inside his own skin, pushed himself off the wall.

"Forget about it. Mavis has a great imagination. Remind me to tell her so later. Let's just go through the house, slow and careful, okay?"

Beau, relieved to see Nick back to normal, nodded, gave him a happy gundog look.

"Okay. Where you want to start?"

"There's a security camera out front. See if you can find a hard drive for it. Maybe there's an image on it we can use."

"Okay," said Beau, moving back up the hall towards the door. Nick shook himself one last time, took in a long, uneven breath, let it out slow, and walked towards the bandbox room.

Pausing in the door, he saw a large octagonal room, pale yellow walls with white crown molding, lined with tall grace-ful windows, a large stained-glass lamp in the ceiling. The wooden floors gleamed with polish and the windows shim-mered with a rain-washed light streaming in through the antique glass.

A pair of stuffed chairs were set down in front of a large fifties-era stereo and a General Electric television set in a huge blond-wood cabinet. A side table next to one of the chairs held a black remote and a heavy crystal glass that was half full of an amber liquid.

Nick bent down, sniffed the glass—scotch, flat and warm, been there all night. A comforter lay on the floor in front of the chair, as if it had slipped off Delia's lap when she got up.

Assuming it was Delia in the chair.

He used a pen tip to touch the remote for the stereo and the room was suddenly booming with the sound of a mournful cello, the volume set at a deafening level. The grocery lady, Alice Bayer, had said that she shut it off when she got into the house. Nick shut it off again, used the pen to flick the televi-sion set on.

The screen bloomed slowly into light and he was looking at the front porch, a color image, obviously taken from the POV of the security camera. He could see Beau kneeling down in the lower left corner of the picture, probably tracing a cable.

Okay.

She's sitting here, having a scotch, listening to some cello music. A nice quiet Friday evening. Something disturbs her. Not the phone. Was there a bell down by the gate? He'd have to look. He didn't think so. Maybe the doorbell. Yes, because before she got up to answer the door, she switched the television to the closed-circuit channel to see who it was at the door.

So whoever was at the door was somebody she wasn't worried about, somebody she knew, a friend maybe? The gardener? Gray Haggard?

Was she expecting him?

If so, why check the security camera?

Maybe she was just a paranoid old bat?

Beau and he would have to go through all her things, her files, her bank accounts, everything. Missing Persons already had her description out with all the local and County guys.

If she had just wandered off—maybe a stroke—they'd find her. But it wasn't likely that they had *both* wandered off, unless she was gone when Haggard got here and now he was off somewhere looking for her. Or they had gone off together?

Without his car?

Or hers?

Did she have a car?

Yes.

A 1975 navy blue Cadillac Fleetwood, a huge barge of a boat that would have stood out if anybody had seen it on the roads. But, according to the file, the car was in the shop for repairs, which was why Alice Bayer was dropping by with groceries.

No. They weren't off on a road trip. There was more to this than a couple of doddering old geezers stumbling off into the night.

So far the house wasn't telling him much, other than that

she owned a lot of very expensive stuff—all of which was still lying around everywhere, so robbery didn't look like a motive. It was clear from the opulence of the house and all that it contained that Delia lived right at the top of the Niceville food chain. But then, she was a Cotton, wasn't she, and that's what they had always been, lords of all they surveyed for over a hundred years.

He stood in the middle of the room, turning slowly around, trying to get some feeling about what might have happened here, and he noticed a set of tall glass double doors, leading, it looked like, into a wood-paneled dining room.

The doors were shut and the ancient glass, as rippled as running water, conveyed only a rough impression of what was beyond them—dark wood and brass and bright shining things and a large chandelier over the table, glittering like a Fourth of July sparkler.

He walked over and stood in front of the doors, looking through the glass, and was about to reach for the gilt handle to open them when he felt something grating under his foot.

He looked down and saw a small lump of what at first looked like red coal, jagged and misshapen, about the size of a thimble. He picked it up and turned it in his hand. It was blood-warm, almost hot, and it wasn't coal.

He knelt down and ran his hand over the floorboards, which were also blood-warm, for some odd reason. Maybe a hot-water pipe ran under the doorway here?

He felt another tiny lump under his searching palm, and picked that up as well, a star-shaped fragment with rough, twisted edges, as if it had at one point been ripped from something much larger, and by a powerful explosive force. To his military mind these lumps looked exactly like shrapnel.

He stood up, pocketing the metal fragments, and looked more carefully around in the doorway. The varnish on the flooring near here was marked, discolored, almost as if it had been scraped or burned away. Whatever it was, the discoloration ran under the closed doors.

He opened both doors wide.

The dining room was neat, spacious, and elegant, the tall lyre-backed chairs lined up in close-order drill, the huge expanse of inlaid wood shining like topaz, reflecting the brilliance of the crystal chandelier above it.

The corroded stain—the burned-out mark—whatever the hell it was—ran for another three feet into the dining room, as if whatever had been spilled here—something strong enough to eat away at layers upon layers of very old varnish—had run out across the flooring and then had been left there long enough to ruin the finish.

This did not fit with the rest of the house, which was beautifully cared for. He stood there, looking down at the stain, and it came to him that the mark, the burn, whatever, was roughly in the shape of a human figure. The head was lying in the bandbox room, the waist across the threshold, and the legs stretching out into the dining room.

Not a small figure either, from the size of the mark, a tall person, six feet at least. He got the impression that the figure—if it had been a man—had been lying on his back with his legs bent over to one side, as if something heavy was lying on top of him, pressing him into the floor.

Well, this was ridiculous.

It is a *stain*, Nick.

A mark. There was no blood, no heel marks to suggest a struggle, no signs of violence at all.

He knelt down again, and touched the floor in the middle of the stain. It *was* definitely warm, several degrees warmer than the surrounding floor.

Check for a hot-water pipe, he thought, *under the boards*. He rubbed at the surface, feeling the raw grain of the old wood. The varnish had been taken off right down to the wood. In the shape of a man. He lifted his fingertip and smelled the residue on his skin. A sharp scorched smell, like burned cloth, and underneath that a bitter coppery reek.

What in the hell happened here?

His radio beeped, and then Beau's voice, crackling with static, a tight hoarse whisper.

"Nick, where are you?"

"In the living room. Where are you?"

"I'm in the basement."

"What are you doing down there?"

"Up until a minute ago, I was tracing the camera cable. There's something down here, I don't know what it is, but, Nick, you got to see it."

Coker and Danziger Complicate Things

The robot Frisbee with the Raytheon GNS logo sat in a blue-velvet-lined cutaway inside its stainless-steel casket on the dining room table between Coker and Danziger, bathed in a circle of hot white light from a halogen desk lamp that Coker had brought in from his office.

A bottle of Jim Beam was set at Coker's right elbow, and a glass, fruity juice-glass-type thing with oranges and grapes all over it, sat at each man's right hand. In the background some smoky music was playing, Jerry Goldsmith's trumpet solo from the *Chinatown* movie.

Coker sucked the last hit off his cigarette, stubbed it out in an ashtray that looked like a NASCAR racing slick, sat back in the chair, making it groan like a rusted gate, and considered Danziger's complexion as Charlie inhaled another drag of his own cigarette.

"You *do* recall you got a bullet hole in that lung you're choking up right now?"

Danziger gave him a squint-eyed look through his personal fogbank.

"I'm not using *that* one. I'm redirecting."

"Redirecting what? Like into the other lung?"

"Yep."

"You die, Charlie, I get to keep it all."

"What about Merle Zane? He call back?"

Coker shook his head, wondering about that.

"I got three calls in about ten minutes. Each time it was his cell number on the display, each time I picked up the call, and all I'm hearing is some sort of hissing, scratching sound, like steam or maybe like leaves or grass being blown around. I'm thinking, maybe some kind of animal, even. Like a raccoon or a possum? I wait for Merle to say something, but nothing comes, the hissing and scratching goes on for about fifteen maybe twenty seconds, and then the call cuts off."

"You phone him back?"

"After the third call. The cell rings a couple of times, and then his voice mail picks up—"

"You leave a message?"

"I said we wanted to meet, straight across, repair the situation, make it right, and all he had to do was name a place."

"And he never called back?"

Coker shook his head, going inside himself for a moment, trying to figure out Zane's game, gave it up for insufficient data.

"No, he didn't. So now I'm giving the Merle Zane matter some additional thought. I come up with anything brilliant, I will let you know."

Coker leaned forward, tapped the steel box.

"Now. About this cosmic-gizmo-Frisbee that lies before us . . . you got any suggestions?"

Danziger was quiet for a while.

In a corner of the room Coker's big flat-screen Samsung television, muted, was showing cop cars clustered randomly around a large redbrick building next to an Art Deco church, and a female broadcaster with helmet hair was talking into the camera in the foreground.

There was a crawl along the bottom of the screen reading:

STANDOFF AT SAINT INNOCENT ORTHODOX CUSTODIAN TAKES
TWO HOSTAGES THREATENS SUICIDE POLICE NEGOTIATING . . .

"I got a question, first," said Danziger finally, taking a sip of his JB, wincing as he choked it down. He hated Jim Beam but in this part of the state it was what got drunk if you were drinking with cops. When he was alone he drank Italian Pinot Grigio so cold it hurt his teeth, but he wouldn't want that to get out and around.

"Shoot," said Coker.

"What was this thing doing in a lockbox at the First Third in Gracie?"

"That's easy," said Coker. "Waiting for you to come along and get us rat-fucked."

"Yeah, well, aside from that."

Coker gave it some consideration.

"Off the top of my head, I'd say there was no good reason at all for it to be sitting there. If it really is some sorta high-tech classified shit, then it would be in a lockdown at the Raytheon HQ in . . . where the fuck?"

"Waltham. That's in Massachusetts."

"Or in whatever the fuck subsidiary in Quantum Park is doing R and D for Raytheon."

"Yeah. That's what I'm thinking."

"Do you know what *is* the Raytheon subsidiary in Quantum Park?"

"Looked it up. Company called Slipstream Dynamics."

"Slipstream Dynamics? Okay, so you figure Slipstream Dynamics might have a problem with one of their super-secret Frisbees lying around in a lockbox at the First Third Bank in Gracie?"

A slow incline of Danziger's head as he glared down at the thing.

"When you were rooting around in the vault, did you happen to notice whose lockbox it was?"

"No," said Danziger. "They never have names. Only numbers."

"So you just picked it . . ."

"Because it was there."

"So . . . if it wasn't *supposed* to be there . . . ?"

"Then this would also explain why nobody on the news
has said anything about some high-tech gizmo being stolen
from the First Third in the first place, which means that whoever was keeping it there was doing something the good folks
at Raytheon probably would not . . ."

"Smile upon?"

"Yeah."

Coker worked that out. Danziger watched him do it.
Watching Coker think was always interesting.

"You're thinking, maybe they'd like it back?"

"That's what I'm thinking."

Coker was quiet for a time, so Danziger poured them both
some more Jim Beam and lit himself another one of Coker's
Camels, thought briefly about giving up smoking, at least
until his right lung healed, rejected that idea, and sat back
with a contented sigh to watch Coker think some more.

"Risky," was what Coker finally said.

Danziger nodded.

"So's killing cops for money. How much did we get, by the
way?"

Coker waved, absently, in the direction of the kitchen
counter, where thirty-nine neat stacks of bundled bills were
lined up with OCD-level precision next to a smaller heap of
rings, jewels, and negotiable bonds taken from the various
lockboxes that Danziger and Merle Zane had found the time
to pry open after they'd loaded up the currency.

"Comes to two million one hundred and sixty-three thousand dollars, plus the miscellaneous shit."

Danziger was visibly shocked.

"Man. I knew it was a shitload."

"Bank is saying they lost two point five."

"They always do that in a robbery."

"Well, we got two mil one sixty-three plus the miscellaneous shit. How come you don't look happy?"

"It's too much money, Coker. That much money, people go nuts looking for it. It's too much."

"Whaddya wanna do? Give some back?"

Danziger looked like he was thinking about it.

"I guess not. But we gotta keep our heads."

"Mine's fine. Hell of a take, Charlie."

"Yes it is. And the Frisbee," said Danziger, privately dividing two mil one sixty-three plus the miscellaneous shit by one and liking the result.

"Yeah. And the Frisbee. You're thinking we ransom this sucker back at 'em? Who would we talk to about that?"

"Probably Byron Deitz. He's the head of security for the whole place."

"And you're saying that Deitz is already sniffing around this thing. Boonie say why?"

"Deitz is saying he just wants to help. Brotherhood of the badge and all that shit. And also part of the Quantum Park cash draw is sitting in there on your kitchen counter, so he's saying that a professional obligation is involved."

"Deitz doesn't give a rusty fuck about anything other than Byron Deitz. Boonie and the Feebs aren't going to let a mutt like him stomp all over their investigation. Nor is Marty Coors. I wouldn't either. You say Deitz is asking about Lyle Crowder?"

"That he is," said Danziger.

"That I don't like. What's our exposure with Lyle?"

Danziger shrugged.

"Even if he rolls, which I don't think he will, because he's looking at death for being an accessory, now that he's killed two old ladies, and anyway nobody around here will let him plea-bargain while he's standing on the graves of four dead cops, and besides he doesn't know who we are."

He took a sip, puffed at his cigarette, ran a hand through his hair, making a bristly burring sound, his eyes on the middle distance.

"No. I mean, all he can say is he got a fat FedEx envelope with five thousand dollars in fifties in it and a note saying what he had to do to get another five thousand, which was to fuck up traffic big time on the interstate at a certain point in time. From what he said to me, I figure Boonie's almost all the way convinced the kid is clean. That's fine with me. We just leave it be. We don't want to change Boonie's mind about any of that. Anyway, killing Crowder will just convince Boonie that he's closer to the guys who did the bank than he thought he was. He'll go back over everything Crowder ever did. They'll find out he got a FedEx delivery, start tracing it backwards."

"Won't lead to us, will it? You used gloves when you packed it, gave a phony address?"

"Yeah. But killing the guy, it's just one of those tricky things that people do in robberies, the one-step-too-far that ends up getting them fucked. Look what happened with Merle. Tried to shoot him, and now he's out there somewhere doing God only knows. We simply paid him off, he's back home with the Bardashi boys happy as a rabbit in rhubarb. We try for Lyle, maybe one of his guards gets in the line of fire? Or we only wing him and now he knows his only chance is to come clean with the Feds. Nope. When in doubt, sit tight. When there's nothing to be done, do nothing. You follow?"

Coker, after some thought, nodded.

"Works for me, if you say so. What you wanna do about the proceeds?"

"Best thing there is to stick to the plan, leave it alone for a year or so, then piece it out careful-like, not doing anything too showy. Which reminds me, what'd you do with the Barrett?"

"Switched out the barrel and the firing pin. Cleaned it up and now it's back in storage, at the depot, where it belongs. Threw the old barrel into Crater Sink. It sleeps with the fishes."

"You'll find no fishes in that black hole, my friend. Place gives me the willies, always has. What about the Python you used to mop up the dead?"

"Also sleeps with the fishes."

"And my shit-box Chevy?"

"Drove it to Tin Town and left it on Bauxite, next to the needle exchange. Left the keys in. Waited around. It was gone in fifteen minutes."

"Damn, Coker. Had my blood in it."

"So what? Don't mean a thing unless they want the DNA. DNA doesn't have a microscopic label saying 'I belong to Charlie Danziger.' Anyway, by the time those hypes get through with it, your blood'll be underneath sixteen layers of icky junkie poop. No crime scene guy in the world is going to get inta that vehicle. It'll be FIDO by the time the NPD even notices it."

"Fuck It Drive On."

"Yep."

Charlie shook his head, smiling at Coker.

"Icky junky poop?"

"I'm trying to be colorful."

"Well, don't."

Coker's phone rang, an old black number sitting behind him on a sideboard.

Coker leaned back, snagged it.

"Coker."

Danziger could hear some sort of soft buzzing sound from the earpiece, a female voice. Coker's expression changed as he listened to the caller.

"Hey Mavis . . . no, I'm good . . . sitting here having a glass with Charlie Danziger . . . yeah, I know, all over the news right now, I can see it—"

He set the phone aside, pointed at the television set, where the Live Eye Seven coverage of the standoff at Saint Innocent had gone national.

"Charlie, can you un-mute that?"

Danziger did, and the room was filled with the overheated breathless coverage of the Live Eye Seven field reporter, a plastic-coated blond chick with helmet hair who looked to be about fourteen.

"And as of this hour there seems to be no progress as Kevin David Dennison is refusing to answer the negotiator's calls—"

Coker and Danziger watched the screen for a moment, and then Coker made a slicing move across his throat and Danziger hit the MUTE button. Coker was back on the phone, listening hard, making a few terse replies, suddenly all business.

"Okay. I got that. What about Marty's guys? . . . Well then call Glynco and get a—what? Benning? Well, that's fucked. No, I get it . . . no, I got no problem with it . . . how soon? Yeah . . . yeah . . . we got an okay from Mauldar to do this? On paper? Right. Good. Relax, Mavis, I'll be there in fifteen minutes. I got the gear in the truck. Yeah. Good."

Coker put the phone down, looked across at Danziger, cracked into a broad grin.

"That was Mavis Crossfire—"

"Yeah. You can see her in the background there, by the squad cars. She needs a police sniper, am I right?"

"Just in case."

"What about Marty's SWAT guys?"

"At Benning, in a competition."

"Bad time to be drawing attention to your sniping skills, Coker."

"What am I going to do, Charlie? Tell her I don't feel like it?"

Coker stood up, killed the last of his JB, set the glass down, his mind already on the job.

"I gotta go change. You wanna come along on this job? Might be interesting."

"And do what? Hold your dick? Fetch coffee and donuts? I'm not a cop anymore. I'm going to go do something about this bionic Frisbee here."

"Like what?"

"Like fuck with Byron Deitz's mind."

"How?"

"We're gonna get him to buy it back, right?"

"Yeah."

"Well, first we gotta get him off balance."

"You got any idea how?"

"I'm gonna dance him all around Tin Town, one damn place after another, Helpy Selfy, Piggly Wiggly, Winn-Dixie, Lowe's, every second peeler bar. By the time I'm through jerking him around, he won't know his ass from a tuna fish sandwich. Then we'll do the deed."

"Yeah? Still be more fun holding my dick."

"Well, I wouldn't know, would I?"

"Ask your mom."

Byron Deitz and Thad Llewellyn Disagree

Byron Deitz, a guy with a limited emotional range, was finding his limitations sorely tested today as he sat in his yellow Hummer in the rain-misted parking lot of the First Third Bank in Gracie. He was staring out through the rainy ripples on the Hummer's tinted window and waiting for a Mr. Thad Llewellyn, the Assistant Commercial Accounts Manager for the First Third Bank in Gracie, to come out and get in the truck and respond to a few simple fucking questions.

However, Llewellyn was not all that anxious to come out and respond to a few simple fucking questions from Byron Deitz.

Nor had he particularly savored his earlier interlude with Phil Holliman, Byron Deitz's Second in Command, his Two IC, as Holliman called himself, which had taken place around daybreak on the front steps of Mr. and Mrs. Llewellyn's rambling ranchero property in a shady glen a mile off Side Road 336, a few short miles south of Gracie, and generally—make that *formerly*—felt by the Llewellyn family—all two of them— to be a safe haven from the dizzying delights of Gracie's social whirl, of which there weren't any.

Sadly, this had not been the case at six this morning, when

Mrs. Llewellyn—born Inge Bjornsdottir—had her hatha yoga
session forcefully derailed by a hammering din on or about
the front door, followed by the stumble-tumble sound of her
husband coming down the hall stairs two at a time and sham-
bling towards the front door with a look of utter panic on his
pinched and birdlike features, his furry lambskin slippers slip-
sliding on the polished parquet.

Mrs. Thad had listened, rapt and avid, to a short but memorable exchange between Thad and the Unexpected Caller,
from what she could see of him over her husband's cringing
figure, a monstrous black man in a charcoal suit not quite up
to containing him.

The words were indecipherable to her, but the tone was
pretty clear—malice and threats have their own unique
cadences—and the interview ended with Thad having his own
front door slammed in his face hard enough for the sidelight
windows to rattle in their custom-built frames.

Inge oozed out into the hall in her sky blue one-piece
yoga suit and her hot-pink bunny-eared slippers and the couple stood there staring at each other as the sound of a big
sedan wheeling around in their circular drive and spraying
pricey quartz gravel all over their Arts and Crafts front porch
gradually faded into a pressure-filled silence.

"*Who* was that *awful* man?" Inge had asked, in tones of
brass, while Thad stood in the front hall, drooping before her
like an under-watered fern.

"His name was Phil Holliman, Inge," Thad had replied, in
a small scorched voice. "He works for Byron Deitz."

"What did he want at this ungodly hour?"

Thad, who had not been totally frank with Mrs. Thad on
the matter of the supplementary income which was allowing
them to maintain this shady retreat, was at a bit of a loss how
to reply.

Watching his eyes dart to and fro while his nose twitched
and his lips quivered, Inge, no slouch herself when it came to

calculations of self-interest and knowing her husband pretty well, had decided that what she didn't know wasn't going to get her indicted.

She harrumphed at him twice, her lips pursed, and then turned sharply around on her suffering bunnies and swept regally back into her yoga room, slamming the door behind her and leaving her husband to contemplate the finer points of domestic discord.

What that awful man had wanted at that ungodly hour, Thad was now trying to cope with, was that he should be ready to pop like a jack-in-the-box out of his cubicle at the First Third Bank in Gracie within a few heartbeats after he saw Byron Deitz's yellow Hummer lurch into the bank's parking lot.

This, according to Phil Holliman, would happen around noon this day.

And it had just now come to pass, exactly at noon, exactly as the unpleasant Mr. Holliman had predicted it would.

Not surprisingly, the sight of Deitz's Hummer had nearly given the excitable banker a stroke of his own, and he took himself off to the bathroom to have a drink of water and pop a couple of what he called his Happy Caps as a way of girding his loins for the fray.

Deitz, sitting in the Hummer and grinding his molars in that way he had which filled his bony skull with those mysterious walnut-cracking noises he was always at a loss to explain, got another phone call on his OnStar system, which made him jump a yard and swallow his gum.

The call display read BELFAIR CULLEN COUNTY CID, so he punched CALL ANSWER and said, "Deitz here."

"Byron, this is Tig Sutter."

Jeez. Now what?

"LT, how are you, sir?"

"I'm good, Byron. I'm good. You got a minute?"

Deitz looked out the window as the glass doors of the First

Third swung open and out popped the reedlike figure of Mr. Thad, holding a red umbrella over his head and scooting in pixie steps across the wet pavement towards the Hummer.

"About to go into a meeting, Tig, but anything I can do—"

"Nick was going to call you about this, but he's sorta tied up on a Missing Persons case—"

Thad Llewellyn had reached the passenger door and was now standing outside, peering in through the tinted glass, blinking at him, looking mournful but resigned, and even a little bit dreamy-eyed.

Deitz reached out and popped the locks and Thad scooted inside, settling into the passenger seat with his back up against the door.

He nodded weakly at Deitz as Deitz held a finger up to his lips, letting Thad know that he was to remain silent until required to speak.

"Always happy to hear from you, LT. How is Nick?"

"He's good," said Tig, in a distracted tone. "Look, you following this hostage thing at Saint Innocent?"

Deitz, who had been following nothing but his own doom-laden lines of thought ever since yesterday evening, had to admit that he had no idea what Tig Sutter was talking about.

Tig laid it out for him, the anonymous e-mail accusing the custodian, Tig's decision to wait for Maryland to get back to him, and then the sudden explosion of publicity, the Live Eye Seven truck and the newspapers and the subsequent cluster-fuck now taking place on Peachtree.

Deitz listened, aware of Thad Llewellyn's rapid breathing and smelling his minty-fresh cologne. He buzzed a window down while wondering where Tig was going. He was sensing an incoming request which he might just be able to exploit for reciprocal info on the bank job, so he was paying close attention.

Tig reached the end of the narrative, and there was a hesitant silence.

Deitz made the leap.

"You want this anonymous creep traced, Tig?"

"Well, that was where we were going. I mean, we could send it down to Cap City, but everybody down there is involved in what happened yesterday, and we just don't have the technical resources—"

"Tig, we have a whole IT section at our disposal. I gotta brilliant guy, name of Andy Chu, he's just sitting around on his butt playing Grand Theft Auto. I'd be happy to offer whatever help you need to follow this thing. Pro bono. of course. I admit we're kinda caught up in doing whatever we can do to find out who pulled that bank job—"

"Well, that's a federal thing now, Byron—"

"True, but a lot of the funds belonged to Quantum Park and as you know—"

"Yes, I do, that's your client, and of course if your guys hear anything—"

"Cap City got any leads yet?"

"Like I said, CID's not in on this. From where I'm sitting, they had insider info, so Boonie Hackendorff is looking at that, at the bank staff and the people at Wells Fargo. And it's pretty obvious the shooter was a pro, and the likely weapon was a Barrett .50—"

"That ought to narrow the list, sir, you know, cross-check Barrett sales with military and professional shooters?"

"Yeah," said Tig, with a sigh. "And that narrows it down to a couple of thousand people, even if we stick with the continental United States. And that's not even counting private civilian shooters, some of whom are as good as any pro. Speaking of that, your guy Holliman is giving us a hell of a headache."

"What's he doing?"

"Well, from what I'm hearing, he spent most of last night going through Tin Town and the club district like General Sherman, putting people up against walls and raising holy hell with all our snitches and CIs. He's back at it right now, down by the Pavilion—apparently it's all about the robbery—which I totally get—like we said—but I gotta tell you, Byron, his methods really suck. Boonie Hackendorff is going to be calling you about him, and Marty Coors is ready to have State CID bust him on interfering with police, so maybe you'll wanna jerk his chain some?"

"Jeez, Tig. I'm real sorry about that. I did tell him to get on the street and talk to people, but not like that. I'll get him to back off, okay?"

"Yeah, well, that would be good. He's getting people all stirred up and too scared to talk. Anyway, this is not why I called. You really think you can help us trace this e-mailer sleazebag?"

"You can confirm it was the same guy who contacted you who sent the e-mails to the press?"

"Yes. I mean, that's the way it looks. We asked for the *Niceville Register* copy, and the one sent to Channel Seven, and the one sent direct to the church. They're all identical. The one we got was sent last night around two in the morning. The other three went out this morning before ten."

"Maybe the guy got impatient. Was looking for something to happen."

"He got the reaction he wanted, in spades, once it got to the television guys. They contacted the church, the pastor was already looking at his copy of the e-mail—had just sent for Dennison, who was already in the building—they were talking about it, still pretty calm—and the news guys started showing up, Dennison freaked, and things went straight to shit. I want this asshole taken down, Byron. When can you get a guy here?"

"Don't need to. Just forward everything you've got to—you got a pen?—okay, write this down—*techserve*—one word—*techserve at Securicom dot com slash AndyChu*. Got that?"

"Yeah," said Tig, reading the address back. "And the name again? Andy . . . ?"

"Andy Chu, only it's one word, *AndyChu*, in the e-mail address. Okay?"

"Got it."

"I'll call Andy right away, give him a heads-up. Andy's the best there is, could have something for you by the end of the day, maybe even sooner."

"Thanks, Byron. I really appreciate this."

"Happy to help. And you know, while I got you, if you think of it, anything you can let me know, how the investigation into the Gracie thing is going—you know, way off the record, cop to cop?—well, I'd take it as a professional kindness. My clients are pretty spooked and I'd like to be able to reassure them. So far, it's just the money, right? Nothing else you're hearing about?"

There was a silence, during which Mr. Thad secretly swallowed his third Happy Cap of the day and Byron ground his molars some more, thinking that he had pushed this too far.

"Don't know what else there could be, Byron. It was a straightforward bank job. Why, has one of your companies reported anything missing?"

Shit, thought Deitz. *Guy's much too quick. Just shut the fuck up, will you?*

"No. Nothing like that. Just trying to narrow the field, see if there was anything that stood out."

"Well, now you know what I know. I hear anything, I'll give you a call. And I'll get that e-mail stuff to you right away."

Tig clicked off, and for a moment the two of them—Thad and Deitz—sat there listening to the rain pattering on the roof and to each other breathing. Deitz suppressed the urge to call Phil Holliman right then, and turned to the banker.

"Okay, Thad, we gotta—holy shit, you okay? You look kinda fuzzy."

Mr. Thad, now almost completely zoned out on his Happy Caps, a few minutes away from being totally blotto and feeling quite serenely invincible, gave Deitz a Buddha-like smile.

"You, my Byronic friend, my . . . my Byronic Man . . . are far too intense."

Thad blinked in slow motion, giving Deitz a slow and clinical once-over.

"Look right there," he said, pointing languidly. "A vein is popping out on your forehead. Your complexion is dangerously flushed. You need to relax, Byron, you really do. Would you like one of my Happy Caps? They are bliss in a bottle, Byron my boy. Bliss in a bottle. Try one?"

Thad held out his bottle, his loving spirit rising to the moment, the Brotherhood of Man welling up in his drug-saturated soul.

Deitz blinked down at the bottle, read the label—ATIVAN—and then looked over at Thad.

"Shit. How many of these have you had?"

"I," said Thad, giving the matter some thought, blinking back at Deitz. "I may have had three. Yes. Three it is."

Deitz reached over, plucked the bottle out of Thad's palm, held it up—it was half full of little beige nuggets—frowned censoriously at Thad—Deitz disapproved of drugs, particularly when used by other people to blunt the Byron Dietz effect. He tossed the pill bottle into the cup holder on the seat divider.

Stared at it for a moment.

A kind of Zen pause here.

Then he backhanded Thad across the right cheek so hard Thad's head bounced off the passenger window with a musical *bonk*. The pink clouds in Mr. Thad's mind parted briefly and a bolt of clarity pierced the rosy mist.

Deitz saw his opening.

"Just one fucking question, Thad. Did you tip anybody off to what was in my lockbox?"

Thad put a hand up and touched the red mark on his cheekbone.

"No. How could I? I didn't know what was *in* the lockbox.

You only told me to keep an eye on it. You never said what was in it. Why? What was it?"

Deitz chewed that thought for a while. Thad was right. He'd never told the banker what was in the box. Why the hell would he?

"None of your fucking business. The guys who did the bank, any idea who they were?"

Thad labored to bring his mind to bear upon this question.

"No. There was nothing . . . two white men, both with those masks on . . . one large, with blue eyes, and another, dark eyes and . . . and . . ."

His voice trailed off and Deitz reached out, pinched the man's nose between his index finger and his thumb, twisted it hard, and let it go, wiping the blood off on Mr. Thad's shirt. Then he took him by the throat and started squeezing.

"Give me something to go on," he said in a grating snarl, his eyes slitted almost shut and his look inhuman, a hot glare his family knew pretty well. "Or I'll snap your fucking neck right here."

Thad, tears of pain on his cheeks, eyes welling up, a trickle of blood running from his red-tipped nose, stared back at Byron Deitz with the totally absent look of a man with less than three brain cells still firing. He could no longer feel his toes and a warm numbness was creeping up his torso.

Deitz shook him like a rag mop, but even Deitz could see that the banker had left the building.

The guy blinked a few times, and then his lids closed and his head fell forward, held up only by Deitz's rigid forearm. After a long silence, and in a dreamy murmur, Mr. Thad said, quite distinctly, "Crito, I owe a cock to Asclepius."

Deitz grunted in disgust, let go of his throat, and Thad commenced to pour himself down into the passenger footwell.

"Boots," he muttered, a moment later, from the depths of

the footwell. "The big man wore navy blue cowboy boots. I have never seen navy blue cowboy boots . . ."

His voice receded into a sighing whisper. The rest was silence, broken only by the sound of one man seething.

Boots? thought Deitz, picking Thad's pill bottle up again and, almost absentmindedly, turning it in his hands.

Beth, his unsatisfactory wife, was always popping Ativans to counter the Deitz Effect. Her Ativans were sort of squared-off little white pills with a T-shaped notch pressed into the top. These looked different, like little beige nuggets, but what the hell. Maybe he could use one himself.

He was sure as hell stressed out enough.

He held the bottle in his thick fingers, listening to Thad Llewellyn wheezing away in the footwell. Obviously the little banker could not handle his meds at all. He sighed, felt a moment of pity for himself, for all the ways in which people in his life were disappointing him. He threw the pill bottle back into the cup holder and started up the truck.

What Deitz was unaware of, wheeling out of the parking lot with an unconscious banker in his passenger seat footwell, was that "the meds" the little banker was currently failing to handle well were not *lorazepam*, the chemical term for Ativan, but a substance known to chemists as *3,4-methylene-dioxy-meth amphetamine* and to overstressed bankers wheezing in footwells as Happy Caps. Its more general name in the wider world of recreational drugs was ecstasy.

In the meantime, round and round again, inside his head, to the accompaniment of that mysterious walnut-cracking sound, ran the little mantra:

Blue cowboy boots?

Merle Zane Rides the Blue Bus

The Blue Bird school bus—painted, a long time back, a bright robin's egg blue—wheezed into the Button Gwinnett Memorial Regional Bus Depot station in downtown Niceville, coming to a stop under the platform's tin roof in a squeal of bad brakes.

The driver, an elderly but military-looking black man with yellow eyes and snow white hair, turned to smile a gold-toothed smile at the passengers, about two dozen roughly dressed leathery-looking workingmen of varying ages and races, who had either been on the bus when it pulled up to the gates of the Ruelle Plantation or had climbed on at Sallytown or Mount Gilead or had just flagged the bus down from the side of the road at various places along the rural routes to Niceville.

"Niceville, gentlemen," he said, standing up and addressing the crowd in a practiced manner. "End of the line. Gathering is at eleven this evening, here at the dock, for those of you going back up the line. Most of the seats are taken, got us a full load, so you be sure to get your return ticket punched on the way out, otherwise you might not get a seat. It's a long weary walk in the dark and many folk get themselves lost. God bless and you all have yourself a fine time in Niceville."

Merle, his back aching and his wound throbbing from five hours of pounding along backcountry roads, got slowly to his feet and picked up his bag, the old Army kit bag that Glynis Ruelle had loaned him. He shuffled slowly down the aisle, following the other men, his boots clanking on the tin floorboards.

Inside the kit bag was a change of clothes, and a 1911 .45-caliber Colt Commander, loaded, along with two spare magazines. Glynis Ruelle could find no ammunition for his 9 mm Taurus, but she had several boxes of .45 rounds for the Colt.

The weight of the bag hanging from his shoulders was comforting, since he was now back in Charlie Danziger's home territory.

There had been heavy rain downstate, but the sky was clearing as he stepped off the bus. When his foot hit the wooden boards of the bus station platform, he could feel the powerful flow of the Tulip River on the other side of the station, now at full flood after all the rain.

The bus station reeked of damp and mold, of cigarettes and cigars and rotting garbage. Beyond the station doors, Niceville crowded around, a decaying old-fashioned city netted over with a black tangle of telephone and power lines.

It looked like a random city, full of narrow lanes, needle-tipped church towers spiking above the ragged rooflines, wrought-iron filigreed galleries held up by ornate cast-iron pillars creating shaded cloisters under them that ran for blocks along the street level.

The quality of the light as the clouds melted away was hazy and luminous, making Niceville look like a calendar shot of prewar America. The humid warmth of spring gave the whole town the earthy aroma of a freshly dug grave.

Maybe it was just that he was spooked and bone-weary and ramped up on fear and painkillers, but to Merle it felt like Niceville had some kind of strange vibe going on, like there was some power running through it, or behind it, or under it, like a live wire, or an underground river, and this *power* wasn't a kindly one. Whatever it was, it didn't like people. There was something just plain *wrong* with Niceville, Merle thought, and that was all he could say about it. He'd be glad to get the hell out, once this was all over.

Whatever *this* was.

While he stood there all the Blue Bird riders drifted off, going their separate ways, no two together. There had been no talk between the riders during the bus trip.

The man sitting next to Merle, a tall skinny white-haired old man with a forlorn look, wearing beige slacks and a plaid shirt, had spent the whole trip staring out the window, his thin blue lips working soundlessly and a puzzled look in his eyes.

Merle asked him his name, but the old man just turned to blink slowly at Merle, as if trying to make him disappear, and then went back to watching the fields and towns tick by, radiating a deep sadness.

A Niceville PD patrol car rolled slowly past, two cops inside, neither of them showing any interest, either in Merle or in much else.

This made him feel easier. If there was a description of him floating around, he obviously didn't match it. After the patrol car turned a corner, Merle moved out into the streets, heading into the town square towards City Hall, unmistakable with that huge round dome.

The redbrick pile next to it would be the library, just where Glynis Ruelle had said it was going to be. Lady Grace Hospital, according to Glynis, was on the far side of the library, about a block along a street called Forsythia.

The rest is up to you, Glynis had said.

He touched the back pocket of his jeans, where there was a

wallet that Glynis had given him, stuffed with cash, as well as a driver's license with a black-and-white picture that could actually have been any middle-aged white male without a beard, identifying Merle as John Hardin Ruelle, address Ruelle Plantation, 2950 Belfair Pike Road, Cullen County Side Road 336.

He shouldered the bag, moved out into the crowds, who paid him no mind at all, heading in the direction of Lady Grace. A navy blue and bright gold streetcar rumbled past him, shiny as a kid's toy. People inside were staring straight ahead, faces fixed and blank.

They looked like corpses.

A block later, at the intersection of Forsythia and Gwinnett, he saw a bank of television screens flickering in a large shop window, and a group of people gathered on the sidewalk, staring at multiple images of the same picture.

Merle stopped at the outside edge of the crowd, tall enough to look over the heads of the other people. From what he could see, some sort of police emergency was going on, squad cars and uniformed cops clustered around a church, and an EMS van waiting in the background.

The sound was off, or too low to be heard through the plate glass of the shop window, but a blond newswoman was talking into the camera, and a crawl along the bottom read HOSTAGE STANDOFF CONTINUES AT SAINT INNOCENT ORTHODOX.

Merle watched the action for a while, which seemed to be at some sort of stalemate, and then moved off up Gwinnett as the sun finally broke out completely. He glanced up past the uneven rooflines of the shops on the street and saw, in the luminous haze, a large stand of trees on top of a high wall of pale limestone, a sheer cliff face that seemed to bend over the town.

Merle vaguely recalled Coker talking about Tallulah's Wall and a limestone sinkhole supposed to be on top of the wall. Crater Sink. Merle got the impression that this sinkhole was a bad place, haunted by something nobody wanted to think about.

If some stupid hole in the ground could spook a hard case like Coker, it was just another good reason to get out of town as soon as possible.

The sunlight was shining on the stand of trees and he could see a cloud of tiny black specks circling the upper branches of a taller tree poking up right in the middle of the forest—crows, a huge flock, he decided, and all stirred up, trying to frighten something away, a hawk or an eagle. He heard a harsh croaking call, this one very close.

Following the sound, he saw a group of crows perched on a sagging power line no more than fifty feet away, on the sunny side of Gwinnett.

They were looking directly at him, their black wings flaring as they shifted and cocked their heads sideways to peer down at him, black beaks sharp-edged in the sunlight, their feathers glittering like glass as they shifted from leg to leg, croaking at him, glaring down at him, as if outraged to see him there, as if personally offended by his presence.

For a moment Merle felt a strange sense of unreality flow over him, and under it a tremor of irrational fear. At that point, the flock, screeching and calling, exploded up into the sky, formed into a tight cloud, wheeled above the oaks that lined Gwinnett, and then fluttered into the high blue sky like scraps of blackened ash from a burning building. When Merle looked back down at the sidewalk, he was staring at Charlie Danziger. Danziger was on the far side of the street. Merle's first impulse was to quietly close in on the man, tap him on the shoulder, and when he turned around, put two rounds through his forehead, smiling as he did so.

He even swung the canvas bag off his shoulder at the same time that he moved back into the shadow of a theater marquee, edging behind the line of young people waiting to get inside—something about Rollerblading vampire spies. Merle stood there in the shade of the marquee for a moment, watching Danziger, who was moving pretty well for a guy who had stopped at least one of Merle's 9 mm slugs yesterday. Up until now, Merle wasn't sure how much damage he'd done to Danziger during their shoot-out. *Not much*, he concluded, with regret.

Danziger was snaking through the crowds on the sidewalk, a big hard-looking cowboy wearing jeans and a suede jacket, those navy blue cowboy boots, walking fast, although obviously favoring his right side, his hands in the pockets of his jacket, his attention fixed on something up ahead of him, Merle had no idea what, but from the look on Danziger's face, even at this distance, he wasn't having kind and loving thoughts. He looked pale, intent, focused, like a man about to do something risky.

It occurred to Merle to get out his cell phone and call Danziger, just to freak him out, and then he remembered that he'd lost his cell phone while he was stumbling through the woods last night.

And he also remembered what he had said to Glynis this morning—*They have no way to spend it. The idea was to keep it hidden for a couple of years. I know who they are. I have time—*

Hell, he didn't even know exactly how much they took out of the bank, although Danziger had figured there was upwards of a million and a half to be had that day, if they pulled it off.

No, he thought, coming off point as Danziger's stalking figure started to get lost in the mist, only his shock of white hair showing above the milling crowd. What he had told Glynis was still a good decision. He would come after them when he was ready, six months from now, when they weren't expecting him.

He waited until Danziger was completely out of sight, came out into the sunlight again, and headed across Forsythia

toward Lady Grace Hospital, threading through the streaming traffic as the afternoon sunlight began to slant through the
trees, making their deep blue shadows stretch slowly out.

The lobby of Lady Grace Hospital was a huge vaultlike
open space with flying buttresses and arches covered in gilt
running fifty feet up to a painted cupola in powder blue dotted
with golden stars. A window wall on the right of the lobby as
he came in shed a yellow light down on a random collection of
couches and armchairs, with a few people sitting on them,
slouched, limp, as if condemned to wait here for a bus that
wasn't coming.

One of the figures, Merle realized as he walked past, was
the craggy old man who had sat next to Merle on the Blue
Bird.

He was here, sitting in the sun, his plaid shirt bleached out
in the afternoon light, his head slowly turning to track Merle
across the floorboards, his pale eyes unblinking, his thin blue
lips working, the same air of dull despair floating around him
like a fog.

At the far end of the black-and-white-checked marble
floor a broad walnut counter stood between two darkened
hallways. The chair behind the desk was empty, but on the
stuccoed wall above the desk a black-ribbed sign with white
lettering indicated the various wings and departments of Lady
Grace.

In a niche above the sign, a statue of the Virgin Mary, her
arms stretched out in benediction, her drapery the same powder blue as the interior of the cupola, smiling a vapid simper-
ing smile, her eyes oddly Chinese, stared directly down at
Merle as he crossed the floor.

Nurses in pale blue uniforms and sensible shoes, cleaning
staff in red, and doctors in scrubs or wearing white lab coats
milled around the main floor, clustered around a Starbucks.

Others, waiting for elevators while studying their clip-
boards, stood in the dim shadows beyond the desk. The

entrance hall looked like a church but instead of sandalwood incense it smelled of coffee and Lysol and wintergreen.

No one paid the slightest attention to Merle as he studied the sign briefly and then walked around to Elevator Bank A, where he waited in silence, surrounded by a chattering cluster of pretty young girls who smelled of hair spray and bubble gum.

While he waited, he sensed a presence behind him and turned around to see the old man from the Blue Bird standing there, staring at the needle indicator as the elevator descended.

Merle looked at him, and the man looked back, blinked once, and then spoke for the first time.

"He's on the fourth floor," said the man, his voice pitched low, a hoarse whisper, as if he didn't want the girls to hear.

"Who is?" asked Merle, cocking his head.

"You'll see," said the man. "You'll have to wake him. He's sleeping. Clara will show you."

There was a low musical *bong*, and the elevator doors, ornate bronzed bars over a thick sheet of stained glass, pulled back with a groan and a flood of staff and visitors poured out. The man let the crowds push him back away from Merle, never breaking eye contact.

"A major loon," said Merle to himself, although the fourth floor was where he was supposed to start looking, according to Glynis.

He rode up with the chattering girls, and got off on the fourth floor, stepping out into a shadowy darkness, a long narrow hallway lit only by tiny amber sconces set into the wall every few feet.

At the far end of the darkened hall there was a pool of cool white light, and a nurse, at her desk, leaning over a computer, staring intently at something in front of her.

Merle came down the hall, walking as quietly as his boots would let him, passing half-open doors with numbers on them, getting fleeting glimpses into darkened rooms where mounded figures huddled under blankets, shadowy spaces full of the beep and rush of machinery, all the drapes drawn tight against the sun.

As he got close to the nursing station, the woman lifted her head and smiled at him. She was young and very lovely, with pale auburn hair and a full sensual figure.

She wasn't in a uniform, but she had on a pale green summer frock that emphasized her curves and reminded Merle of soft dreamy summer nights in exotic places he had never been to.

Her large hazel eyes were full of pale white light. She had a name tag on her breast: CLARA MERCER RN.

"Sir, I'm sorry, but visiting hours are from five until eight."

Merle came to a stop at her station, gave her his best smile, which was pretty good, considering his dark sharp-planed appearance and his beak of a nose. "I realize that, Miss Mercer—"

"Oh please. I'm Clara."

"Nice to meet you, Clara. I'm Merle. I'm sorry to just turn up like this. It's just that I'm only in for the day, got a bus from upstate."

"Did you come in on the Blue Bird?" she asked, giving his farmhand clothes a quick up and down. The question surprised Merle. It was as if she had been expecting him.

"Yes. And I'm not sure how long I have."

"Well," she said, glancing back up the long dark hallway behind him, "I think I know why you're here. We're not supposed to . . . but no one's around right now anyway. Everybody's in a staff meeting and I'm just here to answer the phones. Who would you like to see? Would it be Rainey?"

Merle said yes.

Clara's expression changed, grew more solemn, and the cool light in her hazel eyes got cooler.

"Oh yes. It's his time, isn't it? Such a sad thing. Are you a relative?"

"Yes. Distantly, but I would like to see him, if I can?"

"He won't know you at all," she said, her voice pitched low. "He's almost not here . . . and you can only have a few minutes with him. There's a danger of infection, too, so you'll have to wear a smock."

She pointed to a rack of white coats set in an alcove a few feet away. Merle crossed to it, found one, and pulled it on as the girl ticked something off on a chart. She looked up as he came back, smiled again, full of sympathy.

"He's in four eighteen. It's a private unit, just down this hallway and through the glass door. Remember, you can't go any closer than the white line. I'd come with you, Merle, but I have to cover the phones."

"I'll be careful," said Merle, already moving away, his heart thudding in his ribs and his throat closing up. He got to four eighteen, and stopped outside, looking through the heavy beaded glass window set into the upper half of the door, with the words CRITICAL CARE PRIVATE SUITE. Through the glass he saw a dimly lit interior, blurry and distorted, with a row of green lights flashing above a large hooded white shape.

He reached out, pushed the door open, and stepped into a small but well-equipped hospital room, where a contorted figure lay on its right side, a young boy, twisted into a fetal position, cheek flattened against a terry-cloth pillow.

The boy was covered by a pale blue blanket, his eyes half-open, mouth drooling, and he was surrounded by beeping machinery and IV drips and tubes snaking into and out from under the blankets.

The room was cool and silent, other than the machinery sound, and smelled faintly of urine. There was a white line painted on the floor, with the words PLEASE DO NOT CROSS stenciled along it.

Merle stepped to the edge of the white line and stood looking down at the figure in the bed. The boy's age was hard to tell—maybe twelve or thirteen. He was blue-skinned, emaciated, breathing on his own, but barely, and, other than the rapid rising and falling of his rib cage under the blanket, as motionless as death.

Merle's heart, not a particularly loving one, went out to the kid, but he had business to conduct.

"Rainey," he said, softly but clearly. "Can you hear me?"

No change.

"Rainey, Glynis needs you to wake up now."

On the cardiac screen, the numbers began to climb. The kid's eyelids trembled but did not open.

Merle watched the cardiac monitor as the numbers ticked upwards, worried that any significant change might trigger a visit from whoever was monitoring the machinery, possibly a computer somewhere else entirely, but perhaps a human close enough to get here in a hurry.

He was pretty certain that he had the kid's attention, although how a kid in a coma could have a quality called "attention" was a mystery to Merle.

"You've been asleep, Rainey. Asleep long enough. You need to do something for Glynis, Rainey. Will you do a favor for Glynis Ruelle?"

The eyelids fluttered and the boy's lips began to work, and the small bony hand on the coverlet flexed convulsively. On the monitor, the cardiac rate had climbed to 136 and a red bar was flashing underneath the numbers.

"When you wake up, you have to ask the doctors and nurses for a man named Abel Teague. Can you remember that name? The name is *Abel Teague*. He lives in Sallytown. Glynis Ruelle needs to talk to him, Rainey. Will you tell the doctors that it's very important that Glynis Ruelle hears from Abel Teague very soon. Will you do that?"

The boy's eyes opened, and he stared into the darkness beside his bed, seeing nothing, hearing only a low soothing voice from the shadows, repeating the names *Glynis Ruelle* and *Abel Teague*.

The cardiac monitor over the bed was now showing a solid red band under the heart rate indicator and the machine was beeping loudly.

Merle watched the boy blinking into darkness, his cheeks twitching now, his twisted fingers jerking, and decided that he had delivered Glynis Ruelle's lunatic message, which, against all his solid expectations, seemed to have been heard.

He turned and stepped softly into the hallway, and walked quickly back towards the nursing station. Clara Mercer, the girl with the cool hazel eyes, was not there.

The station was empty. It seemed that the whole floor was deserted. The silence pressed in on him and he felt a strong desire to get back out into the light before he found out what sort of people were in all those darkened rooms along the hall. He slipped off the lab coat, hung it up, and turned to his right to go back up the main hall, past the amber sconces, moving quickly and silently past the shadowed beeping rooms, his skin crawling and his breathing short and sharp.

He got to the elevator bank, pressed the DOWN button, and the doors slipped open at once. There was a man inside the elevator, a tall dark-skinned man with long shiny black hair, in pleated gray slacks and a white shirt.

He had pale sea green eyes, a hard-nosed aggressive air that notched up as soon as he saw Merle in the light from the elevator.

"Who are *you*?" he asked, in a tight, wary tone.

"Who am I? Who the hell are *you*?" Merle barked back, his nerves on edge, his temper short.

The man stared at him for a long moment, as if trying to memorize his face, and then he slipped past Merle, turned, and stood in the hall watching as Merle got into the elevator, holding the door open with his left hand, his right hand shoved into his pocket.

"My name is Lemon Featherlight," said the man. "What

are you doing here? Who are you? Why did you come here? What did you want here?"

"My name is Merle Zane," Merle said, "and I came to see a friend." He hit the button for the first floor.

The doors started to close, but Featherlight caught the slider and blocked it.

"Who sent you?"

"Glynis Ruelle sent me, Mr. Featherlight," said Merle, on a whim, just to raise the devil with the guy. "You have a nice day."

He reached out and jerked the slider free, and he was still grinning at his joke as the doors closed. The man was staring back, his eyes wide and full of strong emotion. Thinking about it later, as he made his way back to the station to wait for the Blue Bird, Merle decided that he had damn near scared the guy to death, which was just fine with him. It was about time he started making things happen in Niceville, because up until now Niceville had pretty much kicked his ass.

Nick and Beau Open a Door

"What the hell am I looking at, boss? Is it like a home theater or something?"

Nick said nothing for a time, standing beside Beau Norlett in the pitch-black basement of Delia Cotton's mansion, at the bottom of the rickety staircase that led down from the kitchen.

Both men were watching a wall of moving light on the far side of the basement, a field of flickering, dancing images in bright greens and deep yellows, pure blues and vivid browns, almost like a movie of an Impressionist painting being shown on a screen, a shimmering field of motion and light that covered the entire wall, a stretch of thirty, maybe forty feet, and about seven feet high.

Both men stared at it in stunned silence, each man feeling a cold crawling ripple on the back of his neck, and a kind of pagan dread.

"I . . . don't know," said Nick, stepping off the last stair and walking out into the dark room. "It sure as hell isn't like any home theater I've ever seen."

The glow from the field of light was strong enough, once his eyes adjusted, for Nick to make out a gigantic old furnace, like a huge squid squatting at the far end of the basement, and a row of storage boxes piled along the wall opposite the field of dancing light. Heavy rough-cut beams ran overhead and the floor was concrete, very clean, no dust, a dry well-kept space, as carefully tended as the rest of the house.

Behind him he heard Beau fumbling around, muttering to himself.

"What are you doing?" said Nick, speaking in a whisper, as if he were afraid to attract the attention of whatever this light-thing really was.

"I'm looking for a light switch," said Beau, also in a whisper.

"No. Don't touch anything. Stay where you are."

"What are you going to do?"

"I don't know," said Nick, moving farther out into the room, staring at the flickering on the basement wall. Bright green bands across the top, swatches and blobs of vivid color here and there, a band of cool sky blue along the bottom . . . cool sky blue?

"Beau, have you got a camera on your cell phone?"

"Yeah," said Beau. "You want me to take a picture of . . . it?"

"Yes. No flash. Can you do that?"

"Just a minute . . . yeah . . . okay."

Nick heard the phony metallic snap sound that cell phone cameras had to make now because of all the locker room perverts who bought cell phones with cameras, and then a rapid series of them—*snickety-snickety-snickety-snick*.

"I can take a video too, you want?"

"Yes. Start now."

"Okay . . . but, boss, please, don't go near it."

"I'm not. I'm just—there's something weird."

"No shit," said Beau, watching through his LCD screen as Nick stepped into the middle of the room, facing the wall of light, his body lit up by the glow, Nick staring at it, fixed and frozen.

He was trying make sense of it when something tripped in

his brain, a visual gestalt, and the puzzle got solved. The color field was *upside down*.

He bent sideways, trying to see it that way, and suddenly he was looking at a tree line, blurry but clear enough, a broad canopy of oaks and chestnuts and a few dark spear points that could be pines or cedars, and, below the tree line, a large tilled field, with people working in it, a brown tractor pulling a flat sled loaded high with what looked like white stones, round as balls.

More dark figures of men, some digging in the black earth, others lifting what looked like long black boxes out of the ground, still others in a ragged line, watching the work.

He tried to get the image to focus, straining his eyes, stepped forward—

"Nick, honest, don't touch it."

"I'm just going to—"

He heard a sound, a low hissing growl that sent a chilly ripple up the back of his neck. At that moment, the field of light flickered, jumped, and changed. Instead of a tree line and a farm field, and workers digging at trenches of some kind, the scene had changed completely, and now he was looking at an upside-down image of a row of slate roofs, big old houses, spreading live oaks with drooping strands of Spanish moss, rolling lawns, and closer in, a wrought-iron fence, a gate, a red and black Jeep with a dark figure beside it—

Nick turned his back on the light wall, and walked across the basement towards a blacker patch high up on the far wall. As he walked, his shadow grew larger on the image, until it blotted it out completely. Nick held his hand up and saw, on his flat palm, a small disk of shimmering light.

He moved his palm forward toward the dark patch until the disk shrank to the size of a quarter.

Now the basement behind him was in total darkness. He looked at the dark patch and saw a tiny circle of light in the middle of it.

He reached out, felt some kind of heavy cloth, and in the middle of the cloth, a small hole, perhaps a rip, about an inch in diameter.

He stepped back, shaking his head, and started to laugh.

"What is it?" asked Beau, as Nick's black shadow receded and some of the color field came back on the wall. Nick reached up and tugged the shade open, and the image on the wall disappeared in a wash of bright sunlight streaming in through a basement window.

Then he drew the shade closed again, and the glowing image on the far wall reappeared, although, Nick realized, not at all like the image he had first seen, that strange unreal scene of a green tree line, and workers in a farm field, a tractor towing a sled of small pale round objects that could have been white stones.

Or skulls, the thought came, but he said nothing. Instead he looked at Beau.

"Ever hear of a camera obscura, Beau?"

"Yeah, I think so. Isn't it like a pinhole camera? We studied them in school, made 'em out of shoe boxes."

"Yeah. That's what this room is right now."

He turned, pointing to the field of light.

"I guess the light's about right for this effect. There's a small hole in this black shade here. When it's closed, the sun comes in through the hole in a narrow beam, just like in a pinhole camera. What you're looking at there is an upside-down picture of the street out front. There's the Armed Response Jeep, that figure is Dale Jonquil standing next to it, those are the gates, the fence, and the houses and the lawns across the street."

Beau stared at it, frowning, and then got it, in that abrupt and startling way that an optical illusion will suddenly reveal itself. He stepped up to the wall, reached out, and felt cold stone under his fingertips.

"Damn, Nick. Scared the living—"

"Me too. First time I ever saw something like this, I was a kid, helping some friends move. We rented a stake truck, with a tarp over it. There was no room in the cab so I rode in the back, under the tarp. I had my back up against the side boards—it was pitch dark—and I realized that there was something flickering on the far side of the truck. There was a small hole in one of the boards, and the daylight was coming through it. Took me a minute or two to figure out I was look-ing at an image of the streets and cars going by, only upside down. A camera obscura. That's what this room is."

"You figure Miss Cotton set it up like this?"

"Don't know. Looks like it was just some sort of freaky accident . . ." he said, his voice trailing off as he tried to deal with the effect that first image had had on him, the image of the farmer's field and the people working in the earth, the image that had abruptly changed into a reflection of the street outside Delia Cotton's mansion.

A ghostly farm, strange twisted trees in a weird golden light, human skulls heaped on a cart, workers—or slaves—digging up . . . digging up what?

Coffins?

"Beau, did you get this on the camera?"

"I think so," said Beau, reaching out, finding a switch, and turning the light on, a large electric bulb hanging from a wire in the middle of the basement. The dark shadows leaped away into the corners and the image on the wall faded into a faint suggestion of colored motion.

The light also showed something underneath the octopus furnace, in the shadows of it, a dark rounded mass.

Beau went over to it, kneeling down to peer under the old tin ductworks. The dark mass receded, almost as if it were liq-uid, pulling itself back deeper into the shadows, but in com-plete silence.

Beau recoiled, sat back on his heels.

"I do not like this house, Nick. I truly do not. Now I know what the jimjams are. What the hell is that thing?"

"I don't know," said Nick, leaning down to look under the pipe, his heart blipping. Beau wasn't the only cop here with the jimjams.

"It's alive, whatever it is," said Beau. "Now I can hear something hissing. How about I just shoot it?"

"You can't just shoot things, Beau. Tig wouldn't like it. He'd make you pay for the bullet. How about you just get down there and go on in and see what it is?"

Beau gave him a look, pushed himself to his feet, stepped back, smiled broadly, and waved Nick on through with a graceful veronica.

"Sir, according to the manual, this is where a highly skilled senior officer is supposed to show the dumb-ass rookie how these things are done."

"According to the manual?"

"Oh yes sir. It surely is. Just like on *NCIS*."

Nick looked sideways at him, sighed, and stepped forward, going down on one knee, leaning over to peer into the darkness.

Whatever was in there, it didn't like that and the low hissing turned into a long, throaty snarl that made all his favorite body parts go tingly and cold. He looked up at Beau.

"We got any gloves in the car?"

"Just those latex jobs," said Beau.

"See if there's any gardening gloves around."

"What is it?" asked Beau, backing away, afraid he was going to miss something interesting.

"Just find some," said Nick, settling back into a crouch, breathing through his mouth and trying to calm down, listening to Beau ramble up the wooden staircase and make the floorboards creak as he walked down the front hall.

Alone in the basement—well, not entirely alone—Nick could feel the big house settling down on him, a great dead weight trying to crush him into the concrete.

He had no idea what had happened to Delia Cotton, but something had definitely happened to her house. The whole place was just . . .

Outside?

Lemon Featherlight's phrase came back, the way he had described whatever had happened to Rainey Teague, how the kid had somehow been . . . transported . . . to an ancient crypt.

Whatever it was, it came from . . . outside.

Nick shook himself, ran his hands through his hair. That was just horseshit. Somebody—somebody real—was screwing around with Niceville, and that was what guys like him were supposed to stop.

He heard the floorboards creaking, Beau coming across the main floor and down the basement stairs. Whatever was under the furnace hissed again, and recoiled farther into the shadows.

"I got these," said Beau, handing him a pair of long, heavy cotton gardening gloves. "And these," he said, holding up a shovel and a rough gray blanket.

Nick slipped the gloves on, tugged his shirtsleeves down, got down on his knees, and crawled under the pipe, tensed, and made a sudden snapping lunge.

He got a fistful of thick fur—felt his glove and his forearm getting raked—the thing hissing and snarling deep down in its throat. Incredibly strong, it writhed under his hand and sank its teeth into the glove—Nick could feel the pinpricks of its fangs just touching his skin. He came back out, holding a large Maine Coon cat by the scruff of its neck.

He grabbed the hind legs with his other hand, struggling to keep a grip on the thing. The cat's eyes were wild and dilated, ears flat back, ruff flared up, tail lashing, lips snarling back and fangs exposed to the gum line, a crazy green light in its irises. It was trying to use its hind-leg claws to rip the flesh off Nick's forearm.

Beau threw the blanket around it and they finally managed to wrap the big cat up tightly inside it, with only its head sticking out, the cat fighting with everything it had, hissing and snarling at them, trying to bend its head around far enough to bite Nick's hand.

"Jeez," said Beau, looking at the cat. "What the hell's got into her?"

"This is Delia's cat," said Nick. "On the report. Mildred . . . something. Mildred Pierce."

Hearing the name, the cat seemed to settle down a bit, not enough for them to let it out of the blanket, but at least it had stopped trying to shred them into human confetti.

Nick could feel the animal trembling under his hands, and the heat coming off her radiated through the blanket.

He generally liked cats better than dogs, and now he held her in close to his chest. She was thrumming like a bowstring as they went back up the stairs and into the kitchen area, Beau keeping a wary eye on the cat, holding the shovel like a baseball bat.

"Put the shovel away," said Nick. "We're not going to brain a goddam house cat, are we?"

"She gets away from you, I am. She's as big as a lynx. Look at her eyes. That cat's insane."

Nick looked at the cat, and the cat, going suddenly still, glared back at him, a fixed lidless stare, and Nick had the momentary illusion that a cold but intelligent entity was looking at him. The feeling passed, and it was just a cat.

"Jesus," said Nick, lifting it up. "What have you seen, cat? What the hell have you seen?"

"We're interviewing a cat?" said Beau.

"She's the only witness we have," Nick answered. "I think she's got some blood on her fur. Let's start by seeing whose blood it is."

Bock Gets More Consequences
Than He Can Handle

Bock had been one of the few people in Niceville, other than Byron Deitz, who had gone about his Saturday chores blissfully unaware of the hostage situation unfolding at Peachtree and Gwinnett.

Once committed to a course of action, no matter how swinish, Bock possessed a work ethic second to none. After firing off three copies of the Kevin David Dennison e-mail to the church, the local newspapers, and Live Eye Seven quite early in the day, he had spent the rest of his Saturday morning diligently at work on the Littlebasket file, hunting for, locating, and then downloading the most sexually graphic, or simply graphically humiliating, of the hidden-camera shots Morgan Littlebasket had taken of his daughters, Twyla and Bluebell, as they flowered into womanhood.

The selection had required some close concentration—how to choose for maximum pain and humiliation—but he finally got the job done around two, listening with half a mind to NPR on Sirius Satellite Radio, a rebroadcast of Garrison Keillor's *Prairie Home Companion*—"The Joke Show," as it happened, one of his all-time favorites.

He'd have had a different morning if he'd been tuned to Fox, but he wasn't.

After Bock finished up the Littlebasket project—another difficult job well done—he used a hush-mail IP in Iceland to forward what he had titled *The Greatest Tits of the Littlebasket Girls* to the one person in Niceville who would get the biggest jolt out of them. Then he sat back with that *Tonto, our work here is done* feeling people get after a difficult job. He poured himself a celebratory Stella and used his remote to fire up his immense Sony Bravia flat screen.

Thirty seconds later, he was on his feet with his heart in his throat and Stella all over him. Bock stood there, riveted, transfixed, and, once he had confirmed that the hostage-taker at Saint Innocent Orthodox was in fact a Kevin David Dennison, a custodian at the church, for a short time wonderfully exhilarated by the adrenaline rush of raw power he was feeling, the godlike ability to hurt, anonymously, and from a safe distance.

And then, gradually, as he considered the event more carefully, not so much.

Although vicious, Bock was far from stupid, and as he absorbed the scope and severity of the incident playing out on his screen, his exhilaration ebbed away, eventually leaving him with yet another case of the crawling dreads.

What had he kicked off, and what would be the repercussions, if the e-mails he had sent out, the tips that were the root cause of this confrontation, were traced back to his personal computer?

The phrase *reckless endangerment* along with graphic visions of a tiny prison cell shared with toothless throwbacks from that *Deliverance* film came bubbling up from his lizard brain.

He gave some thought—fleeting, rueful—to an attempt to retrieve the *Greatest Tits* file he had sent off only a short while ago, but gave it up as hopeless. Once sent, as others have learned to their sorrow, e-mails were as irretrievable as the snows of yesteryear, although they tended to last a hell of a lot longer.

During this unhappy period, he had gotten up and hustled his naked butt into the bathroom, showered, and shaved and, in a way, tried to stiffen himself for sirens in the distance and squad cars filling up Mrs. Kinnear's driveway and police bull-horns telling him to come out with his hands up.

He even dressed in his best clothes—the same sober busi-ness suit he had worn to the custody hearing—how long ago?

God, less than twenty-four hours.

At any rate, he put it on again, along with a clean white shirt and his best black lace-ups. If he was about to get cuffed and perp-walked, he wanted to look as good as possible while it was happening. One never got a second chance to make a first impression.

He also checked his bank account—online—to make sure he had enough ready money to make bail and he also got his lawyer's business card off the dresser—Ms. Evangeline Bar-row, Attorney-at-Law.

Barrow wasn't a criminal lawyer, but she knew her way around the courthouse, and maybe she'd be able to keep Judge Theodore W. Monroe from hanging Bock out to twist in the wind while crows plucked his eyes out like fat green grapes.

With that lurid image in his head, he spent another few minutes setting up a shredding program to begin the compli-cated work of erasing every conceivable digital trace of any-thing incriminating from his hard drive, a slow, exacting, but thankfully automatic process that would nevertheless take sev-eral hours to complete.

Then he pulled himself together—with an effort—and turned his attention back to the television—he was recording the thing on his TiVo—just as a dark green Crown Victoria pulled up to the squad car tangle in front of the church and a tall broad-shouldered silver-haired man in a dark gray suit got slowly out, his angular face set and cold-looking.

This guy, in civilian clothes but obviously a senior cop of some kind, was met by the large red-haired female cop, Staff Sergeant Mavis Crossfire, the NPD cop in charge, according to the news broad, and by the State Police guy, a lean blond cop in a crisp gray and black uniform, identified as Captain James Candles. The man from the green Crown Vic was not identified, but he stood out even in that elite company, an impressive-looking Clint Eastwood type with hard eyes and seamed leathery skin who moved well and radiated a kind of quiet menace, at least to Bock, who was very sensitive to menace wherever he encountered it, which was almost everywhere he went. The news pixie was speculating on who this guy might be when the cop walked around to the trunk, popped it, and extracted what was unmistakably a rifle case, which caused Bock's throat to close up and his knees to go weak.

Holy Shit.

They were ready to kill the guy.

Holy Leaping Jesus.

And they were letting the weapon be seen on camera, sending a clear signal to the citizens and specifically to Kevin David Dennison inside the rectory office that things were being kicked up a level. Bock had already heard that the record on the guy wasn't accurate—horseshit, by the way, Bock did not make mistakes about data—and they were hinting that maybe there was some doubt about just how guilty this Kevin David Dennison guy really was. But apparently that wasn't going to stop them from blowing his brains out on national television.

And if *that* happened, if they did that, the root cause of this guy's death—along with the deaths of anybody else who might get whacked this afternoon—the root cause of it all would be . . .

Tony Bock, that's who.

Jesus Christ, he was thinking, sitting down on the couch and staring at the screen, *what the hell have I gotten myself into?*

This cop standoff was serious shit.

Even if nobody got killed, those cops down there in the street, maybe even that silver-haired movie-star assassin in the dark gray suit, they were all going to come looking for the busy little asshole who started all this.

And that busy little asshole was sitting right here, on his big leather sofa, staring at them from the other side of his flat-screen Sony.

Bock flopped backwards into the couch, heart hammering, cold fear rippling up and down his belly and chest—he had a terrific aptitude for dread—his agile rodent mind darting about the basement floor of his life looking for some rat hole to duck into. It was at this unpleasant juncture that his phone rang. He leaned down to stare at the call display, which read: SECURICOM TECHSERVE.

Okay.

Not good.

But not the cops.

Bock reached out, picked up the receiver, swallowed hard, and said, "Bock here."

"Mr. Christian Bock?"

A mild meek voice, definitely not a cop voice. Some cubicle-rat for a telemarketing firm.

Bock reached down deep for intimidating syntax.

"Yes. Whom is this to whom I am speaking?"

"My name is Andy Chu. Have you got a moment?"

"I don't know an Andy Chu. What's this about?"

"I'm the IT tech here at Securicom, Mr. Bock. I can hear your television set in the background. Are you by any chance watching the coverage of the hostage-taking at Saint Innocent?"

"Yes. I am. Everyone is. So what?"

On the screen, something was happening—the cops were all ducking behind their cars or racing for cover behind buildings. The news pixie was talking too fast into her mike, breathlessly squealing *Shots fired shots fired OMG.*

"My goodness," said Andy Chu, a placid voice with a hint of Asian in it. "Looks like things are going downhill pretty fast, doesn't it?"

"Look, whoever you are, what the hell do you want with me?" asked Bock, faking puzzled impatience, although his heart was telling him to brace himself for something deeply ugly.

Chu paused, and then, although in the mildest and most conciliatory of tones, he spoke the four words that will always strike mortal terror into the hearts of even the most stalwart men.

"We need to talk."

Coker Sorts the Wheat from the Chaff

Coker had taken a firing position five feet back from an open window inside a vacant apartment over a pizza parlor across Peachtree from the rectory of Saint Innocent Orthodox, with a good clear line of sight through the thin glass window of the rectory, where, beyond the partially closed venetian blinds, he could see the figure of a stout apple-faced middle-aged man with a bald head and tortoiseshell half-glasses perched on his flushed, sweaty face.

The man was wearing a dark green uniform with the name KEVIN stitched on the front right pocket. He was holding a black phone to his ear with his right hand and was waving a small stainless-steel pistol around in his left.

In the background, directly behind the man, Coker could see three people lined up on an overstuffed couch, a willowy-looking young man with his arms protectively wrapped around two little boys, all three of them literally bug-eyed with fright.

Coker was also aware of what they were sitting on—an overstuffed couch in bug-splatter orange with big blue flower blotches all over it; a classic seventies atrocity that Coker felt could only be improved by bloodstains and bits of human skull.

From where Coker was sitting, the young priest could just as easily have been using the kids as shields to hide behind, but then Coker was a suspicious sort of guy, although he did try to think well of civilians, even if they were gutless pencil-neck pastors with lousy taste in furniture.

Coker was sitting in a wooden chair, his suit jacket draped neatly over the back of it. He always wore a nice dark business suit with a shirt and a tie for this sort of thing, feeling that the serious nature of the work called for serious clothing.

He had his shirtsleeves rolled up and his elbows braced on top of a heavy dining room table that he had forced two grumpy Niceville cops to hump up the back stairs from the pizza parlor downstairs.

His right eye was hovering close to one end of the Leupold scope he had fitted to an SSG 550 semi-auto sniper rifle firing a 5.56 round, a Swiss-made jewel of a killing machine, with adjustable cheek-piece and shoulder-butt support, a two-stage trigger he had fine-tuned himself, a heavy hammer-forged barrel, a forward bipod, and an anti-reflective screen over the long barrel, so that heat rising off the barrel wouldn't cause air ripples in the scope image: all in all, a sniper's dream and a privilege to kill with.

Through the scope he could see the short round man pacing back and forth through his crosshairs, and in his ear he could hear the laconic talk going on between Mavis Crossfire, who had command of the scene, and Jimmy Candles, Coker's platoon mate.

Mavis and Jimmy were discussing the informal pool that had started up between the various cops attending regarding the likely outcome of this afternoon's festivities, with Mavis putting ten dollars into the guy getting his fontanel remodeled by a couple of HV rounds from Coker's SSG, and Jimmy Candles going for a disappointing but peaceful resolution of the thing, mainly on the grounds that word had come down from Tig Sutter that while the guy in the janitor's suit really was a convicted sex offender back in Baltimore, it was a lousy beef.

"Waddya mean a lousy beef?" said Nate Crone, one of Tig's CID guys. They were all sitting around the office watching the thing on the squad room television. "What about the cell phone cluster around the schoolyards and swing sets?"

"He's a *gym coach*," said Tig, grumpy, trying to watch the screen. "Part-time. He was coaching the parish soccer team."

"Horseshit, boss. He's dirty as my dick," said Nate, who was young enough to still think that all civilians were just degenerates who hadn't gotten up the balls to go do something unspeakable yet.

Tig sighed, thinking, *Okay, a teachable moment, as the president likes to say.*

"Nate, all of you. Listen and learn. This is why I didn't want to do anything before we got the Maryland report. It turned out the charge was based on some photos he had taken of his two-year-old daughter in her bath and then been stupid enough to take to a photo-mat, where a radical feminist clerk, caught up in that mid-eighties horseshit thing about Satanic child abuse, calls in the cops."

"Why's he taking nudie shots of his naked kid?"

"This was *then*, Nate. The eighties. Nobody does it now, because we're all scared shitless, and this kind of crap is exactly why. The Baltimore ADA, another feminist crusader, bulls the case through, getting a conviction in spite of the appeals of the guy's wife and his employer. So he does six months, getting beaten up and butt-fu . . . getting sexually assaulted every other day by actual sex offenders."

"Good. Pedophile creep. Hope he gets some more of it when he gets back there."

"Nate, button it. Anyway, he finally gets early release. Since he wasn't actually a *real* sex offender, he found it pretty easy not to assault his children over the next twenty years. He raises two kids, loses his wife last year, goes on being a solid citizen right up to today, and by the way, both of his kids are being flown in right now from Baltimore to beg the guy to give himself up."

"Then why's he waving a gun around at two kids and a pastor?" said Nate, unwilling to surrender the warm glow of his self-righteous preening.

"I think I just explained that. Guy's been through a lot, now here it's all happening again. Thanks to one sleazebag snitch with a grudge against him. He just . . . lost it. It happens."

"Screw him," said Nate, whom Tig was beginning to actively dislike. "Coker should just drill him and end it."

"Nate, no offense, but you're actually kind of an asshole," Tig said, more in sorrow than in anger, giving up on Nate and going back to the television, where it looked like things were coming to some sort of crisis point.

Coker's earpiece popped and cracked—he heard a sound like a small firecracker from across the street—all the cops down in the street flinched—and then he was hearing the voice of Jimmy Candles in his earpiece, his official voice, now speaking for the record.

"Coker, Little Rock thinks we can't let this run on. He's not cooperating at all, he's just fired a warning shot into the ceiling, the kids are going nuts, the priest just peed himself, and the guy's getting freakier every second."

"If you want him, Jimmy," said Coker, in a flat, businesslike tone, looking through the scope at the target, and then looking harder. "I got him. Anytime. But maybe you want to put a pair of binoculars on that Llama .32 he's waving around, before you green-light this thing."

"Just a minute," said Jimmy, clicking off. Coker looked

away from the scope and watched as Jimmy Candles, the tall blond guy in the black fatigues standing in the middle of the platoon ring, raised a pair of binoculars to his eyes and stood there for a while, focused, silent.

Coker went back to his scope and steadied his crosshairs on the janitor's left hand, which was not being waved around so much while the guy was on the phone to the negotiator.

The small steel pistol, a semi-auto with a slide on the left-hand side of the frame, had a small brass tube sticking straight up from the ejector slot. Coker spent some time making sure of that brass tube, and then he watched the janitor talking on the phone.

He had studied the backstop and come to the tactical conclusion that even through the glass of the office window he could still put a nice neat hole in the guy's temple without hitting the folks on that butt-ugly couch.

Then he went back and made sure of the brass casing sticking up out of the ejector slot, sighed, and waited. Jimmy Candles was back in a minute.

"Am I seeing a stovepipe round, Coker?"

"That's what I'm seeing. Little piece like that, you don't hold it steady when you fire it, the slide won't come back far enough, and the spent casing gets jammed right there, sticking up out of the ejector slot."

"Does he look like he sees it?"

"No," said Coker, after checking. "He's busy with the phone. But that ain't going to last."

Coker heard a muttered side-talk conference over the headset, muted and muffled by Jimmy Candles' hand. Then he was back.

"Hold on, will you?"

"I'm here. But hurry up. I got to piss."

A silence, and then Mavis Crossfire came on.

"Coker, you sure about this?"

"I'm sure it's a stovepipe jam, Mavis."

"He doesn't come across like a guy knows weapons. How long you figure it would take an amateur to clear that jammed casing, rack a round, and fire at somebody coming in through the door?"

"Jeez, Mavis. Where are you? I can't see you. I can hardly hear you."

A silence, then a whispered reply.

"We're right outside the office door. In the hallway. We got a ram with us."

Coker really liked Mavis Crossfire.

Everybody did.

She was a stand-up and a cop's cop. He'd rather see that moron janitor get his ticket punched than have anything happen to Mavis Crossfire.

He leaned into the scope, zeroed the crosshairs on the guy's temple, slipped his finger inside the trigger guard, eased the blade back a hair . . . another faint tick he could feel in his finger . . . as the sniper he had the right to make a judgment shot . . . he could do it now . . . tick . . . tick . . .

Shit.

He pulled his finger out, softened a bit.

"Okay, how about this? I keep the scope on him, we count down from five, you take the door, come in fast but keep out of my line of fire. I want to have a clear head shot if he manages to un-jam that thing. You know where I am?"

"We do," she said, a faint whisper now. "You're across the street, the second floor, the open window above Perky's Pizza Palace."

"Okay. We're going to do this? You sure?"

"Long as you're right about that stovepipe. 'Cause if you're wrong and I get killed, my ghost is going to come haunt your belfry."

"I don't have a belfry. You'll have to haunt my garage. You ready?"

In his mind Coker could see them, out in the hall, looking at each other, doing a gut check.

"Okay. We're ready."

"Okay. Here goes, Mavis. Countdown. Start. Five . . . four . . . three. . ."

He put his eye to the scope, settled into calm, finger on the trigger, let out a slow breath . . .

"Two . . . one . . ."

Kate Puts Dad on the Hook

On his way to the lab with Delia's cat, Nick got on the phone to Kate, catching her on her way back to the house.

"Kate, where are you?"

"Almost home. Where are you?"

"On the way to the crime lab with a cranky bloodstained house cat that's gotta weigh in at fifty pounds."

"So just another day at the office, then?"

Nick laughed, but there was still something odd in his voice, and she could hear it.

"You okay, babe?"

Nick was going to tell her *yes*, but then he thought, what the hell. She wouldn't have asked if she hadn't heard very clearly in his voice that he was far from okay.

Beau was staring at him sideways, obviously still shaken and upset by what he had seen in Nick's face at Delia's house in The Chase.

Nick figured Beau was seeing the first hairline crack in his idol. Good. Beau needed to be his own man, not somebody else's sidekick.

Kate was still waiting for an answer.

So Nick gave her the basics, telling it without any editorial spin, or any attempt to play it down. She asked a couple of good questions but mainly she just took it in.

The fact that Beau had been through it too made the whole thing easier to tell, and now, as Nick came to the end of the story, they were both hanging on Kate's answer, as if she could make some sense out of it, maybe because she was a woman.

"The black figure you saw in the glass—?"

Nick's chest closed up.

She was going right for the heart of it.

"That sounds like something you might have seen in the Middle East, doesn't it?"

"Yes," said Nick, staring out at the traffic, very aware of Beau in the seat beside him, holding the cat as if she were about to bite him. For her part, the cat seemed pretty calm. She had curled up in Beau's lap and gone straight to sleep.

"I mean, women in burkas, that's what they look like, just shapes in black. So it makes sense that you might interpret a black reflection that way."

"True," said Nick, hoping she'd leave it there.

"But you think there's more, don't you?"

"Like what?"

"From the sound of your voice, I'd say you think the house itself was to blame. That the house was making you see things from your past, things that upset you."

Nick was quiet for a time.

"Yeah. That's what it felt like."

"Is there anything about a figure in a burka that would upset you?"

Silence.

"Yes. There is."

The Wadi Doan, a leafy little gorge carved out of the horny brown hide of central Yemen, a chain of villages as old as the world. Three figures in head-to-toe burkas, walking all wrong, shoes all wrong, stumbling on the stones, eyes fixed on the middle distance, heedless staring robots, coming closer and closer to their idling Humvee.

Exactly the profile of suicide bombers.

The Wadi Doan.

"I'm not going to ask you about it—"

"Thanks, Kate. Just the war, I guess. We used to call them BMOs. Black Moving Objects."

This unknown thing that had happened back in the war, it was still the one unsayable thing between them. Maybe someday Nick would talk about it. Tig had said so himself, when she was plying him with multiple mojitos at the Moot Court bar.

She doubted it, and it was true that part of her didn't really want to know about it in the first place.

"But this BMO thing, it does explain how a reflection like that would get to you, especially if you're all keyed up, looking for a missing woman. Did Beau see anything?"

Nick looked over at Beau, asked him the question. Beau shook his head.

"No. Not Beau. Just me. Mavis Crossfire said she saw something; but she wouldn't say what. And there was a guard there, Dale Jonquil; he said he saw a young woman in a green dress, holding a cat."

That shook Kate.

She remembered her dream, the young woman in a green dress. Holding a cat.

So did Nick.

"Didn't you have a dream last night about a girl in a green dress and a cat?"

She hesitated.

There was no point in saying no.

"Yes. I did."

"Okay. Now *that's* a tad freaky, isn't it?"

"Yes. It is. Did the guard, this Dale Jonquil guy, did he see the cat you have with you?"

"Yes. We showed it to him on the way out. It's the same

one he saw in the mirror. But then he knew the cat from before. Her name is Mildred Pierce. She's Delia's cat, and Dale works security in her neighborhood, so that makes sense. But he doesn't like Delia's house much either."

He glanced across at Beau, checking him out, seeing the expression on his face.

"Neither does Beau."

"Did Beau see a girl with a cat?"

"You see a girl with a cat?"

Beau shook his head.

"No."

"But he did see the image on the basement wall. Did you try to take a picture of it?"

"Yes. Beau took some shots with his cell phone camera."

"Did he get anything?"

"Yeah. A short video."

"Can you make anything out of it?"

"We haven't tried yet. Beau's going to transfer it to a computer and pull off an mpeg."

"But you both saw it?"

"Yeah. Both of us."

"What did you see?"

Nick hesitated.

People working in a field.

Coffins.

Skulls.

"The picture shifted. First a farm, and then it turned into the street outside the Cotton place."

"I'd love to see it."

"I'll get a copy and bring it home."

Silence.

"Kate, I have to say, that house is . . ."

"Weird?"

"No. More like insane."

They were at the lab.

"We're here, Kate. Gotta go. Love you."

"Love you too, babe."

She was turning into her driveway, into the home her father and mother had lived in for thirty years.

Dillon and Lenore.

Niceville.

She climbed out of the SUV, remembering to take her Glock out of the glove box. The house was warm and musty, and the clouds were breaking up. The house was dim but pierced everywhere with afternoon light shining in through the tall sash windows.

She thought about Nick's experiences at Delia's mansion in The Chase for a while, looked at the clock. It was the middle of the afternoon, a Saturday. Her dad would be in his office at the library, watching the cadets drill on the VMI parade square. She picked up the phone—held it in her hand, listening to the dial tone—and put it back down again.

Getting Dillon Walker to give her a straight answer to anything about the Niceville abductions had been like chasing fireflies. Ever since Rainey had been found, her dad would happily talk to her about anything at all—football, politics, the military, chocolate chip cookies, Beth's marriage, Nick's war fever, why red wine drinkers live longer. Anything at all, except the Niceville disappearances.

Even the news that Sylvia had disappeared, and that Rainey had been found—alive—sealed inside an ancient grave, hadn't been enough to shatter his reserve. He listened politely to the news, offered no comments, and wished the boy a speedy recovery.

Miles' suicide a few days later hadn't seemed to surprise

him at all. If anything, it had sealed the matter for him, as if a kind of blood debt had been paid. When Kate, as Sylvia's cousin, had been appointed Rainey's guardian, her father had approved of it, but in a distant and guarded way, limiting himself to what seemed at the time to be a cryptic comment about making sure Rainey's adoption papers were kept somewhere safe, just in case.

"In case of what?" she had asked at the time.

"In case they're . . . needed."

"Why would they be needed, Dad?"

"No idea. Just being a worrier, I guess."

She was in the sunroom, a glassed-in conservatory addition to the house. She sat there in the yellow and white room, surrounded by lush ferns and bougainvillea, looking out at the ancient pine forest that crowded the lower end of the lawn. A little stream ran through it, and a steep hill rose up on the far side of the forest, the rocky ground covered with red pine needles. Even with the afternoon light lying over it, the pine forest seemed to have a rich violet darkness inside it that looked deeper and more solid than simple shadows. Just like Niceville.

This had gone on long enough.

Clearly her father was keeping something from her. Knowing him as she did, Kate was sure he thought he was doing it for her own good.

Lovely man, Dillon Walker, but he could also be a condescending, stiff-necked . . .

She let it go.

She was a grown woman, and now the strangeness of Niceville seemed to be closing in on her own family. That was the point here. Rainey Teague was in a coma. Nick was seeing mirages on a basement wall. She was dreaming of green-eyed girls in sundresses. Delia Cotton and Gray Haggard were missing.

Something was terribly *wrong* in Niceville, and she was convinced her dad knew something about it. It was time to drag it out of him.

She pulled in a breath, held it, let it out slowly, sat up straight on the couch.

Reached for the phone.

Dialed the number.

It rang twice, and then she heard her father's whiskey baritone, his soft Virginia accent. She saw him at his desk at VMI, in his book-lined study, a fine-featured man with a weathered face, intelligent, calm, deep lines around his eyes.

"Kate, you're calling early."

She usually called him at the end of the day, a ritual as comforting to him as it was to her.

"Is this a bad time?"

"Never a bad time to hear from my favorite daughter."

"I thought Beth was your favorite daughter."

"She is when I'm talking to her. How are you?"

Kate went through the formalities, but her father knew her pretty well.

"Okay. Something's wrong, honey. I can hear it in your voice. What is it? Is it Beth?"

"If you mean is she still with Byron, yes, she is. For now."

"Nick and Reed should go talk to that man."

"Nick wants to. And it's all we can do to keep Reed from doing something so extreme about Byron that it would get him fired from the State Patrol. But Beth has to be ready. It's no good until she is. And she has the kids to think about, Dad."

"That's exactly why she should leave that thug. Nick agrees with me. He said so last week."

"It's Beth who has to agree, Dad. Not you and Nick and Reed. This can't just get decided by the menfolk."

This was a sensitive topic, and one they had been over

many times before. Her father was picking up the tightness in her voice now.

"So Beth isn't why you called early?"

"No, Dad."

"Well, something's on your mind. Let's hear it."

She took a moment to get her thoughts in line. When she got right down to the essentials, she found that the question was actually pretty simple.

"Dad, what's wrong with Niceville?"

A long silence.

"Niceville's a Southern town, honey. The Old South. It's haunted by history, Kate. That's all."

"Dad. I love you. You know that. But things are happening here right now, and I need you to be straight with me. For once."

She heard him breathing.

She could almost hear him thinking too.

Looking for an exit.

"For once? That's a little harsh."

"I'm sorry, Dad. You know what I'm talking about. Niceville. The families. Why it is the way it is."

"I see."

"Do you?"

Resignation was in his answer.

"Yes, Kate. I do. You said things have been happening. What kind of things?"

She told him.

He listened without interruption.

Kate laid it out as clearly and as simply as she could, leaving out details that she felt were . . . unreliable . . . such as her dream about a girl with a cat. When she finished, he was quiet again. She waited him out.

"So Gray Haggard's gone?"

"No trace of him."

Her father was quiet for a long time.

"Kate," he said finally, his voice weary and full of sadness, "I'm going to tell you something that you can never tell your brother and sister. Do you think you can do that?"

"I . . . yes, I can do that. If that's what you want."

"You know Reed thinks your mother died because of a drunk driver."

Kate took that in.

"She *didn't*?"

"I don't know. Maybe a drunk driver had something to do with it. But I do know she was speeding, speeding dangerously, when she died."

"I heard about that. The OnStar system?"

"Yes. It's a GPS system too. OnStar has computers that can tell an investigator how fast a car was going at the moment of a crash. By the speed at which the car moved from one point to another. Are you certain this is something you want to get into, Kate? Once you hear it, you may wish you hadn't."

"Okay, Dad. I can take it."

A pause.

"Your mother was doing in excess of a hundred and forty-five miles an hour when the OnStar system registered her rollover. Now this is something you're not going to like to hear, honey."

"Dad. Please."

"When a vehicle is being driven in excess of the speed limit by that much, sometimes the OnStar operator picks up on it. Sometimes the operator will place a call to the vehicle, to see if something is wrong with the driver. Or even the vehicle, perhaps a gas pedal malfunction. Or is she drunk, or having an attack, or has she been hijacked. That sort of thing. When your mother's car got to a hundred and forty, a minute or so before the accident, the OnStar lady tried to contact Lenore. She opened the cell connection."

Kate had never heard a breath of this story.

"Did Mom answer?"

"Yes."

"What did she say?"

Dillon was quiet for so long she thought she had lost him.

"Lenore said, *She uses the mirrors.* She said it several times, in a panicky voice."

Kate tried to make sense of it, failed.

"*She uses the mirrors?* What does that mean?"

"I've thought about that ever since she died. The only conclusion that I was able to come up with was that your mom was having some kind of stroke, that she was seeing things in the car mirror, and that whatever she was seeing was terrifying her."

"You mean, she was speeding to get *away* from something she saw in her rearview mirror? That's crazy, Dad. Crazy. That state trooper, Charlie Danziger, he was with her when she died. He never said anything about this to us."

"He did to me."

"He did?"

"Yes. At the funeral. In the garden. She was still talking like that when she died. Charlie Danziger stayed with her, held on to her, right to the end. She literally died in his arms. He thought I should know what she was saying, at the end."

"Did it mean anything to you? What she said?"

"Not a thing—at the time. But it was disturbing. That's why I let the drunk driver story stand, at least for Reed and Beth."

"For me too, Dad," she said.

"I know. That was why I wanted you to stay away from the mirror that was in Uncle Moochie's window. You still have it, don't you?"

"Yes," she said, after a moment. "It's still upstairs, in the closet."

"Why didn't you get rid of it? Give it back to the cleaning lady, or to Moochie, or to Delia?"

"Nobody wanted it. After the story got out about Rainey, we couldn't give it away."

"Then you should break it. Smash it."

"Dad . . . I don't get this. Any of it. Why did you stop working on what was going on in Niceville?"

"I stopped because your mother died."

"That's *when* you stopped. Was it *why* you stopped?"

It took a time for him to answer.

"In a way. I think I got the idea what I was doing was . . . unlucky."

"For whom?"

"For us. The Walkers. And for the rest of the families."

Her father always used that phrase when he was talking about the Founding Four, the Walkers and the Cottons, the Teagues and the Haggards.

The families.

As if they were all drifting down the river of time together, trapped on the same unlucky boat.

"How could it be unlucky? You were just looking things up in the archives. Who would care?"

"Because I found something in the archives. It troubled me. When your mother was killed, I began to worry that maybe what had happened to her was . . . part of it. Part of the disappearance question."

"What did you find out?"

"I found out something that seems to link all those disappearances over the years. The thing they might all have in common."

"And what is that?"

"It's possible that every person who disappeared was related in one way or another to the families."

Kate took that in, and then rejected it.

"That's absurd. Are you talking about, what, like a family curse? That's simply nuts, Dad."

"Not a curse, no. But the linkage appears, and it's the only connecting factor I could ever develop. Everyone who went missing was connected in some way to the same four families."

"Dad, you could almost say that everybody in Niceville fits that description."

"I took that into account. The correlation was still strong, higher than any statistical glitch. As a matter of fact, there was an even narrower connection. Everyone who had disappeared had, in one way or another, been related in some way to people who knew a young woman named Clara Mercer."

"Clara Mercer? I . . . do I know that name? I seem to remember something . . . she killed herself? Went into Crater Sink?"

"Nobody knows exactly what happened to her. She was a distant relative of ours. A pretty wild girl. Back before the Great War, while still very young, she had an affair with one of the Teagues. She got pregnant by him."

"Oh dear. Back in those days . . ."

"Yes. It amounted to ruin, an unmarried girl."

"What happened to the baby?"

A pause here.

"Clara was sent away for a while. In 1913, or thereabouts. To a private clinic in Sallytown. When she came back, there was no child with her. The story was that she lost the child in a miscarriage. That was where it was left."

"Do you know the man who did this to her?"

"Abel Teague. He was what they used to call a rake. He wouldn't marry her, in spite of being confronted by several of her male friends. Somehow, by some device, he avoided several duels. Nobody seems to know quite how he did that."

"What happened to Clara?"

"In effect, as far as I could determine, when she came home after being . . . sent away . . . she had what they used to call a nervous breakdown. Her family tried to care for her—"

"Who was her family?"

"Her older sister, Glynis—"

"*Glynis?*"

"Yes, that was her name. Why?"

"You *know* why, Dad. I told you last year that someone named Glynis R. signed her name to a card glued to the back of the mirror. It would have to be the same woman, wouldn't it?"

A pause.

"Yes. I believe it is. I thought so at the time. Glynis Mercer had married into the Ruelle family. The Ruelles had extensive plantations south of Gracie. They took Clara in and did what they could. But then the local do-gooders stepped in. Somebody somewhere made a determination that she was a danger to herself and others. The records aren't clear, because of that fire in '35, but I got the impression that some medical officials came and forcibly removed her from the Ruelles and locked her up in that asylum in Gracie."

"Good God. Not Candleford House?"

"Yes. I'm afraid so."

"Dear God. Poor thing. How long did she last?"

"Nobody knows. According to the records, what bits are left, I was able to work out that something serious happened in 1931. She was on a medical trip to Niceville, with an escort. She needed some sort of surgery. They took her to Lady Grace and she underwent some kind of procedure—from what I can figure out, it was very likely an abortion."

"Resulting from a rape?"

"Probably. The guards at Candleford House were utterly corrupt. Little better than animals. No, worse. At any rate, during her recuperation, she broke her restraints and ran away. Three days later her dress and shoes were found at the edge of Crater Sink. Her body was never found."

Silence.

"But how did this story connect with all those disappearances?"

"The disappearances began soon after Clara's escape from Lady Grace. And all the victims were people who had, in one way or another, injured Clara Mercer, either by being members of the Teague . . . I don't know . . . *faction*, if you like, or because they put her, or allowed her to be put, in Candleford House against her will"

"Dad. You're a historian, not a Victorian novelist. The whole thing is . . . crazy."

"I couldn't agree more. I'm just giving you the facts as they presented themselves to me."

"Did you ever tell Nick any of this?"

"Yes. I did. He dragged it out of me, just as you're doing. Not in this kind of detail, but the basics."

"When?"

"I guess maybe a month ago."

"What did he think?"

"Same as you. Found the whole thing crazy."

"But he listened?"

"Kate, he was there when they pulled Rainey Teague out of Ethan Ruelle's grave. You may not like this—neither do I— but there's no denying some kind of pattern here."

She uses the mirrors.

In her mind she could see the writing on the linen card—

With Long Regard — *Glynis R.*

"*She uses the mirrors?* That's what Mom said?"

"Yes."

"Who do you think 'she' was? Was it Glynis?"

"Glynis Ruelle is dead and buried."

"Nick didn't tell me about any of this."

"I didn't think he would."

"Why not?"

"Because you're a Walker. One of the families."

"You mean he's afraid someone is stalking me?"

"You could say that."

"The same person who is stalking the other members of the families? Do you really think that?"

A long pause.

"I'm *wondering* about it. That's all."

"Dad. Think about it. You're saying that people have been disappearing in Niceville since the late twenties? There's no way one person could have done all that. He—or she—would have to be . . ."

"A reasonable guess would be a hundred years old. Possibly older."

"That's impossible. Is that really what you think?"

"No. Of course not. It just nags at me. You asked me what was wrong with Niceville. I agree that it's absurd. If there really is anybody behind this, it will probably turn out to be a descendant, a relative, acting out a private obsession. But the fact is that Clara Mercer's body was never found."

"Dad, nothing that goes into Crater Sink ever comes back out. Everybody knows that."

She shook her head, waved it all away with an open palm, a gesture her father couldn't see but one he sensed as she did it.

"And *this* is what's wrong with Niceville?"

"Perhaps something more basic is going on, Kate. Evil invites retribution, evil generates chaos and cruelty. You and I both know that bad acts have a way of reverberating down through families. Dealing with that sort of thing is how you make a living, Kate."

After a time, Dillon spoke again.

"You may have heard this. The Creek and the Cherokee both have a legend about a cursed place, a place where some kind of evil presence lived. It's in the archives, recorded by a fellow named Lanman, working back around 1855. The Cherokees believed that somewhere in the vicinity of the Savannah River—Lanman was vague about exactly where—there was a high stone bluff, and at the top of the bluff was what he called '*a terrible fissure.*' From his description, I gathered it was some sort of crack or opening in the mountain."

"Dad. You're not trying to tell me that Crater Sink—"

"Crater Sink has been here longer than we have, Kate. Far longer. Thousands, perhaps millions of years. And it's a very strange place, you'll have to grant. It's not surprising that the Cherokee would have some mythology around it. We do ourselves. I mean, we Niceville people. *Things go into Crater Sink, but nothing ever comes out*? You just said it yourself. You grew up with those stories. We all did."

"Campfire tales. Ghost stories to make the kids shiver. Every town has some scary place."

"True, but Lanman says the Cherokee called the place Talulu, which sort of nails the location down. Mind you, this is all hypothetical stuff. Hearsay. Nothing I'd care to repeat in a court of law. Look, sweetheart, we've gotten a little off the track. Do you still have my records there. In the basement?"

"Yes."

"The families had a jubilee, at Johnny Mullryne's plantation in Savannah. In 1910. There's a picture of it, of all the families together. There's some writing on the back of the picture. I think that's when this all started."

"What's written on the back?"

"All the names of the people in the picture. One name is underlined. And next to the name that's underlined is a single word. The word is *shame*."

"What's the name?"

"I mentioned him earlier. Abel. Abel Teague."

"As in Rainey Teague?"

"Yes. Although, as we know, Rainey was adopted. Miles Teague was Abel Teague's grandson. Abel Teague's father was Jubal Teague, and *his* father was a man named London Teague. Back in the 1840s, London Teague had a plantation in southern Louisiana called Hy Brasail. There was some talk that London Teague arranged for the murder of his third wife, Anora Mercer—the lady they named the golf club after? It's a matter of record that John Gwinnett Mercer, Anora's godfather, fought a duel with London Teague over Anora's death.

So the Teagues have a checkered past, don't they? Do you still have Rainey's papers?"

"How could I not? You ask about them a lot."

"Where are they?"

"In Rainey's file, at my office."

"You went back over them, didn't you? Just to be safe, to make sure he was the only inheritor?"

"Yes. Due diligence."

"Of course. His birth parents, the Gwinnetts, the record is they died in a fire, right?"

"Yes. When he was two. They had a farm outside Sallytown. They raised Clydesdale horses. A hay fire started in the horse barn. They were both killed trying to get their animals out. They had no relatives, so Rainey went into foster care."

"In Sallytown?"

"Yes."

"You were able to confirm all this?"

"Not really. But the papers were in order, as far as I could determine."

"And did you manage to talk to the foster parents when you were taking on Rainey's file?"

"No. I was told they left the state a year after Rainey was adopted. I tried to trace them—just so one day I could tell Rainey about his past, if he ever asked—but I never found them."

"Do you recall their names?"

"Yes. Palgrave. Zorah and Martin."

"No trace of them? Either of them?"

"Not that I could find. I didn't look all that hard. They were sort of peripheral to the issue."

He was quiet again.

Kate waited patiently.

"Who initiated the adoption process, Kate?"

"Miles did, according to the papers. Sylvia had just gone through a long series of in vitro attempts. I remember Miles thought she was suicidal. We were all pretty worried about her."

"So, the story is, Miles went out and, somehow, found a boy who might actually be a distant relation to the family, an unknown boy in a foster home two hundred miles away in Sallytown?"

"Yes. I guess so. Why? Is there anything strange about that?"

"This lawyer named Leah Searle, did you ever speak to her?"

"No. She died, a year later."

"How?"

"Drowned, according to her daughter-in-law."

"Where?"

"Not in Crater Sink, Dad. Come on, you're starting to scare me. Are you saying there's something odd in Rainey's adoption?"

Another long silence. Her father was quiet for so long she began to think she'd lost her connection. Eventually he spoke.

"Kate, would you mind if I came down?"

"Dad, we'd *love* it. When?"

"I can be there in four hours."

Bock Meets Chu and Chu Meets Bock

Bock and Chu had agreed to meet at a place called the Bar Belle, on the Pavilion overlooking the Tulip River, a nice sunny patio with round metal tables and umbrellas flapping overhead that advertised Dubonnet and Heineken and Stella Artois, the same place where, as it happened, Nick and Beau had been wrapping up their lunch break.

Bock had made it a point to get to the Bar Belle before Chu—a good hour early. This was a tradecraft trick he had learned while watching *The Bourne Identity*. He sat alone at a table next to the railing, where he could get his back up against the wall, just like Matt Damon would do. On the other side of the teak panels the Tulip River was hissing like a big brown python.

Bock was wearing all black for the meet because he felt it made him more intimidating, whereas it actually made him look like an off-duty mall cop. He ordered a drink they were calling a Tequila Mockingbird and received it from a girl with her knockers overflowing their C cups like melting ice cream cones and a smile that would have warmed the cockles of a dead man. Bock might as well have been a dead man, for all he gave a damn right then, although they were lovely to look at, in an abstract if-only-my-life-were-different way.

Most of the tables had been empty when he got there, except for one a few yards away, where he noticed a couple of guys sitting quietly, one white guy, lean and kind of scary-looking, in charcoal suit pants and a crisp black dress shirt, with short black hair going white at the temples and these odd gray eyes that, when he had glanced over to watch Bock take a chair, seemed to have him bagged and tagged in under two seconds.

This unsettling guy was sitting with another guy, a black guy as large as the federal deficit and so muscular that if he'd wanted any more muscles he'd have had to hire someone to carry them around for him. The black guy was sitting canted to the left as if he had hurt his right butt cheek or something.

These guys were up and gone a few minutes after Bock arrived, long before he got the Tequila Mockingbird down to its slurpy bits, the lean white guy giving Bock a long backwards glance as they paid up and split.

Perhaps they sense my power, Bock was thinking, before the profoundly humiliating purpose of this meeting came crashing back to his surface.

In that connection, Bock, being a man of the world and capable of bold strokes in a crisis, especially a self-inflicted one, as most of his were, had taken some precautions about this meeting with Andy Chu. Firstly, he had a small voice-activated Pearlcorder hidden in his pants, attached by a thread-thin cable to a mike that looked like a button sewn into the pocket of his black shirt, and he had a tiny video camera hidden inside a fake pen stuck in the same shirt pocket.

Furthermore, in case this Andy Chu person got violent, Bock had an impressive mail-order badge made of genuine chromium-plated German silver and a laminated ID card that certified Bock as a Bail Bond Recovery Agent fully empowered with all the power that mail-order badges can confer.

And, as a backup, he had a collapsible steel baton stuffed into the back of his pants.

Tactically speaking, this last had not been such a good idea, since it kept sliding down into the crack of his ass. Next time he'd put it in his pocket, but it was too late to move it now.

So, there Bock sat, generally pleased with all these careful preparations, plus feeling the fortification that comes naturally from the rapid inhalation of three consecutive Tequila Mockingbirds in under thirty minutes. He was becoming much more confident that, in the event that bold assertive action should ensue, he would be ready to do whatever was needed in the sacred cause of Tony Bock Getting Away with Stupid Shit.

Over the next hour, as Tony Bock lapped up a fourth Mockingbird, the deck tables filled up with happy chatty college types in loud shirts and cargo shorts with their ball caps on backwards.

Bock watched one guy with his ball cap turned around so the bill was hanging down his neck and the guy was literally shading his eyes from the sun with his left hand.

What a complete putz—turn the cap around, you dipshit dork.

He was still looking at the guy with withering contempt when a skinny shadow fell across his table and he looked up at the silhouette of a slender bite-sized guy in a white short-sleeved shirt and beige nerd-slacks.

Bock, who had forgotten that he too had his ball cap on backwards, used his left hand to shade his eyes and managed to make out the features of a small-boned Asian guy, beard-less, wearing wraparound iridescent bug-eye sunglasses and a diffident smile. The guy actually put out his hand.

"Mr. Bock, I am Andy Chu."

Bock, seizing the high ground right off, glared at the boy's hand as if it were a dead bat. The boy withdrew it and took a chair, still smiling.

"How do you know who I am?" asked Bock. "We've never met. I don't know who the hell *you* are."

"Well, I am Andy Chu and forgive me if I feel we have already met," said Chu, picking up the menu and looking more at ease than Bock felt a sleazeball blackmailing midget gook wearing the Full Geek had any right to look.

"I know what you look like," the kid went on, speaking in a conversational tone, "since I have seen the naked pictures you take of yourself in front of the computer, sitting on that big black leather sofa."

Quite suddenly, Bock found that he had nothing snappy to come back with. His heart had jumped up his throat and was now trying to squeeze out his left ear. His hearing was gone and his voice was nowhere to be found.

The kid seemed to understand this.

"Try to be calm, Tony. I mean you no harm. But you see I *have* been all through your computer. I have seen all of your dirty-picture collection and your dirty-story collection. I know the websites you go to and how long you stay there and I have seen the webcam pictures you take of yourself while you are there."

He paused, saw the way Bock was taking this—he looked like he was going to either faint or throw up or both. Chu patted Bock's arm in a comforting way, and then went back to his menu, speaking in the same calm voice.

"Settle down, Tony. Don't take this so seriously. This is not so bad. I only meant to say—I hope I can call you Tony?— that in the two hours I have had to study you, I feel that I know you better than I know my older brother in Macao, who is also a man who likes to use Photoshop to take the heads off his girlfriends and sisters and put them on the bodies of naked whores."

Bock's eyes were on his hands.

A vein was hammering at his temple and from somewhere deep down an alarm was going off.

Heart attack stroke heart attack stroke.

Chu, if he was aware, rolled on anyway.

"Once, if you will believe this, he even did this to a picture of our mother. He and I do not talk anymore after I let him know that I knew what he was doing, but he also stopped doing it. And so will you, if you are wise, and let me help you. I think I will have the red snapper and the wild rice. It looks good. Will we have some wine too? A white wine? Maybe a cold Pinot Grigio?"

This was said in the same calm, clear voice, Chu smiling at Bock as he handed the menu across.

Book took it in shaking hands, his guts turning into dishwater and flushing pink in the sun. He found that his lips were stiff and his cheeks cold and slack, as if all the blood had left them. He felt that he was melting down into himself, that the only solid and steely part left of Antony Bock was a collapsible baton located somewhere deep down in his underwear.

He stared at what was left of his fourth Tequila Mockingbird, his hands in his lap, clutching the menu, and could not for any price have brought himself to look up at Andy Chu.

"Please. You look sickly. I do not judge you," said Andy Chu, not unkindly. "From what I can see, until yesterday, you have just used those pictures to please yourself, and I am not the one to say you are bad to do so. I would not be surprised to hear that everyone around us on this patio has sexual secrets they would not like to see exposed. That is just human nature."

Chu paused, changed his tone, and was now mildly scolding him.

"But what you have done to that poor man down at the church, and to those innocent police officers who risked their lives—now that was very wrong. And I think you sent an e-mail this morning around ten thirty to somebody named Twyla Littlebasket. It had a very large attachment, after which you shredded a graphic file. I was unable to retrieve all of it. Was this more of your troublemaking, Tony?"

Book worked his mouth, trying to find enough spit to be

able to talk, because something had to be said, if only to stop
this kid from saying anything more. Chu, sensing this, handed
him a glass of water and watched with cool sympathy as Bock
drank it down in one long swallow.

"You *couldn't*. I shredded all my—"

"*Tried* to, Tony. I got most of it. Enough."

"Look . . . Mr. Chu . . ."

"Please, call me Andy."

"Look . . . Andy . . . this stuff, this is just too crazy to be
talking about here . . . we oughta go—"

The waitress with the ice cream bazookas shimmered up
and smiled down upon them. Chu ordered his red snapper—
well grilled—and the wild rice, and, glancing at Bock, seeing
the state he was in, ordered the same for him.

"May we also have a bottle of Santa Margherita, on ice, if
you would?"

The girl beamed upon them some more and shimmered
off. Chu looked at Bock for a time over the top of his glasses,
and then leaned back.

"I think, since you are finding it hard to talk, I should tell
you what is going on in my own mind. Is that okay? Do you
need a pill or something? No?"

In his ramble through Bock's hard drive Chu had come
across Bock's medical records. The guy had a serious choles-
terol problem and was probably going to need multiple arterial stents sometime in the future, if he was ever going to see
the north side of fifty. The last thing Chu wanted right now
was for Tony Bock to pitch a myocardial infarct.

He waited a bit, anxiously studying Bock's complexion,
which had settled down somewhere between waxy and clammy.
Chu figured he wasn't going to die yet.

"Okay, well, first, Tony, this shame you are feeling, this is a
good sign. If you were really a bad person, I would think you
would not be half so ashamed. Like I said, I don't judge you

about the sex thing. I am Chinese, from Macao, one of the most crowded cities on the planet. How do you think it got so crowded?"

Chu waited for a smile at his joke, got only a bug-eyed stare and a froglike gasping.

He went on, speaking as if he had given this thing a lot of thought, which he had.

"Okay . . . let me say this carefully. We agree that—oh, by the way, I have made a complete copy of everything on your drives, just so we are okay together, in the same place, yes?"

"How . . . how did you find . . . ?"

Chu smiled at him.

"There are amateurs and there are professionals, Tony. You are an amateur. I have spent six years—postgraduate—at MIT and Caltech—studying only the way computers and the Net encounter each other. You are, I hope I get this correct, an energy auditor for Niceville Utility, yes? A graduate also of East-Central-Mid-State-Poly?"

Bock was going down again, so Chu kept talking.

"Anyway, you might want to know that all of these so-called hush-mail sites—even the ones in Iceland, which is an outlaw state with regard to the Internet—they are all watched. Agencies have set up these virtual watchers at the outer gates of all these portals and whenever somebody uses one, a note is made of the IP. It took me less than fifteen minutes to find out your IP location, and less than that to break your firewall and take over your machine. I see this is not pleasant to hear, so I'll go on . . . will I? . . . with why I am here."

The meals came, and Chu daintily devoured his. Bock rallied enough to attack the wine but food was out of the question.

Mostly he was thinking, *Run run run.*

Change my name.

Get out of town.

"First, Tony, I am not here to blackmail you."

Bock stopped at the bottom of his glass, stared through it at Chu, set it down.

"No?"

"No. No offense, Tony, but I know to the penny what you make every month, what you have in the bank, and in savings, and what you have to pay to your ex-wife, Miss Dellums, and your daughter, and for your rent to Miss Kinnear. Tony, my friend, I make ten times what you make. Some years twenty. I have made investments. I am very comfortably off for a man only in his thirties."

Thirties? thought Bock. *I thought you were fifteen years old.*

"So I am not interested in your money. Do you know what an American H-One visa is, Tony?"

Bock shook his head, his mind still turning over the phrase *Not here to blackmail you.*

"Okay, H-One visas are usually given to people with extraordinary ability in an area of highly specialized knowledge. Such as information technology and computer science. I am such a person. I am a citizen of the People's Republic of China, and my residency here is, to be blunt, at the discretion of my employer. Under the H-One rules, my visa has to be supported by something called a Labor Certification. The rules are complex, but the short story is if my employer wishes to, he can withdraw my Labor Certification, and my visa is gone. I can appeal, but, if an employer has influence, one can be forced to go back to his homeland and reapply for another H-One visa. Do you follow this?"

"Yes, I think I do."

"Good. To put it simply, my employer and I are not on good terms, but I do not wish to return to the People's Republic of China."

"Now?"

"Now or ever. To be honest, were I to be confronted with the certainty of deportation back to Macao, I would put a bullet in my head."

"Yow," said Bock. "You really don't want to go back, do you? Why not?"

Chu studied Bock for a while.

"I won't make it a big lecture. I will keep it simple. Aside from a very strong personal reason which has to do with the animosity between myself and my older brother, who is something of a gangster in Macao, it is simply that in America I am a free man. In China, on the other hand, I am a snot-rag. I can be nose-blown upon and tossed away by anyone with power over me. China is not a free place. Everybody knows that it is a *busy* place, a beehive nation of industry, with lots of money being made. Nobody in the West cares how that nation of industry treats its people. In China it is possible now to prosper but it is not possible to live without fear of the government. The government has absolute power over everyone. If you are not pleasing the government terrible things will happen to you without warning and without hope of the slightest mercy. This is no way for a human to live. It is degrading. It makes cowards of the good people. And cringing informants of the rest. I refuse to live like this."

Here he paused, going quiet, seeing something dark, and the shadow of it flitted across his unmarked face. He shook it off, brightened.

"So, in spite of the difficulties of my present employment—I work for a most unpleasant man—here is still better than there, and I am not going back to China to live like a serf just because Byron Deitz doesn't like me."

"Byron Deitz? I've heard of him."

"Yes? A powerful figure in Niceville?"

"Yeah. Owns a big security company."

"Yes. He does. He is my boss. He is also a traitor to your country. And we are going to punish him."

"We?"

"Yes. You and I."

"How?"

It took Chu a few minutes to explain. At the end of it, Bock had multiple objections but they could be succinctly conveyed by the two phrases *No fucking way* and *Are you totally fucking nuts?*

"Yes," said Andy Chu, with a smile. "I am."

Lenore

After his call to Kate, Dillon Walker located a text file on his computer and hit PRINT. Outside the window of his office in the Preston Library a soft afternoon light lay on the drill square and the old Federal-style buildings.

The weather had been fine all that day, cool and clear, with just a shadow of cloud along the top of the Blue Ridge.

He could hear, through the half-open window of his book-lined study, the rhythmic cadence of a cadet platoon running through the grounds, the steady tramp of their feet like a muffled drum on the quad, the words as familiar to him as when he had first learned to chant them himself, as a young soldier in the 101st Airborne so many years ago. He listened for a moment longer to the chant. His hands on the keyboard in front of him were knotted and bent with arthritis, barely able to type. It was hard to see them as they had been on that June day in 1944, firmly clutching his parachute straps as he floated down into a firestorm at Normandy. He had not known it at the time, but he had been within a mile of his friend Gray Haggard, who was at that same moment trying not to drown in the bloody foam off Omaha Beach.

The running cadence faded into the distance and a cool

wind stirred the blinds, making them rattle in their traces and fluttering his papers on the broad rosewood desk.

Someone called his name, softly, from out in the dim corridor of the library, beyond his office door. This was odd, since the place was closed on Saturday afternoons, all the cadets out on an exercise, the library usually deserted.

He sat back in his creaking chair, cocked an ear. "Hello? I'm in here? Who is it?"

Silence, and then it came again, a soft whispering voice, at once familiar and very strange.

A muscle in his cheek quivered and he put a finger to his throat, feeling the carotid throb.

He was seventy-four and although he had nothing in particular wrong with him, that was just another way of saying that *everything* was wrong with him.

The voice was a voice he knew, although he had not heard it for years. It was Lenore, and this was why, as a rational man, he was checking his pulse, since he was apparently having some sort of seizure.

He reached out for the water bottle on the credenza behind him and sipped at it, fumbling in a drawer for an aspirin. The voice spoke again, closer now, and a slender figure appeared on the other side of the pebbled glass door of his office.

He watched the figure, young, female, dressed in either a white form-fitting dress or nothing at all, watched as she lifted an arm and knocked once, softly, on the glass.

"Dilly, it's Lenore. It's *time*, honey. We have to go. Everything is ready. Everyone is waiting."

Dillon Walker felt a shudder of fear ripple through him, which, hating any form of cowardice, he crushed at once.

Dilly.

Lenore always called me Dilly.

He stood up and came around the desk, pausing in front of the door. He looked around the room with regret, and then back at his desk, half expecting to see his dead body slumped across the papers. But the chair was empty and he was here in his slippers and his comfortable olive-drab corduroy slacks and his black polo shirt, feeling very much alive.

The figure, now that he was close, was very naked and very much in the shape of his dead wife. The image knocked again and called his name.

She uses the mirrors, Lenore had said, moments before her death. *She uses the mirrors.*

He felt himself at the edge of some great thing, on the brink of a great revelation, an encounter with something powerful and strange—something . . . *outside*.

Not to open that door would be an act of cowardice, a sniveling and greedy attempt to scrape a few more seconds of life off his plate. His work here was not done, but it would be completed by others. No man was indispensable. He thought about Kate, and Reed, and Beth, about Rainey Teague and his adoption, about Miles and Sylvia, and the essential strangeness of Niceville. If what was beyond the door was really Lenore, then everything that was hidden from him would be revealed, and he would one day see all of his family again. Sooner or later, for every living man, the time came to leave.

He opened the door, thinking he would see Lenore, but instead darkness flew at him, black wings, razor-edged beaks, claws ripping, yellow eyes with a green light, a crushing force thick with rage and hate. The feeding began. Like Gray Haggard, he lasted far too long.

Kate Kavanaugh Has a Visitor

For a long time Kate refused to think about what her father had said about the mirrors, refused to even attempt to make sense of it. She put her head back, closed her eyes for a while, felt a warm wave of fatigue roll over her.

She slept.

The phone rang.

She picked it up, looked at the call display—L. STEINERT.

"Lacy?"

"Hi, Kate. I'm sorry to call you at home."

"You sound tense."

"Not tense, no. But I'm trying to get in touch with Nick and he's not answering his cell. Tig says he was out on a disappearance, and that he had gone to get some bloodstains checked, but he's not at the police lab either."

She looked at the time—after four—he'd be home around nine, if nothing went crazy at work.

"He usually cuts out for lunch around this time, if he's working. You could try the Bar Belle at the Pavilion. It's his favorite lunch spot. I have their number, if you like?"

A pause.

"No, it's not . . . I've left messages. He'll call back sooner or later."

"Okay. I'm sorry. Was it urgent?"

"No. Well, I think he'd like to know."

"Is it good news? He could use some."

"Nobody knows this yet, so keep it close until I can get to Nick. You need to know about it too, since you're his legal guardian. It's about Rainey Teague—"

"Oh hell. Not dead?"

"No. He woke up."

"What?"

"Yes. Well, I mean, he didn't just suddenly sit up and ask for a cookie. The doctors are with him. But he's come out of the . . . whatever it was, and he's . . . 'responsive' . . . was the way they put it. You remember I was talking to you about Lemon Featherlight?"

"Yes. He wanted to see Nick."

"Lemon was the one who found him. Awake, I mean. Lemon had gone to see him after he spoke to Nick this morning—he tell you about that?"

"No. He hasn't. What was Lemon doing there?"

"Lemon and Rainey were friends. I know, sounds odd, but Lemon took what happened to Rainey pretty hard, so after he spoke to Nick he thought he should go down and see the kid again. Anniversary of it, I guess, or whatever. Lemon's a strange guy, but he's got a good heart. Anyway, he walks into the CCU room and the nurses are all clustered around the bed, bells and whistles are going off, and he can hear Rainey crying and asking for some guy named Abel Teague. Nobody knew who the hell he was, maybe a relative. Anyway, it was all pretty chaotic, but now Lemon wants to see Nick again. Like, ASAP, if he can. So I'm calling around—"

Kate broke in.

"Did you say *Abel Teague*?"

"Yes. Abel Teague."

"Rainey was asking for somebody named Abel Teague?"

"Yes. Kate, you sound funny."

"I feel funny."

No time to try to explain this to Lacy.

"Have you tried his beeper?"

"A *beeper*? Who has a beeper these days?"

"Nick does. It's for just us. He hates the cell and a lot of times he just shuts it off for lunch. But the beeper he keeps on, in case I really need to get in touch with him."

"Oh jeez. I'm not using *that*, then. How about you just tell him, if he calls, to get in touch with me right away. Lemon is going nuts."

"I'll do it, Lacy. And that is good news, about Rainey, isn't it?"

"I sure hope so. Does the name Abel Teague mean anything to you?"

"Why?"

"Because when I said his name your voice went all tight. What's going on?"

"Yes. The name means something to me."

"What?"

"Lacy, when I know, you'll know."

"Promise?"

"I promise. Bye-bye."

Kate stared at the phone for a time, thinking about using the beeper.

But Lacy was right. If it went off, Nick would jump a mile. If he was driving, he could fly off the road and die.

On the other hand . . . Rainey Teague.

Awake.

She was still trying to decide what to do when she noticed that someone was standing at the bottom of her lawn, down by the pines, half in the shade of the slender trees. A girl, a full-grown girl, not a child, her arms down at her side and staring up at the windows of the conservatory. Quite still, her expression solemn and remote.

Kate set the phone aside and stood up, going around to the glass doors that opened onto the lawn. She stepped out on the edge of the grass, shading her eyes against the afternoon sun, looking at the girl, who was about a hundred feet away, just standing there. She was wearing a sundress, pale green, dappled with what looked like poppies or roses or maybe strawberries.

Just like the girl in her dream.

Or she was changing her memory to fit the girl, which people tended to do. She suppressed a superstitious shudder and stiffened herself. She wasn't going to cower in her house like a frightened child.

"Hello," she called, opening the door and coming down the lawn, half afraid that she would frighten her away. "Are you lost, honey?"

Kate was barefoot and she could feel the green grass, still moist from the rains, cool and wet between her toes. She was less than fifty feet away from the girl, who was looking at her with cool hazel-colored eyes, her full red lips slightly parted, as if she were . . . hungry. Now that she was nearer, Kate could see that the girl was old enough to have a full figure, curved and ripe and sensuous.

The girl in her dream had been just a child.

Hadn't she?

Kate was also close enough to see that the flowers on her pale green sundress were not flowers at all but stains, red irregular stains. She had seen enough pretty young women with those kinds of stains on them to know dried blood when she saw it.

"What's your name, honey? Has somebody hurt you? Come with me, we'll get you all cleaned—"

The girl—the young woman—turned away abruptly and

stepped into the shade of the forest, a pale green flicker in the violet shadows.

Dammit, thought Kate, looking at her bare feet. *I can't chase you in my bare feet.*

Kate paused there for a moment, trying to decide whether to go back to the house and get some shoes or just to plunge into the woods and get hold of the girl, who quite obviously needed help.

There was nowhere for her to go in there, just the creek, which was full of slippery stones and mossy roots, and then the hill on the other side, which was much too steep to climb.

"Honey, please come out of there, will you?"

Kate saw a shape deep in the tree shadows. The girl was still in there, inside the woods, watching her. *Waiting* for her?

Kate heard a voice that seemed to come from inside her own head—a familiar voice, although silent for years.

Lenore's voice.

Kate, said her dead mother, *don't go in there.*

Unable to help herself, and angry at this sudden attack of female hysteria on her part, Kate spoke out loud.

"Oh, for God's sake, Mom. I'm not a child."

And the answer came back, in a voice less like her mother's and more like her own.

Neither is that.

Byron Deitz Motivates His People

Deitz was waiting in the fading sunlight outside Kwikky Kleen Kar Kare on Long Reach Boulevard, watching the Tulip River, at full flood, boiling past the muddy banks, the broad back of the river mud brown, the surface of it rippling and roiling with the current.

Deitz was drinking a lime slushy and waiting for a wiry Filipino kid to scrub Mr. Thad's nose blood off the leather passenger seat of the Hummer.

He had a new BlackBerry and was trying to get it to dial a number for him, but it didn't really want to. He had to use his thumbs to type the number in manually. He had extremely large thumbs. Things were not going well.

Finally he got through to his IT section.

"Andy there?"

A moment of silence, and Deitz had time to wonder again where the hell that walnut-cracking sound was coming from.

"Sir?"

"Andy. You got anything yet for Tig Sutter?"

"I'm afraid not yet, sir. It is very complicated. The sender was—"

"I need something for Tig, Andy," he said, literally in a growl. "Something fucking soon. I need Tig to owe me big. I need it fast. This is *not* the time for you to fuck up again, kid."

"I will most definitely not fuck up again. I am on it very hard."

"How long?"

"End of the day, I hope."

The walnut-cracking sound inside Deitz's head got very loud and the Tulip River went all reddish.

"*End of the day?* Fuck *that*. Get it now. Get it right *fucking* now. Be back to me in one hour or start clearing out your desk. You follow?"

A long silence, while Deitz wondered where he was going to get an IT guy as good as Andy Chu, deciding finally that the woods were full of IT geeks just as good as Andy Chu. Maybe better. In the meantime, like any good manager, you had to motivate your people.

Andy's voice again, cool and calm.

"I follow, sir."

"I'm fucking clear?"

"Yes sir. You are . . . extremely clear."

"Good. Get it done," said Deitz, clicking off.

He stood there, staring down at the screen, thinking, as had been his habit lately, black and complicated thoughts, including an inventory of everyone he had ever met who owned a pair of navy blue cowboy boots—not many—when he heard his name called, in a strange lisping accent.

He turned to watch as a long black Lincoln Town Car— the one that looked like a turtle in a tuxedo—came to a stop at the curb by the car wash, a lean and sallow face peering at him out of the rear window—*another goddam zipperhead*—an Asian man with narrow wrinkled eyes as black as buttons, the too large head completely bald, on closer examination, a distinctly unpleasant look, with a large misshapen forehead, bumpy irregular cheekbones, a squashed mushroom of a nose, and a thin-lipped slash of a mouth with an incongruous soul patch under the lower lip.

Deitz threw the slushy into the Tulip and came over to the curb, his expression not welcoming and his mood unimproved by this unexpected arrival.

"I'm Byron Deitz. Who the fuck are you?"

The head bobbed and showed its teeth, tiny, even babyish, stained with tobacco, fencing off a fat white tongue that bobbed around inside the man's bloodred mouth like a moray in a cave.

"Will you join me?" he said, opening the door and pulling back inside the rear seat to give Deitz some room to slide in. "It is much cooler inside."

Deitz looked at the man for a moment, feeling the weight of his Sig in his belt holster, considering the man's expensive pearl gray suit, his satiny shirt, a much paler gray, the lavender silk tie, and the gold collar bar, the slender Italian shoes, the lavender silk socks.

The man made an ingratiating head bob and flashed those teeth again, and the name came to Deitz out of an old black-and-white film with Humphrey Bogart.

Joel fucking Cairo, he said to himself. *In the flesh. What next? A fat man with a black bird?*

"Who are you and who you with?" he said, in a steely snarl, staying firmly planted on the sidewalk.

"I'm sorry. My name is . . ." Here he mumbled something that sounded to Deitz like *Hickory Dock*.

"Come again?"

"I am Zachary Dak," he said, more carefully. "Here is my card."

He reached into his suit jacket and brought out a silver card case, extracted one, offered it to Deitz with both hands, palms up, smiling at him.

Deitz took the card, read it.

Zachary Dak, LLB, PhD
Director of Logistics
Daopian Canton, Inc.
2000 Fortunate City Road, Shanghai
PR China 200079
86.022.63665698

Deitz slid the card into his suit jacket, looked around the place, giving each car and every person in the area a careful appraisal.

He slipped into the car, leaving the door open, keeping one foot on the curb. The interior of the car smelled of Chinese cigarettes, which smelled exactly the way he figured they would smell.

"We're supposed to meet at the Marriott."

Dak nodded his head, glancing briefly at the back of the driver's head, a cannonball head that rode on a hairy neck as wide as a tree stump.

"Yes. That was the arrangement. And I am sorry to alter it. May I ask, do you have the item with you at this time?"

Deitz looked around the black leather interior of the car, thinking mikes and wires.

"I have no knowledge of any *item*, Mr. Dak."

Dak squirmed in his seat, indicating his extreme embarrassment and discomfort.

"Quite right. I misspoke. I refer only to the meeting which we have arranged. As you know, time is important here. Our Learjet waits at Mauldar Field. We must take flight on Monday morning."

"What if we're going to need more time than that?"

"Sadly, not possible. The deadline is fixed. Urgent business takes us to Dubai. Accordingly, my people are anxious to have this . . . consultation . . . take place as soon as it can."

"How did you find me?" asked Deitz, cutting in.

"Your car is most singular, Mr. Deitz."

"Horseshit. I don't get this. Why show up here, and why show up now?"

Something flitted across Dak's face, and it changed in a subtle but memorable way. Deitz was suddenly glad he had one foot on the curb and a Sig Sauer in his belt. What Zachary Dak looked like was less than what he was.

"Please get in and shut the door," he said.

Deitz got in and shut the door. The car immediately accelerated into traffic. Deitz was watching Dak's hands but did not see how the Glock got there. It was just there.

"This is only a precaution," said Dak, "so that you might listen with attention and do nothing rash. We are aware that you have had a problem with the item. We are aware that you cannot produce it."

Deitz managed to keep his expression steady. Dak smiled and went on.

"This upsets you. I understand. This is upsetting to us as well. But there is no point in being disputatious, as our interests happily coincide. You wish to regain the item promptly. We wish it to be promptly regained."

"OnStar," said Deitz, having worked it through. "You've had my truck phone hacked. You're inside the OnStar system. You heard me get a call about the . . . item."

Dak looked pleased.

He literally beamed.

"The People's Republic has made heroic strides in opening up certain areas of the communications systems of several of our trading partners. There is no hostility in this. It is simply prudent to know the positions of your good friends in business. To illustrate, we know that you are acting in perfect faith and that the theft of the object was as unexpected and distressing to you as it was to us. You share our sense of urgency. You are making energetic inquiries, as is your associate, Mr. Holliman."

Christ, thought Deitz. *They know how to turn on the OnStar microphone even if I'm not on it. They've heard everything I've said in the truck.*

"We are here to help, in any way we can, which is why we have come out into the field to assist you."

"Moving around Niceville in this limo will just attract attention. The best thing you could do is to go back to the Marriott and wait. I'll get the thing. You can count on it."

"We do count on you, Mr. Deitz. But we must still have it in our possession by Sunday evening at the very latest. To properly analyze the device will take several hours, and its extraction from the Slipstream vaults must never be discovered. You must return it without discovery, or the entire project will lose much of its value. Many millions are in play. Much effort has already been expended. I must answer to my superiors. We have discussed this matter of the robbery among ourselves. Have you reached any conclusions?"

"Yeah," said Deitz. "I have."

Dak inclined his head, glanced at the driver, and then brought his attention back.

"They are?"

"It was partly an inside job. I'm sure of it. So far I've eliminated the banker—"

"The unfortunate Mr. Llewellyn?"

"You heard that?"

Dak smiled.

"A most vigorous interrogation. We gather he had drugged himself? He is recovered, we hope?"

"I dropped him off at his house. He'll live."

"The matter of the blue boots. Was that useful?"

"Not a lot. But Phil found out that there was blood at the barn where they were hiding. We figure one of the guys on the job was hurt."

"So. Inside job, you think. One man hurt. You have only to determine who among the list of possible insiders has sustained an injury."

"Not quite. The insider could have provided the info. That doesn't mean he was actually on the job. Any two pros could have pulled that job."

"We are assuming that either one or both of them was wounded by the police in pursuit—"

"Or the two of them had a fight."

"A *pistolero* disagreement?" asked Dak, who was studying Spanish as a slight diversion from the toils of international espionage.

"They recovered several brass casings from the fire at the barn. Melted, but a lot of them."

"So, many rounds? And blood on the ground?"

"Yeah. A real firefight."

"But no hospital calls, naturally?"

"No. Not one."

"It would be useful to know the current state of the official investigation."

"Yeah. Fucking useful."

"You can accomplish this?"

"Not easily. What about you?"

"We could do such a thing, given time. We do not have time. Our search must become more vigorous. We have only a few hours in which to succeed. However, we have great hopes of success. May I make a prediction?"

"Sure. Need a fortune cookie?"

Dak presented a smile which showed no amusement of any kind, only a flicker of impatience.

"The item was contained in a box of some sort? With identifying signs of some type?"

"Yeah. A steel box, with a Raytheon logo."

"So this device would clearly signal its worth to any intelligent thief?"

"Yeah. Sure as hell."

"And you would describe the people who accomplished this robbery as intelligent?"

"Yeah," said Deitz, grudgingly. "I would."

"Then our prediction is that you will shortly be contacted by the thieves, or by a representative of the thieves. The object has no value to them, and is actually a clear and present hazard to their security. The penalty for being found in possession of such a thing would be very dire, would it not?"

"Fucking dire," said Deitz, thinking about how much he personally would dislike thirty-to-life in Leavenworth.

Dak inclined his head. "So. Two scenarios are likely. One, they have destroyed it, and you and I find ourselves in a difficult position. Two, they will attempt to return it in exchange for a consideration. Since you are chief of the security apparatus for the research park, their next logical step would be to contact you."

He held up a hand as he watched Deitz's temper flame up again.

"Vengeance is an indulgence, Mr. Deitz. A form of weakness, if it is allowed to derange our affairs. You must not allow this to happen. When you are contacted, you must agree to whatever terms are asked and proceed with the utmost dispatch—"

"Terms? The terms will be damned expensive."

"No doubt. You are being generously recompensed for your exertions on our behalf. You will pay what is asked promptly and without—"

"*I'll* pay—"

"*You* will pay, Mr. Deitz," he said, with serene emphasis, "since the original responsibility to deliver the item to us lies with you."

"What if they want too much? What if they want more than you're giving me? What if they want more than I can pay?"

Dak made a *so-sorry-too-bad* gesture.

"If for any reason you are unable to effect the exchange then you will be set aside and we will deal with them directly."

Deitz had a pretty good idea of what Dak meant by the phrase *set aside*. He had to admit that when it came to threatening somebody, Dak was a hell of a lot better at it than he was. Dak was looking at his watch and Deitz, glancing out the window, saw that they were back at the car wash. The limo rolled to a stop. Deitz popped the door, and the steamy heat of the afternoon poured inside.

"What if they don't contact me in time?"

"You will of course continue to make your inquiries. As will we. We have some resources you do not have. We will call upon them. In the meantime, you should even now reestablish contact with all of your means of communication, at home and at your offices. It is quite possible that a contact has already been initiated. If so, act on it in a swift and certain manner. Be effective and do not give in to revenge fantasies. Your sole concern must be to regain possession of the object. You have my card. On the back there is a cell number. Be in touch with me in sixty minutes."

"Or I could just talk into the roof of my fucking truck," said Deitz, with an edge.

"Or that," said Dak, with a polite smile. He closed the door and the car powered out into traffic. The Tulip rolled on and so did Niceville. The Filipino kid had the seat cleaned and Deitz gave him a fifty for his trouble.

He got into the truck, slammed the door hard, and sat back in the interior, which smelled of acetone and saddle soap and Deitz's cigars. He started the car, turned up the air conditioner, turned his BlackBerry back on. There was a text message waiting for him, with no sender ID.

PIGGLY WIGGLY
VINE AND BAUXITE
THE CORKBOARD
NOW

Nick and Beau Get Word

Beau and Nick were only a block north of where Byron Deitz and Zachary Dak were concluding their discussions. Nick was still brooding on Bock.

"You get a look at that guy at the table by the railing? All in black?"

Beau stopped to think.

"I saw him," he said. "He drove up in that lime green shit-box Camry. Why?"

"I know the guy. His name is Tony Bock. He's the guy in the Dellums custody case. Kate handed him his ass on Friday afternoon."

"Weird-looking guy."

"Yeah. Did you see what he had shoved down the crack of his ass? He had one of those collapsible steel batons. What do they call them? An ASP? Must have been damn uncomfortable."

Beau nodded. "Or maybe he had his dick on backwards."

"Yeah," said Nick, pulling out his cell phone. "Happens to me all the time."

Nick's cell phone rang as soon as he turned it on. He got

into the car on the passenger side—a couple of Advils had
eased the pain in Beau's butt cheek enough for him to drive.

Nick hit ANSWER.

"Lacy?"

"Nick, I've been trying to reach you."

Her voice was tight and urgent, but not the tone she had
when she was calling with a problem.

"I can see that. Four times in the last hour. Is everything
okay?"

"Yes. No. Well, maybe."

"That pretty much covers the ground."

"Nick, Rainey Teague woke up."

The words ran around in his skull like those tigers chasing
the black kid in that book nobody was allowed to read anymore. For some crazy reason he remembered it from his
childhood. *Little Black Sambo.* His mother had waved it around
as an example of what she called endemic racism. On some
level Nick knew he was thinking of that stupid book right now
because what Lacy had just said completely rocked his world.

"How awake?" he asked when he could speak.

"They're saying he's responsive. He's talking. He's been
immobile for a year, so he can't sit up or control very much.
But he's definitely not in a coma or a caledonia or whatever it
was."

Nick turned to Beau.

"Lady Grace, Beau. Right now."

"What's up?"

Nick told him.

Beau took it in, made a U-turn to a chorus of outraged
honks, accelerated into the street with the siren on. Cars on
both sides swerved to the curb to give them room. Nick, busy
getting the story from Lacy, only half registered Byron Deitz
in his big fat yellow Hummer driving slowly north, staring at
them as they flew south down Long Reach Boulevard.

Lacy had gotten to the part about Lemon seeing a man in the elevator.

"What does he mean? Like, a ghost?"

"No," said Lacy, who wasn't sure what the hell Lemon had been trying to say. "Just a guy with a really wicked vibe. Lemon said he sort of radiated crazy. Crazy and spooky. I don't know. Whoever he was, he scared the hell out of Lemon, which is pretty hard to do."

"He get a description?"

"Yeah. He'll tell you when you get there. He's in the lobby, waiting for you."

"You got his cell?"

Lacy gave it to him.

"What was Lemon doing there in the first place?"

"After he talked to you, he wanted to go see the kid. He says he went to smoke the room."

"What? You mean like that bug-killing stuff?"

"No, you mutt. It's a tribal thing he does. All the Indians have it. He takes some sweetgrass and burns it in a bowl and calls the kid's name."

"Looks like this other guy had a better method for calling the kid. What's this name Rainey was saying again?"

"He was asking for somebody named Abel Teague."

"*Abel Teague?* You sure?"

"Yeah. He was also talking about a woman named Glynis Roo . . . something. Glynis Ruelle. I don't know what this all means," said Lacy, "but you better go find out."

"I will," said Nick. "Thanks, Lacy."

"Keep me in the loop, will you?"

"When I know, you'll know. Bye."

He switched off, hit AUTO-DIAL. The phone rang six times, and then went to voice mail.

"Kate, when you get this, call me on my cell. You sitting down? Great news. Rainey Teague just woke up. Yes. Woke up. He's responsive, whatever that means, but he's got a ways to go to be all right. Still great news. Anyway, I wanted you to be the first to know. Love you, babe. Call me."

"Not home?" asked Beau.

"Probably out in the yard," said Nick, hitting a speed-dial number. Tig Sutter answered on the second ring.

"Nick—you heard?"

"I heard. We're on our way to Lady Grace now. Do we still have the jurisdiction here?"

"Oh yeah. Case is still open. I've already called the doctors down there. They're saying the kid's not coherent, but he's definitely conscious. They're going to do a bunch of tests on him, but I told them to keep him alert until you got there."

"Incredible, Tig," said Nick, his heart lightening in a way it hadn't ever since the case kicked off. "You know I've never even talked to the kid?"

"Yeah, well, remember, he doesn't know his parents are dead. That's going to be a tricky call."

"He's not going to hear it from me. Not today, anyway—"

"He'll be asking."

"Yeah. I can't reach Kate. She's his legal guardian. She ought to be there, see to what he needs, sign whatever has to be signed."

"Nick, this is going to sound crazy, but the docs are saying the kid calmed down when he heard Lemon Featherlight's voice. If Kate's not available, maybe you could go in that direction?"

"We should think about that, Tig. Guy's a CI, a drug dealer—"

"Lemon connected with the kid last year. Even Tony Branko at Vice thought Lemon's heart was in the right place. I think it's worth a shot."

Nick thought it over.

"Okay. I'll give him a try. Did you hear from the lab yet?"

There was nothing more to be said.

After a pause, Albert began to count.

"One."

"Two."

"Three."

Both weapons came up, and they fired at almost the same second, the heavy thump of the Colt, the brittle crack of the .38. The sound died out quickly, muffled by the dense mist. Crows began to caw and chatter in the distance.

They stood there for a few seconds, staring at each other, and then Merle went down on one knee, the heavy Colt falling to the grass, blood pumping out of a small round hole in his throat, just under the Adam's apple. He had a much larger hole in the back of his neck. Albert ran over to him, bending down, catching him as he fell.

Abel Teague took a step forward, staggered, took another, went down on one knee.

He had a large bloody hole in his left cheek, just below the eye. The eye itself had exploded outwards like a shattered egg. The back of his skull was gone, and his brains were scattered all over the lawn behind him.

Abel Teague fell sideways, rolled over onto his back, looked up at the sky, gasping. He could hear the crows calling and from far away he heard Albert Lee's voice, fading away. He closed his mind, trying to keep the spark going, thinking that if they could get to him in time the docs could do wonders. When he opened his mind a heartbeat later, he was looking up at Glynis Ruelle, a high blue sky behind her, her green eyes on him, her rich black hair shining in the sunlight.

"Get up," said Glynis. "You have work to do."

Kate Meets Clara

Sleep was out of the question, especially since Linus Calder had phoned back on Nick's cell three times, and now Nick was out in the backyard again, talking the guy through every detail of what had happened at Delia Cotton's house in The Chase.

Kate listened with part of her mind to the back and forth, theories about how it might have happened, how to explain these two events without stepping off the edge of the known universe.

Her father was not in his office or his flat, that much she knew. His car was in its parking space at the VMI lot. Kate had even begun to hope that he was just out for a long walk, or gone on a bender because the idea of driving down to see her and talk about Niceville had freaked him out.

Which she knew he would never do.

His car was still there.

He had never reached it.

So he was officially missing.

But Nick was on it, and this detective up in Virginia, Linus Calder, seemed to know what he was doing, and Reed had called her to tell her he was at VMI now and also on the case.

And then she had made a call to her sister, Beth, and found out that she was having yet another fight with that man.

She told Beth what was going on, got the impression that she wasn't listening very carefully, which was understandable, tried to make it sound as if Dad had just gone on a trip without telling anybody, felt she had half convinced Beth.

And then Deitz had started bellowing at Beth again, something about the air conditioner being out of order and what was she doing on the fucking phone, and she could hear the kids crying in the background, so Kate put the phone down, thinking that there was really nothing more she could do about anything. Except maybe one thing.

The last thing her father had said to her.

His records, in the basement.

Now that she was wide awake again, she got up off the couch and poured herself a large black coffee and went along the back hall to the kitchen and on down the stairs into the basement.

Up in the backyard, under the stars, the yellow glow of the yard lights shining on the trees at the bottom of the yard, Nick was listening—patiently—to Linus Calder, a guy every bit as exhausted as Nick was, but still at the crime scene, and Linus Calder was going over it again.

"There's no organic material in the stain site. I mean, if it was . . . what . . . spontaneous combustion? . . . you'd find something organic—not that I believe in spontaneous combustion—but . . . Jesus . . . what the hell *else* could it be? I swear, Nick, you say something like alien abduction, I'll shoot my dog. I don't actually own a dog. But I'll go out right now and buy one and shoot it."

"I'm not going to say alien abductions, okay?"

"Your CSI guys file a report yet?"

"They're off the scene, but no report yet."

"You going to come up here, take a look? I mean, we already got the hotshot brother—"

"What's Reed doing?"

"Driving me nuts. Until I hooked him up with some Virginia State Patrol guys. He knows people they know. Don't get me wrong. Nice kid, bit scary, bit *out there*, reminds me of those thousand-yard-stare guys we had in Vietnam. Anyway, he's out with the Virginia troopers and they're doing a canvass of everybody at VMI, see if anybody saw anything—"

"At *this* hour?"

"These kids are military. They don't mind. But that's all harness work, stuff the uniform guys can do instead of munching honey-dip crullers up at Beanie's. I need a real detective up here, not another steroidal keener."

"I hear you. I'll chopper up in the morning."

"We going to get everything you've got? I mean, this prof was a well-loved guy. This is VMI. They don't like scary random shit at VMI."

A pause, a wheezing sigh.

"Seriously, Kavanaugh, what're we going to do about all this? I been a cop since forever and I've never seen anything like this. Outside of the horror movies. You got *anything* for me?"

Nick thought about it, and then told the cop what he was thinking. Calder listened all the way through, and then he said, "Dear God. I was right all along. You *are* a fucking fruitcake."

"I tried to warn you. What's *your* theory?"

"Okay. Here's one. This Delia Cotton broad, she's loaded, right?"

"The Cottons are probably the richest family in Niceville. Maybe in the whole state."

"Okay. There you go. But Haggard, he's a poor lonely old

gardener, and he's best buds with our Dillon Walker guy here, they were at Omaha Beach together and all that heroic shit, so they decide to take her out—"

"The Walkers and the Haggards are loaded too."

"Okay. Then it's some sort of mysterious family vendetta, a terrible secret buried in the past. But now it's about to come out, so they kidnap the old lady and make themselves disappear at the same time. They get hold of some scraps of shrapnel, get hold of a few leftover bone pins—"

"From your friendly local secondhand bone-pin and shrapnel shop?"

"Then they toss a bucket of acetone on the floor, slop it around, strip the varnish off in the shape of a body, maybe use a blowtorch on it to dry it all off—"

"Hence the warm spots?"

"Hence the warm spots. Scatter the metal around, and off they go—everybody thinks they're like disappeared by these man-eating ghosts, I mean, everybody who's a fucking fruitcake believes that, but really they're on their way to Costa Rica with all of Delia Cotton's money. Or secrets. Or whatever the hell it is."

"Makes more sense than my theory."

"Sure as shooting it does, my friend. But you're still a fruitcake. Nobody says 'hence' anymore. Get some sleep. I'll see you tomorrow morning."

Nick rang off, looked into the house through the conservatory glass, and saw Kate in the family room just beyond it, taking things out of a large cardboard box, her hair hanging down over her forehead, her fine-boned hands white in the downlight, her expression intent and determined.

Kate looked up at him, her eyes strange. She was holding a stack of old photos.

"Nick. This is Dad's file box, from that research he never finished. He said I should look at it. Want to see something interesting?"

"Sure," he said, sitting down beside her on the couch. She smelled of old cardboard and cobwebs and there was dust all over her shirt.

She riffled through some faded sepia pictures, found one, a very large one, perhaps eight by ten, pulled it out, and set it down on the coffee table.

It was a formal picture, slightly faded but still quite clear, a turn-of-the-century family group, fifty or more people posed on a large stone staircase in front of a massive archway, live oaks draped in Spanish moss all around, horses in the fore-ground, a prosperous and attractive group, the men and boys in stiff black suits and starched collars, the women and the girls with high-piled Gibson-girl hair and lace collars and full billowing bosoms, waists cinched in tight, dainty feet visible under the hems of their lacy petticoats.

The photo was printed on stiff cardboard and framed in sinuous Art Nouveau engravings. Below the picture the card company—Martin Palgrave & Sons—had printed, in a fine copperplate script:

Niceville Families Jubilee
John Mullryne's Plantation
Savannah Georgia 1910

Kate flipped the card over.

On the back, someone with a free-flowing script had recorded all the names of the people in the picture, in order, starting at the upper left and going all the way through to the bottom right. One name had been underlined: Abel Teague.

Written beside his name, in a different hand, was one word: *shame*.

"Okay," said Nick, watching her face. "Abel Teague is the man Rainey was asking for when he came out of the coma."

"Yes. Lacy told me. There's more. And I don't want you to think I'm a . . . what do cops always say?"

"A fruitcake?"

"Yes. There's a face I want you to look at."

Kate flipped the card over, tapped the image of a pretty young girl with her light-colored hair piled high, a long, graceful neck, a full figure under the lacy bodice, large direct eyes, pale in color, full lips partly open. Most of the women in the shot were very pretty. This one was a stunner, with an air of almost defiant sensuality that conveyed itself across more than a century and seemed even now to look directly into Nick's eyes.

"Wow. She's a heart attack."

"Yes, she is. And she also looks *exactly* like the girl I saw at the bottom of the garden this afternoon."

She said this without drama, but with an air of quiet certitude that Nick had learned to take seriously. Which he did.

"So then she's a relative, an ancestor?"

"Yes, she must be."

"Who is she? Her name on the back?"

"Yes. Her name is Clara Sylvia Mercer. The famous Clara Dad was talking about. Dad thinks she's probably a distant relative by way of the Mullrynes and the Walkers. Mom was a Mullryne and her mother was a Mercer."

Nick looked at the picture more closely.

Looks a lot like Kate.

"Now, you're not thinking this is the *same* girl, Kate? I mean, here she is in 1910 and she can't be more than fifteen or sixteen. She'd be . . . what, almost a hundred and seventeen now?"

"Is this a fruitcake check?"

"No. Not at all."

"It's not her, I know that. It *can't* be her, but it's somebody who looks very much like her."

"Is Abel Teague in this shot?"

Kate moved her fingertip, placed it on the body of a broad-shouldered medium-sized well-set young man with a high clear forehead and eyes so pale they had to be either blue or light gray.

Abel Teague had a good face, thought Nick, intelligent, with humor in it, maybe a touch of arrogance, but they all did. He wasn't wearing a jacket, just a shirt and what looked like striped pants in a military cut.

"So what's the *shame* thing?"

Kate gave him one of her looks.

"Dad said he talked to you about what was wrong with Niceville. About the disappearances. About Clara being shut up in Candleford House."

"Yes. The State Police finally began to investigate the place back in 1935, but somebody set it on fire before they could find out very much."

"Same year as the fire in the Niceville Town Hall," said Kate. "It's almost as if somebody was wiping out the traces . . ."

"Traces of what?"

"I don't know, Nick. Maybe to Rainey?"

"To Rainey?"

"Dad was asking me a lot of questions about Rainey's adoption."

"What about it?"

"How Miles found Rainey in the first place. Up in Sallytown. How his birth parents had died—"

"The Gwinnetts. A barn fire, right?"

"Yes. Another fire. Then his foster parents go missing—"

"They did? You never told me."

"Well, at least I could never find them. And then the lawyer who did the adoption for Miles—Leah Searle—she drowns a year later."

Nick found his inner cop waking up.

"So, what you're saying is, fires and drownings in 1935—"

"And more fires and drownings seven years ago."

"And all connected to the Teague family."

"Yes."

Nick looked at the file box on the floor and then up at Kate.

"I could look into all of this tomorrow, if you want?"

"Tomorrow's Sunday."

"FBI link still works on Sundays. Computers all work. Census records—it's all—"

The phone rang.

Kate picked it up, was deep in an intense conversation within thirty seconds. She looked up at him, mouthed the words *Lemon Featherlight*.

Nick nodded, picked up the jubilee card again, turned it over, ran his fingertip down the list of names, looking for a particular one.

He found it halfway down the third row.

Glynis Mercer Ruelle

He flipped the card over, found her in the third row, a tall strong-faced woman with an erect bearing, aristocratic, with gleaming black hair ribboned around a long, well-turned neck.

She had a direct, penetrating gaze. Her eyes were pale in the sepia-tinted shot and Nick figured they might possibly be green.

Although she had an air of sensuality, she wasn't smiling at all, and seemed in some indefinable way to be unhappy with the company.

Looking at her, Nick decided that she would have made a good friend and a loving wife but she would not forgive an insult easily and probably had a full measure of the Southern flair for honor, for the vendetta. He looked again at the word written against Abel Teague's name.

shame

Something about the handwriting.

Where had he seen it?

Kate was still on the phone.

Nick went up the stairs to his office, dug around in the closet, full of his old Class As and two sets of dress blues, his blues studded with medals and gleaming gold braid.

He found the package right at the back, lifted it out, a medium-sized rectangle, wrapped in a cotton duvet, tied with yellow ribbon, heavy and solid. He unwrapped it carefully.

It was the mirror that Rainey Teague had been looking at—or had seemed to be looking at—when he simply flicked out of existence. The frame was baroque, the metal silver plated in gold, and the mirror glass was not original, but was much older than the frame, a type of silvered glass that, according to Moochie, dated back to the middle of the seventeenth century, possibly from Ireland.

Nick looked at his own reflection in the mirror, staring into the thing as if defying it to come alive in his hands.

His face looked distorted and strange in the glass, which was pitted and rippled, with patches of the silver coating on the back scraped away. The thing was heavy in his hands, and although he kept his office cool because of his computer, the frame felt warm, almost hot.

He turned the frame over, looked at the linen card on the back, at the signature.

With Long Regard—Glynis R.

He had the jubilee card with him. He held it up beside the handwritten card.

He was no calligrapher, but even he could see the hand-writing was identical. If Glynis Ruelle had written the card on the back of the mirror, then Glynis Ruelle had also written the word *shame* beside Abel Teague's name.

Kate was calling him.

When he got back to the family room, carrying the mirror, Kate had her laptop open and was clicking through to her e-mail service.

She looked up at him.

"That was Lemon. The streetlights are off over at Garri-son Hills."

Nick sat down, suddenly very tired.

"What about his inside lights?"

"All working. He says it looks like something is pressing up against the glass."

Something deep in his lizard mind made Nick say what he said next.

"Tell him not to open a door. Or a window."

Kate stared at him.

"Why?"

"I have no idea. Just a feeling. Call him back, tell him that. Please."

Kate picked up the phone again, dialed.

A silence.

A minute long.

She put the phone down.

"He's not answering."

A pause.

"Power failure, probably."

"Yes. Probably. I'll try his cell."

Kate did, got switched to Lemon's voice mail.

"Not answering."

"What did he call about?"

"He found something on Sylvia's computer. He sent it to me as an attachment."

She turned the machine around, showed him the screen. He could see two images, apparently scanned-in copies of some turn-of-the-century paperwork. And a third, a scanned-in newspaper column, also very old-looking.

Nick leaned in and studied the official papers.

"What are they?"

"They're conscription notices," said Kate. "Made out in June of 1917. Two of them. They're made out to John Hardin Ruelle and Ethan Bluebonnet Ruelle. Look at the signature of the conscription clerk at the bottom."

Jubal Custis Walker, Clerk of Records

"Jubal? That's your grandfather, isn't it?"

"Yes. It is. Lemon found these on Sylvia's computer, along with a copy of the 1910 census. On the census, John and Ethan Ruelle are listed as Sole Supporters of Family. Lemon says that means they should never have made it onto a conscription list in the first place. Guess who was listed as John Ruelle's wife?"

"Glynis Ruelle."

"That's right. Lemon also sent along a copy of a column in the *Cullen County Record*, dated December 27, 1921." She hit a tab and the attachment appeared.

GREAT WAR HERO KILLED IN ILLEGAL DUEL

Authorities are investigating the unlawful death of Lieutenant Ethan Bluebonnet Ruelle in a pistol exchange that took place outside the Belfair Saddlery on Christmas Eve last. According to witnesses, Mister Ruelle, a hero of the Great War who had lost an eye and his left arm at Mons, was accosted outside the Saddlery by Lieutenant Colin Haggard. An argument ensued and both men agreed to a stand there and then. In the exchange Lieutenant Ruelle was shot in the face and died on the spot. Lieutenant Haggard, also a veteran of the Great War, was detained by citizens.

When questioned by the authorities as to the nature of the quarrel, Lieutenant Haggard stated that Lieutenant Ruelle had impugned his honor in connection with an action in the Great War. Charges are being considered but have not yet been applied.

The feeling of the citizenry runs against Lieutenant Haggard. Many feel that Lieutenant Haggard belongs to what is known as the Teague Camp in a long-standing disagreement between the Ruelle Family and Abel Teague in connection with what the Ruelle family has long regarded as a Breach of Promise matter involving Clara Mercer. Clara Mercer is the younger sister of Lieutenant Ruelle's sister-in-law, Glynis Ruelle, the widow of Captain John Ruelle, killed in the same battle in which Lieutenant Ethan Ruelle received his wounds. Miss Clara Mercer suffers greatly from this clash of families and is in the loving care of the Ruelle family as of this writing.

Lieutenant Haggard is reputed to have been involved in a number of illegal stands over the years and is considered to be a gun hand, which has drawn the ire of the local citizenry.

The Chief Constable of Belfair County, the Honorable Lewis G. Cotton, has so far declined to act in the matter.

"They're all there," said Nick, after reading it twice. Kate nodded.

"My own grandfather signed the conscription papers sending them off to the war. So they couldn't keep going after Abel Teague. I can't believe it. What a terrible thing to do."

It was hard to disagree with that, so Nick didn't try.

"Is there any other record of the Ruelles' actually doing that? Challenging Abel Teague?"

"Lemon couldn't find one. He's still looking. But Dad felt that it had to have happened, given the times, and that Abel Teague dodged the challenge. Maybe more than once."

"So John dies in the war. Ethan comes back—"

"Wounded. Crippled."

"And of course the resentment is still there," said Nick, looking at the article. "Probably much worse. Maybe he went back after Abel Teague again?"

"He would have had plenty of reason. His brother's dead and Clara's back at the farm going quietly insane and there's Abel Teague, walking around the town with a smile on his face."

"So somebody—probably Abel himself—brought in a ringer to finish it. This Colin Haggard guy."

"Ethan should have declined the fight. No one would have thought any the less of him."

"Except for him," said Nick.

Kate looked at the jubilee card, all those faces, all those lives. She dropped it back into the box, flipping the lid shut, leaned back into the couch.

"Did you get an mpeg made from whatever you saw in Delia's basement?"

"Yes. Beau gave me a flash drive."

"Do you have it here?"

"Yes."

"May I look at it?"

"Why?"

"Because I'm your wife."

"And you're . . . what? Curious?"

"Just show it to me. Please."

Nick hesitated, reached into his pocket, drew it out, a small Sony USB drive.

Kate took it and plugged it into her laptop. The machine worked on it for a while, and then the media player popped up and the clip began to run, grainy, stuttering, but clear enough.

Nick saw himself standing in front of a long stone wall, lit up by the reflected glow of what was flickering on the wall of Delia Cotton's basement, a shimmering field of green, a brown bar, a blue glow along the bottom. The image jumped and righted itself. Beau had found a way to turn the image right side up when he copied the tape.

Now the image showed a broad line of pines and oaks, a thick forest line hemming in a tilled field, people working in the field, spades chopping into the earth, something long and dark being lifted up. A sled pulled by a tractor.

"Can you stop it there, Kate?"

She froze the video.

"Can you zoom in?"

Kate hit a button and the image jumped closer. Nick leaned in and focused on the sled, on the pile of white stones. Kate was leaning in close, so close he could smell her scent and feel the heat of her body. He felt her stiffen, and she drew back.

"Nick. Are those skulls?"

"Yes," he said. "That's what I thought. Let it run some. A thing happens, about now. I want to see if I was right."

Kate hit PLAY and the video jerked into life again. Nick was still in the picture. On the sound track they could hear Beau's voice.

"*Nick, honest, don't touch it.*"

"*I'm just going to—*"

And then a hissing sound, deep and resonant, loud enough to fill the room.

Nick leaned into the screen, intent.

A moment of time, and then the image of the farm flickered and disappeared, changing all at once into a section of rolling green lawn, a black iron fence, a red and white security van at the curb, a young black man in a uniform.

"What *was* that?" Kate asked. "What happened? What was that hissing noise?"

"Delia's cat. She was under a furnace pipe. What happened was the picture *changed*. It was a field with people digging in it, a tree line—"

"A sled piled with skulls—"

"Yes. And then it changed into the street scene outside Delia's house."

A silence.

"What does it mean, Nick?"

"I have no idea."

"It was a real place, wasn't it?"

"Looked real enough. Maybe a burial ground? The South is full of them."

"We could search the photo archives, see if we can find a match. The pines, the countryside, it looks like someplace in the Belfair Range."

"The Ruelles had a place south of Sallytown. Your dad mentioned it. That would put it right in the middle of the Belfair Range. That's where you'd see a stand of old pines like that. Can you save this video?"

"Yes," she said, hitting SAVE AS.

The video shut down.

There was a flicker outside, and the streetlights blinked off.

"Oh, great," said Kate. "I guess we're next."

"Kate. A power failure, okay?"

"Go do something manly about it, then."

Nick got up, went to the living room window. Not a glimmer from outside, but the house lights were still on. Nick could see lights through the trees, which meant the power was still on in the other homes along the street. Kate was sitting on the floor, staring up at him, her face white.

"Like I said. A rolling blackout."

"Then why are the house lights still on?"

"The streetlights are on a different cable."

Nick picked up the phone, listened to the steady dial tone, dialed the number for Sylvia's house, listened to it ring and ring. He set it down, looked back out at the street.

All he could see was his own reflection in the window, a figure in the light, Kate on the floor beside him, staring out.

"I'll go check the breaker panel."

"In the horror movies, the first guy who gets killed is the guy who goes to the basement to check the breaker panel."

"This is not a horror movie."

"Then maybe it's a ghost story."

"I think you need a drink."

"Yes. I do. So do you."

Nick went down the narrow hall to the kitchen, glancing at the conservatory at the back of the house. It was lit with a warm yellow glow, and their yard lights were still on, a soft warm pool on the back lawn, lighting up the linden trees at the bottom of the slope.

He was pouring two glasses of Louis Jadot Beaujolais when he heard the front doorbell ring, turned around, started back up the hall. A figure was standing there. A woman in a black burka.

He heard Kate walking into the front hall.

"Don't answer that," Nick called out.

The black figure hovered in the hallway, shifting, indistinct, but full of menace.

Kate was at the door now. Through the tall stained-glass sidelights she saw, bathed in the amber glow of the porch light, a familiar figure in a trench coat and a scarf, rumpled, fatigue in every line. A familiar voice.

"Kate. Honey, it's Dad. You home?"

Her heart stopped.

"Nick, it's Dad."

"Kate," said Nick, "that's not your dad."

Kate found herself moving towards the door, her hand reaching out for the brass knob as if it were detached from her body.

Nick forced himself to *move*, ran straight at the black fig-

ure in the hall—passed right through it—a fleeting sensation
of intense heat—like being too close to an IED exploding—a
rush of white-hot rage, and the feeling of something *hungry*
tearing at his skin—he fought free, ran down the hall. The
front door was wide open.

Something black and formless seemed to flow into the
hallway, filling it up, billowing out towards Kate. Nick pulled
Kate back and away. The shape paused, reformed, gathered,
shuddered, and then seemed to explode out at them. A voice
spoke from behind them, a woman's voice.

"Clara. Stop."

They turned and saw a woman in the middle of the living
room, a tall weather-worn woman with a strong, handsome
face, deep-set green eyes, a shapely body, long black hair in a
shining fall. She was barefoot, wearing a white summer dress.

She was directly in front of the gilt mirror with her signature on the back. The mirror's glass was a blaze of pale green
light, shining on the figure, placing her inside an aura of shimmering light strong enough to show her naked body through
the thin fabric of her summer dress.

"Clara. Stop. Come home."

Nick and Kate turned to face the black shape again, but it
was gone. A young woman in a green summer dress was hesitating in the hall, a pretty young woman with soft brown eyes
and rich auburn-colored hair. Clara Mercer.

Clara shook her head, took a step backwards, moving into
the downlight from the lamp over the porch. Her shape grew
less clear. The other woman—Glynis Ruelle—spoke again,
with more force, an edge of impatience, pleading with her.

"Clara. Abel is dead. I have him now. He's for the harvest.
It's over. Come home."

The tension between the two women became an audible
humming vibration. The vibration increased, grew louder,
rose in frequency, reaching a single piercing painful note at

the farthest pitch of hearing. The room was filled with the vivid green light pouring out of Glynis Ruelle's mirror.

Clara spoke.

"Abel is dead?"

"Yes."

"Did he face your man?"

"Yes. And we have been given satisfaction."

Clara hesitated, seemed to flicker into and out of focus— the black cloud came back and then vanished into the darkness beyond the door.

Clara stepped forward, passed directly through Nick and Kate's bodies as they stood there in the hall—both Nick and Kate felt her passing—sadness, grief, loss, rage. Clara moved into the green aura and stood in front of Glynis.

The light from the mirror grew, flickered, and was suddenly gone, and they were alone in the front hall, by the open door, the glow from the porch light pooling on the stone floor of the hallway.

After a while, inside the hush that had fallen, Kate pushed the door closed, turned the dead bolt with a shaking hand, crossed the floor to the mirror, which was leaning against a chair, reached out to touch it—it was as warm as blood— brought it forward and laid it on the carpet, facedown.

Sunday Morning

Byron Deitz Finally Gets It

Deitz and Phil Holliman were sitting on a pair of lawn chairs set out by the pool. The awning was flapping in a hot wind and the sun was blazing down on them, setting the air on fire, even at this early hour.

Holliman looked cool and calm in a seersucker suit and a white shirt, bare feet in thin Italian slippers, but Deitz looked hot, his face flushed and damp. He poured some more gin into his glass, dropped some cubes into it with a tinkly *plonk*, and swilled it all down, his thick throat working.

"Jeez," said Holliman, "you don't look good."

Deitz put the glass down hard, glared at Holliman, his bug-eye iridescent sunglasses reflecting a distorted image of Holliman back at him. He made a back-there gesture, indicating a white panel van with NICEVILLE UTILITY COMMISSION printed on the side.

"AC ditched it last night, middle of the fucking night. Whole system crashed—fucking computerized shit—guy's in there now, trying to fix it."

"Where's Beth and the kids?"

"She's not here right now."

Holliman didn't ask why.

He had a pretty good idea.

"Where is she? Her sister's?"

"Nah. She's gone to a hotel. Took the kids. Heat sorta got to us both last night, she had a hissy fit, on account of her fucking old man's gone AWOL up in fucking VMI and I wasn't—" he made ironic quote marks with his hooked fingers—"*sympathetic*, the fucking bitch. I guess I smacked her one. I know, I know, but it's been a bad week. So, ba-*bing*, she takes the Cayenne and the kids, blew the doors off going down the drive."

Holliman saw something in Deitz's face.

"She marked up?"

"Nothing a pair of sunglasses won't cover. Thing is, Kate's married to Nick, and Nick's already called. Says we gotta meet."

"Sounds like a duel."

Deitz looked down at the pool.

"Yeah, well, I put him off until tomorrow, on account of business, but when we do meet, I'm going to haveta straighten the guy out. I mean, I can't let some fucking brother-in-law, I don't care if he is a fucking war hero, get in between me and my family. If I gotta, I'll punch his fucking lights out, and, you know, Phil, I'm about ready to do that, because I'm fucking tired of taking shit from people, and I'm really okay if it starts with him. You follow?"

Holliman, a diplomat, had some of his G and T, because if Deitz and Nick Kavanaugh were going to go at it, he'd have to think long and hard about where he'd put his money.

"Okay, I follow, and let me know when it happens, so I can come watch. Now back to business, boss. I called the Chinks, you know, to arrange picking up the . . . thing. I get their voice mail."

"Okay," said Deitz. "No problem. Early yet. Gone down for breakfast."

"Okay. Breakfast. Alla them at the same time. I can see that. Chinks move in packs, right?"

"Yeah. Well, I see your point. Stay on it. I got something else I want you to look at. See what you think."

He reached out, gathered up a section of the *Niceville Register*, laid it out in front of Holliman, pressed it flat with a sweaty palm.

Phil leaned over and read the news item.

BODY FOUND IN FOREST

State police officers doing a search of the woods in the vicinity of last Friday's fire at the historic Belfair Saddlery discovered the partially decomposed body of a man about a half mile from the site of the fire. The man, described as a white male in his mid-forties, was found lying against a tree. His body showed signs of being partially eaten by coyotes and other scavengers. Initial estimates place the time of death at between four and six o'clock on Friday afternoon. Cause of death was initially thought to be exposure but a preliminary examination at the scene revealed a gunshot wound to the lower back, which nicked an artery, another wound which severed the left ear, and a third wound in the middle of the throat, which caused severe brain damage and a fatal loss of blood. Fingerprint Recognition at the FBI identified the deceased as Merle Louis Zane, an ex-convict who had served time for attempted manslaughter at the Louisiana State Prison in Angola. Police Captain Martin Coors states that investigators are now looking to see if there is a connection between the dead man and the armed robbery carried out a few hours earlier at the First Third Bank in Gracie, where four police officers were gunned down during a pursuit.

The investigation continues.

"The third man," said Phil. "Gotta be the third guy. Looks like they had a disagreement, after the fucking robbery."

"Pukes always do," said Deitz. "But who'd he disagree with, that's the question. Now look at this," he said, turning over the fold, flattening out a large full-color spread above the fold.

"That's a picture of the hostage thing, down there at Saint Innocent Orthodox."

Holliman studied the picture, a tangle of cop cars, two cops sticking a green-shirted guy into the back of a cruiser, some cops and civilians standing around talking, big grins all over.

"Yeah, I saw this. Silver-haired guy in the gray suit, that's Coker, he's the sniper. Dozer dyke is Mavis Crossfire. And the guy watching, looks like Wyatt Earp, that's Charlie Danziger. Bunch of other guys, cops. Jimmy Candles."

"Look at Charlie Danziger. Anything stand out?"

Holliman leaned over, lifted his sunglasses to see the shot more clearly.

"Yeah. He's got gay cowboy boots on."

"Gay? Why gay?"

"They're fucking blue, Byron. Who the fuck wears blue cowboy boots? Richard Simmons?"

"Nothing ringing your bell here?"

Holliman sat back, taking the paper with him, holding it out into the sunlight.

"Oh fuck."

"Yeah. Oh fuck."

"The guy with the blue boots? At the bank?"

"Danziger. And that fucking Coker."

"No way."

"Think about it. Danziger knows the payroll is coming in. He finds a wheelman, Merle Zane, some pro he knows from his days with State. Coker is the shooter, waiting for those poor schmucks down on Route 311. He's using a Barrett out of Stores, cleans it and puts it back before anybody is the wiser."

"Coker's a cop. Danziger was a cop. No way they'd pop four of their buddies like that."

"For two and a quarter mil I'd pop your mother. I'd pop *my* mother. And that Coker's a chilly motherfucker, and Charlie Danziger's got a beef with State, goes way back."

Holliman stared at the picture, taking it in.

"That means they're also the guys who—"

"Ran my ass off yesterday afternoon, making me buy back that Raytheon thing. I mean, who the fuck else would have the balls? It's them, Phil, take it to the bank. It's them."

Holliman looked at Deitz.

"Holy shit."

"Yeah. My sentiments exactly."

"What do you want to do?"

"I'm going to go out to Charlie Danziger's place and I'm going to start blowing holes in him until he tells me where my fucking money is, and then I'm going to kill him."

"Deitz, you can't do that. I mean, we got a business going here, we're making good money for easy work, why blow it all?"

"Yeah? What would you suggest, Phil?"

"I'd call Boonie Hackendorff and Marty Coors and tell them what you think, that's what. Shit, if Thad told you about the blue boots, he sure as shit told the FBI. Maybe they're already onto him."

"That's the problem, Phil. If the Feds get to Danziger before we do, then sooner or later he's going to tell them about the Raytheon thing, just to buy himself a deal."

"There's no deal for being accessory to killing four cops. It's the needle for sure, him and Coker. The Raytheon thing wouldn't buy him a donut."

"You want to take that chance, Phil?"

"You go out there and beat the shit out of Charlie Danziger if you want, Byron, if you can, but I'm not going out there with you."

"I don't want you with me. You gotta go get that thing back from the Chinks. That's gotta be back in the tray at Slipstream by the end of the day tomorrow—"

"Excuse me—Mr. Deitz?"

Both men looked up at a young guy in black wearing an NUC smock, waiting by the open patio doors, holding a big black metal toolbox. Black hair, pale white skin, bug-eye sunglasses just like Deitz's.

"Yeah . . . Bock, yeah. Hey, Bock, how's it going?"

Bock gave him sort of a half salute, a big toothy grin— *maybe some wiseass in it*, Holliman was thinking, watching the guy.

"It's all fixed, Mr. Deitz. I ran a full diagnostic. It was the motherboard for the SensoMatic module—"

"Great, Bock, great," said Deitz, waving him off. "I owe you anything?"

"No sir," said Bock, smiling at him. "All on warranty. We're sorry for the inconvenience to you and your family."

"Okay, well, thanks."

Bock turned to go, but Deitz called him back

"Oh, wait, one thing," he said, as Bock's knees turned to rubber. "This is for you," he said, holding out a fifty.

Bock hesitated.

"Ah, sir, we're not allowed to accept—"

"Fuck that. You been here fucking two hours. Buy yourself some breakfast, kid. Okay."

Bock came forward, folded the bill into his hand, stuffed it into the pocket of his smock.

"So, it's all good now?" said Deitz.

"Oh yes," said Bock. "It's all good now."

They watched Bock walk down the drive, get into his van, drive slowly away.

Deitz leaned forward.

"No, look, Phil, this is how we play this. You go get the thing from the Chinks, take it back to Slipstream right away, no point holding it any longer than we have to—"

"It's early. They don't have to give it back until noon."

"Okay, so go sit in the lobby until noon. Have a lime rickey and a Waldorf salad. Just get it in your hands and put it back where it belongs."

"What are you going to do?"

"Stop looking so freaked, Phil. I heard you. I'm not gonna do anything nutso. I'm just going to go out to Charlie's place, like a buddy, dropping in, like, and I'm going to ask him a few hard fucking questions and get some fucking answers."

"What about Coker? Those two are tight, and Coker's even crazier than Danziger."

"I can handle Coker. I get what I need out of Danziger, I got Coker by the balls. I work this right, we get my money back, maybe I might even let those two keep some of what they took from Gracie. Thing is, I roll Charlie Danziger, we own *both* their asses, now and forever. We win and everybody else loses. That's how I like it. Now go. I gotta get some gear together."

Phil stood up, looking nervous.

"Deitz, I think you should sit on this until I get back. We should talk about it some more."

"Fuck talk," said Deitz. "You work for me, Phil. Go earn your pay."

Holliman flipped his glasses on, nodded his head, and walked away towards his truck. Deitz watched him go, thinking, *Jigs, they're all the same.*

He was in his Hummer and halfway to Danziger's ranch north of the city when his OnStar phone rang.

It was Andy Chu.

"Chu, what is it? I'm busy here."

"This won't take a minute, boss."

"If it's about that fucking e-mail snitch, Andy, then you're a day late and a dollar short."

"It's not that, sir."

"Then what the fuck is it?"

"Perhaps you'd like to pull over first?"

"What the fuck for?"

"Mario La Motta. Desi Muñoz. Julie Spahn. Arthur Desoto."

Shit.

Shit shit shit.

"Look, Andy . . . those names? Can I ask where—"

"Pull over now."

"But . . ."

"Mr. Deitz, with respect, if you wish to complete your business with Mr. Dak and not go to a federal prison for the remainder of your life, you would be well advised to comply with my request."

Deitz shut up and pulled over.

He was still listening to Andy Chu explain exactly how a new day had just dawned and how Byron Deitz now had a new silent partner when he got a call on his cell.

He looked at the call display: PHIL HOLLIMAN.

"Look, ah, Andy, can I put you on hold for a minute? Okay? Would that be okay?"

"Certainly. Please do. I will wait."

Deitz flicked his cell open.

"Yeah, Phil, what's the—"

"They're gone, Deitz."

"Gone? Who's gone?"

"Zachary Dak and his whole crew. They checked out thirty minutes ago. They're in the wind."

"Jesus. What about the item?"

"I'm standing in their room. There's nothing here. Nothing. They're taking the item with them. They were *always* going to take it with them."

"Jesus H. Christ on a Fucking Crutch."

"Yeah, well, I'll give Him a call then, if you think He'll help."

"No, wait—the Lear. It's at Mauldar Field. That's a half hour from the Marriott. Call the field boss, tell him not to give that Lear clearance to take off until I get there—"

"I'm a just security guard, Deitz—"

"Tell him whatever. Make sure that fucking plane never gets spooled up. Go. Now."

Deitz flipped the cell phone shut.

His head was so full of that walnut-cracking sound that he thought it was coming from the entire fucking universe, that the whole universe was made up of this walnut-cracking sound, like from the Big Bang. He got back to Andy Chu.

"Andy, I got to go—"

"We have much to discuss."

"I know, look, and I hear you, I really do, it's just that I've got this emergency, it affects the company—"

"I think of it as *our* company now, yes?"

"Yeah, of course, Andy, you and me, a whole new thing, I'm totally okay with all that, you know, business is business, right? We can talk about the details later, but right now I really—"

"I understand fully. Please have a very nice day. And remember to drive carefully."

"Good. Yeah. Okay. I promise. Gotta go."

He hit the OFF button and was already wheeling the Hummer around, almost putting it on two wheels. He punched the pedal flat, gritting his teeth all the while, thinking about the best route to take to get to Mauldar Field—*straight down 366 and then hang a left on Pewter and cut across on Shiloh*—he had the engine howling and was now doing a flat one-forty going

southbound on Arrow Creek Road and he could see traffic flying by at the intersection of Arrow Creek and 366—he looked
at his watch—he could not believe the day he was having—
fucking wily Asiatics.

He was fumbling for his cell phone to make a call to Mauldar Field himself—*make sure that God-damned Lear never gets
wheels up*—he took the curve onto 366 at eighty and almost
rolled it, recovered, punched it again as he got zeroed onto the
straightaway, pushed it to one forty-five, had the cell, punched
in the numbers, and got Mauldar Field Tower—

"Yeah, Mauldar, let me have your controller."

"Who's calling?"

"Byron Deitz, I'm the head of Securicom. Have you got a
Chinese Lear spooling up?"

"It's fourth in line to go. Why?"

"You gotta stop it, okay? Gotta stop it."

"Who are you again, sir?"

Deitz tried not to lose it.

"I'm the head of Securicom for Quantum Park—"

"Are you a law enforcement official?"

"No, listen, wait, yes, I'm FBI. You—"

A siren.

He could hear sirens.

He looked in his rearview mirror.

There was a State Police car right on his ass, his lights
flashing, his rack strobing like a fucking clown car.

Oh fuck.

"May I have your ID number, sir?"

"My ID num— Look, you fucking asshole—"

The State car was pulling alongside, the window coming
down—

"Sir, without an ID number I can't stop a—"

"Yes, you fucking·can, you dumb cock—"

The line went dead.

Deitz looked to his left and he was looking at a young black female cop who was looking back at him and making a *pull-the-fuck-over* sign.

Deitz powered his window down.

"Look, I'm FBI, okay—"

The wind was whipping his words away.

She shook her head at him, made an emphatic gesture for him to pull over.

Now the driver was on his bullhorn.

Pull to the right and stop.

Pull to the right and stop now.

Deitz thought about pulling away. He also thought about shooting them both dead and *then* pulling away. He could not *believe* the day he was—

Bam.

He jumped in his seat, the wheel going bats under his hand, looked to his left and the young lady cop was holding a Remington 12-gauge out the window and she was aiming it at his left front wheel again, steadying it on the window frame.

The truck was already wobbling and he had to fight to keep it from rolling—it was weaving crazily from side to side, lurching like a moose on a log—he jammed on the brakes, the nose took a dive, and he managed to get it settled enough to roll it onto the right shoulder.

He shut the engine off and looked up at two highly pissed-off State cops leaning on the far side of the cruiser hood and he was also looking down the muzzles of a Remington 12-gauge and a Glock 17.

He popped the door, thinking how was he going to chill these cops, maybe even get them to stop the Lear—no, he'd have to tell them why and then he'd be—

"Stay in your vehicle," the lady cop was shouting. "Stick both hands out the side window. Do it now."

Deitz did as he was told.

"You shot my fucking car!"

"Just stay where you are."

The male cop moved out to the left to get a line of fire that allowed the lady cop to come up to the driver's-side window without getting in his way. She still had the shotgun in her hand, but the muzzle was pointed down.

She stood there at his window for a second, breathing hard, her eyes wide and angry. Deitz had his license out and he handed it to her.

"You shot my car, officer!"

"No idea what you're talking about. You had a blowout while speeding . . . Mr. Ditz."

"Deetz, officer. It's pronounced Deetz."

She looked down at his license, shoved it into her uniform pocket.

"Insurance and registration, Mr. Ditz."

"Deetz. Not Ditz. Look, officer, I'm sorry about—"

"Insurance and registration. Now."

Deitz leaned over to open the storage panel beside him. As he did this, he felt the shotgun muzzle come up again. She was one totally wired cop, that was for sure. He moved very slowly, riffled through the compartment, came up with the vehicle ownership and the insurance binder.

She was watching his hands as he did so and when he gave her the papers he saw her eyes slip past and focus on something in the cup holder. Her expression got even harder.

He looked where she was looking.

Saw the pill bottle.

Thad Llewellyn's Happy Caps.

"You taking medication, Mr. Ditz?"

Deitz looked at the bottle, and then back at her.

"No. Ah, those belong to a friend—"

"May I see the bottle, please?"

Illegal search, he was thinking. *This is just a speeding bust. Gives her no rights to search the fucking truck. I don't have to show her dick all.*

"Ah, look, officer . . ." He looked at her name tag. "Officer

Martinez. I'm the head of Securicom—I'm ex-FBI—I'm real sorry about all this and I'm sincerely apologizing for the speeding. I'm in the middle of an emergency here and I sorta lost it back there, but how about you just write me up and let me—"

"The bottle, Mr. Ditz."

"Look, lady, I'm a cop too, in case you fucking missed it, and the fact is, I don't have to show you any fucking thing other than my license and—"

"Plain sight, Mr. Ditz. That bottle is in plain sight. During a traffic stop, I have the right to examine any object in plain sight. Are you refusing to show me that bottle?"

Deitz sighed, picked the bottle up, and handed it to her through the window. She turned the bottle in her left hand, reading the label.

"This prescription medication is not in your name, Mr. Ditz. It's in the name of a T. Llewellyn."

"Yeah. I know. He's my banker. I guess he left it in the car the other . . ."

His voice trailed off as she unscrewed the cap and looked inside the bottle.

She looked up at him again.

"Do you know what these are, Mr. Ditz?"

His belly took a slow roll and his neck muscles tightened. He was afflicted with a terrible doubt. This must have showed on his face.

"I believe they're Ativans, Officer Martinez."

"I believe they're ecstasy, Mr. Ditz. An illegal substance. Please get out of the vehicle."

Deitz blew up.

"Look, for fuck's sake, you goddam bitch—"

This was not helpful.

Ten minutes later he was sitting in the back of the cruiser, scraped and bruised and pepper-sprayed, his hands cuffed behind his back. Two more State cars and one deputy car had arrived and he was watching them all jerking around playing grab-ass while Officer Martinez, who was obviously a major whack job, went through his truck from grill to taillights, who the fuck knew why—probably, if he knew cops at all, looking for something else, anything else, to nail him for, along with speeding and failure to stop and possession of a controlled substance.

He wasn't all that worried about the ecstasy beef. Even a third-year law clerk could lay that off on Thad the Banker without breaking a sweat.

What he was worried about, sitting there watching Officer Martinez tear his truck apart, was that fucking Learjet, now wheels-up and heading for the wild blue yonder at six hundred miles an hour, taking the Raytheon GPS back to China. Something massive would have to be done about that. Exactly what would take some thought.

In the meantime, he watched her go at it, riffling through the rear storage compartments, intensity in every line of her compact body.

Fucking Dickless Tracies.

They were all the—

Something in her body language shifted.

He heard her call out to the other cops.

She turned and came striding back to the rear window of the cruiser, full of grim purpose, and she slammed something up against the glass, grinning down at him like a shark. In her hand was a fat stack of mint hundred-dollar bills. He could see the First Third Bank logo on the wrapper.

The other cops were all gathering around and talking real fast and getting on their radios and only then did Byron Deitz begin to suspect how totally and completely fucked he really was.

Bock's Sunday Was Memorable

Bock parked his truck in the tiny little space Mrs. Kinnear had assigned to him, got out, and his mind elsewhere, slammed the door loud enough to wake up Mrs. Kinnear's shi-tzu. Bock could hear his frenzied barking through the thin wooden boards of the house, and then the harsh croaking squawk of Mrs. Kinnear's voice, trying to shut the little ratso up. *Good luck with that*, Bock thought, climbing the stairs to his flat over the garage, turning over the events of the last two days, thinking about how much he could wangle out of Andy Chu for his services.

Dearie me, he thought, *a guy can get a lot of living done in thirty-six hours*, wondering idly, as he turned his key, if he had any Stellas left in the cooler. He opened the door, stepped inside—*home again home again hippity-hop*—and felt something cold and steely pressed up against the back of his head. A young woman was sitting on the black leather couch, drinking one of his Stellas and smiling at him, not a nice smile at all. A deep growling voice very close to his ear, heavy with the scent of cigarettes, said:

"Tony Bock, meet Twyla Littlebasket."

Twyla lifted the Stella, gave him a tight smile. A strong

hand on his shoulder turned him around and he was looking at the Clint Eastwood cop he had seen on his television yesterday afternoon, the silver-haired sniper from the hostage-taking incident at Saint Innocent. Bock's legs became unreliable and he started to go down, but Coker had him in an iron grip. He perp-walked him over to the couch, shoved him down beside Twyla, and sat down in Bock's matching black leather chair, a large blue-steel revolver in his right hand.

He made a ceremony of lighting up a cigarette, exhaled with quiet satisfaction, blowing the smoke in Bock's direction. Bock swallowed, tried to say something, choked on it, his lips working but nothing coming out other than a few strangled chirps, as if he had swallowed a budgie.

Coker raised a hand, palm out, smiled.

"Kindly shut the fuck up, son. You know why we're here. We all know why we're here. Twyla, anything you want to say before we begin?"

"Jesus," said Bock, in a squeak, feeling his bones go soft and his cheeks sag. His head felt like a helium balloon and the room turned to white light. He sagged to the right, flopped over onto the arm of the couch, his lids fluttering. Bock had left the building. Twyla watched him for a moment, reached out and pressed a finger into the side of his neck, took it back and wiped it off on her jeans. She looked over at Coker.

"Fainted."

Coker twirled the heavy revolver, grinned through the smoke at Twyla.

"Tough guy."

"Are you going to kill him?"

Coker twirled the gun again.

He liked doing that.

"I don't know. Do you *want* me to kill him?"

Twyla considered the flabby pile of guts in front of her. After a while, she shook her head.

"No. He's just too . . . pathetic."

"What *do* you want to do with him? You want to geld him, gonna be messy. We'll have to find tin shears, a drop cloth, maybe some duct tape."

Coker was only half kidding.

She thought about it.

"We could bring him to court?"

"Court? Which court?"

"Your court. Coker's Court of No Appeal."

"Why? What use is he? Donny Falcone's a rich dentist. This guy's just a skanky little pervert."

Twyla looked at Bock's fish-belly skin and his pouchy face, listened to his labored breathing, and then she took in his room packed with computers, his communications gear, his wide-screen monitors, his ham radio, his CB set, his printers and scanners and all the piled-up storage disks.

"But maybe he's more than that too. Maybe he's an *enterprising* skanky little pervert. I cannot believe, looking at this setup he's got here, that Bluebell and I were the only people he's been fucking over. I think it's his hobby."

Coker took that in. She had a point.

"So," he said, meditating upon it, "when he comes around, maybe we start asking him what the fuck *else* he's been doing?"

"And who he's been doing it to."

Coker looked at her, reappraising. He felt himself growing quite fond of Twyla. You never knew where life's opportunities were to be found. She was a smart girl. She had depths. She'd have to be watched, but she had depths.

So they waited, listening to Bock wheeze and snuffle and flutter. Twyla poured them both another Stella and Coker worked through two more Camels.

A while later Bock came around with a jerk and a snort and a yelp worthy of Mrs. Kinnear's shi-tzu, his eyes blinking, his hands flapping like little pink flippers. He sat up, saw that they were still sitting in front of him, took in the fact that it hadn't all been some horrible dream. He began to weep in a drizzly, snuffling sort of way.

"Jeez," he said, after a bit, wiping his nose on the back of his hand, "what do you guys *want*?"

"What have you got?" asked Coker, twirling the revolver again and smiling at Bock through a cloud of smoke. Bock brightened a bit, looked hopeful.

"You mean like money?"

"Nope. Got enough money already."

"Then . . . what?"

"Twyla here thinks you're an enterprising young guy. What I wanna know, is she right?"

"I don't know what she means."

Coker cast his gaze to heaven, then back.

"Sure you do. Twyla here figures she's not the only person you've been fucking over. She thinks that fucking strangers over from the safety of your little hideout here is kind of your hobby. What you do for kicks. Know what? I think she's right."

Coker leaned forward, got in Bock's face.

"So here's the deal, Tony. I like to know useful things. If you can tell me a useful thing, maybe I won't let Twyla here start in on you. She's Cherokee, you know that? I think you guys invented scalping, didn't you, Twyla?"

"That was the Huron. We did noses and lips."

Coker shrugged, smiled at Bock through the smoke. Bock blinked back, glanced over at Twyla, flinched away from her flat glare, swallowed hard, took a moment, and totally ratted out Andy Chu.

Nick and Kate and Kate and Nick

They were sitting at the breakfast table with the morning papers, toast and jam and black coffee. Neither of them had slept at all. They'd stayed up and talked all night. Nick was supposed to take a chopper up to VMI to look into Dillon Walker's disappearance, but he wasn't ready to leave, and Kate wasn't ready to let him go yet. The morning was sunny and fresh and cool and it was hard to square the view out the window with what had happened last night. Nick was scanning the front page and Kate was watching him, thinking about the events of the night, trying to walk it back to something she could understand, something she could work into her view of the world as it had always been. So far she wasn't getting anywhere. Nick stiffened, glanced at her, and then back at the paper.

"What is it?"

Nick kept his head down, folded the paper up and set it aside, reached for his coffee.

"Oh no you don't," said Kate, picking up the paper. "What did you see?"

Nick sat back, sipped at his coffee.

"First page, under the fold, side banner."

Kate found it.

BODY FOUND IN FOREST

State police officers doing a search of the woods in the vicinity of last Friday's fire at the historic Belfair Saddlery discovered the partially decomposed body of a man about a half mile from the site of the fire. The man, described as a white male in his mid-forties, was found lying against a tree. His body showed signs of being partially eaten by coyotes and other scavengers. Initial estimates place the time of death at between four and six o'clock on Friday afternoon. Cause of death was initially thought to be exposure but a preliminary examination at the scene revealed a gunshot wound to the lower back, which nicked an artery, another wound which severed the left ear, and a third wound in the middle of the throat, which caused severe brain damage and a fatal loss of blood. Fingerprint Recognition at the FBI identified the deceased as Merle Louis Zane, an ex-convict who had served time for attempted manslaughter at the Louisiana State Prison in Angola. Police Captain Martin Coors states that investigators are now looking to see if there is a connection between the dead man and the armed robbery carried out a few hours earlier at the First Third Bank in Gracie, where four police officers were gunned down during a pursuit.

The investigation continues.

She put the paper down.

"Merle Zane. Nick, is this the same man who went to see Rainey in the hospital? The man Lemon saw in the elevator?"

"Lemon saw the man in the elevator on Saturday after-noon. This guy's been dead since Friday."

"Could they have the time of death wrong?"

"Probably not. Certainly not by twenty-four hours."

"So it's not the same Merle?"

"How could it be?"

Kate reread the item, set the paper down.

"Of course. You're right. How could it be? Just a coincidence—the name, I mean. An unusual name."

"Yeah. Just a coincidence. Talking about Rainey, what are your plans for him?"

"My plans?" said Kate.

"Yes. You're his legal guardian. You're all he has now. He'll need weeks of physio, and probably some psychological counseling, but sooner or later they'll release him. Where's he gonna go?"

Kate watched Nick's face carefully.

"Are you ahead of me on this?"

"I'm thinking maybe I am."

"It would be a big change for us, taking on a kid."

"Yes, it would."

"You're not crazy about the idea?"

"I'm worried about it."

"You mean, the responsibility?"

"No. We can handle that."

"Then what is it?"

"It's the kid himself. I'm not sure how I feel about having him . . . here. In the house. With us."

Kate sat back, her expression hardening.

"I'm not sure I follow. Nobody worked harder to find that child, nobody cared more about seeing him come out of that coma. I don't understand this."

"I don't either."

"Is it that you know something about him that I don't? Is that it?"

Nick said nothing.

"Nick . . . ?"

"Okay. Reed sent me something this morning. E-mail with an attachment."

"What was it?"

"Something he found on your dad's computer."

"What is it? Where is it?"

Nick got up, walked down the hall to his office, came back with a printout, laid it down in front of her. A single page, close type, unsigned.

Rainey Teague DOB questions: memo for Kate Searched Cullen County census for period surrounding R's DOB with Gwinnetts found no entry. No entry in surrounding parishes no entry in Belfair, no State or County Records show any certificate of R's birth or baptism. No record in adjoining states, counties, or parishes. No sign R was born or baptized anywhere in US, Canada, or Mexico in any date range corresponding to his stated age. Foster parents Zorah and Martin Palgrave: found entry Cullen County Registry of Birth Martin Palgrave born Sallytown November 7 1873 married Zorah Palgrave Sallytown Methodist March 15 1893. Palgraves received credit letter signed G. Ruelle April 12 1913 "for care and confinement Clara Mercer and delivery of healthy male child March 2nd 1913."

Martin and Zorah Palgrave operated printing shop that created tintype print Niceville Families Jubilee 1910.

Indications Leah Searle made same findings re Rainey adoption and communicated same to Miles Teague at his office in Cap City on May 9 2002 prior to adoption from alleged "Palgrave foster home," no actual trace of which can be found in any taxpayer list or census other than in Cullen County census of 1914.

Conclusion: further study required to verify place of birth, true identity, and origins of person now known as Rainey Teague.

Query Miles Teague suicide possible result of his realization that Rainey Teague's recovery from Ethan Ruelle

crypt was related to R's uncertain origins. Otherwise it is
inexplicable.

Must place all this before Kate now, since she, as his legal
guardian, will be the obvious choice to provide him home
until he comes of legal age. These issues need to be resolved
ASAP.

Kate read it twice, a third time.

"What does this mean, Nick?"

"What it says. Clara Mercer delivered a healthy male child
at the Palgrave home on the second day of March in 1913."

"But I looked into the Palgraves. Martin and Zorah. The
records were right there, in Leah Searle's files."

"But you never found them, did you? The Palgraves? No
trace anywhere?"

"No. But Leah Searle must have. She laid it all out in her
records. Including Rainey's birth certificate."

"When was Rainey born?"

Kate went inward, remembering. Her expression shifted
and her lips went a little blue.

"March 2, 2000."

"Where?"

"In Sallytown. Nick, this is . . . it's all wrong. I don't know
where Dad is going with this—"

"I'd say, neither did he. But he was coming down to talk it
out with you. Reed found a copy of this file sitting in your
dad's printer. He found the digital copy on his computer. The
document had been modified only a few minutes before he
printed it out, and he printed it out at 14:37 yesterday."

"Right after he talked to me?"

"That's what the file says."

Kate looked at Nick.

"Rainey . . . Rainey is *not* . . . he's not—"

"Ninety-nine years old?"

"You *cannot* believe that?"

For a while Nick said nothing.

"No, I guess I don't."

"Then what *do* you believe?"

"What do I believe, Kate? I believe I don't want that boy living in my house, not right now."

"You *can't* mean that, Nick. Not you. He has nowhere else to go. I have no choice. I'm all he has. I'm his guardian. *We're* all the family he has now. You and me. You know we have to take him in. You *know* that. You're all about duty and service and honor. That's what this is. I know you understand that."

"Yes. I do."

She was quiet for a while.

"And, for all we know, all this confusion about Rainey's documentation could just be some kind of bureaucratic bungle. God knows we've both seen enough of that, between the law and the Army."

Nick had to admit she was right, and it showed on his face. Kate softened.

"I know this is a lot to take in, honey."

"Yes. But I think you're right. It's something we owe the kid. He has no one else."

"So . . . you're okay with it?"

"Yes. I'm okay with it."

"You sound like it's a death sentence."

"Do I?"

"Yes. You do. It's in your voice. Is that what you think it is?"

"No. Not that."

"What, then?"

Kate waited a full minute for Nick's answer.

"I'm afraid we're letting the *outside* come in. But I'm with you. I'll stand by him."

Kate smiled, kissed his cheek, sat back.

"Come what may?"

"Come what may."

Morgan Littlebasket
Weaves It All Together

Morgan Littlebasket was in his Cessna, soaring like an eagle, gliding in a perfect arc along the rim of Tallulah's Wall, skimming the treetops so close he was getting lash marks on the leading edge of his wing tips and really upsetting the crows. He was wearing his favorite rig, his Flying Tigers jacket and his Army Air Corps–issue Ray-Ban aviators, and he had the cockpit mirror set so he could see himself at the controls. The engine note was a pleasing baritone hum and his hands on the controls were rock steady.

Overhead the sun was climbing into a blue sky over Niceville and far below his starboard wing the Tulip River looked like a ribbon of golden light as it snaked through the city center. A haze was lying over Niceville, smoke and fumes and mist, but to his eyes it gave the town a soft-focus 1940s look that went very well with his outfit. He was feeling like a fighter pilot, cruising for Nips in the South China Sea, Van Johnson as a wingman and Betty Grable waiting for him back at the field. He banked left, sliding away and down, and flew right along the Tulip for a while, at a very illegal thousand feet, but he didn't do that for long. He pulled back on the stick and the plane rose again, the lift so strong he could feel it in his cheeks and along his thighs, and now he was heading for Tallulah's Wall again, the limestone cliff filling up his windshield. He had a picture of his family on the sun visor and he reached up to touch a fingertip to Lucy's cheek, thinking how lucky she had been to have known him. He dipped the stick a degree, steadied his course, and flew his Cessna straight into the side of Tallulah's Wall at what they later estimated to be roughly two hundred miles an hour.

The impact caused the fuel tanks, just topped up an hour earlier, to explode, and a red and black flower of flame blossomed across the face of the cliff, drawing everyone's attention down in the town. The concussive wave rippled across the rooftops of the city, bouncing people out of their Sunday-morning sleep. It shook the windows of Brandy Gule's flat over the needle exchange hard enough to wake up Lemon Featherlight, who had just now fallen asleep while she watched over him, and it thumped pretty hard against the glass of the conservatory where Kate and Beth were having a long heart-to-heart about Byron Deitz, and it rattled all the windows in Tony Bock's flat, briefly distracting Coker and Twyla Little-basket from the very interesting story Tony Bock was, at that point, only halfway through.

But the shock wave had faded into a distant rumble by the time it reached Charlie Danziger's place, where he was sitting on his porch with a glass of Pinot Grigio and a loaded Winchester on his knees, half expecting either Byron Deitz or Boonie Hackendorff or maybe the devil himself to come wheeling up his driveway, guns a-blazing.

The concussive wave drew people all over Niceville out onto their porches and lawns and balconies to stare up at Tallulah's Wall, where the roaring fire on the face of the cliff had spooked a large flock of crows that lived there. The flock took flight, a huge black swarm, and headed west across the upper part of the city, their flight followed by almost every citizen in the town.

The flock, later estimated at maybe three thousand birds, entered the airspace over Mauldar Field about ten minutes after Morgan Littlebasket's plane, what was left of it, carrying Morgan Littlebasket, what was left of him, went cartwheeling down into the rocky base of the cliffs.

The black mass of crows, moving in unison like a school of fish, banked to the south-southeast over Mauldar Field, a move that put the flock directly into the path of a Learjet that had just cleared the runway after a short delay caused by a crank call the tower had received a few minutes earlier from an unknown citizen.

The jet, banking right and rising, reached the same height as the flock of crows, into the midst of which it flew at more than four hundred miles an hour. The twin jets sucked in enough crow meat and bone and blood to lock up the turbines and, since the windscreen was so smeared with crow blood and crow guts that neither of the pilots could see a damn thing, the plane entered into a death spiral so steep that not even the archangel Michael could have stopped the Learjet from doing what it did sixty-four seconds later, which was to augur fifty feet into the ground at a little more than four hundred miles an hour and turn Mr. Zachary Dak and everything else on board, including the cosmic Frisbee, into a volcanic fireball that exploded outwards all over the fourteenth green of the Anora Mercer Golf and Country Club.

As the fireball and the molten shrapnel hurtled out in a 360-degree arc the explosion narrowly missed a slender reed of a man with red-rimmed eyes and a large bandage over a badly broken nose who was addressing a ball buried deep in a sand trap sixty yards away from the fourteenth green, but, sadly, in a strange quirk of fate, the fireball caught and utterly incinerated his beloved wife, Inge, who was standing in the dead center of the fourteenth green, holding the flag and bellowing at him, in tones of brass, *For Christ's sake, Thad, will you just hit the goddam—*

The fireball then shrank to a towering pillar of black smoke with a flaming core. Now the flock of crows, decimated but still a coherent mass, gathered together again, seeming to turn into a single solid entity, dense, cold, black, impenetrable, as curved as a scythe.

This shape swooped low over the rooftops and church spires and forested blocks of Niceville, darkening the town as it passed. Then it rose up, soaring into the blue, wheeled suddenly to the northwest, and flew back to the crest of Tallulah's Wall, where it settled into the ring of ancient trees that grew around Crater Sink, the birds clustering there in fluttering ranks, strung along the ancient branches, chittering and squawking, yellow eyes shining, sharp beaks clacking like scissors, staring down into Crater Sink.

And there they stayed, for an unnaturally long time, until well after sundown, motionless and strangely silent, two thousand crows watching the perfect circle of cold black water with a fixed intensity, as if they were all waiting for something, finally, to come back out of Crater Sink.

Acknowledgments

All my gratitude goes to my agent, Barney Karpfinger; my guardian angel, Cathy Jaque; and my editor, Carole Baron, all of whom made a good book infinitely better; and to Danielle Adair, Emily Stroud, Tom Macdonald, Susan Hodgins, Suzanne Hutchinson, Debbie Fowler, Barbara Wojdat, and Lisa Hong, all of whom know why.

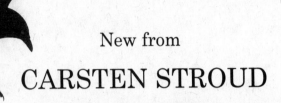